The Russian Concubine

The
Russian
Concubine

KATE FURNIVALL

BERKLEY BOOKS, NEW YORK

THE BERKLEY PUBLISHING GROUP
Published by the Penguin Group
Penguin Group (USA) Inc.
375 Hudson Street, New York, New York 10014, USA
Penguin Group (Canada), 90 Eglinton Avenue East, Suite 700, Toronto, Ontario M4P 2Y3, Canada
(a division of Pearson Penguin Canada Inc.)
Penguin Books Ltd., 80 Strand, London WC2R 0RL, England
Penguin Group Ireland, 25 St. Stephen's Green, Dublin 2, Ireland (a division of Penguin Books Ltd.)
Penguin Group (Australia), 250 Camberwell Road, Camberwell, Victoria 3124, Australia
(a division of Pearson Australia Group Pty. Ltd.)
Penguin Books India Pvt. Ltd., 11 Community Centre, Panchsheel Park, New Delhi—110 017, India
Penguin Group (NZ), 67 Apollo Drive, Rosedale, North Shore 0745, Auckland, New Zealand
(a division of Pearson New Zealand Ltd.)
Penguin Books (South Africa) (Pty.) Ltd., 24 Sturdee Avenue, Rosebank, Johannesburg 2196,
South Africa

Penguin Books Ltd., Registered Offices: 80 Strand, London WC2R 0RL, England

This is an original publication of The Berkley Publishing Group.

Copyright © 2007 by Kate Furnivall.
Cover photo of poppy by Kevin Summers/Getty Images. Cover photo of woman sitting by Lisa Spindler
Photography Inc./Getty Images. Cover photo of the Forbidden City by John Wang/Getty Images. Cover
photo of Chinese drapery by Jack Hollingsworth/Getty Images.
Cover design by Rich Hasselberger. Text design by Kristin del Rosario.

First edition: August 2007

Library of Congress Cataloging-in-Publication Data

Furnivall, Kate.
    The Russian concubine / Kate Furnivall.—1st ed.
        p. cm.
    ISBN 978-0-425-21558-6
    1. Russians—China—Fiction.   2. China—History—1912–1937—Fiction.   I. Title.

PR6116.U76R87 2007
823'. 92—dc22
                                                                        2006103255

PRINTED IN THE UNITED STATES OF AMERICA

10   9   8   7   6

In memory of my mother,
Lily Furnivall,
whose story inspired my own. With love.

ACKNOWLEDGMENTS

My warm thanks go to Jackie Cantor at Berkley for her constant enthusiasm and to Teresa Chris and Patty Moosbrugger for their unfailing belief in the book. Many thanks also to Alla Sashniluc for providing me with Russian language with such energy and to Yeewai Tang for providing Chinese language with such grace.

A big thank-you to Richard for opening the door in my mind that took me into China, and to Edward and Liz for their invaluable encouragement. I would also like to thank the Brixham Group for listening to my woes and giving good advice, and Barry and Ann for taking me out to play when I needed it. And most of all, huge thanks to Norman for all his insight, his support, and his cups of coffee.

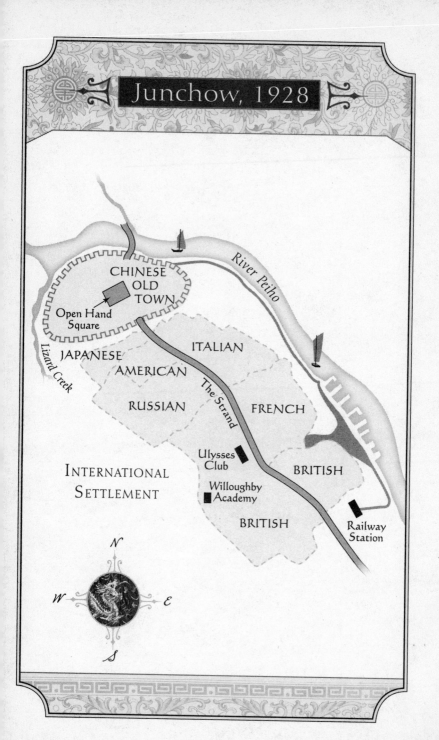

Junchow, 1928

CHINESE OLD TOWN

Open Hand Square

River Peiho

Lizard Creek

JAPANESE

ITALIAN

AMERICAN

RUSSIAN

The Strand

FRENCH

INTERNATIONAL SETTLEMENT

Ulysses Club

Willoughby Academy

BRITISH

BRITISH

Railway Station

N
W E
S

1

Russia
December 1917

THE TRAIN GROWLED TO A HALT. GRAY STEAM BELCHED from its heaving engine into the white sky, and the twenty-four freight carriages behind bucked and rattled as they lurched shrieking to a standstill. The sound of horses and of shouted commands echoed across the stillness of the empty frozen landscape.

"Why have we stopped?" Valentina Friis whispered to her husband.

Her breath curled between them like an icy curtain. It seemed to her despairing mind to be the only part of her that still had any strength to move. She clutched his hand. Not for warmth this time, but because she needed to know he was still there at her side. He shook his head, his face blue with cold because his coat was wrapped tightly around the sleeping child in his arms.

"This is not the end," he said.

"Promise me," she breathed.

He gave his wife a smile and together they clung to the rough tim-bered wall of the cattle wagon that enclosed them, pressing their eyes to the slender gaps between the planks. All around them others did the same. Desperate eyes. Eyes that had already seen too much.

"They mean to kill us," the bearded man on Valentina's right stated in a flat voice. He spoke with a heavy Georgian accent and wore his astrakhan hat well down over his ears. "Why else would we stop in the middle of nowhere?"

"Oh sweet Mary, mother of God, protect us."

It was the wail of an old woman still huddled on the filthy floor and wrapped in so many shawls she looked like a fat little Buddha. But underneath the stinking rags was little more than skin and bone.

"No, *babushka*," another male voice insisted. It came from the rear end of the carriage where the ice-ridden wind tore relentlessly through the slats, bringing the breath of Siberia into their lungs. "No, it'll be General Kornilov. He knows we're on this godforsaken cattle train starving to death. He won't let us die. He's a great commander."

A murmur of approval ran around the clutch of gaunt faces, bringing a spark of belief to the dull eyes, and a young boy with dirty blond hair who had been lying listlessly in one corner leapt to his feet and started to cry with relief. It had been a long time since anyone had wasted energy on tears.

"Dear God, I pray you are right," said a hollow-eyed man with a stained bandage on the stump of his arm. At night he groaned endlessly in his sleep, but by day he was silent and tense. "We're at war," he said curtly. "General Lavr Kornilov cannot be everywhere."

"But I tell you he's here. You'll see."

"Is he right, Jens?" Valentina tilted her face up to her husband.

She was only twenty-four, small and fragile, but possessed sensuous dark eyes that could, with a glance, for a brief moment, make a man forget the cold and the hunger that gnawed at his insides or the weight of a child in his arms. Jens Friis was ten years older than his wife and fearful for her safety if the roving Bolshevik soldiers took one look at her beautiful face. He bent his head and brushed a kiss on her forehead.

"We shall soon know," he said.

The red beard on his unshaven cheek was rough against Valentina's cracked lips, but she welcomed the feel of it and the smell of his unwashed body. They reminded her that she had not died and gone to hell. Because hell was exactly what this felt like. The thought that this nightmare journey across thousands of miles of snow and ice might go on forever, through the whole of eternity, that this was her cruel damnation for defying her parents, was one that haunted her, awake and asleep.

Suddenly the great sliding door of the wagon was thrust open and fierce voices shouted, *"Vse is vagona, bistro."* Out of the wagons.

★ ★ ★

THE LIGHT BLINDED VALENTINA. THERE WAS SO MUCH OF IT. After the perpetually twilit world inside the wagon, it rushed at her from the huge arc of sky, skidded off the snow, and robbed her of vision. She blinked hard and forced the scene around her into focus.

What she saw chilled her heart.

A row of rifles. All aimed directly at the ragged passengers as they scrambled off the train and huddled in anxious groups, their coats pulled tight to keep out the cold and the fear. Jens reached up to help the old woman down from their wagon, but before he could take her hand she was pushed from behind and landed facedown in the snow. She made no sound, no cry. But she was quickly yanked onto her feet by the soldier who had thrown open the wagon door and shaken as carelessly as a dog shakes a bone.

Valentina exchanged a look with her husband. Without a word they slid their child from Jens's shoulder and stood her between them, hiding her in the folds of their long coats as they moved forward together.

"Mama?" It was a whisper. Though only five years old, the girl had already learned the need for silence. For stillness.

"Hush, Lydia," Valentina murmured but could not resist a glance down at her daughter. All she saw was a pair of wide tawny eyes in a heart-shaped bone-white face and little booted feet swallowed up by the snow. She pressed closer against her husband and the face no longer existed. Only the small hand clutching her own told her otherwise.

THE MAN FROM GEORGIA IN THE WAGON WAS RIGHT. THIS was truly the middle of nowhere. A godforsaken landscape of nothing but snow and ice and the occasional windswept rock face glistening black. In the far distance a bank of skeletal trees stood like a reminder that life could exist here. But this was no place to live.

No place to die.

The men on horseback didn't look much like an army. Nothing remotely like the smart officers Valentina was used to seeing in the ballrooms and *troikas* of St. Petersburg or ice skating on the Neva, showing off their crisp uniforms and impeccable manners. These men were different. Alien to that elegant world she had left behind. These men were hostile. Dangerous. About fifty of them had spread out along the length of the train, alert and hungry as wolves. They wore an assortment of greatcoats against the cold, some gray, others black, and one a deep muddy green. But all cradled the same long-nosed rifle in their arms and had the same fanatical look of hatred in their eyes.

"Bolsheviks," Jens murmured to Valentina, as they were herded into a group where the fragile sound of prayers trickled like tears. "Pull your hood over your head and hide your hands."

"My hands?"

"Yes."

"Why my hands?"

"Comrade Lenin likes to see them scarred and roughened by years of what he calls honest labor." He touched her arm protectively. "I don't think piano playing counts, my love."

Valentina nodded, slipped her hood over her head and her one free hand into her pocket. Her gloves, her once beautiful sable gloves, had been torn to shreds during the months in the forest, that time of traveling on foot by night, eating worms and lichen by day. It had taken its toll on more than just her gloves.

"Jens," she said softly, "I don't want to die."

He shook his head vehemently and his free hand jabbed toward the tall soldier on horseback who was clearly in command. The one in the green greatcoat.

"He's the one who should die—for leading the peasants into this mass insanity that is tearing Russia apart. Men like him open up the floodgates of brutality and call it justice."

At that moment the officer called out an order and more of his troops dismounted. Rifle barrels were thrust into faces, thudded against backs. As the train breathed heavily in the silent wilderness, the soldiers pushed and jostled its cargo of hundreds of displaced people into a tight circle fifty yards away from the rail track and then proceeded to strip the wagons of possessions.

"No, please, don't," shouted a man at Valentina's elbow as an armful of tattered blankets and a tiny cooking stove were hurled out of one of the front wagons. Tears were running down his cheeks.

She put out a hand. Held his shoulder. No words could help. All around her, desperate faces were gray and taut.

In front of each wagon the meager pile of possessions grew as the carefully hoarded objects were tossed into the snow and set on fire. Flames, fired by coal from the steam engine and a splash of vodka, devoured the last scraps of their self-respect. Their clothes, the blankets, photographs, a dozen treasured icons of the Virgin Mary and even a miniature painting of Tsar Nicholas II. All blackened, burned, and turned to ash.

"You are traitors. All of you. Traitors to your country."

The accusation came from the tall officer in the green greatcoat. Though he wore no insignia except a badge of crossed sabers on his peaked cap, there was no mistaking his position of authority. He sat upright on a large heavy-muscled horse, which he controlled effortlessly with an occasional flick of his heel. His eyes were dark and impatient, as if this cargo of White Russians presented him with a task he found distasteful.

"None of you deserve to live," he said coldly.

A deep moan rose from the crowd. It seemed to sway with shock.

He raised his voice. "You exploited us. You maltreated us. You believed the time would never come when you would have to answer to *us*, the people of Russia. But you were wrong. You were blind. Where is all your wealth now? Where are your great houses and your fine horses now? The tsar is finished and I swear to you that—"

A single voice rose up from somewhere in the middle of the crowd. "God bless the tsar. God protect the Romanovs."

A shot rang out. The officer's rifle had bucked in his hands. A figure in the front row fell to the ground, a dark stain on the snow.

"That man paid for *your* treachery." His hostile gaze swept over the stunned crowd with contempt. "You and your kind were parasites on the backs of the starving workers. You created a world of cruelty and tyranny where rich men turned their backs on the cries of the poor. And now you desert your country, like rats fleeing from a burning ship. And you dare to take the youth of Russia with you." He swung his horse to one side and moved away from the throng of gaunt faces. "Now you will hand over your valuables."

At a nod of his head, the soldiers started to move among the prisoners. Systematically they seized all jewelry, all watches, all silver cigar cases, anything that had any worth, including all forms of money. Insolent hands searched clothing, under arms, inside mouths, and even between breasts, seeking out the carefully hidden items that meant survival to their owners. Valentina lost the emerald ring secreted in the hem of her dress, while Jens was stripped of his last gold coin in his boot. When it was over, the crowd stood silent except for a dull sobbing. Robbed of hope, they had no voice.

But the officer was pleased. The look of distaste left his face. He turned and issued a sharp command to the man on horseback behind him. Instantly a handful of mounted soldiers began to weave through the crowd, dividing it, churning it into confusion. Valentina clung to the small hand hidden in hers and knew that Jens would die before he released the other one. A faint cry escaped from the child when a big bay horse swung into them and its iron-shod hooves trod dangerously close, but otherwise she hung on fiercely and made no sound.

"What are they doing?" Valentina whispered.

"Taking the men. And the children."

"Oh God, no."

But he was right. Only the old men and the women were ignored. The others were being separated out and herded away. Cries of anguish tore through the frozen wasteland and somewhere on the far side of the train a wolf crept forward on its belly, drawn by the scent of blood.

"Jens, no, don't let them take you. Or her," Valentina begged.

"Papa?" A small face emerged between them.

"Hush, my love."

A rifle butt thumped into Jens's shoulder just as he flicked his coat back over his daughter's head. He staggered but kept his feet.

"You. Get over there." The soldier on horseback looked as if he were just longing for an excuse to pull the trigger. He was very young. Very nervous.

Jens stood his ground. "I am not Russian." He reached into his inside pocket, moving his hand slowly so as not to unsettle the soldier, and drew out his passport.

"See," Valentina pointed out urgently. "My husband is Danish."

The soldier frowned, uncertain what to do. But his commander had sharp eyes. He instantly spotted the hesitation. He kicked his horse forward into the panicking crowd and came up alongside the young private.

"Grodensky, why are you wasting time here?" he demanded.

But his attention was not on the soldier. It was on Valentina. Her face had tilted up to speak to the mounted *soldat* and her hood had fallen back, revealing a sweep of long dark hair and a high forehead with pale flawless skin. Months of starvation had heightened her cheekbones and made her eyes huge in her face.

The officer dismounted. Up close, they could see he was younger than he had appeared on horseback, probably still in his thirties, but with the eyes of a much older man. He took the passport and studied it briefly, his gaze flicking from Valentina to Jens and back again.

"But you," he said roughly to Valentina, "you are Russian?"

Behind them shots were beginning to sound.

"By birth, yes," she answered without turning her head to the noise. "But now I am Danish. By marriage." She wanted to edge closer to her husband, to hide the child more securely between them, but did not dare move. Only her fingers tightened on the tiny cold hand in hers.

Without warning, the officer's rifle slammed into Jens's stomach and he doubled over with a grunt of pain, but immediately another blow to the back of his head sent him sprawling onto the snow. Blood spattered its icy surface.

Valentina screamed.

Instantly she felt the little hand pull free of her own and saw her daughter throw herself at the officer's legs with the ferocity of a spitting wildcat, biting and scratching in a frenzy of rage. As if in slow motion, she watched the rifle butt start to descend toward the little head.

"No," she shouted and snatched the child up into her arms before the blow could fall. But stronger hands tore the young body from her grasp.

"No, no, no!" she screamed. "She is a Danish child. She is not a Russian."

"She *is* Russian," the officer insisted and drew his revolver. "She fights like a Russian." Casually he placed the gun barrel at the center of the child's forehead.

The child froze. Only her eyes betrayed her fear. Her little mouth was clamped shut.

"Don't kill her, I beg you," Valentina pleaded. "Please don't kill her. I'll do . . . anything . . . anything. If you let her live."

A deep groan issued from the crumpled figure of her husband at her feet.

"Please," she begged softly. She undid the top button of her coat, not taking her eyes from the officer's face. "Anything."

The Bolshevik commander reached out a hand and touched her hair, her cheek, her mouth. She held her breath. Willing him to want her. And for a fleeting moment she knew she had him. But when he glanced around at his watching men, all of them lusting for her, hoping their turn would be next, he shook his head.

"No. You are not worth it. Not even for soft kisses from your beautiful lips. No. It would cause too much trouble among my troops." He shrugged. "A shame." His finger tightened on the trigger.

"Let me buy her," Valentina said quickly.

When he turned his head to stare at her with a frown that brought his heavy eyebrows together, she said again, "Let me buy her. And my husband."

He laughed. The soldiers echoed the harsh sound of it. "With what?"

"With these." Valentina thrust two fingers down her throat and bent over as a gush of warm bile swept up from her empty stomach. In the center of the yellow smear of liquid that spread out on the snow's crust lay two tiny cotton packages, each no bigger than a hazelnut. At a gesture from the officer, a bearded soldier scooped them up and handed them to him. They sat, dirty and damp, in the middle of his black glove.

Valentina stepped closer. "Diamonds," she said proudly.

He scraped off the cotton wraps, eagerness in every movement, until what looked like two nuggets of sparkling ice gleamed up at him.

Valentina saw the greed in his face. "One to buy my daughter. The other for my husband."

"I can take them anyway. You have already lost them."

"I know."

Suddenly he smiled. "Very well. We shall deal. Because I have the diamonds and because you are beautiful, you shall keep the brat." Lydia was thrust into Valentina's arms and clung to her as if she would climb right inside her body.

"And my husband," Valentina insisted.

"Your husband we keep."

"No, no. Please God, I . . ."

But the horses came in force then. A solid wall of them that drove the women and old men back to the train.

Lydia screamed in Valentina's arms, "Papa, Papa . . . ," and tears flowed down her thin cheeks as she watched his body being dragged away.

VALENTINA COULD FIND NO TEARS. ONLY THE FROZEN EMPTI-ness within her, as bleak and lifeless as the wilderness that swept past outside. She sat on the foul-smelling floor of the cattle truck with her back against the slatted wall. Night was seeping in and the air was so cold it hurt to breathe, but she didn't notice. Her head hung low and her eyes saw nothing. Around her the sound of grief filled the vacant spaces. The boy with dirty blond hair was gone, as well as the man who had been so certain the White Russian army had arrived to feed them. Women wept for the loss of their husbands and the theft of their sons and daughters, and stared with naked envy at the one child on the train.

Valentina had wrapped her coat tightly around Lydia and herself, but could feel her daughter shivering.

"Mama," the girl whispered, "is Papa coming back?"

"No."

It was the twentieth time she had asked the same question, as if by continually repeating it she could make the answer change. In the gloom Valentina felt the little body shudder.

So she took her daughter's cold face between her hands and said fiercely, "But we will survive, you and I. Survival is everything."

2

THE AIR IN THE MARKETPLACE TASTED OF MULE DUNG. THE man in the cream linen suit did not know he was being followed. That eyes watched his every move. He held a crisp white handkerchief to his nose and asked himself yet again why, in the name of all that's holy, he had come to this godforsaken place.

Unexpectedly, the firm English line of his mouth dipped into the hint of a smile. Godforsaken it may be, but not forsaken by its own heathen gods. The lugubrious sound of huge bronze bells came drifting down from the temple to the market square and crept uninvited into his head. It reverberated there in a dull monotone that seemed to go on forever. In an effort to distract himself, he selected a piece of porcelain from one of the many stalls shouting for business and lifted it up to the light. As translucent as dragon's breath. As fragile as the heart of a lotus flower. The bowl fitted into the curve of his palm as if it belonged there.

"Early Ch'ing dynasty," he murmured with pleasure.

"You buy?" The Chinese stallholder in his drab gray tunic was staring at him expectantly, black eyes bright with feigned good humor. "You like?"

The Englishman leaned forward, careful to avoid any contact between the rough-hewn stall and his immaculate jacket. In a perfectly polite voice he asked, "Tell me, how is it you people manage to produce the most perfect creations on earth, at the same time as the foulest filth I have ever seen?"

He gestured with his empty hand to the crush of bodies that thronged the market square, to the sweat-soaked mule train with blocks of salt creaking in great piles on the animals' unbreakable backs as they barged their way noisily through the crowds and past the food stalls, leaving their droppings to ripen in the grinding heat of the day. The smallpox-scarred muleteer, now that he'd arrived safely in Junchow, was grinning like a monkey, but stank like a yak. Then there was the white mess from the hundreds of bamboo birdcages. It coated the cobbles underfoot and merged with the stench of the open sewer that ran along one side of the square. Two young children with spiky black pigtails were squatting beside it, happily biting into something green and juicy. God only knew what it was. God and the flies. They swarmed over everything.

The Englishman turned back to the stallholder and, with a shrug of despair, asked again, "How do you do it?"

The Chinese vendor gazed up at the tall *fanqui*, the Foreign Devil, with a total lack of comprehension, but he had promised his new concubine a pair of satin slippers today, red embroidered ones, so he was reluctant to lose a sale. He repeated two of his eight words of English. "You buy?" and added hopefully, "So nice."

"No." The Englishman lovingly replaced the bowl beside a black-and-white lacquered tea caddy. "No buy."

He turned away but was allowed no peace. Instantly accosted by the next stallholder. The flow of chatter, in that damn language he couldn't understand, sounded to his large Western ears like cats fighting. It was this blasted heat. It was getting to him. He mopped his brow with his handkerchief and checked his pocket watch. Time to make tracks. Didn't want to be late for his luncheon appointment with Binky Fenton at the Ulysses Club. Bit of a stickler about that sort of thing, was old Binky. Quite right too.

A sharp pain cut into his shoulder. A rickshaw was squeezing past, clattering over the cobbles. Damn it, there were just too many of the darn things. Shouldn't be allowed. His eyes flicked toward the occupant of the rickshaw with irritation, but instantly softened. Sitting very upright, slender in a high-necked lilac cheongsam, was a beautiful young Chinese woman. Her long dark hair hung like a cloak of satin far down her back and a cream orchid was fastened behind her ear by a mother-of-pearl comb. He couldn't see her eyes, for they were lowered discreetly as she gazed down at her tiny hands on her lap, but her face was a perfect oval. Her skin as exquisite as the porcelain bowl he'd held in his hands earlier.

A rough shout dragged his attention to the struggling rickshaw coolie, but he averted his eyes with distaste. The fellow was wearing nothing but a rag on his head and a filthy loincloth round his waist. No wonder she preferred to look at her folded hands. It was disgusting the way these natives flaunted their naked bodies. He raised his handkerchief to his nose. And the smell. Dear God, how did they live with it?

A sudden shrill blare of a brass trumpet made him jump. Rattled his nerves. He stumbled back against a young European girl standing behind him.

"I'm so sorry, miss." He touched his panama hat in apology. "Please excuse my clumsiness. That vile noise got the better of me."

She was wearing a navy blue dress and a wide-brimmed straw hat that hid her hair and shaded her face from him, but he gained the distinct impression she was laughing at him because the trumpet proved to be nothing more than the local knife grinder's way of announcing his arrival in the market. With a curt nod, he crossed the street. The girl shouldn't be there anyway, not without a chaperone. His thoughts were sidetracked by the sight of a carved image of Sun Wu-kong, the magical monkey god, on one of the other stalls, so he did not stop to ask himself what possible reason an unattended white girl could have for being alone in a jostling Chinese market.

LYDIA'S HANDS WERE QUICK. HER TOUCH WAS SOFT. HER fingers could lift the smile from the Buddha himself and he'd never know.

She slid away into the crowd. No backward glance. That was the hardest part. The urge to turn and check that she was in the clear was so fierce it burned a hole in her chest. But she clamped a hand over her pocket, ducked under the jagged tip of the water carrier's shoulder pole, and headed toward the carved archway that formed the entrance to the market. Stalls piled high with fish and fruit lined both sides of the street, so that where it narrowed at the far end, the crush of people deepened. Here she felt safer.

But her mouth was dry.

She licked her lips. Risked a quick glance back. And smiled. The cream suit was exactly where she'd left him, bent over a stall and fanning himself with his hat. Her sharp eyes picked out a young Chinese street urchin wearing what looked like coarse blue pajamas, loitering meaningfully right behind him. The man had no idea. Not yet. But at any moment he might decide to check his pocket watch. That's what he'd been doing when she first spotted him. The stupid melonhead, didn't he have more sense?

She'd known straight off. This one was going to be easy.

A little sigh of pleasure escaped her. And it wasn't only the adrenaline talking after she'd made a good nab. Just the sight of the Chinese market spread out before her gave her a kick of delight. It was the energy of it she adored. Teeming with life in every corner, bursting out in noise and clatter, in the high-pitched cries of the vendors and in the bright yellows and reds of the persimmons and watermelons. It was in the flow of the rooftops, the way they curled up at the edges as if trying to hook a ride on the wind, and in the loose free-moving clothes of the people below as they haggled for crayfish or bowls of baked eels or an extra *jin* of alfalfa shoots. It was as if the very smell of the place had seeped into her blood.

Not like in the International Settlement. There, it seemed to Lydia, they had whalebone corsets clamped round their minds as well as round their bodies.

SHE MOVED FAST. BUT NOT TOO FAST. SHE DIDN'T WANT TO attract attention. Though foreigners in the native markets were not uncommon, a fifteen-year-old girl on her own certainly was. She had to be careful. Ahead of her lay the broad paved road back to the International Settlement and that's exactly where the cream suit would expect to find her if he came looking. But Lydia had other plans. She turned sharp right.

And ran straight into a policeman.

"Okay, miss?"

Her heart hammered against her ribs. "Yes."

He was young. And Chinese. One of the municipal recruits who patrolled proudly in their smart navy uniform and shiny white belt. He was looking at her curiously.

"You lost? Young ladies not come here. Not suitable."

She shook her head and treated him to her sweetest smile. "No, I'm meeting my *amah* here."

"Nurse ought know better." He frowned. "Not good. Not good at all."

An angry shout suddenly rang out from the marketplace behind Lydia and she was all set to run, but the policeman had lost interest. He touched his cap and hurried past her into the crowded square. Instantly she was off. Up the steep stone steps. Under the stone arch that would take her deep into the heart of the old Chinese town with its ancient walls guarded by four massive stone lions. She didn't dare come here often, but at times like this it was worth the risk.

It was a world of dark alleyways and darker hatreds. The streets were narrow. Cobbled and slippery, dirty with trampled vegetables. To her eyes the buildings had a secretive look, hiding their whispers behind high stone walls. Or else low and squat, lurching against each other at odd angles, next to tearooms with curling eaves and gaily painted verandas. Grotesque faces of strange gods and goddesses leered down at her from unexpected niches.

Men carrying sacks passed her, and women carrying babies. They stared at her with hostile eyes, said things to her she couldn't understand. But more than once she heard the word *fanqui*, Foreign Devil, and it made her shiver. On one corner an old woman, wrapped in rags, was begging in the dirt, her hand stretched out like a claw, tears running unchecked down the deep lines of her skeletal face. It was a sight Lydia had seen many times, even on the streets of the International Settlement in recent days. But it was one she could never get used to. They frightened her, these beggars. They threw her mind into panic. She had nightmares where she was one of them, in the gutter. Alone, with only worms to eat.

She hurried. Head down.

To reassure herself she wrapped her fingers round the heavy object in her pocket. It felt expensive. She longed to inspect her spoils but it was far too dangerous here. Some local tong member would chop her hand off as soon as look at her, so she forced herself to be patient. But still the tiny hairs on the back of her neck stood up. Only when she reached Copper Street did she breathe more easily and the sick churning in the pit of her stomach begin to subside. That was the fear. Always the same after she'd made a nab. Trickles of sweat ran down her back and she told herself it was because of the heat. She tweaked her scruffy hat to a smarter angle, glanced up at the flat white sky that lay like a stifling blanket over the whole of the ancient town, then set off toward Mr. Liu's shop.

It was set back in a dingy porch. The doorway was narrow and dark but its shop window gleamed bright and cheerful, surrounded by red latticework and draped with elegantly painted hanging scrolls. Lydia knew it was all part of the Chinese need for *face*. The façade. But what went on behind the public face was a very private matter. The interior was barely visible. She didn't know what the time was but was sure she had overrun the hour allotted for lunch. Mr. Theo would be angry with her for being late back to class, might even take a rule to her knuckles. She had better hurry.

But as she opened the shop door, she could not resist a smile. She might be only fifteen, but already she was aware that expecting to hurry a Chinese business deal was as absurd as trying to count the fluttering pigeons that wheeled through the sky above the gray tiled roofs of Junchow.

INSIDE, THE LIGHT WAS DIM AND IT TOOK A FEW MOMENTS for Lydia's eyes to adjust. The smell of jasmine hung in the air, cool and refreshing after the humid weight of the air in the streets outside. The sight of a black table in one corner with a bowl of fried peanuts on it reminded her that she had eaten nothing since a watery spoonful of rice porridge that morning.

A thin stick of a man in a long brown robe shuffled out from behind an oak counter. His face was as wrinkled as a walnut, with a long tufty beard on the point of his chin, and he still wore his hair in the old-fashioned Manchu queue that trailed like a gray snake down his back. His eyes were black and shrewd.

"Welcome, Missy, to my humble business. It does my worthless heart good to set eyes on you again." He bowed politely and she returned the courtesy.

"I came because all Junchow says that only Mr. Liu knows the true value of beautiful craftsmanship," Lydia said smoothly.

"You do me honor, Missy." He smiled, pleased, and gestured toward the low table in the corner. "Please, sit. Refresh yourself. The summer rains are cruel this year and the gods must be angry indeed, for they breathe fire down on us each day from the sky. Let me bring you a cup of jasmine tea to soothe the heat from your blood."

"Thank you, Mr. Liu. I'd like that."

She sat down on a bamboo stool and slipped a peanut into her mouth as soon as his back was turned. While he busied himself behind a screen inlaid with ivory peacocks, Lydia's gaze inspected the shop.

It was dark and secretive, its dusty shelves so crowded with objects they tumbled over each other. Fine Jiangxi porcelain, hundreds of years old, lay next to the very latest radio in shiny cream Bakelite. Delicately painted scrolls hung from a ferocious Boxer sword and above them a strange twisted tree made of bronze seemed to grow out of the top of a grinning monkey's head. On the opposite side two German teddy bears leaned against a row of silk top hats handmade in Jermyn Street. A weird contraption of wood and metal springs was propped up beside the door and it took Lydia a moment to realize it was a false leg.

Mr. Liu was a pawnbroker. He bought and sold people's dreams and oiled the wheels of daily existence. Lydia let her eyes glide over the rail at the back of the shop. That was where she loved to linger. A glittering array of elegant evening gowns and fur coats, so many and so heavy that the rail bowed in the middle as if flexing its back. Just the sight of such luxury made Lydia's young heart give a sharp little skip of envy. Before she left the shop she always made a point of sidling over there to run her hand through the dense furs. A glossy muskrat or a honey mink, she had learned to recognize them. One day, she promised herself, things would be different. One day she'd be buying, not selling. She'd march right in here with a bucketload of dollars and whisk one of these away. Then she'd drape it around her mother's shoulders and say, "Look, Mama, look how beautiful you are.

We're safe now. You can smile again." And her mother would give a glorious laugh. And be happy.

She slipped two more peanuts into her mouth and started tapping her tight little black shoe on the tiles with impatience.

At once Mr. Liu reappeared with a tray and a watchful smile. He placed two tiny wafer-thin cups without handles on the table alongside a teapot. It was unglazed and looked very old. In silence the old man filled the cups. Oddly, the aroma of jasmine blossom that rose from the stream of hot liquid did indeed soothe the heat from Lydia's mind and she was tempted to place her find on the table right there and then. But she knew better. Now they would gossip. This was the way the Chinese did business.

"I trust you are keeping in good health, Missy, and that all is well within the International Settlement in these troubled times."

"Thank you, Mr. Liu, I am well. But in the Settlement . . ." She gave what she hoped was a woman-of-the-world shrug. "There is always trouble."

His eyes brightened. "Was the Summer Ball at Mackenzie Hall not a success?"

"Oh yes, of course it was. Everyone was there. So elegant. All the grandest motorcars and carriages. And jewels, Mr. Liu, you would have appreciated the jewels. It was just so . . . ," she couldn't quite keep the wistfulness out of her voice, "so perfect."

"I am indeed pleased to hear it. It is good to know the many nations who rule this worthless corner of China can meet together for once without cutting each other's throats."

Lydia laughed. "Oh, there were plenty of arguments. Around the gaming tables."

Mr. Liu bent a fraction closer. "What was the subject of the dispute?"

"I believe it was . . . ," she paused deliberately to sip the last of her tea, keeping him hanging there, listening to his breath coming in short expectant gasps, ". . . something to do with bringing over more Sikhs from India. They want to reinforce the municipal police, you see."

"Are they expecting trouble?"

"Commissioner Lacock, our chief of police, said it was just a precaution because of the looting going on in Peking. And because so many of your people are pouring into our Junchow International Settlement in search of food."

"*Ai-ya*, we are indeed in terrible times. Death is as common as life. Starvation and famine all around us." He let a small silence settle between them, like a stone in a pond. "But explain to my dull brain, if you would, Missy, how someone like you, so young, is invited to attend this most illustrious occasion at Mackenzie Hall?"

Lydia blushed. "My mother," she said grandly, "was the finest pianist in all Russia and played for the tsar himself in his Winter Palace. She is now in great demand in Junchow. I accompany her."

"Ah." He bowed respectfully. "Then all is clear."

She didn't much like the way he said that. She was always wary of his impressive command of English and had been told that he was once the comprador for the Jackson & Mace Mining Company. She could imagine him with a pickax in one hand and a lump of gold in the other. But it was whispered he had left under a cloud. She glanced at the shelves and the padlocked display case of sparkling jewelry. In China, thieving was not exactly unknown.

Now it was her turn.

"And I hope that the increase of people in town will bring advantages to your own business, Mr. Liu."

"*Ai!* It pains me to say otherwise. But business is so poor." His small dark eyes drooped in exaggerated sorrow. "That son of a dung snake, Feng Tu Hong, the head of our new council, is driving us all into the gutter."

"Oh? How is that?"

"He demands such high taxes from all the shops of old Junchow that it drains the blood from our veins. It is no surprise to my old ears to hear that the young Communists skulk around at night putting up their posters. Two more were beheaded in the square yesterday. These are hard times, Missy. I can hardly find enough scraps to feed myself and my worthless sons. *Ai-ya!* Business is very bad, very bad."

Lydia managed to bite back her smile.

"I grieve for you, Mr. Liu. But I have brought you something that I hope will help your business become successful once again."

Mr. Liu inclined his head. A signal that the time had come.

She put her hand in her pocket and drew out her prize. She laid it on the ebony table where it gleamed as bright as a full moon. The watch was beautiful, even to her untutored eyes, and from its handsome gilt case and heavy silver chain drifted the smell of money. She observed Mr. Liu carefully. His face did not move a muscle, but he failed to keep the brief flash of desire out of his eyes. He turned his face away from it and slowly sipped his tiny cup of tea. But Lydia was used to his ways, ready for his little tricks.

She waited.

Finally he picked it up and from his gown produced an eyeglass to inspect the watch more closely. He eased open the front silver cover, then the back and the inner cover, murmuring to himself under his breath in Mandarin, his hands caressing the case. After several minutes he replaced it on the table.

"It is of some slight value," he said indifferently. "But not much."

"I believe the value is more than slight, Mr. Liu."

"Ah, but these are hard times. Who has money for such things as this when there is no food on the table?"

"It is lovely craftsmanship."

His finger moved, as if it would stroke the silver piece once more, but instead it stroked his little beard. "It is not bad," he admitted. "More tea?"

For ten minutes they bargained, back and forth. At one point Lydia stood up and put the watch back in her pocket, and that was when Mr. Liu raised his offer.

"Three hundred and fifty Chinese dollars."

She put the watch back on the table.

"Four hundred and fifty," she demanded.

"Three hundred and sixty dollars. I can afford no more, Missy. My family will go hungry."

"But it is worth more. Much more."

"Not to me. I'm sorry."

She took a deep breath. "It's not enough."

He sighed and shook his head, his long queue twitching in sympathy. "Very well, though I will not eat for a week." He paused and his sharp eyes looked at her assessingly. "Four hundred dollars."

She took it.

★　★　★

LYDIA WAS HAPPY. SHE SPED BACK THROUGH THE OLD town, her head spinning with all the good things she would buy—a bag of sugary apricot dumplings to start with, and yes, a beautiful silk scarf for her mother and a new pair of shoes for herself because these pinched so dreadfully, and maybe a . . .

The road ahead was blocked. It was a scene of utter chaos, and crouching at the heart of it was a big black Bentley, all wide sweeping fenders and gleaming chrome work. The car was so huge and so incongruous in the narrow confines of streets designed for mules and wheelbarrows that for a moment Lydia couldn't believe she was seeing straight. She blinked. But it was still there, jammed between two rickshaws, one lying on its side with a fractured wheel, and up against a donkey and cart. The cart had shed its load of white lotus roots all over the road and the donkey was braying to get at them. Everyone was shouting.

It was just as Lydia was working out how best to edge around this little drama without attracting notice that a man's head leaned out the rear window of the Bentley and said in a voice clearly accustomed to command, "Boy, back this damn car up immediately and take the road that runs along the river."

"Yes, sir," said the uniformed chauffeur, still hitting the cart driver with his peaked cap. "Of course, sir. Right away, sir." He turned and gave his employer an obedient salute, then his eyes slid away as he added, "But is impossible, sir. That road too narrow."

The man in the car struck his own forehead in frustration and bellowed something Lydia didn't hang around to hear. Without appearing to hurry, she ducked down a small side street. Because she knew him, the man in the car. Knew who he was, anyway. That mane of white hair. That bristling moustache. The hawkish nose. It could only be Sir Edward Carlisle, Lord Governor of the International Settlement of Junchow. Just the old devil's name was enough to frighten children into obedience at bedtime. But what was he doing here? In the old Chinese town? He was well known for sticking his nose in where it wasn't wanted, and right now the last thing Lydia needed was for him to spot her.

"*Chyort!*" she swore under her breath.

It was to *avoid* contact with white faces that she came here, risked trespassing on Chinese territory. Selling her ill-gotten gains anywhere in the settlement would be far too dangerous. The police were always raiding the curio shops and pawnbrokers, despite the bribes that flew into their pockets from all directions. *Cumshaw*, they called it. It was just the way things were done here. Everyone knew that.

She glanced around at the street she had sneaked into, narrower and meaner than the others. And a flicker of anxiety crawled up the back of her neck like a spider. It was more an alleyway than a street and lay in deep shadow, too cramped for sunlight to slide in. Despite that, lines of washing stretched across it, hanging limp and lifeless as ghosts in the dank heat, while at the far end a man under a broad coolie hat was trundling a wheelbarrow toward her. It was piled high with dried grass. His progress was slow and laborious over the hard-packed earth, the squeal of his wheel the only sound in the silent street.

Why so silent?

It was then she spotted the woman standing in a squalid doorway, beckoning. Her face was made up to look like one of the girls that Lydia's friend Polly called Ladies of Delight, heavy black paint round the eyes and a slash of red for a mouth in a white-powdered face. But Lydia had the impression she was not as young as she would seem. One red-tipped finger continued to beckon to Lydia. She hesitated and brushed a hand across her mouth in a childish gesture she used when nervous. She should never have come down here. Not with a pocketful of money. Uneasily she shook her head.

"Dollars." The word floated down the street from the woman. "You like Chinese dollars?" Her narrow eyes were fixed on Lydia, though she came no nearer.

The silence seemed to grow louder. Where were the dirty raga-muffins at play in the gutter and the bickering neighbors? The windows of the houses were draped with oiled strips of paper, cheaper than glass, so where was the sound of pots and pans? Just the squeal, over and over, of the barrow's wheel and the whine of black flies around her ears. She drew a long breath and was shocked to find her palms slick with sweat. She turned to run.

But from nowhere a scrawny figure in black stood in her path. *"Ni zhege yochou yochun de ji!"* he shouted in her face.

Lydia couldn't understand his words but when he spat on the ground and hissed at her, their meaning was only too clear. He was very thin and despite the oppressive heat he wore a fur cap with ear flaps, below which hung wisps of gray hair. But his eyes were bright and fierce. He shook a tattooed fist in her face. Stupidly her eyes focused only on the dirt beneath his torn fingernails. She tried to think straight, but the thudding of her heart in her chest was getting in the way.

"Let me pass, boy," she managed to say. It was meant to be sharp. In control. Like Sir Edward Carlisle. But it didn't come out right.

"Wo zhishi yao nide qian, fanqui."

Again that word. *Fanqui.* Foreign Devil.

She tried to step around him but he was too fast. He blocked her way. Behind her the squeal of the wheelbarrow stopped, and when she glanced over her shoulder the woman and the wheelbarrow man were now standing together in the middle of the alleyway, swathed in dark shadows, watching her every move with hard eyes.

A thin hand suddenly clamped like a wire noose around her wrist.

She panicked and started to scream. Then the demons of hell itself seemed to let loose. The street filled with noise and shouts as the woman ran forward, shrieking, on hobbled feet, and the man abandoned his barrow and hurled himself with a growl toward Lydia, a long curved scythe at his side. And all the time the old devil's grip on her wrist tightened, his nails sinking like teeth into her flesh the more she struggled.

With no sound a fourth person stepped into the street. He was a young man, not much older than Lydia herself but tall for a Chinese, with a long pale neck and close-cropped hair and wearing a black V-neck tunic over loose trousers that flowed when he moved. His eyes were quick and decisive but there was a stillness to his face as he took in the situation. Anger flared in his dark eyes as he stared at the old leech hanging on to her wrist, and it gave Lydia a flicker of hope. She started to shout for help, but before the words were out of her mouth the world seemed to blur with movement. A whirling foot crashed full into the center of the old man's chest. Lydia clearly heard ribs splintering, and her tormentor was sent sprawling onto the ground with a yelp of pain.

She stumbled as he fell, then caught herself, but instead of fleeing, she remained where she stood, eyes wide with astonishment. Entranced by the movements of the young Chinese man. He seemed to float in the air, hover there, and then swing out an arm or a leg as fast as a cobra strike. It reminded her of the Russian ballet that Madame Medinsky had taken her to at the Victoria Theater last year. She'd heard about such fighting skills but never seen them in action before. The speed of it made her head swim. She watched him approach the man with the scythe and swing backward with elbows raised and hand outstretched, like a bird about to take flight, and then his whole body twisted and turned and became airborne. His arm shot out and crashed down on the back of the man's neck before the scythe could even begin its swing. The Chinese woman's red mouth opened in a wide scream of terror.

The young man turned to face Lydia. His black eyes were deepset, long and almond-shaped, and as Lydia looked into them an old memory stirred inside her. She'd seen that look before, that exact expression of concern on a face looking down at her in the snow, but so long ago she'd almost forgotten it. She was so used to fighting her own battles, the sight of someone offering to fight them for her set off a small explosion of astonishment in her chest.

"Thank you, *xie xie*, thank you," she cried, her breath ragged.

He gave a shrug of his broad shoulders, as if to indicate the whole thing were no effort, and in fact there was no gleam of sweat on his skin in spite of the speed of his attack and the stifling heat in the alley.

"You are not hurt?" he asked in perfect English.

"No."

"I'm glad. These people are gutter filth and bring shame to Junchow. But you should not be here, it is not safe for a . . ."

She thought he was going to say *fanqui*.

". . . for a girl with hair the color of fire. It would fetch a high price in the perfumed rooms above the teahouses."

"My hair or me?"

"Both."

Her fingers brushed aside one of the locks of her unruly mane that had fallen loose from under her hat, and she caught the stranger's slight intake of breath and the softening corners of his mouth as he watched. He lifted his hand and she was convinced he was about to put his fingers into the flames of her hair, but instead he pointed at the old man who had crawled into the shadow of a doorway. A black earthenware jar stood in one corner of it, its wide mouth stoppered by a cork the size of a fist. Bent double with pain, the man lifted the jar and with a scream of rage that brought spittle to his lips, he hurled it at the ground in front of Lydia and her rescuer.

Lydia leapt back as the jar shattered into a hundred pieces, and then her legs turned weak with fear when she saw what burst out of it.

A snake, black as jet and more than three feet long. A few seconds, that's all it took for the creature to slither cautiously toward Lydia, its forked tongue tasting her fear in the air. But abruptly it swept its head in a wide arc and disappeared toward one of the cracks in the wall. Lydia almost choked with relief. Those few seconds were ones she would not forget.

She looked back at the young man and was shocked to see that his face had grown pale and rigid. But his eyes were not on the snake. They were fixed on the old devil where he lay hunched in the doorway, staring up at them both with malice and something like triumph in his eyes.

Without dropping his gaze, the young Chinese said in a quick urgent voice, "You must run."

Lydia ran.

3

Theo Willoughby liked his pupils. That's why he ran a school: the Willoughby Academy of Junchow. He liked the raw untarnished eagerness of their young souls and the clear whites of their eyes. All unblemished. Untainted. Free from that damned Apple with its knowledge of Good and Evil. Yet at the same time he was fascinated by the change in them during the years they were under his wing, the gradual but irresistible journey from Paradise to Paradise Lost that took place in each of them.

"Starkey, stop chewing the end of that pen. It's school property. Anyway, you'll catch woodworm from it."

A faint titter ran round the classroom. The pupil in the second row of desks dug inky fingers into his mop of brown curls and threw his teacher a look of pure hatred.

Theo, at thirty-six years old, was as adept as any Chinese poker player at keeping his expression blank, so he didn't chuckle. Just gave a curt nod. "Back to work."

That was another thing he liked about them. They were so malleable. So easy to provoke. Like kittens with tiny little claws that barely scratched the surface. It was their eyes that were their true weapons. Their eyes could rake your heart to shreds if you let them. But he didn't let that happen. Oh yes, he liked them all right, but only up to a point. He was under no illusions. They stood on the opposite side of the fence and it was his job to haul them over it into a well-equipped adulthood, whether they wanted to or not.

"I would remind you all that the essay on Emperor Ch'eng Tsu is due in tomorrow," he said briskly. "No slackers, please."

Instantly a hand went up at the front of the class. It belonged to a fifteen-year-old girl with neatly bobbed blond hair and a sweet dimple in each cheek. She looked slightly nervous.

"What is it, Polly?"

"Sir, my father objects to the fact we are learning Chinese history. He says I must ask you why we are finding out what some heathen barbarians got up to hundreds of years ago, instead of . . . ?"

Theo brought down the wooden-backed board eraser with such a crash on his desk that it made the whole class jump. "Instead of what?" he demanded. "Instead of English history?" His arm shot out, pointing to a pupil in the front row.

"Bates, what is the date of the Battle of Naseby?"

"1645, sir."

The arm swung around to the back of the class. "Clara, what was the name of Henry the Eighth's fourth wife?"

"Anne of Cleves."

"Griffiths, who invented the spinning jenny?"

"James Hargreaves."

"Who was prime minister during the passing of the Reform Bills?"

"Lord Grey."

"When was the introduction of macadamized roads?"

"1819."

"Lydia . . . ," he paused, "who introduced the rickshaw to China?"

"The Europeans, sir. From Japan."

"Excellent." Theo slowly uncoiled his long limbs from his seat, his scholar's gown billowing around him like great black wings, and walked over to Polly's desk. He stood looking down at her, as a crow might look at a wren with its tiny foot in a snare. "So, Miss Mason, does that indicate a lack of knowledge in our little group of the history of our noble and victorious country? Would your father not be impressed by such a display of historical facts?"

Polly started to turn pink, her cheeks ripening to the color of plums. She stared down at her hands, fiddling with a pencil, and stammered something inaudible.

"I'm sorry, Polly," Theo said smoothly, "I didn't quite catch that. What did you say?"

"I said, yes, sir." But still her words were mumbled.

Theo turned to face the room. "Class, could any of you hear what Miss Mason said then?"

In the back row Gordon Trent stuck up a hand and grinned. "No, sir, I couldn't hear nothing."

"We will ignore that appalling use of the double negative by Mr. Trent and return to Miss Mason. So, let me remind you of my question, Polly," he said quietly. "Would your father not be impressed by such a display of historical facts?"

Before Polly could reply, Lydia jumped to her feet.

"Sir," she said politely, "it seems to me that Chinese history is much like Russian history to an English person."

With deadly calm, Theo abandoned the bowed blond head before him and moved back to his own desk. "Do enlighten us, Lydia. In what way is Chinese history much like Russia's to an English person?"

"They are both irrelevant, sir, to an English person who is living in England. I think what Polly means is that only out here in China do they matter at all. And all of us in this class will one day soon be living in England, more than likely."

Polly cast her friend a grateful glance, but Theo was not aware of it. He was staring at Lydia in silence. His gray eyes narrowed and something tightened around his mouth. But instead of the outburst his class expected from him, he sighed.

"You disappoint me. Not only are you late for class this afternoon but now you exhibit a gross misunderstanding of the country you are living in."

At that moment a sudden crackle of noise and explosions outside in the street broke up the tension in the room.

"Firecrackers," Theo said with a wave of his hand toward the open window. "A Chinese wedding or celebration of some kind." He leaned forward with sudden interest. "And why do they traditionally use firecrackers at such times, Lydia?"

"To frighten away evil spirits, sir."

"Correct. So in spite of condemning all Chinese history as *irrelevant*, you do actually know at least something about it." He pointed a finger at Polly in the front row. "Tell me, who invented gunpowder, Miss Mason?"

"The Chinese."

His finger traveled once more along the young faces.

"Who invented paper?"

"The Chinese."

"Who invented canal locks and the segmented arch?"

"The Chinese."

"Who invented printing?"

"The Chinese."

"The magnetic compass?"

"The Chinese."

"And are these things irrelevant, Lydia? To a person living in England?"

"No, sir."

He smiled. Satisfied. "Good. Now that we've cleared up that point, let us move on to a study of the Han dynasty. Any objections?"

Not one hand went up.

THEO KNEW LI MEI WAS AT THE WINDOW UPSTAIRS. THE TApering tips of her fingers rested on the glass, as if she would touch him through it. But he didn't turn. Or even glance up at her.

He stood beside the school gates, his tall frame very upright, his back melting in the fierce heat radiating off the wrought-iron gates as the afternoon showed no promise of relief. It wasn't the high temperatures that bothered him. It was the humidity. Throughout the summer it battered you down and robbed you of any energy until you cried out for the bright clear days of autumn. But it was the end of the school day and as always his light brown hair was freshly combed, his gown discarded and replaced by a crisp linen jacket. A headmasterly smile, cool yet approachable, firmly in place to greet mothers as they arrived to collect their children. The *amahs* and chauffeurs he ignored.

He did not approve of mothers who were too busy drinking tea or taking tennis lessons or playing endless rounds of bridge to collect their offspring themselves, but sent servants to do the job. Any more than he approved of fathers who poisoned their daughters' minds. Mr. Christopher Mason sat clearly in that category. Theo experienced a familiar ripple of frustration. What chance did this great country have when men like that, men who worked in the administration itself, regarded China's remarkable history as a waste of time? As not worth knowing. It disgusted Theo.

"Hello, Mr. Willoughby. Looks like rain again tonight."

"Good afternoon, Mrs. Mason. I do believe you're right."

The woman who had stopped in front of him was short and smiling, a dimple in each cheek like her daughter. Her fair hair was pulled back by a velvet ribbon and her round face was flushed with exertion. Little drops of sweat beaded her upper lip and glinted in the light.

Theo smiled. "Did you enjoy your ride?"

Anthea Mason laughed, leaning against her bicycle, which was a bright green tandem, one hand fiddling with the bell so that it gave off little chirrups. "Oh no, I never enjoy the ride here, it's uphill all the way." She was wearing a light cotton blouse and cycling slacks, but both looked creased and damp. Her blue eyes sparkled with anticipation. "But that means the trip home is a breeze. Especially with Polly on the backseat."

Theo decided to bring up the subject of Chinese history. "Mrs. Mason, there is something I feel I should . . ."

But her gaze was already scanning the regimental rows of pupils in navy uniform, all lined up in the courtyard under the watchful eye of Miss Courtney, one of his junior teachers. The school was a handsome redbrick building with a wide driveway at the front, a lawn on one side, and the courtyard on the other. It was a place of freshly waxed floors and clean blackboards.

"Ah, there's my girl." Mrs. Mason lifted a hand and waggled her fingers at her daughter. "Yoo-hoo, Polly. Crumpets for tea, sweetheart."

Polly blushed furiously with embarrassment, and on this occasion Theo did feel sorry for her. She detached herself from her companions and came over, dragging her heels. Beside her walked Lydia, their heads close together, one smooth and golden, the other a mass of long unruly copper waves stuffed under her boater. They were whispering to each other, but years of practice had enabled Theo to develop a batlike ability to decode a pupil's barely audible mutterings.

"Oh my God, Lyd, you could have been killed. Or worse." Polly's voice was breathless, her eyes wide, her hand clenched round her friend's thin arm as if she would drag her from the mouth of hell.

"I wish you'd seen him, the way he—" Lydia stopped abruptly, aware of Theo's eyes on them. "Bye, Polly," she said casually and stepped to one side.

"Hello, Lydia," Mrs. Mason called out in a cheery voice, though Theo saw her regard the girl with concern. "Would you like to come home with us for tea? I could call over one of the rickshaws."

"No, thank you, Mrs. Mason."

"We're having crumpets. Your favorite."

"I'm sorry, I can't today. I'd love to but I have some errands to run."

"For your mother?"

"That's right."

Polly was staring at her, plainly worried. Theo couldn't work out what was going on. But his attention was taken by a request from Anthea Mason as she placed one smart two-tone shoe on her pedal.

"Oh, Mr. Willoughby, I almost forgot. My husband asked me to mention that he'd like a few words, and would be grateful if you could meet him at the club tomorrow evening." She shook her head prettily and laughed, as if to make light of the summons. "You men, where would you be without your billiards and brandy?"

Then off she pedaled with her daughter on the seat behind her, both pairs of legs going in unison, and as Theo stared after them his smile slipped. His shoulders slumped.

"Damn," he murmured under his breath.

He turned and almost fell over Lydia, who was hovering behind him. They were both momentarily confused. Both apologized. She ducked her head, hid under her straw hat's brim. But too late to prevent him from seeing her face. She had been standing, as he had been, staring after the disappearing tandem as it wove its way with a tinkling bell through the busy street. But what shocked Theo was the expression in her amber eyes. They were full of such naked longing. The intensity of it created a little stabbing pain like an echo in his own heart.

What was it she wanted so badly?

The bicycle? He was well aware that the girl was poor. Everyone knew that her mother was one of the Russian refugees, with no man to earn a decent wage for the family; well, not a permanent man anyway. But this wasn't about the bicycle. No, Lydia wasn't that sort. So was it for Polly she yearned? After all, he'd known more than a few schoolgirls who had fallen in love with someone of their own sex, and certainly they were close, those two. He looked down thoughtfully at the straw boater. He noticed it was yellowing with age and was stained in numerous places on the crown where she had dumped it down carelessly or gripped it with a grubby hand when the wind blew in off the great northern plain. If it were anyone else, he'd tell her to ask her parents to buy a new one instantly.

So was it the mother she wanted?

Hardly. Her own mother, though she rarely came to the school unless specifically requested, was far more beautiful and infinitely more enticing than the homely Mrs. Mason. But then his own taste in women always ran to the dark and exotic. Even when he was a boy and could pop his penny in the peepshows or peer secretly at his father's book on the paintings of Paul Gauguin. A sudden influx of cars and parents demanded his attention, a flurry of smiles and polite handshakes, so it was not until ten minutes later when the courtyard was almost empty that he glanced around and found the young Russian girl still at his elbow.

"Good heavens, Lydia, what are you doing still here?"

"I've been waiting. I wanted to ask you something, Headmaster."

Theo chuckled to himself. He'd noticed before that pupils were very free with his courtesy title when they wanted something from him. Nevertheless he smiled encouragingly. "What is it?"

"You know all about China and Chinese ways, so . . ."

He snorted a derisive laugh. "I've only been here ten years. It would take a lifetime of study to know China, and even then you'd only have scratched the surface."

"But you speak Mandarin and you know a lot." Her eyes held his and there was an urgency in them that intrigued him.

"Yes," he agreed quietly. "I do know a lot."

"So can you tell me the name of something, please?"

"That depends on what this *something* is."

"It's the Chinese way of fighting. The one where they fly through the air and use their feet. I need to know what it's called."

"Ah, yes, the Chinese are famous for their martial arts. There are numerous kinds, each one with a different style and philosophy behind it. My own favorite is *tai chi chuan*. That's difficult to translate because it carries many meanings, but roughly it is the Yin Yang Fist." He noticed the girl was listening with a level of attention he wished she would apply to her ordinary school lessons. "But it sounds as if you're talking about *kung fu*."

"*Kung fu*," Lydia repeated carefully.

"That's right. It translates literally as Merit Master. The Japanese call it *karate*. That means empty hand. In other words, it's unarmed combat."

She smiled to herself, a soft smile of delight that warmed her slender face. "Yes. That's it."

"But why on earth do you need to know about unarmed combat?"

She gave him a bold, mischievous grin. "Because I want to learn more about Chinese ways, so that I can decide for myself whether they are relevant or irrelevant, sir."

"Well, I am pleased that you are so eager to learn more about the land you're living in, whatever the reason. Now off with you, young lady, as I have other things to do."

For a split second Lydia let her eyes slide to the upstairs window, and then without even a good-bye, she was gone.

Theo sighed. Lydia Ivanova was never going to make life easy for him. Only today he'd had to take the ruler to her knuckles because she was late for afternoon classes yet again. The girl had scant respect for rules. Not insolent exactly. But there was something about her, the way she walked into class, the independent way she held her head and in the way she raised her gaze to his slowly when he asked her a question. It was there in the back of her eyes. As if she knew something he didn't. It irritated him.

But not as much as Mr. Christopher Mason irritated him. He reached up and locked the heavy gates, shutting out the world. Only then did he allow himself the exquisite pleasure of looking up at the window.

"IT IS NOT WISE TO TWEAK TAIL OF TIGER, MY LOVE."

"What do you mean?" Theo kissed the delicious hollow at the base of Li Mei's throat and felt the pulse of her blood under his lips.

"I mean Mr. Mason."

"To hell with Mason."

They were lying naked on the bed, the shutters half-closed against the heat, allowing only a narrow shaft of light to steal into the room. It lay like a dusty sash of gold across Li Mei's body, as if it couldn't keep its fingers from her breasts any more than he could.

"Tiyo, my love, I am serious."

Theo raised his head and kissed the point of her chin. "Well, I'm not. I've been serious all day long with a whole school full of monkeys and now I want to be very unserious."

She laughed, a delighted sound that was so soft and low it made the souls of his feet tingle. Her skin smelled of hyacinths and tasted of honey, but infinitely more addictive. He brushed his lips down her sleek body, over the curve of her hip, and rested his cheek against her slender thigh with a sigh of pleasure.

"So you go see Mr. Mason tomorrow?"

"No. The man's a menace."

"Please, Tiyo."

She reached down and caressed his head, the tips of her fingers beginning a gentle massage of his scalp, until he could feel all the tension melting from his brain. He adored her touch. It was like no other woman's. He shut his eyes to block out everything else but that one swirling, emptying sensation.

"Tomorrow is Saturday," he murmured, "so I shall take you out on the river. There the air is cooler and in the evening we shall stop off at Hwang's and eat phoenix tail prawns and *kuo tieh* until we burst." He rolled over onto his side and smiled at her. "Would you like that?"

Her dark eyes were solemn. Gracefully she removed the cream orchid and the mother-of-pearl comb from her hair, placed them on the bedside table, and looked at him very seriously. "I very much like that, Tiyo," she said. "But not tomorrow."

"Why not tomorrow?"

"Because you see Mr. Mason tomorrow."

"For heaven's sake, Li Mei, I refuse to go running over there like a puppy every time he crooks his finger in my direction."

"You want lose school?"

Theo pulled away. Without a word he left the bed and went over to the open window where he stood staring out, his naked back rigid. After a long silence, he said, "You know I couldn't bear to lose my school."

A rustle of sheets and she was there with him. Her slight body pressed tight against his back, her arms clasped around his chest, her cheek on his shoulder blade. He could feel her long lashes whisper over his skin. Neither spoke.

From this high up on the hill Theo looked down at the tiled roofs of the town that had been his home for the last ten years, a home he loved, and a refuge from the whisperings he'd left behind in England. He gazed out over the sweep of the whole International Settlement, a little speck of China that seemed to have mutated into a part of Europe. It possessed a curious mix of architectural styles, with solid Victorian mansions sitting cheek by jowl with the more ornate French avenues and long Italian terraces with wrought-iron balconies and exuberant window boxes.

The Europeans had stolen this parcel of land from the Chinese as part of the reparations treaty after the Boxer Rebellion in 1900. They had elbowed the ancient walled town to one side and set about constructing their own much larger town right next to it, seizing control of the waterway with gunboats that nosed their way like gray crocodiles up the Peiho River. The International Settlement, they termed it, a bustling center of Western trade and commerce that delighted the masters back home in Britain but stuck in the craw of the Chinese government.

Theo shook his head. The British were too damn good at it, this whole controlling-the-world thing. Because though the settlement was international, there was no question that it was the British who controlled the place, Sir Edward Carlisle who set his signature with a flourish on every new document, just as he stamped his stern character on the International Council. Officially the town was divided into four quarters—British, Italian, French, and Russian—lined up neatly next to each other like old friends, but it didn't work out like that, not in practice. They bickered constantly. Argued over land distribution. Theo had heard them at it in the Ulysses Club. And somehow the British ended up owning nearly half the town while small areas were taken from the Russians and ceded to the Japanese and

Americans in exchange for very large payments of gold. But then money always talked. Money and gunboats.

As Theo's eyes scanned the town, he had to admit that compared to the ramshackle Russian Quarter over to his left, where many of the houses were cramped and shabby, the British Quarter was impressive. It gleamed like a well-fed cat. The church steeples, the clock tower of the Town Hall, the classical façade of the Imperial Hotel, the immaculately tonsured rose beds in the parks, no wonder the natives called them devils. Foreign Devils. Only a devil can steal your soul and turn it into alien territory. To the Chinese of Junchow the International Settlement was a different planet. Yet in the distance the river glinted like polished metal and the merchant ships at anchor alongside the clusters of sampans all added to the foolish illusion of permanence.

He became aware that Li Mei's fingers were caressing his chest in slow spinning circles.

"In market today, Tiyo, I see your friend. Newspaper man."

"Who do you mean?"

"Your Mr. Parker."

"Alfred? What was he up to down there?"

She gave a soft little laugh that rippled through him. "I think he look for something old. But I think he in trouble."

"How's that?"

"He too English. Not keep eyes wide awake. Not like you."

She wrapped her arms more tightly around Theo and gave an encouraging giggle, but he did not respond. Disappointed, she shook her head and the perfume from the silky curtain of her hair billowed around him. Somewhere out in the street a car sounded its Klaxon but the room remained in silence. A handful of pigeons fluttered past, the whistles attached to their tails making a whirring noise that sounded like the laughter of the gods.

"Tiyo," Li Mei said at last, "you want I should ask my father?"

Theo swung around, his gray eyes suddenly hard. "No. Don't you *ever* ask him."

4

THE GAS LAMP IN THE HALLWAY WASN'T WORKING, PROBA-bly needed a new mantle, but Lydia didn't even notice. She hurried down the gloomy passage from the front door, instinctively avoiding the holes in the linoleum, dumped her packages on the bottom of the stairs and knocked on Mrs. Zarya's sitting-room door.

"Who is it?"

"It's me, Lydia."

The door opened and a tall middle-aged woman looked out at Lydia suspiciously. *"Kakaya sevodnya otgovorka?"*

"Please, Mrs. Zarya, you know perfectly well I don't speak Russian."

The woman laughed as if she had scored a point, a great big laugh that shook the thin walls. She was a large woman with a broad fleshy face and a bosom like the great steppes of Russia. She frightened Lydia because her tongue could be as fierce as her hugs and it was important to stay on the right side of her. Olga Petrovna Zarya was their landlady and occupied the ground floor of her small terraced house. The rest she let out to tenants.

"Come in, little sparrow, I want to speak to you."

Lydia stepped inside the room. It smelt of borscht and onions, de-spite the window being open onto the narrow strip of flagstones she called her backyard, and was full of heavy furniture too large for the cramped space. In pride of place on an embroidered runner that hid the stains on the top of the mahogany piano stood a framed photo-graph. It was of General Zarya. In full White Army uniform, his arms folded, his gaze stern and accusing. Lydia always avoided his sepia eye if she could. There was just something about it that made her feel a failure.

"My patience is over," Olga Zarya announced, planting herself firmly in front of Lydia. "Tell that lazy mother of yours that she has taken wicked advantage of me, of my good nature. You tell her. That next week I throw her out. *Da*, into the street. And what does she expect, if she doesn't . . ."

"Pay the rent?" Lydia placed a neat pile of dollar bills on the table and stood back.

Mrs. Zarya's jaw dropped for a split second, and then she snatched up the money and flicked through it quickly, counting to herself in Russian.

"Good. *Spasibo*. I thank you." The woman stepped closer, her long shapeless black dress wafting the smell of mothballs toward Lydia, and put her big face so close Lydia could see her mouth twitch with irritation as it said sharply, "But not before time."

"The two months we owe and this month. It's all there."

"*Da*. It's all here."

"I'm sorry it was so late."

"She's been playing again? To earn this?"

"Yes."

The landlady nodded and reached out a well-padded arm as if she would enfold the girl in an embrace, but Lydia eyed the bosom with alarm and backed out the door.

"*Do svidania*, Mrs. Zarya."

"Good-bye, little sparrow. Tell that mother of yours that . . ."

But Lydia shut her ears. She scooped up her packages and dashed up the stairs. The treads were uncarpeted, the bare wood scuffed and dusty, so her feet made a clattering sound she knew her mother would hear from above.

"Hello, Mrs. Yeoman," she sang out as she shot past the second-floor rooms. They were rented by a retired Baptist missionary and his wife who had decided, inexplicably, in Lydia's view, to eke out their pension in the country they had devoted their lives to.

"Good afternoon, Lydia," Mr. Yeoman called back in his usual cheery manner. "You sound as if you're in a hurry."

"Is my mother home?"

There was a slight pause, but she was too excited to notice. "Yes, I do believe she is."

Lydia took the last flight of narrow steps up to the attic room two at a time and burst through the door. "Mama, look what I've got for us, Mama, I've . . ." She stopped. The smile died on her face.

Her foot kicked the door shut behind her. She felt all the happiness of the day drain from her body and trickle onto the floor alongside the broken crockery, the crushed flowers, and the thousands of cushion feathers that made the room look as if it had been attacked by a swan. At her feet lay the pieces of a shattered mirror. In the middle of the chaos lay the small figure of Valentina Ivanova, curled up on the carpet as neat as a cat. She was fast asleep, her breath coming in soft, regular little puffs. Under the table lay a vodka bottle. It was empty.

Lydia stood staring, struggling for control. Then she dropped her armful of parcels and brown paper bags carelessly on the floor and tiptoed over to her mother, as if she feared she might disturb her, though in reality she knew that only a bucket of water could wake Valentina now. She knelt down beside her.

"Hello, Mama," she whispered. "I'm here. Don't you worry, I'll . . ." But the words wouldn't come. Her throat ached and her head felt as if it might burst.

She reached out a hand and brushed a dark strand of tousled hair from her mother's face. Valentina usually wore it up in an elegant twist or sometimes tied back girlishly behind her head, like Lydia's own, but today it lay spread out in long loose waves of dense color on the drab carpet. Lydia stroked it. But Valentina did not move. Her cheeks were slightly flushed but even in a drunken stupor her beautiful features managed to look clean and fine. She was dressed only in an oyster-colored silk chemise and a pair of stockings. Under one eye was a dried smear of mascara, as if she had been crying.

Lydia sat back on her heels but continued to stroke her mother's hair, again and again, calming herself by the feel of it under her fingers. At the same time she told her in detail about her narrow escape in the old town today and about her Chinese protector and how terrified she'd been of the disgusting snake.

"So you see, I might not have come home today, Mama. I might have fallen into the clutches of a white slave trader and been shipped down to Shanghai to become a Lady of Delight." She made a sound that was supposed to be a laugh. "Wouldn't that have been funny? Don't you think so, Mama? Really funny."

Silence.

The place smelled sour. Of cigarette smoke and ash. The windows were closed and the heat was stifling. Lydia picked up the empty vodka bottle and hurled it with a cry of rage against the wall. It exploded into a thousand pieces.

It took Lydia more than an hour to clean the room. To sweep up the pieces of china, the glass, the petals, and the feathers. By far the worst were the feathers. They seemed to come to life and mock her efforts at capture as they floated teasingly just out of reach. By the end of it, she had a cut knee from where she'd knelt on a tiny stiletto of porcelain, an ache in her back from all the brushing, and a handful of feathers in her hair. On top of everything else, she was now unbearably hot, so she threw off her clothes and walked around in just her bodice and navy knickers.

Valentina slept through it all. At one point Lydia eased a pillow under her head on the floor and kissed her cheek. The windows were open but it made little difference, as all the heat of the house rose and gathered in their airless aerie under the roof. The attic was just one long room with slanted walls and two dormer windows, not improved by a smattering of down-at-the-heels furniture. A threadbare carpet, which might once have been colorful but was now a washed-out gray, covered the center of the floorboards. Each end of the room was partitioned off by a curtain to form two windowless bedrooms, and though the curtains managed to give the illusion of privacy, sounds carried through them with ease. So both mother and daughter had learned the courtesy of silence.

Lydia unwrapped her packages. But the sudden abundance of good food did not tempt her now. Nor did she bother with the meal she had planned to cook. She had no heart for it. Nor stomach either. Automatically she rinsed the fruit and vegetables in cold water because the Chinese were disagreeably fond of using human manure in their fields, but then she left them discarded on the drain board, unchopped and uncooked.

She made herself a drink, a cup of milk with a spoonful of honey in it, and dragged a chair to the window to sit with her elbows on the sill, looking down on the street below. A dingy terrace. Narrow houses. With doors that opened straight onto the pavement. Nothing nice about it in Lydia's eyes, nothing to lift her mood of despair. The Russian Quarter, they called it, packed with Russian refugees who were stuck here with no papers and no jobs. The lowly paid work went to the Chinese, so unless you could turn a trick at sword swallowing for coppers in the marketplace or had a wife willing to walk the streets, you starved. Simple as that.

Starved or stole.

But she kept looking, kept watching. The bald man with the white stick from next door, the two German sisters strolling arm in arm, the scrawny dog stalking a butterfly, the baby playing with a rattle in a doorway, the cars crawling past, the bicycles, even a grim-faced man with a pig in a wheelbarrow.

The only one to glance up in her direction was a big bear of a man, unmistakably Russian with his mass of oily curls sneaking out from under an astrakhan hat and a heavy beard that smothered the lower half of his face. A black eye patch gave him a gloomy, sinister appearance. Just like the picture of Bluebeard, the pirate in one of her library books, except this one didn't carry a knife glinting between his teeth, and as he passed she noticed that his knee-high boots seemed to have a howling wolf tooled into the side. She felt like howling herself. But instead she continued to look at each person with interest, anything rather than look at what lay in the room behind her.

The sky was growing darker as the heavy clouds on the horizon marched nearer and the evening air began to smell of rain. To keep her mind off the one thing that was filling it, she wondered whether it was raining in England. Polly said it always rained in England but Lydia didn't believe her. One day she was determined to go there and find out for herself. It was odd the way Europeans came to China by choice when, from what she'd read, there seemed to be everything that was beautiful and sophisticated and desirable in Europe already. In London, in Paris, in Berlin. Well, maybe not Berlin anymore. Not since the war. But London, yes. The Ritz. The Savoy. Buckingham Palace and the Albert Hall. And all the clubs and shops and theaters.

Regent Street and Piccadilly Circus. Everything. Just everything you could possibly ever want. So why leave them?

She gave a deep shuddering sigh, and a trickle of sweat crept from her ear to her chin like a tear. Oh God, she didn't know what to do. What to say. Her heart was kicking like a mule in her chest and all she could think of was whether it was raining in England. That was so stupid. She dropped her head on her arms and lay quite still, until her breathing grew calmer.

"Papa, what should I do for her? Please, Papa. Tell me. Help me."

No one knew that Lydia whispered to the memory of her father when she was in trouble. Not even Polly. And certainly not her mother. Her mother never mentioned him, didn't even use his surname anymore.

"Papa," she whispered again, just to hear the sound of that word coming out of her mouth.

Finally she abandoned the window and turned back to the room. It was a grim place to live, with its low sloping ceiling, its moody little paraffin cooking stove and its chipped earthenware sink, but her mother had done everything she could to make it bearable. More than bearable. She'd made it colorful and flamboyant. The nasty brocade sofa and armchair, worn through at the arms, had vanished from sight under swathes of material in wonderful purples, ambers, and magentas that seemed to glow with life. Armfuls of cushions everywhere in gold and bronze gave the room an atmosphere of bohemian looseness, which her mother called risqué and which Olga Zarya called lascivious. A fringed shawl the color of Lydia's hair was draped over the pine table, and candles were gathered on a brass dish in the center so that their flames flickered and reflected on the coppery silk.

To Lydia it was home. It was all she had. She went over to the sleeping figure once more. In the fading light of day she sat on the gray carpet and held her mother's gray hand in hers.

"DARLING." VALENTINA LIFTED HER HEAD FROM THE PILLOW on the floor and blinked slowly like a cat stirring itself. "Darling, I fell asleep. What time is it?"

"The church clock just struck one." Lydia did not look up from the book in front of her on the table.

"In the morning?"

"It's not this dark at one o'clock in the afternoon."

"Then you should be in bed. What are you doing?"

"Homework." Still she refused to look at her mother.

Valentina stretched, easing the kinks out of her spine, sat up and noticed the pillow. She closed her eyes for a brief moment and shuddered.

"Darling, I am sorry."

Lydia shrugged indifferently and turned a page of her *Outlines of English History*, though the words in front of her eyes jumped around without meaning.

"Don't sulk, Lydia, it doesn't suit you."

"Lying on the floor doesn't suit you either."

"Maybe if I were lying under it, we would both be better pleased."

"Don't, Mama."

Valentina gave a soft laugh. "I apologize, my little one."

"I am not your little one."

"No, you're right, I know." Her deep brown eyes skimmed over her daughter's bent head and coltish naked legs. "You're grown up now. Too grown up."

She stood and stretched again, pointing each bare foot in turn like a ballet dancer, and shook out her long hair so that it shimmered around her shoulders, catching the candlelight in its rich dark folds. Lydia pretended not to notice. But instead of reading about the Riot Act of 1716, she was watching her mother's every move through lowered lashes and found herself both relieved and infuriated by how calm and well-rested she looked. More than she had any right to be. Where were the ravages of all that pain? The elfin upsweep of Valentina's eyebrows was even more pronounced than usual, as if the whole of life were just one silly joke, not to be taken seriously.

Valentina sat down on the sofa and patted the cushion beside her. "Come and sit with me, Lydia."

"I'm busy."

"It's one o'clock in the morning. You can be busy tomorrow."

Lydia shut her book with a sharp little snap and went over to the sofa. She sat there stiffly, maintaining a decent gap between her mother and herself, but Valentina reached across it and ruffled her daughter's hair.

"Relax, darling. Where's the harm in a few drinks now and again? It keeps me sane. So please don't sulk."

"I'm not sulking," Lydia said sulkily.

"My God, I'm so thirsty, I . . ."

"We only have one cup left and no saucers."

Valentina burst out laughing, and despite herself Lydia sneaked a smile. Her mother looked around the floor and nodded. "You cleaned it all up for me?"

"Yes."

"Thank you. I bet Mr. Yeoman downstairs thought the world was coming to an . . ." She broke off and stared at the bare patch of wall by the door. "The mirror. It's . . ."

"Broken. That means seven years bad luck."

"Oh God, Olga Petrovna Zarya will kill me and charge us twice what it was worth. But the next seven years can't be any worse than the last seven, can they?"

Lydia said nothing.

"I'm sorry, sweetheart," Valentina murmured, but Lydia had heard those words before. "At least the cups were ours. Anyway, I always hated that mirror. It was so ugly and it made me look so old."

"I've made a jug of lemonade. Would you like some?"

Valentina turned and stroked her daughter's cheek. "That would be heavenly. My throat is parched."

When she was sipping the cool liquid out of their one remaining teacup—any glasses had been pawned long ago—she placed a hand on top of her head each time she tipped it back, as if to hold it on.

"Any aspirin?" she asked hopefully.

"No."

"I thought not."

"But I bought these for you." With a shy smile Lydia produced from behind her back a chocolate-filled croissant and a long silk scarf in a deep dramatic red. "I thought it would look good on you."

Valentina put down the teacup on the carpet and took the croissant in one hand and the scarf in the other. "Darling," she said, drawing the word out like a caress. "You spoil me." She stared at both gifts for a long moment, then swirled the scarf around and around her throat with delight and took a huge bite out of the pastry. "Wonderful," she murmured with her mouth full. "From the French patisserie. Thank you, my sweet child." She leaned over and kissed Lydia's cheek.

"I've been doing some jobs to help Mr. Willoughby at school and he paid me today," Lydia explained. The words came tumbling out a fraction too fast, but her mother didn't seem to notice.

A tiny muscle that had been clenched tight in Lydia's forehead relaxed for the first time that evening. Everything would be okay again now. Her mother would stop. No more craziness. No more tearing their fragile world apart. She picked up the cup from the floor and took a mouthful of lemonade for herself to unstick her tongue from the roof of her mouth.

"Was it Antoine again?" she asked in a casual voice with a sidelong glance at Valentina.

Instantly she regretted it.

"That filthy bastard, *podliy ismennik!*" Valentina exploded. "Don't even speak his name to me. He's a lying French toad, a sneaky snake in the grass. I never ever want to see him again."

Lydia felt a tug of sympathy for Antoine Fourget. He adored her mother. Would have married her tomorrow if he had not already been married to a French Catholic who refused to divorce him and by whom he had four children clamoring for attention and financial support. He always took Valentina dancing on a Friday night and stole a secret hour or two with her during the week whenever he could take a long lunch from his office while Lydia was at school. But she knew when he'd been there. The room smelled different, altogether more interesting, of cigarettes and brilliantine.

"What did he do?"

Valentina jumped to her feet and started pacing the room, both hands clamped firmly to her head. "His wife. She is expecting another baby."

"Oh."

"The cheating bastard had sworn to me he never went near her bed anymore. How could he be so . . . so unfaithful?"

"Mama, she *is* his wife."

Valentina tossed her head angrily, then closed her eyes as if in pain. "In name only, he promised me."

"Maybe she loves him."

Her eyes snapped open and in a challenging gesture she placed her hands on her hips. Lydia couldn't help noticing how thin they were under the silk slip.

"Does it occur to you, Lydia, that maybe *I* love him too?"

This time it was Lydia's turn to laugh. "No, Mama, it does not occur to me. You are fond of him, you have fun with him, you dance with him, but no, you do *not* love him."

Valentina opened her mouth to protest, but then shook her head skittishly and collapsed once more onto the sofa, lying back among the cushions. She draped one arm across her aching head.

"I think I'm going to die, darling."

"Not today."

"I do love him a little bit, you know."

"I know you do, Mama."

"But . . . ," Valentina looked out from under her arm, her eyes narrowed as she gazed up at her daughter's face, at her strong straight nose, her high Scandinavian cheekbones, and the copper blaze of her hair, ". . . but the only man I've ever loved—or ever will love in this life—is your father." She shut her eyes firmly.

Silence settled on the room. Lydia felt her skin prickle with pleasure. A damp breeze carrying spots of rain slipped in through the open windows and cooled her cheeks, but nothing could cool the delicious warmth that drifted through her body, as seductive as opium.

"Papa," she whispered and in her head she heard his rich deep laugh echo till it filled her young skull. She saw again the world swing in a crazy kaleidoscope as strong hands swept her up high in the air. If she tried harder still she could conjure up the masculine smell of him, an intoxicating mix of tobacco and hair oil and damp bristly scarves that tickled her chin.

Or was she making that up?

She was so frightened of losing the little scraps of him she had left. With a sigh she stood and blew out the candles, then curled up among the cushions again next to her mother and fell asleep as easily as a kitten.

THE SOUND OF A CAR KLAXON IN THE STREET WOKE LYDIA with a jolt. The pale yellow light that filtered through the partition curtains of her miniature bedroom told her it was morning and later than it should be. Saturday meant only a half day at school but she was still expected there at nine. She sat up and was surprised that her head felt disconnected and swirled away from her, but then remembered she'd had nothing to eat the day before. With a sinking heart she recalled why.

But today would be better. Today was her birthday.

The hooting in the street started up again. She jumped from her bed and leaned out of the nearest window to look at what was going on. The overnight rain had stopped, but everything was still wet and glistening, and the air was already showing signs of heating up again. The slates on the roof opposite were beginning to steam. Above her the sky was a dull and lifeless gray but down below on the street was a bright splash of color that lifted her spirits. A little open sports car was parked right outside their door and in it sat a dark-haired man wearing a yellow polo shirt and clutching a vast bouquet of red roses. He looked up and waved the flowers at her.

"'Allo, *ma chérie*," he called. "Is your *maman* up yet?"

"Hello, Antoine." Lydia smiled and quickly put up a hand to cover her grubby bodice. "Is that your new car?"

"This? Yes, I won her last night, at cards. Isn't she adorable?" He kissed his fingers in an extravagant French gesture and laughed, showing healthy white teeth.

Every time Lydia saw him she thought he was the most handsome man she'd ever met, not that she'd met that many of course, but it wasn't hard to imagine how easy it would be to have fun with him. He was in his thirties, Mama said, but to Lydia he seemed younger, he was so full of boyish charm.

"I'll see if she's awake," she shouted back and rushed across the room to peek behind her mother's curtain.

In sharp contrast to the colors and sensuality of the sitting-room area, Valentina kept her sleeping section stark and plain. White unadorned walls, white bed linen, even a white-painted old wardrobe with doors that were warped and hard to open. The curtain had once been a pair of white bedsheets that were now discolored with age. It was an unforgiving and soulless cell. Sometimes Lydia wondered what it was she was trying to atone for.

"Mama?"

Valentina was lying in a tangle of sheets, her hair twisted into a dark muddle of misery on her pillow, and shadowy hollows bore witness under her eyes. Her eyelids were closed but not for one second did Lydia believe she was asleep. All the signs were of a restless, tormented night.

"Mama, Antoine is here."

The eyes did not open. "Tell him to go to hell."

"But he's brought you flowers." Lydia sat down on the end of the bed, not something she normally did unless invited. "He looks very sorry and . . . ," she thought quickly for something else to tempt her, "and he's driving a sports car." She omitted to mention that it was very small and rather odd looking.

"So it will be easy for him to drive himself straight into the river."

"You're too cruel."

Valentina's eyes shot open at that and they were not pleased. "You're too soft on him. Just because he's a man."

Lydia blushed and stood up. In her worn-out bodice and knickers she knew she lacked dignity, but she lifted her chin and said, "I shall go down and tell him you are asleep."

"If you really want to make yourself useful, tell him to bring me some vodka."

Lydia swept out past the curtain and risked no comment. She splashed chilly water from the sink over her hands and face, rubbed her teeth with a finger dipped in salt, and scrubbed at her forehead with the heel of her hand to try to dislodge the tight band of fear that gripped it. It only took the word *vodka* to panic her. She pulled on her school uniform, grabbed her satchel, and picked up a couple of sugared dumplings. She was walking out the door when her mother's voice called out. Softly this time.

"Lydia."

"Yes?"

"Come here, my sweet."

Reluctantly Lydia entered the white bedroom. She stood just inside the curtain and stared down at her scuffed black shoes. She was used to them hurting, like she was used to her head hurting.

"Lydia."

She looked up. Her mother was lying languorously back against her pillows, her hair brushed out in a gleaming fan, and she was smiling, holding out one hand. Lydia was too cross to respond and stayed where she was.

"Darling, I haven't forgotten what day it is."

Lydia stared at her shoes, hating them.

"Happy birthday, sweetheart. *S dniom rozhdenia, dochenka.* I didn't mean it about the vodka, honestly I didn't. Come and give me a kiss, darling. A birthday kiss."

Lydia did so, brushing her warm cheek against her mother's cool one.

"Sit down a minute, Lydia."

"But Antoine is . . ."

"Damn Antoine." Valentina waved a hand dismissively. "I want to say something to you."

Lydia sat down on the bed. Abruptly she realized she was hungry and took a bite out of the dumpling, her tongue chasing the sugary bits around her lips.

"Darling, listen to me. I am glad to see you eating something nice on your birthday but sorry I was not the one to give it to you."

Lydia stopped eating, the sweetness in her mouth suddenly soured by a vague sense of guilt. "That's all right, Mama."

"No, it's not all right. It makes me sad. I have no money to buy you a present, we both know that. So instead I invite you to come with me when I play at the Ulysses Club tonight. You can be my page turner."

A cry of delight burst from Lydia and she threw her arms around her mother. "Oh, Mama, thank you, it's the very best birthday present."

"Mind your dumpling in my hair."

"It's what I've wanted for years."

"As if I didn't know that. You've always pestered me to come to the recitals, but now at sixteen years old I think it is time. And it means I won't have to wear myself out afterward telling you that Sir Edward said this or Colonel Mortimer argued that, and what all the ladies were wearing. Please, sweetheart, do take your sticky fingers away from me."

Lydia jumped up and brushed her hands on the sides of her skirt. "I'll make you proud of me, Mama. We can practice this afternoon on Mrs. Zarya's piano. You know how she likes to hear you play."

"Only if the miserable old dragon hasn't thrown us out on the street by then."

"Oh no, I didn't tell you, I've paid the rent we owed. And next month's is in the blue bowl on the shelf. So don't worry about Mrs. Zarya any more."

"This work you do for Mr. Willoughby must be extraordinarily well paid."

Lydia nodded awkwardly. "Yes, it is. I've been marking the schoolwork of the children in the lower classes, you see. Almost like a teacher really." She scooped up her satchel. "Thanks again, Mama." She rushed for the door.

Her mother's voice followed her. "And tell that lying rat in the car downstairs to stick his flowers alongside his promises, down in the sewer where they belong."

Lydia shut the door quickly before Mr. and Mrs. Yeoman could hear.

"But it's only got three wheels," Lydia objected.

"It's a Morgan, so what do you expect?" Antoine Fourget patted one of the car's shiny black fenders. "She has won the races all over the world."

"Is it the same as the one Isadora Duncan was killed in last year?"

"*Non.*" He crossed himself quickly. "That was a Bugatti. But this is a *magnifique* little lady. I was lucky last night at cards." He turned hopeful eyes on Lydia. "But am I lucky today? *Eh bien,* what did your *maman* say?"

"Not good."

"She won't see me?"

"Sorry, no."

"The flowers?"

She shook her head.

Antoine slumped into the driving seat and made a low rumbling sound in the back of his throat. Lydia felt an overwhelming urge to reach out and smooth his ruffled black hair, to feel how soft it was, to do something, anything to ease the misery her mother had inflicted. But she kept her hands to herself.

"Can I have a ride, Antoine?"

He summoned up a smile, "Of course, *chérie*. A ride to school?"

"Yes, please."

He lifted the flowers off the passenger seat and she jumped in, clutching her hat on her lap. "It's my birthday today," she said.

"Ah, *bonne anniversaire*." He leaned across and kissed her on both cheeks. "*You* shall have the flowers instead. For your birthday, from me."

He presented the bouquet to her with a flourish that made her blush and started the car. Lydia knew she was not the one he wanted seated beside him, but nevertheless she enjoyed the ride. What she didn't tell her mother's lover was that this was her first time in a car. She'd never even sat in one before. The constant movement of the gear stick and the fiddling with the controls fascinated her, as well as the distortion of the pavement flying past at full speed and the wind rushing into her face over the tiny windshield, tearing at her hair, making her blink and gasp for breath. When the Morgan hooted at a rickshaw, making it dive out of their way, she beamed with delight.

"Lydia."

"Mmm?"

The roads were becoming wider now as they left the meaner beggar-ridden streets that made up the Russian Quarter and headed through the better part of town where the shops and cafés were already opening. Sikh policemen in turbans stood on little platforms at each major junction, flapping their white-gloved hands to direct the flow of traffic. Lydia leaned over the low door of the car and waved to one just for the fun of it.

"Lydia," Antoine repeated more urgently.

"Yes?"

"Do you think she will forgive me?"

"Oh Antoine, I don't know. You know what she's like."

He uttered a faint groan, and she became frightened he might crash the car in a wild Gallic gesture of despair, so she hurried on, "But I expect she'll get over it quickly. Just give her a few days."

The grand Town Hall with its pillars and Union Jack shot past in a blur, then Victoria Park with a smattering of prams and nannies. Lydia felt her cheeks gripped by the wind as Antoine put his foot down.

"I love her, you know," he said. "I didn't mean to hurt her. I should never have mentioned the baby."

"Yes, maybe that was a mistake."

"Does she love me?"

"Yes, of course she does."

"Really, *chérie*?"

"Really."

The glorious smile he gave her was worth the lie. It sent a tingle all down her spine, right to her fingertips, and it was then that an idea occurred to her.

"Antoine, do you know what I think might help?"

"What?" He stuck out an arm and swung left up Wordsworth Avenue, the car's motorbike engine growling as it launched itself at the incline.

"If you gave Mama a present she really wanted, I think it might win her over."

His dark eyes darted a look of alarm at her. "I'm not rich, you know. I cannot bestow her with jewels and perfumes like she deserves. And when I did once offer her a little money, you know, just to help, she refused it."

Lydia looked at him in surprise. "But why?"

"She shouted at me, threw a book at my head. Said she was not a whore to be bought."

Lydia sighed. *Oh Mama*. Such pride came at a price.

At the top of the hill in the British Quarter the houses were large and elegant, built of pale stone and surrounded by well-tended lawns and neat hedges. The school was coming into sight. She must hurry.

"No, I don't mean anything expensive. I was thinking of something . . . to comfort her when you're not there." She glanced at him warily. "When you're with your wife."

He frowned. "Like what do you mean?"

She swallowed and said it quickly. "A rabbit."

"What?"

"Yes, a white rabbit with lovely long ears and sweet pink eyes."

"*Un lapin?*"

"That's right. She owned one when she was a little girl in St. Petersburg and has always longed for another."

He looked at her closely. "You surprise me."

"It's true."

"I'll ask her."

"No, no, don't do that. You'll spoil the surprise." She smiled at his profile encouragingly and thought what a beautiful Roman nose he had. "She'll be reminded of you every time she runs her fingers through its soft white fur."

She could see he was thinking about it. The corners of his mouth curled up and he shrugged in his eloquent French way that said so much more than English shrugs.

"Maybe," he said, "*c'est possible.*"

"A red ribbon would be nice too. On the rabbit, I mean."

But she wasn't sure he heard straight. He was maneuvering around a large black Humber out of which three girls in Willoughby Academy uniforms were tumbling and staring at Lydia with envy. Clutching the bouquet of roses in her arms, she kissed her handsome companion's cheek in full view of them and sauntered into school. The day was starting well.

It was only later, when dreaming out of the window in class, that she allowed herself to think about the lithe young figure she'd noticed half hidden in the shadow of the rickshaws across the road, of the pair of black Chinese eyes watching her as she entered the school gates.

5

THE ULYSSES CLUB WAS AS PRETENTIOUS AS ITS NAME. Theo hated it. It stood for everything he despised about colonial arrogance. Self-important and disdainful. The building was at the heart of the British Quarter, set back from the road, as if disassociating itself from the noise and bustle of the town behind a dense barrier of rhododendron bushes and a sweep of manicured lawn. It boasted a grand white façade with towering columns, pediment, and portico, all carved to the glory of the conqueror.

As he took the great wide steps that led up to the entrance, they made him think of a shrine, and to some extent that's exactly what the place was. A shrine. To the god of conservatism. To preserving the status quo. And it went without saying that any yellow-skinned person, of that unholy tribe who lied to your face and sold their children, was not invited through its hallowed portals, except via the back door and clad in a servant's uniform.

Theo loathed it. But Li Mei was right. Between kisses that set his loins on fire and soft words that reshuffled his brain, she taught him to see it as a game. A game he had to play. Had to win.

"WILLOUGHBY, OLD BOY, GLAD YOU COULD MAKE IT."

Christopher Mason was striding toward him across the marble floor of the reception hall with his hand outstretched, his smile as affable as a snake's. He was in his midforties, kept his figure trim by horse riding, and carried himself like an army officer, though Theo knew for a fact he'd never seen a parade ground in his life. Mason had at an early age opted for a desk career in government and sought a post in China only when he heard of the fortunes to be made out there if you knew what you were doing. His eyes were round and shrewd, his dark brown hair combed straight back from a widow's peak, and though he was several inches shorter than Theo, he made up for it by talking loudly as they headed across the hall.

"Heard the news? Heart-stopping stuff. Damned premature, if you ask me."

"What news is that?" Theo was wary.

He knew that in the busy, claustrophobic hive in which they all lived, *news* could mean that Binky Fenton had stormed out of a croquet match over accusations of cheating, or that General Chiang Kai-shek was drawing up radical legislation to sweep the foreigners off his land and into the sea. Both would be *news*. Both would be *heart-stopping*. But accusations of cheating would be seriously bad form, whereas nobody expected the Chinese to stick to their promises in the first place. Theo waited to hear what it was that was turning Mason's cheeks the color of chopped liver.

"It's our troops. The Second Battalion of Scots Guards. Going home from China on the *City of Marseilles* in the New Year. Bloody cheek of it. Leaving us undefended in this benighted country. Don't they know the Nationalist Kuomintang Army is running riot in an orgy of murder and plunder over in Peking? Good God, man, we need more troops, not less. After all, we're the ones earning the trade profits that keep Baldwin and his blasted government in funds back home. Have you seen what state the financial market is in?"

"We'll have to learn to stand on our own two feet then, won't we?" Theo said with a shrug calculated to annoy. "Why keep an army in place if we claim we want to remain at peace with the Chinese?"

Mason stopped in his tracks.

"What we need," Theo continued, "is a treaty we can all stick to for once, one that is reasonable, not punitive. We *have* to give concessions or we'll have another Taiping Rebellion on our hands."

Mason stared hard at him, then muttered, "Bloody Chink lover," and strode off toward the bar, indifferent to the gentlemanly elegance of the hall's fluted pillars and Venetian chandeliers. Native servants drifted past silently, neat and docile in their white tunics buttoned high at the neck, silver trays in hand, polite expressions frozen on their faces. Yet Theo knew that each one of them was worth no more than yesterday's newspaper to the members of the Ulysses Club, probably less. From the long veranda at the rear of the building a sharp high laugh barked out. Lady Caroline was at the pink gin.

Theo almost turned on his heel. To walk out and leave Mason stranded would give him keen pleasure, but Li Mei's words in his head kept him rooted there.

"You have to play the game, Tiyo. You have to win."

She was so clever, his Li Mei. He loved the way she used his weaknesses and took hold of his ridiculous English public-school desire to regard life as some sort of stupid game you had to win.

He followed Mason through the carved double doors into the bar and looked around. It was packed, as usual, at seven-thirty in the evening. Here they all were, Britain's empire builders. The great and the good. And the not so good. Some stiff and upright in military uniform on the deep leather chesterfields, others sprawled with a cigar in hand in the light new Lloyd Loom chairs that were introduced to make the place more inviting to the female members.

As Theo made his way past the crush of drinkers at the bar, he nodded to the faces he recognized but didn't stop to talk. The sooner this interview was over, the better, as far as he was concerned. But his heart sank when he saw Mason veer off toward a group of four men seated around a low mahogany table. A pall of cigarette smoke hung over them in a grubby halo despite the large brass fans that whirred incessantly on the ceiling, shuffling the heat and the flies around. Theo felt his stiff shirt collar like a garrote at his throat, but if you wanted to join in the game, you had to wear the party clothes. He paused, lit himself a Turkish cigarette, and threw his first dice.

"Good evening, Sir Edward," he said in a voice full of bonhomie. "I hear you're chucking the U.S. Marines out of Tientsin at last."

Sir Edward Carlisle looked up from his whisky tumbler, his hawkish face surprisingly benign in repose, and smiled at Theo. A chuckle flickered around the group, though Police Commissioner Lacock didn't join in. Binky Fenton, a bustling customs officer who was always banging on about interference from the Americans, raised his glass with a hearty, "About time too."

Theo found himself a seat next to Alfred Parker, the one man he regarded as a friend among this little cabal. Alfred gave him a welcoming nod and stuck out a hand. He was a few years older than Theo and new to China, a journalist on the local rag, the Junchow *Daily Herald*. Not bad at it either, Theo reckoned. His last was a scorching piece on foot binding of women. A hideous habit. No longer mandatory since the collapse of the Manchu dynasty in 1911, but still widely practiced. Thank God Li Mei's parents had spared her that particular barbarity. And Alfred Parker was right. He argued that what was the point of crippling half your workforce while your country was starving and dying in the streets? It didn't make sense.

"Evening, Willoughby," Sir Edward said, and sounded genuinely pleased to see him. But then he was a masterly diplomat, so Theo could never be sure. "Yes, you're right, though where you get your information, damned if I know. The secretary of the U.S. Navy has ordered an immediate withdrawal from Tientsin."

"How many men?" Parker asked with interest.

"Three thousand five hundred marines."

Binky Fenton whistled loudly and cheered. "Bye-bye, Yankees, good riddance."

"And our own Scots Guards going in January," Mason grumbled, and flicked a finger in the air. A Chinese waiter instantly materialized at his elbow. "Scotch and soda, boy. No ice. Willoughby?"

"Straight scotch."

Sir Edward nodded approval. He hated to see people ruin good whisky with water. "The Kuomintang Nationalists are in control now," Sir Edward said firmly, but gave no sign as to whether that pleased him. "In Peking as well as Nanking, which means they have control of both the northern and southern capitals. So we have to recognize that the civil war is finally over, among the warlords, if not against the Communists. Marshal Chang Tso-lin and his Northern Army are done for. And that is why, gentlemen, the British Government has decided that the need for so many troops to protect our interests in China is reduced."

"Is it true that Marshal Chang Tso-lin and his men are being given safe passage to Manchuria?" Alfred Parker asked, making the most of the opening.

"Yes."

"But why? The Chinese usually make a habit of slaughtering their defeated enemies."

"You'd better ask General Chiang Kai-shek that one." Sir Edward drew on his cigar, his sharp eyes alert.

He was an impressive figure, early sixties, tall and elegant in a close-fitting formal dress suit, white tie, and high wing collar. His shock of white hair was in contrast to his military mustache, which was stained the color of toffee by a daily concoction of nicotine, tannin, and fine Highland whisky. As governor of Junchow he had the impossible task of keeping the peace between the various foreign factions: the French, Italians, Japanese, Americans, and British—and even worse, the Russians and Germans who, since the end of the Great War in 1918, had lost their official status in China and were there on sufferance.

But the main thorn in his flesh was the blasted Americans, who tended to go off at things half-cocked on their own, and turn up to discuss the situation only when the damage was done. No bad thing to see the back of a parcel of them, even if it did leave Tientsin more exposed. With luck the contingent in Junchow would follow suit. But then there were still the Japs to look out for. That lot made his blood run cold.

His gaze shifted and found Theo Willoughby observing him. Sir Edward again gave an almost imperceptible nod of approval. He liked the schoolteacher. That young man could go far. If only he'd drop this damned obsession with all things Chinese. The business of his affair with the native woman didn't matter a jot. Any number of men of his acquaintance dipped into the yellow pool occasionally. Not that he'd been so inclined himself. Good God, no. Dear old Eleanor would turn in her grave if he did. He still missed the old girl. Like a toothache, it was. But no quack's nostrum could dull that kind of pain. She'd liked Willoughby too. A darling boy, she'd called him. A darling pain in the arse, if Mason's face was anything to go by. Something up, there. Too much tension between the two men, and it was obvious Mason thought he had the upper hand. But he should watch out. That boy was not to be underestimated. Had a tendency to be unpredictable. In the blood, you see. Just look at what his father did back in England. A disgrace, that was. No wonder his boy was hiding away over here on the other side of the world.

He took a long shot of his whisky and rolled it around his tongue with relish. "Willoughby," he said with a glare from under his spidery eyebrows, "you'll stay for tonight's recital by the Russian beauty." It wasn't a question.

"I'd be delighted, sir." Bugger the old devil. Now he'd not see Li Mei all evening.

"Surprised to find you here, Theo," Alfred Parker remarked. His voice was as courteous as ever, but he could not hide his curiosity.

They were standing at the bar together, just the two of them. Replenishing glasses and seizing a respite from a heated discussion on the perils of extraterritoriality and whether the Nationalists would have gained control of Shanghai the previous year without the help of Big-Eared Du and his Green Gang triad.

Theo was always uneasy when the subject of Chinese triads was raised. It made the hairs stand up on the back of his neck. He'd heard whispers about their activities in Junchow. Throats cut, businesses suddenly engulfed in flames, a headless torso found floating in the river. But it was the beauty of China he adored. It was breathtaking. It had stolen his heart. Not just the exquisite delicacy of Li Mei, but the sumptuous curve of a Ming vase, the upward sweep of a calligraphy brush, the hidden meanings in a watercolor of a man fishing, a vivid sun sinking behind a raft of sampans, bathing their stinking filth in a golden unearthly glow. These things filled his senses. Sometimes he couldn't breathe, his passion for them was so strong. Even the foul sweat and broken teeth of a rickshaw puller or a field coolie spoke of the beauty of a country that existed by means of the sheer backbreaking toil of its millions and millions of peasants.

But the triads. Well, they were like rats in a grain barn. Devouring, spoiling, poisoning. Theo wiped a large red handkerchief across his brow and stuck a finger down his collar to loosen its grip on his throat.

"I'm not here by choice," he said. "Mason wants a word."

"That man is too hungry. Fingers in too many pies."

Theo gave a laugh that held no humor. "He's a mean bastard, out for everything he can get. He'll shoot down anyone who gets in his way."

"Then don't get in his way."

"Too late for that, I'm afraid."

"Why, what did you do to annoy the fellow?"

"Take your pick. He doesn't like his daughter learning Chinese history or the fact that I've made physical education compulsory for the girls as well as the boys. And I banned Saturday morning rifle target practice down at the butts. For that one, I was almost strung up by a mob of irate fathers."

Parker laughed, a good strong chuckle. He was a large deep-chested man who possessed a cordial manner, but he seemed ill at ease today. He rummaged in his pocket for his pipe, took his time lighting it, and then shook his head in reproach. "You do it to provoke."

Theo stared at him, surprised. The journalist meant it. Alfred might be a greenhorn when it came to getting to grips with the Oriental way of doing things, but he had an instinct for seeing through the bluff and blah of people's deceptions. That's what made him a good newspaperman and that's why Theo had taken to him. Yes, he could be a pompous ass at times, especially in the company of the fair sex, but otherwise he was a decent chap with the sense to wear a crisp linen jacket and soft collar, instead of the full evening regalia. But his comment left Theo slightly rattled. Because he feared it might be true.

"Alfred, listen to me. I just want to open up the minds of these children."

"Banning them from the things they enjoy, like rifle practice, isn't going to get you further down that path, you know. Quite the opposite, I'd have thought."

"Look, we've not long ago been through a terrible time of war in Europe. And nearly two decades of civil war out here in China, as well as the Opium Wars and the Boxer Rebellion. And look at what's going on in India now. When will we learn that saber rattling is not the answer?"

"Steady on, Theo. We've brought civilization and moral decency to these heathens. And salvation to their souls. Our navy and army were necessary to open the doors."

"No, Alfred. Violence is not the answer. Our only hope for the future is to teach our children that a foreign skin or a foreign tongue does not make an enemy of another human being." He placed a hand on his friend's arm. "This country needs our help desperately. But not our armies."

"Not a bloody conchie, as well as a Chink lover, are you, Willoughby?" It was Mason.

Theo did not turn. He felt the anger rise through his chest. In the long mirror that ran behind the bar, he could make out Christopher Mason standing behind him, his chin pushed out as if asking for it to be knocked off.

"Mr. Mason," Alfred Parker cut in smoothly, "I'm glad to have this opportunity to speak to you. I've been wanting to have a word. Our readers of the *Daily Herald* would be interested to learn your views as chief of education in Junchow. I'm doing a piece on opportunities for young people out here. May I set up an interview with you?"

Mason looked surprised, knocked off balance for a moment, and then permitted himself a smile. "Certainly, Parker. Give my office a call on Monday morning."

"My pleasure."

Mason rocked back and forth on his heels. Then said abruptly, "Now, Willoughby, time for our chat, I do believe."

"Latin."

"Pardon?"

"Why are you teaching my daughter Latin?"

"To broaden her understanding of language."

"And you've got her mixing dangerous chemicals too."

"Mr. Mason, every pupil in my school learns Latin and science, male or female. You knew that when you enrolled her with me three years ago."

"Latin poetry," Mason said, ignoring Theo's comment. "Dissecting frogs and pulling legs off beetles. Chinese history with all that stuff about concubines and beheadings. Gymnastics that make girls leap over horses and do cartwheels wearing next to nothing and boys goggle-eyed while they do it. This is not right for young women. None of it."

"The horses aren't real. They're gymnasium equipment."

"Don't make fun of me, young man."

"I'm not. Just pointing out that they are inside a gymnasium. The boys and the girls have these classes separately, so the boys cannot stare at the girls, who, by the way, are perfectly respectably dressed in chitons while they exercise. Nobody sees them except Miss Pettifer."

"I tell you it's not good for them. Mrs. Mason and I don't like it."

Theo refrained from bringing up the subject of Mrs. Mason arriving on the tandem each day to pick up Polly. Clearly a fan of brisk exercise for the female sex. He stared into the amber depths of his whisky glass and tried to work out what it was Mason was after. They were sitting in private at the far end of the long veranda. At the opposite end in small gatherings among the potted palms were the women, their soft voices drifting in a light murmur that didn't disturb the two men.

"You could always send Polly to a different school, Mr. Mason," Theo offered quietly. "You may find St. Francis High School more accommodating."

Mason's large round eyes fixed on him with dislike. But there was something else in their slate-gray depths that sent a tremor of alarm skittering up Theo's spine.

"That's not my point, Willoughby."

"So what *is* your point?" Theo started to raise his glass to his lips.

"I'm thinking of closing you down."

It stopped him cold. He felt the blood drain from his face. With an effort he replaced his scotch on the table. He blinked, looking out across the croquet lawn, which was the color of lavender in the evening light, and the silver surface of the lake had turned as gray and solid as a dragon's tail. He needed a drink, badly, but didn't dare pick up his glass. Mason was leaning forward with a hard, penetrating stare. Theo made himself concentrate. Slowly he sat back in his chair, crossed his legs, and returned the stare.

"Am I to understand you intend to withdraw the Willoughby Academy's license?" he asked coldly.

"It's a possibility."

"I think you'll find your desk swamped with parental objections to such an absurd move. It's the best school in Junchow and you know it. A broader education for girls is no reason to . . ."

"It's not just that."

Theo frowned. "What else?"

"It's the money."

That was when Theo knew he had lost.

"JUST LOOK AT THAT WOMAN OVER THERE. ISN'T SHE A peach! Enough to set any chap's head spinning." The words came from a noisy group of uniformed army officers as they emerged from the billiard room.

Theo was striding across the marble floor in the direction of the smoking room. He needed time alone. Away from this insane circus. Time to think. To work out what the hell his next move should be. His temples were pounding and a noise like a thousand locusts was buzzing in his ears, but the officer's words made him cast a glance over his shoulder.

It was Valentina Ivanova.

Suddenly Theo recalled the recital this evening. Damn Sir Edward's invitation to attend. Mason would be there of course, with his smug smile and his greedy eyes, his fingers tapping his big white teeth in that predatory way of his. But the sight of Valentina Ivanova abruptly cleared Theo's brain. It reminded him of what he had to fight for, because at her side as she swept through the entrance hall was one of his pupils. Young Lydia. The one so keen to know about Chinese martial arts.

Together they were very striking. Heads turned as they passed. Other women's mouths tightened. The mother looked wonderful. She was quite small but made up for it in the way she walked, the sway of her slender hips and the proud manner in which she held her head. Her skin was pale and flawless, and the waves of shining dark hair were swept up on top of her head, making her taller, more imposing. But it was her eyes, dark and luminous, whose sensuous vulnerability could make a man go weak at the knees.

Theo had seen her several times before, but never quite like this. Tonight she was dressed in an evening gown of shimmering blue Shantung silk. It was cut low to show off the rise of her breasts and her elegant throat. She wore long white gloves to above the elbow but no jewelry. She didn't need any. In his mind he compared her to

Li Mei. Admittedly Mei's figure was less voluptuous, more under-stated in her appeal, but for him there was a purity about Li Mei, a kind of untouched sexuality that no Western woman could match. Like Chinese porcelain next to Wedgwood. Only one broke your heart with its beauty.

"Good God, man, who the hell is that gorgeous creature?" It was one of the army officers.

"I believe she's the concert pianist," said a young major. "The club committee is putting on some entertainment and she is it."

A crude laugh greeted this remark. "She can come and entertain me any time she wants."

"No, I'll take the young one, the lion cub. She looks like she's ready for it."

"Well, I'd want to know what's under that dress before I . . ."

Theo stepped away. Too much to drink. It fouled their mouths. But in a community where the men outnumbered the white women by at least ten to one, it was not uncommon. Brothels thrived, stocked mainly with Russian girls or with Eurasians, the half-castes; both were the rejects in a rigid class-ridden society. Theo felt a fierce urge to walk out of there and leave them all in the inferno they had created for themselves, but he didn't. The evening was not finished yet. And there was still Mason.

At that moment Lydia's eyes caught his and she smiled, shyly, self-conscious in her finery. A lion cub, yes, the man was right. Tawny eyes and gleaming red mane. Something untamed about her. Tonight she looked a lovely young woman, but even gilded in a dress that was the color of apricots and the height of fashion with its dropped waist and knee-length hem, she gave off a vibration of excitement. Of dan-ger, even. Yet when he smiled back at her, she blushed like a schoolgirl.

6

OUTSIDE THE ULYSSES CLUB, THE STREETLAMPS OF Wellington Road cast yellow pools of light out into the darkness. But the darkness of this country was vast and dense. It claimed for itself the fragile world the foreigners thought was theirs.

The darkness gave sanctuary. To the narrow-eyed thief who stood at the bedside of the young major's sleeping child while his *amah* played mah-jongg downstairs. To the stinking honey wagon, the cart piled high with human manure destined for the fields. To the knife at the throat of a white man who thought a debt to a Chinese bookie was not binding.

And to Chang An Lo. As evening closed in, he was invisible in the darkness, his shadowy young figure merged with the mottled trunk of one of the plane trees that lined the road. He didn't move. Even when a silver streak of lightning carved through the sky and rain sheeted down, making the leaves clatter above his head and the cars turn into . glistening black monsters as their headlights swung through the wrought-iron gates of the club. A military guard with peaked cap and rifle checked every entrant.

Chang An Lo leaned his head back against the rough bark and shut his eyes to recapture the sight of the girl as she jumped down from the rickshaw that had carried her here. He pictured again the fire in her hair as it danced around her shoulders, the excitement in her step. He'd watched her face lift to study the giant marble pillars and his sharp eyes noticed the moment's hesitation of her feet. Were her eyes still as full of astonishment, he wondered, as when he saw her yesterday? In the filthy *hutong*, the back alley.

Why had she come to that alley?

He'd asked himself that question many times. Had she strayed by accident? But how could you wander into the old Chinese town without noticing? Yet the ways of the *fanqui* were strange, the paths of their mind smudged and indecipherable. He rubbed a hand over the dense black stubble of his hair, felt the wet sheen of rain on it and pressed his fingers harder into his skull as if he could drag an answer from within it by force alone.

Was it the gods who had brought her to him?

He shook his head, angry with himself. The Europeans were no friend to the Chinese, and the gods of the Middle Kingdom would have nothing to do with them. Chang An Lo himself would have nothing to do with them except to drive their voracious souls back into the sea from which they came, but the strange thing was that when he saw her in the *hutong* yesterday, he didn't see a Foreign Devil. Instead he saw a snarling, snapping fox. Like the one he once freed from a snare in the woods. It had sunk its teeth into him and torn a strip of flesh out of his arm, but it had fled to safety. At that time Chang had caught a glimpse of himself in the animal, trapped and fierce and fighting for its freedom.

And now there was this girl. With that same wildness. A fire raging inside her, as well as in her copper hair and in her wide *fanqui* eyes. She would burn him. He was as certain of it as he'd been that the snared fox would savage him when he touched it. But now he was bound to her, his soul to her soul, and he had no choice. Because he'd saved her life.

In his mind rose the image of the alleyway, a foul degrading sewer that no one would choose to enter. He would have passed it without a glance. But the gods stopped his stride and turned his head. She lit up the whole stinking black hole with her fire. His eyes had never before seen anyone like her.

Abruptly his thoughts were dragged back to the rain and the rumbling night sky, his attention distracted by the sound of footfalls and the brisk tap of a cane, a man passing only a few feet away. He wore a top hat and heavy raincoat, huddled under an umbrella, and hurried past Chang without even knowing he was there. But before he reached the club two shapes threw themselves at his feet on the sodden pavement.

Beggars, a man and a woman. Natives of the old town, their voices raised in high-pitched pleas.

Chang spat on the ground at the sight of them.

The man threw a handful of coins at the ragged creatures with a guttural curse, then brought his cane whistling down on their backs as they groveled for them. Chang watched him walk away. Up the wide white steps and in through the entrance, so grand it looked like a mandarin's palace. He didn't hear the man's words, but he knew the actions. He'd seen them all his life in China.

For the next hour his gaze was drawn again and again to the tall, brightly lit windows, as a bird is drawn to yellow corn. She was in there, the fox-haired girl. He'd watched her mount the steps with the other woman beside her, but between them the gap of unused air bristled with an anger that made their shoulders stiff and their heads turn away from each other.

He smiled to himself as the rain ran down his face. The fox girl, she had sharp teeth.

7

Lydia moved through the club quickly. There was little time and much to see.

"Stay here. I won't be long, ten minutes, that's all," Valentina had said. "Don't move."

They were standing to one side of the sweeping staircase, where an antique oak settle seemed somewhat at odds with the brilliance of the chandelier overhead and the polished newel post in the shape of a giant acorn. Everything was on such a huge scale: the paintings, the mirrors, even the mustaches. Bigger and better than Lydia had ever seen before. Not even Polly had been inside the club.

"And don't speak to anyone," Valentina added, her voice sharp as she glanced around at the interested eyes and saw the men murmur to each other. "Not to anyone, you hear?"

"Yes, Mama."

"I have to go to the office to see what the arrangements are for this evening." She gave a discouraging glare to a young man in evening dress and silk scarf who was drifting closer. "Maybe I should take you along with me."

"No, Mama, I'm fine here. I like watching everyone."

"The trouble is, Lydochka, they like watching *you*." She hesitated, undecided, but Lydia sat down demurely on the settle, hands in lap, so Valentina gave her a squeeze on the shoulder and walked off toward a corridor on the right. As she left, Lydia heard her mutter, "I should never have bought her that bloody dress."

The dress. Lydia touched the soft apricot georgette with her fingertips. She loved it more than her life. She had never owned anything so beautiful. And the cream satin shoes. She lifted a foot and admired it. This was the most perfect moment of her life, sitting here in a beautiful place, dressed in beautiful clothes, while beautiful people looked admiringly at her. Because their eyes *were* admiring. She could see that.

This was living. Not just surviving. This was . . . this was being alive, instead of half dead. And for the very first time she thought she really understood a little of the pain that burned in her mother's heart. To lose all this. It must be like blundering blindly into one of the sewers and making your home with the rats. Home. For a moment Lydia felt the pulse at her wrist start to thump. Home was the attic. But for how much longer? She took a handful of the apricot material and scrunched it up hard in her fist. Her feet slipped under the seat so that the shoes were hidden from view.

Look what I've bought you, darling. For tonight. For your birthday.

When Valentina said those words so full of delight after Lydia had rushed home from school this afternoon, Lydia smiled and expected a ribbon for her hair or even her first pair of silk stockings. Not this. This dress. These shoes.

She had frozen. Unable to move. Unable to swallow. "Mama," she said, her eyes fixed on the dress. "What did you use to pay for it?"

"The money in the blue bowl on the shelf."

"Our rent and food money?"

"Yes, but . . ."

"All of it?"

"Of course. It was expensive. But don't look so upset." Valentina suddenly broke off and her bright eyes grew full of concern. She touched her daughter's cheek. "Don't worry so, *dochenka*," she said softly. "I will be paid well for my concert tonight and maybe it will bring me other bookings, especially with you looking so pretty at my side. See it as an investment in our future. Smile, sweetheart. Don't you love the dress?"

Lydia's head nodded but only a tiny movement, and her lips wouldn't smile however hard she tried. "We'll starve," she whispered.

"What rubbish."

"We'll rot in the gutter when Mrs. Zarya throws us out."

"Darling, you are being melodramatic. Here, try it on. And the shoes. I still owe payment for the shoes but they are so pretty. Don't you think?"

"Yes." She could barely breathe.

But the moment the dress floated down over her head, she fell in love with it. Two delicate rows of beading lined the armholes and the geometric neckline, a sash of shimmering satin at the hips and a daring little slit up one side to just above the knee. Lydia twirled round in it, feeling it rustle against her body and give off the faintest scent of apricots. Or was that in her head?

"Like it, darling?"

"I love it."

"Happy birthday."

"Thank you."

"Now stop being cross with me."

"Mama," Lydia said softly, "I'm frightened."

"Poof, don't be so silly. I buy you your first elegant dress to make you happy and you say you are frightened. To own something beautiful is not a crime." She leaned her dark head against Lydia's and whispered, "Enjoy it, my beautiful young daughter, learn to enjoy what you can in this life."

But all Lydia could do was shake her head. She loved the dress, yet hated it. And she despised herself for wanting it so much.

"You make me cross, Lydia Ivanova, cross as an old goat," her mother said in a stern voice. "You don't deserve the dress. I shall take it back."

"No." The word came out as a shout and betrayed her.

It was only later, when Valentina had finished brushing Lydia's hair and pinning it into a sophisticated curl on one side, that Lydia noticed her mother was wearing new evening gloves.

A NAVAL OFFICER APPROACHED HER AS SHE EDGED AWAY from the smoking room, where she'd taken a quick peek around the door. The air in there was thick with the smoke from a dozen cigars and a brace of pipes, a blue smog that caught at the back of her throat and made her sneeze.

"Can I help you, miss? You look as if you're lost, and I hate to see such a charming young damsel in distress." The officer smiled at her, very dashing in his startlingly white uniform and a smattering of gold braid.

"Well, I . . ."

"Permit me to buy you a drink?"

His eyes were so blue and his smile so playful, offering her an invitation that so far had only been spoken in her dreams. *Permit me to buy you a drink.* It was the dress that was doing it, she knew that. The dress and the sophisticated curl. She was tempted. But in her heart she knew that this elegant officer, with his row of well-fed teeth, would expect something in return for his interest. Unlike her Chinese protector yesterday. He'd asked her for nothing, and that touched her in a way she didn't quite understand. It was so . . . so unfamiliar to her. Why would a Chinese hawk want to rescue a *fanqui* sparrow? The question burrowed inside her.

She recalled the flash of anger in his dark eyes and wondered what lay behind it. She wanted to ask him. But first she'd have to find him and she didn't even know his name.

"A drink?" the uniformed officer asked again.

Lydia turned her head away in disdain and said coolly, "I am with my mother, the concert pianist."

He melted away. Lydia felt a little trill of delight flutter up her spine and moved on toward the next door. It was set back in a small niche off the entrance hall. Reading Room, a plaque announced in brass letters, and the door was already half open. She walked in. The banging of her heart subsided only when she realized there were no more than two people in residence, an elderly man asleep in a leather wingback chair with *The Times* rising and falling over his face as he snored gently. The other man, over by the window where the rain was rattling against the dark panes, was Mr. Theo.

He was sitting very upright with his eyes closed. From his mouth came a sort of long drawn-out *oom* noise, over and over monotonously, the way her mother did piano scales. He was breathing deeply and his hands were turned palms upward like empty begging bowls on the arms of his chair. Lydia watched, fascinated. She had seen natives do this, especially the shaven-headed monks in the temple up on Tiger Hill, but never a white man. She looked around the room. It was dimly lit and one wall was obscured by dark shelves of leather-bound books, and placed at intervals were ebony tables covered in newspapers, magazines, and journals. On the nearest one Lydia could read the headline: CAPTAIN DE HAVILLAND SETS NEW RECORD IN GYPSY MOTH.

She tiptoed over to one of the tables. Very occasionally she found a magazine discarded in Victoria Park and would pore over it for months until it finally fell apart, but these were new and irresistible. She picked up a magazine with the enticing title *Lady about Town* and an illustration of a long-limbed lady beside a long-limbed hound on the cover. Lydia held it close to her face to inhale the scent of strange chemicals that wafted off the crisp pages, then turned the first page. Instantly she was captivated. A picture of two women posing on the steps of the National Gallery in Trafalgar Square, London. They looked so modern in the latest helmet hats and dresses so like her own that she was able to dream herself right into the photograph. She could hear their laughter and the pigeons cooing at their feet.

"Get out."

She almost dropped the magazine.

"Get out of here."

It was Mr. Theo. He was leaning forward and staring straight at her. Only it wasn't the usual Mr. Theo. She nearly did as he said, she was so used to jumping to obey his orders at school, but something in the sound of his voice caught at her, made her stare back. The wretchedness she saw in his eyes shocked her.

She took a hesitant step toward him. "Headmaster?"

His whole body seemed to wince as if she'd laid a finger on an open wound, and he ran a hand over his pale face. When he looked back at her, he had regained control.

"What is it, Lydia?"

She had no idea what to say. How to help. She was unsure of herself, but her feet in their little satin shoes refused to walk away.

"Sir," she said, uncertain what would come next, ". . . are you a Buddhist?"

"What an extraordinary question. And a very personal one, I may say." He tipped his head back against the maroon leather and suddenly looked very weary. "But no, I am not a Buddhist, though many of his sayings tempt me to try out the path to peace and enlightenment.

God knows, those are rare commodities in the blackened soul of this place."

"Of China?"

"No, I mean here, this place, our International Settlement." He gave a harsh laugh. "Where nothing is *settled* except through greed and corruption."

The bitterness of his words found its way into the corners of Lydia's mouth, like the taste of aloes. She shook her head to be rid of it and abandoned the magazine on a table. "But sir, it seems to me that for someone like you . . . well . . . you have, I mean . . . everything. So why . . . ?"

"Everything? You mean my school?"

"Yes. And a house and a car and a passport and a place in society and a . . ." She was going to say *mistress*, a beautiful exotic mistress, but stopped herself in time. She didn't mention the money either. He had money. Instead she said, "Everything anyone could want."

"That," he said rising abruptly to his feet, "that is all mud. As Buddha points out with such clarity, your *everything* soils the human soul."

"No, sir. I can't believe that."

His stare fixed on her with a narrowing of his eyelids that was intimidating, but she refused to drop her gaze. Unexpectedly his mouth broke into a smile, but it didn't have the strength to reach his eyes.

"Little Lydia Ivanova, all togged up in your finery, looking like a delicate ripe magnolia bud about to burst open. You are so innocent, you have no idea what goes on. So unspoiled. This is a world of corruption, my dear. You know nothing about it."

"I know more than you think."

At that he laughed outright. "Oh, I'm sure that's true. I don't take you for a docile dormouse, like some of your classmates. But you're still young and you still have the capacity to believe." He sank down into the chair once more and let his head rest on his hands. "You still believe."

Lydia looked down at the long, tormented fingers buried in his fine, light brown hair and she felt a knot of anger rise on her tongue. She moved close to the chair as the faint sound of a snore drifted from the other side of the room, and she bent forward, so that she was almost speaking into his ear.

"Sir, whatever future I want, I'm the only one who can make it happen. If that's believing, then yes, I believe." The words came out in a fierce little hiss.

He tilted his head to look at her, a hint of admiration lurking behind the frown. "Passionate words, Lydia. But empty. Because you don't know where you are. Or what it is that makes the wheels of this sordid little town turn. It's all filth and corruption, the stench of the gutter . . ."

"No, sir." Lydia shook her head vehemently. "Not here." She gestured toward the leather-bound books, the ormolu French clock quietly ticking their lives away, and the door that led to the elegant world watched over by Sir Edward Carlisle, where everything was stable and serene.

"Lydia, you are blind. This town was born out of greed. Stolen from China and packed full of greedy men. I warn you, by God or by Buddha, it will die by greed."

"No."

"Yes. Corruption is in its heart. You of all people should know that."

"Me? Why me?" A kick of panic in her chest.

"Because you go to my school, of course."

Lydia blinked, baffled. "I don't understand."

Abruptly Theo withdrew into himself. "Go away, Lydia. Take your shining hair and your shining beliefs and dazzle them out there. I shall see you on Monday morning. You will be in your Willoughby Academy uniform, your wrists sticking out too far from your fraying cuffs as usual, and I will be in my headmaster gown. We will forget this conversation ever took place." He waved a hand at her in dismissal, reached for a cigarette, and lit it with an air of quiet despair.

LYDIA SHUT THE DOOR BEHIND HER BUT THE CONVERSATION would not be forgotten. Not by her.

"Lydia, my dear, how lovely you look."

Lydia turned and saw Mrs. Mason, Polly's mother, descending on her. At her side was a woman in her forties, tall and elegant, who made Anthea Mason look dumpy by comparison.

"Countess, let me introduce Lydia Ivanova. She's the daughter of our pianist tonight." She turned to Lydia. "Countess Natalia Serova is also Russian, from St. Petersburg, though I suppose I should really call her Madame Charonne now."

Countess. Lydia became breathless at the thought. Her evening dress was of watered silk, the color of deep burgundy, but it seemed oddly old-fashioned to Lydia with its full skirt and leg-of-mutton sleeves. Her aristocratic back was straight and she held her head high, pearls clustered at her throat, her pale blue eyes surveying Lydia with cool interest. Lydia had no idea what was expected of her, so she bobbed a small curtsy.

"You have been well taught, child. *Devushki ochen redko takie vezhlivie.*"

Lydia stared at the floor, unwilling to admit she didn't understand.

"Oh, but Lydia doesn't speak Russian," Anthea Mason said helpfully.

The countess raised one skillfully arched eyebrow. "No Russian? And why not?"

Lydia felt like digging a hole in the floor and climbing into it. "My mother brought me up to speak only English. And a little French," she added quickly.

"That is disgraceful."

"Oh, Countess, don't be so harsh on the girl."

"*Kakoi koshmar!* She should know her mother tongue."

"English *is* my mother tongue," Lydia insisted, though her cheeks were burning. "I'm proud to speak English."

"Good for you," said Anthea Mason. "Fly the flag, my dear."

The countess reached out, tucked a finger under Lydia's chin, and lifted it an inch. "*That* is how you would hold it," she said with an amused smile on her lips, "if you were at court." Her Russian accent was even stronger than Valentina's, so that the words seemed to roll around inside her mouth, and she gave a little shrug of her shoulders but her cool gaze examined Lydia intently, so that Lydia felt she was being peeled, layer by layer. "Yes, you are a lovely child, but . . . ," Countess Serova dropped her hand and moved back, "far too thin to wear a dress like that. Enjoy your evening." She seemed to glide away across the hall with her companion.

"I heard today that Helen Wills has won Wimbledon," Anthea was saying. "Isn't it thrilling?" She gave an apologetic little wave in Lydia's direction.

For a full minute Lydia didn't move. The hall was filling up as the evening grew busier but there was still no sign of her mother. A sharp pain had lodged just behind her breastbone and misery had soiled the new dress like a grubby stain. She was now acutely aware that she was all bones sticking out, her breasts too small and her hair the wrong color. Too spiky in her mind, as well as her body. She was masquerading in the dress, just as she was masquerading at being English. Oh yes, she spoke it with a perfect English accent, but who did that fool?

At the end of a minute she raised her chin an inch, then went in search of her mother because the recital was due to start at eight-thirty.

THE TWO FIGURES STOOD CLOSE TO EACH OTHER. Too close, it seemed to Lydia. One, small and slender in a blue dress, had her back against the wall of a passageway, the other, broader and needier, was leaning over her, his face almost touching hers, as if he would eat her up.

Lydia froze. She was halfway down a well-lit corridor inside the club, but off to the right ran the narrow passageway that looked as though it led to somewhere like the servants' quarters or the laundry. Somewhere hidden away. It was dim and overwarm, the large potted palm at its entrance throwing long shadowy fingers snaking along the tiled floor. She knew her mother instantly. But the man leaning over her took longer to place. With a shock she realized it was Mr. Mason, Polly's father. His hands were all over her mother, all over the blue silk. On her thighs, her hips, her throat, her breasts. As if he owned them. And she did nothing to push him away.

Lydia felt a swirl of sickness in her stomach. She longed to turn, to break the pull of it, but couldn't, so she stood there, watching, unable to drag her eyes away. Her mother stood absolutely still, her back and her head and the palms of her hands pressed against the wall behind her, as if she would climb right through it. When Mason's mouth seized Valentina's, she let it happen but the way a doll lets its face be washed. Taking no part, eyes open and glazed. With both his hands clutching her body against his, Mason slid his mouth down her neck to the warm cleft between her breasts, and Lydia heard his groan of pleasure.

A small gasp escaped Lydia's mouth, she couldn't help it. Even though it was low and stifled, it was enough to make her mother twist her head. Her huge dark eyes widened when they fixed on her daughter's and her mouth opened, but no sound came out. Lydia's legs at last responded and she stepped back out of sight, into the corridor where she raced back around one corner and then another. Somewhere behind her she heard her mother's voice. "Lydia, Lydia."

That was when she saw someone she knew, a man she was sure she'd met somewhere before. He was heading for the main exit but his face was turned in Lydia's direction. It was the man whose watch she'd stolen yesterday in the marketplace. Without thinking, she burst through the first door on the left and shut it behind her. The room was small and silent, a cloakroom, full of rows of coats and stoles, capes and Burberrys, as well as racks of top hats and walking canes. Off to one side was a small archway into a separate area where an attendant waited at a counter to receive or retrieve the guests' outer garb. The attendant was not in sight at the moment but Lydia could hear him talking to someone in Mandarin.

She was trembling, her knees shaking beneath her, her teeth rattling in her head. She took a deep breath, made herself walk over to a glorious red fox wrap that hung nearby. Gently she rested her cheek against it and tried to calm her heaving stomach with the rich warmth of gleaming fur. But it didn't work. She slid to the floor and wrapped her arms around her shins, rested her forehead on her knees, and tried to make sense of the evening.

Everything had gone wrong. Everything. Somehow everything had changed inside her head. All back to front. Her mother. Her school. Her plans. The way she looked. Even the way she spoke. Nothing was the same. And Mason with her mother. What was that about? What was going on?

She felt tears burn her cheeks and dashed them away furiously. She never cried. Never. Tears were for people like Polly, people who could afford them. With a shake of her head, she rubbed a hand across her mouth, jumped to her feet, and forced herself to think straight. If everything was wrong, then it was up to her to put it right. But how?

With hands still shivering, she brushed the creases from her dress and, more out of habit than intention, started to hunt through the pockets of the coats in the cloakroom. A pair of men's leather gloves and a Dunhill lighter quickly came to hand but she put them back, even though it hurt to do so. She had nowhere to keep them, no evening bag or pocket, but a lady's lace handkerchief she tucked into her underclothes; it would sell easily in the market. Next, a heavy black raincoat, still wet from the rain, a bulge in the inner pocket. Her fingers scooped out the contents. A soft pouch of deerskin.

Quickly, before someone comes. Loosen its neck, tip it upside down. Into her hand tumbled a glittering ruby necklace, lying like a pool of fiery blood in the center of her palm.

8

CHANG WATCHED.

They came like a wave. Up from the heart of the settlement. A dark tidal wave of police that suffocated the street. With guns snug on their hips and badges proud on their peaked caps, as threatening as a cobra's splayed hood. They leaped from cars and trucks, headlights carving the night into neat yellow slices, and they circled the club. A man in black and white finery, with medals bristling on his chest and a single glass lens over his right eye, strode down the steps toward them. He threw orders and gestures around, the way a mandarin scattered gold coins at his daughter's wedding.

Chang watched, his breath cool and unhurried. But his thoughts probed the darkness, feeling for danger. He slid away. From the shadow of the tree and into the blackness while around him others scampered out of sight. The beggars, the vendor of sunflower seeds and the hot-tea seller, the boy, thin as a twig, performing backflips for pennies, all melted away at the first stink of police boots. The night air turned foul in Chang's lungs and he could almost hear the cloud of angry nightspirits flitting and flickering past his head as they fled from yet one more barbarian invasion.

The rain still fell, heavier now, as if it would wash them away. It polished the streets and bowed the heads of the blue-uniformed devils, streaked their capes as they stationed themselves along the perimeter wall of the Ulysses Club. Chang watched as the man with the glass at his eye was swallowed up inside the building's hungry mouth and the heavy doors closed behind him. An officer holding a rifle was placed in front of them. The world was shut out. The occupants shut in.

Chang knew she was in there, the fox girl, walking through its rooms the way she walked through his dreams while he slept. Even by day she appeared in his head, making herself at home there and laughing when he tried to push her out. He closed his eyes and could see her face, her sharp teeth and her flaming hair, her eyes the color of molten amber, and the way they seemed to gleam from within when she'd looked at him, so bright and curious.

What if she didn't want to be shut in the white devil's building? Caged. Trapped. He had to loosen the snare.

He eased away from the wet bricks behind him and set off through the darkness at a low run, as silent and unseen as a cat snaking toward a rat hole.

HE CROUCHED. INVISIBLE UNDER A BROAD-LEAFED BUSH, while his eyes adjusted to the blackness at the back of the building. A high stone wall girded its grounds but no streetlights reached out to disturb the habits of the night. His quick ears caught the sharp screech of a creature in pain, in the talons of an owl or the jaws of a weasel, but the rattling of the rain on the leaves drowned out most other sounds. So he crouched and waited patiently.

He did not need to wait long. The round yellow beam of a flashlight announced the patrol of two police officers, with heads bent and shoulders hunched against the heavy rain as if it were an enemy. They hurried past, scarcely a glance around, though the beam danced from bush to bush like a giant firefly. Chang tipped his head back, lifting his face to the downpour, the way he used to do in the waterfall as a child. Water was a state of mind. If you think it your friend when you swim in the river or wash away the dirt, why call it your enemy when it comes from the heavens? From the cup of the gods themselves. Tonight it was their gift to him, to keep him safe from barbarian eyes, and his lips murmured a prayer of thanks to Kuan Yung, the goddess of mercy.

He stepped forward onto the road, inhaled deeply, drawing together the elements of fire and water, and launched himself at the wall. A leap, fingers finding an uneven stone for half a second, then a twist in the air and legs flying high up above his head to the top of the wall. A silent drop to the ground on the other side. All one smooth flowing movement that attracted no eyes. Just a toad voiced its surprise at his feet.

But before he had taken even one step, a single streak of lightning split the sky in two and lit up the club's grounds for just long enough to rob Chang of his night vision. His throat tightened and his mouth went dry. An omen. But for good? Or evil? He didn't know. For a moment his mind chased in wild circles. He knelt in the deeper blackness that followed, his body as slick as an otter's in the rain, and feared that the omen was sent to tell him he was acting blindly. That the gods wanted to warn him that the *fanqui* girl would cost him too high a price. The smell of the drenched earth rose to his nostrils and he reached out, seized a handful of it, and raised it to his face. China's earth, the yellow loess, rich and fertile, stolen by the barbarians. It felt cold when he crumbled the wet soil in his fingers, as cold as if it had died. Death marched with the foreigners wherever they went.

He knew he should leave.

But he shook his head impatiently and flicked out his tongue to lick the raindrops from his lips. Leave? It was not possible. His soul was tied to hers. He could no more turn and leave this place than a fish could leave its river. A hook was deep in him. He could feel it like a pain in his chest. To leave would be to die.

He moved swiftly and silently over the wet grass, becoming part of the trees, his shadow merging with theirs. Acres of neat lawns spread all around him, a small lake, flower gardens, and tennis courts on one side, a swimming pool big enough to drown an army on the other, all dimly illuminated by the lights from the building. To Chang it looked more like a fortress from the back, with two small round turrets, but then the foreigners had lost courage and softened its face with a long veranda and wide steps down to a crescent-moon terrace. A wisteria curved and writhed over the veranda roof, but the interior was hidden from view because long bamboo blinds had been lowered to keep out the storm. He could hear the blinds as they gusted and shook in the wind, billowing and rattling against the frame like the bones of the dead.

Uncertain which path to take, Chang swung away to the right. As he did so, something small and light fluttered into his face and clung to his cheek driven by the rain. His hand plucked it off and he was about to toss it away as an ill-fated moth, when he glanced at it more closely. A petal. A soft pink rose petal. Only then did he see that he was standing in the middle of a rose garden where the blooms were being slashed and torn by the wind and the rain. He stared at the single petal curled in the palm of his hand. *This* was a sign too. A sign of love. He knew now that he would find her, and anticipation surged hot in his veins. The gods were close tonight, whispering in his ear. He tucked the delicate offering of the petal inside the wet folds of his tunic, and his bare skin tingled at the touch of it. His pulse beat stronger.

He skimmed around the edge of the circle of light, keeping in the shadows, black on black, until he crossed a path to what was clearly the kitchens. The lights shone brightly from the windows and Chang could make out the cluttered surfaces and steaming pans, but no one was in there except a solitary black barbarian in police uniform standing near the door. Where were the workers with their noisy chatter and their cursing? Had the foreigners eaten them? What was going on tonight?

Soundlessly he slipped farther along the building and came to the window of a room that made his heart cry out with envy. It took him by surprise, this envy, and he tried in vain to tear it out. For he despised the Westerners and all they had brought to the East. Except for one thing: their books. He loved their books. And this room possessed a whole wall full of them, just lined up along each shelf for anyone to reach up and read. Not like the delicate scrolls of Chinese learning that were kept for the scholars only. These were sturdy and leather bound and full of knowledge.

Years earlier, Chang had been taught English. That was in the days before his father was beheaded behind the walls of the Forbidden City in Peking, the days he could no longer bear to let into his head because they turned his thoughts into stinging bees. His tutor had used Munrow's *History of the Great British Empire* as reading matter for his pupil, and Chang had almost choked with shame when he discovered how small England was, a miserable piece of spit compared to the great ocean that was China.

The sound of angry words dragged his attention from the books to the two men in the room. One was Glass Eye, seated at a table, stiff and upright, his hand curled in a tight fist before him, his mouth throwing words like weapons. The other was white haired, standing tall and commanding in the center of the room, his eyes fierce above a nose as hooked as a falcon's beak. He did not flinch when Glass Eye crashed his fist down on the table and shouted so loud Chang could hear the words, "I will not stand for it. Under my very nose. As chief of police I insist that everyone be . . ."

The bark of a dog ripped through the night. Off to Chang's left, somewhere unseen behind the cloak of rain. It lifted the hairs on his neck and he moved swiftly around the next corner where the windows were long and arched, giving him a view into a grand chamber that glittered and shimmered as brightly as the sun on the Peiho River. For a second he thought the room was full of birds, fluttering their fine feathers and trilling their sweet songs, but his eyes cleared and they were women in evening dress, chattering behind their fans. This is where she'd be, in this golden cage, and suddenly he had a feeling of moths inside his chest.

There were no men in the room. It was laid out with chairs in straight rows, all facing an object at one end that made Chang gasp with amazement because it looked like a monstrous giant turtle. It was all black and shiny on tall spindly legs and beside it sat a beautiful dark-haired woman occasionally touching its white teeth with one finger and sipping from a tall ice-filled glass. Her eyes looked bored and lonely.

He recognized her. He had seen her before, on the front steps of the club beside the fox girl. His breathing grew so shallow it hardly disturbed the air as his eyes sought a flash of copper hair among the crowd. Few of the women were seated; most were standing in groups or drifting around with a glass or a fan in hand, painted lips curved down in annoyance. Something was displeasing them. He moved closer until he was tucked tight against the stonework beside the window and suddenly he saw her. The world seemed to come at him and turn brighter.

SHE WAS STANDING APART AGAINST ONE OF THE MARBLE pillars, almost hidden from view behind a fat woman with a clutch of ostrich feathers in her hair. By contrast the girl looked frail and pale except for the rich color that glowed in her hair. Chang watched her. He saw her eyes flit uneasily to the door again and again and then grow dark with alarm when it opened abruptly and two women marched in. To Chang they looked like death bringers, all clothed in stiff white robes and strange white headdresses that reminded him of the nuns who had tried to make him eat their living god's flesh and pour their god's blood into his mouth when he was young. His stomach still spasmed at the memory of such barbarism. But these wore no boastful cross around their necks.

With polite smiles they escorted two of the younger women out of the room and it was only when the door closed behind them that some of the tension flowed out of the fox girl's body and she started to prowl around the outer edge of her cage, her arms still stiff at her sides, one hand plucking at the soft material of her dress. He saw her drop a lace handkerchief on the floor as if by chance, but to Chang's eyes her fingers knew exactly what they were doing, and he wondered why. The ways of foreigners were strange.

A tall woman in a gown the color of ripe sloes spoke to her as she passed, but the girl returned no more than a nod of the head and a slight coloring of the cheeks. She was approaching the windows now and Chang's chest tightened as he saw her come closer. Her cheekbones were finer than he remembered and her eyes more wide-set, but around her mouth the skin was blue, as when a child feels sick.

He leaned forward, reached out and touched the wet pane of glass that separated him from her, his fingers rattling a quiet drumbeat on its cold surface that could have been the rain. She stopped midstride, frowned, and looked out into the storm with her head cocked to one side like his father's young hunting cur used to do. Before she could move away, he stepped into the circle of light thrown out from the window and gave her a respectful bow.

Her eyes and her mouth grew as round as the moon with surprise, and then came recognition and a smile. For a brief second he held out the open palm of his hand to her in a mute offer of help, and that was when something hard and cold slammed into the side of his head. Waves of blackness swept over him. The night splintered into sharp fragments of black glass, but his muscles tensed instantly for action.

With one sweep of his leg he could disable this attacker who breathed whisky fumes and curses in his face, or snap his worthless windpipe with a knife blade strike of his hand. But a sound stopped him.

A snarl. It spoke of death.

On the wet grass at his feet a wolf-dog was crouched, its body hunched ready to spring, its teeth bared in a low-throated growl that made Chang's blood choke in his veins. The hound hungered to tear his heart out.

He did not want to kill the dog, but he would.

Slowly Chang turned his gaze from the animal to the man. He was wearing a blue-devil cape against the rain and was tall, with long gangling limbs and empty cheeks, the kind of tree it was easy to fell. In his hand was a gun. Chang could see his own blood glistening on it. The man's thin lips were moving but the wind seemed to be roaring in Chang's ears and he could barely hear the words.

"Yellow piece of shit."

"Thieving Chink."

"Peeping Tom."

"Don't you stare at our women, you bloody . . ." And the gun rose to strike once more.

Chang dipped to one side and rotated his waist, and like the crack of a bullwhip his leg snapped out in an upward strike. But the dog was fast. It hurled itself between attacker and master and sank its teeth into the vulnerable flesh of Chang's foot, forcing him onto his back on the wet earth. Pain raced up his leg as fangs tore at bone. But he inhaled, letting go of the tension in his body, and instead controlled the energy of the fear. He released it in one rippling movement that sent his other foot exploding into the face of the hound.

The animal dropped its grip and collapsed on its side without a whimper. Instantly Chang was up on his feet and running before the night had even drawn breath.

"Take one more step and I put a bullet in your bloody brain."

Chang stilled his mind. He knew this man was going to kill him for what he'd done to the dog. It had robbed the blue devil of face. So to stay or to flee made no difference, the end would be the same. He felt a knifepoint of regret in his lungs at leaving the girl. Slowly he turned and faced the man, saw the violence in his face and the steadiness of the black eye of the gun.

"Dong Po, what on earth do you think you're doing?"

The voice burst through the rain and cut the thread that joined the policeman's bullet to Chang's brain. It was the girl.

"I told you to wait inside the gate, you worthless boy. I shall get Li to give you a good beating for disobedience when we get home." She was glaring at Chang.

At that moment Chang's heart stopped. It took all his strength to prevent a wide smile from growing on his lips, but instead he ducked his head in humble apology.

"I sorry, mistress, so sorry. No be angry." He gestured at the window. "I look for you to see okay. So much police, I worry."

Behind the girl stood another blue devil. He was trying to hold a black umbrella over her head, but the rain and the wind were snatching at it, so that her hair hung in rats' tails and had turned the color of old bronze. Over her shoulders was thrown a servant's thin white jacket, but already it was wet through.

"Ted, what's up with the dog?" The second policeman was middle-aged and heavy.

"I'm telling you, Sarge, if this yellow bugger has killed my Rex, I'll . . ."

"Ease up, Ted. Look, the dog's moving, just stunned probably." He turned to Chang, noting the blood on his face. "Now look, boy," he said, not unkindly, "I'm not sure what's gone on here but your mistress got real upset, she did, when she saw you skulking around these windows. She says you were told to wait at the gate, to act as escort, see, for her and her mother when they need one of them rickshaws. Those rickshaw buggers are right dangerous, so you should be ashamed of yourself, letting her down like this."

Chang stared in silence at his bloodstained foot and nodded.

"No discipline," said the blue devil, "that's the trouble with you lot."

Chang pictured sending a tiger-paw punch into his face. Would that show him discipline enough? If he'd intended the dog to be dead, it would be dead.

"Dong Po."

He looked up into her amber eyes.

"Get off home right now, you miserable boy. You aren't to be trusted, so tomorrow you shall be punished."

She was holding her chin high and could have been the Grand Empress Tzu Hsi of the Middle Kingdom the way she gazed at him with haughty disdain.

"Officer," she said, "I apologize for my servant's behavior. Please see that he's thrown out of the gate, will you?"

Then she started walking back along the path as if she were taking a stroll in the sunshine instead of in a raging summer storm. The blue sergeant followed with the umbrella.

"Mistress," Chang called after her against the roar of the wind.

She turned. "What is it?"

"There no need to kill mosquito with cannon," he said. "Please be merciful. Say where I be punished tomorrow."

She thought for a second. "For that added insolence, it will be at St. Saviour's Hall. To cleanse your wicked soul." She stalked off without a backward glance.

The fox girl's tongue was cunning.

9

"MAMA?"

Silence. Yet Lydia was sure her mother was awake. The attic room was pitch black and the street outside lay quiet, cooler after the storm. From under Lydia's bed came a faint scratching sound that she knew meant a mouse or a cockroach was on its nightly prowl, so she drew her knees to her chin and curled up in a tight ball.

"Mama?"

She had heard her mother tossing and turning for hours in her small white cell and once caught the soft sniffing that betrayed tears.

"Mama?" she whispered again into the blackness.

"Mmm?"

"Mama, if you had all the money in the world to buy yourself one present, what would it be?"

"A grand piano." The words came out with no hesitation, as if they had been waiting on the tip of her tongue.

"A shiny white one like you said they have in the American hotel on George Street?"

"No. A black one. An Erard grand."

"Like you used to play in St. Petersburg?"

"Just like."

"It might not fit in here very well."

Her mother laughed softly, the sound muffled by the curtains that divided the room. "If I could afford an Erard, darling, I could afford a drawing room to put it in. One with hand-woven carpets from Tientsin, beautiful candlesticks of English silver, and flowers on every table filling the room with so much perfume it would rid my nostrils of the filthy stench of poverty."

Her words seemed to fill the room, making the air suddenly too heavy to breathe. The scratching under the bed ceased. In the silence, Lydia hid her face in her pillow.

"And you?" Valentina asked when the silence had lasted so long it seemed she had fallen asleep.

"Me?"

"Yes, you. What present would you buy yourself?"

Lydia shut her eyes and pictured it. "A passport."

"Ah yes, of course, I should have guessed. And where would you travel with this passport of yours, little one?"

"To England, to London first and then to somewhere called Oxford, which Polly says is so beautiful it makes you want to cry and then . . ." her voice grew low and dreamy as if she were already elsewhere, "to America to see where they make the films and also to Denmark to find where . . ."

"You dream too much, *dochenka*. It is bad for you."

Lydia opened her eyes. "You brought me up as English, Mama, so of course I want to go to England. But tonight a Russian countess told me . . ."

"Who?"

"Countess Serova. She said . . ."

"Pah! That woman is an evil witch. To hell with her and what she said. I don't want you talking to her again. That world is gone."

"No, Mama, listen. She said it is disgraceful that I can't speak my mother tongue."

"Your mother tongue is English, Lydia. Always remember that. Russia is finished, dead and buried. What use to you would learning Russian be? None. Forget it, like I have forgotten it. And forget that countess too. Forget Russia ever existed." She paused. "You will be happier that way."

The words flowed out of the darkness, hard and passionate, and beat like hammers on Lydia's brain, pounding her thoughts into confusion. Part of her longed to be proud of being Russian, the way Countess Serova was proud of her birthright and of her native tongue. But at the same time Lydia wanted so much to be English. As English as Polly. To have a mother who toasted you crumpets for tea and went around on an English bicycle and who gave you a puppy for your birthday and made you say your prayers and bless the king each night. One who sipped sherry instead of vodka.

She put a hand to her mouth. To stop any sounds coming out, in case they were sounds of pain.

"Lydia."

Lydia had no idea how long the silence had lasted this time, but she started to breathe heavily as if asleep.

"Lydia, why did you lie?"

Her chest thumped. Which lie? When? To whom?

"Don't pretend you can't hear me. You lied to the policeman to-night."

"I didn't."

"You did."

"No, I didn't."

A sharp pinging of bedsprings from the other end of the room made Lydia fear that her mother was on her way over to confront her daughter face to face, but no, she was just shifting position impatiently in the darkness.

"Don't think I don't know when you're lying, Lydia. You tug at your hair. So what were you up to, spinning such a story to Police Commissioner Lacock? What is it you're trying to hide?"

Lydia felt sick, not for the first time tonight. Her tongue seemed to swell and fill her mouth. The church clock struck three and some-thing squealed at the end of the street. A pig? A dog? More likely a person. The wind had died down, but the stillness didn't make her feel any better. She started counting backward from ten in her head, a trick she'd learned to ward off panic.

"What story?" she asked.

"*Chyort!* You know perfectly well what story. The one about see-ing a mystery man at the French window when you were in the read-ing room with Mr. Willoughby tonight. Suggesting this strange person could be the thief who stole the rubies from the club."

"Oh, that."

"Yes, that. A big bearded man with an eye patch and astrakhan hat and long patterned boots, that's what you said."

"Yes." It came out more timid than she'd hoped.

"Why tell such lies?"

"I *did* see him."

"Lydia Ivanova, may your words scorch holes in your tongue."

Lydia said nothing. Her cheeks were burning.

"They'll arrest him, you know," Valentina said fiercely.

No, how could they?

"Your description marked him out clearly as a Russian. They'll search around here in the Russian Quarter until they find a man that fits. Then what?" Her mother's voice wouldn't let up.

Please don't let them find him.

"It was a foolish lie to tell, Lydia. It puts others at risk."

Still Lydia didn't open her mouth. She was afraid what words might creep out.

"Pah! Go into one of your sulks, if you must." Valentina's voice was heavy with annoyance. "Dear God, what a terrible night this has been. No concert, so no fee, searched by an insolent nurse, and now a daughter who not only ruins her beautiful dress by running around in the rain but also insults me with her lies and silence."

No response.

"Go on, go to sleep then, and I hope you dream of your bearded Russian phantom. Maybe he'll come after you with a pitchfork to thank you for your lies."

Lydia lay in her bed staring out into the darkness, too frightened to shut her eyes.

"Hello, dear, you're up bright and early this morning. Come to tell Polly all about the thrills of last night, have you? Goodness me, what a kerfuffle it was."

Anthea Mason beamed with pleasure at Lydia, as if she could think of no better way to start a Sunday morning than having her daughter's friend arrive on her doorstep before breakfast.

"Come and join us on the terrace."

This wasn't exactly what Lydia had planned, because she needed to speak to Polly in private, but it was better than nothing, so she smiled a thank-you and followed Mrs. Mason through the house. It was large and very modern, with pale beechwood floors, and always seemed filled with light as if it had somehow swallowed the sun, which danced off the plain cream-painted walls and caressed the shiny brass horn of the gramophone that Lydia coveted with a passion. No peeling wallpaper or dingy corners for cockroaches here. And Polly's house always smelled so enticing. Of beeswax polish and flowers and something homemade baking in the oven. Today it was coffee and fresh rolls.

As she emerged onto the terrace with its view over a sun-dappled lawn and yellow tea roses, the image was idyllic. A table was covered in starched white linen and spread with teacups that had fragile little handles and gold rims, and a silver coffeepot was surrounded by perfectly matching silver bowls of sugar, butter, marmalade, and honey. Mr. Mason was relaxing in his shirtsleeves and riding boots at one end of the table, with a newspaper in one hand, a slice of toast in the other, and Achilles on his lap. Achilles was a fat cat with long gray fur and a voice like a foghorn.

"Hi, Lyd." Polly smiled from the other side of the table and tried to hide her surprise.

"Hello."

"Good morning, Lydia," said Mr. Mason. "A bit too damned early for visitors, wouldn't you say?" His tone was one she'd heard him use to the boot boy. She couldn't bear to look at him. Instead she stared at the delicate finger bowl beside him, and became curious about the slice of lemon floating in the water.

"Yes, sir."

"So why are you here?"

"Oh, Christopher," said Anthea Mason, "we're always happy to see Lydia any time, aren't we, Polly? Sit and have a bite to eat, dear."

But Lydia would rather swallow her tongue than sit down at the same table with the man who last night had been molesting her mother. Both she and Valentina had carefully avoided mentioning the subject of what they both knew Lydia had seen, but the pictures were still vivid inside her head.

"No, thank you," she said politely. "I just want a word with Polly, if I may."

Mason leaned back in his chair and tossed the paper to the ground. "Now then, young lady," he said, "whatever you want to say to our daughter can be said in front of us. We have no secrets round here."

The barefaced lie. It made Lydia blink, and she opened her mouth to utter a sharp retort, but Polly forestalled her. She jumped to her feet, grabbing the napkin from her lap. Lydia knew for a fact it had come from London, from a shop called Givan's on New Bond Street, twenty-nine shillings and ninepence for a dozen, Polly had told her proudly, all fine Irish damask. Whatever that was.

"Daddy, we'll just find Toby and walk him down to the park."

"That'll be fun for him. Take his ball and don't forget to wear your hat," Anthea Mason said with a look at her husband.

He turned his face away from her and gave a smile to the cat draped across his lap, its yellow eyes watching him closely. "Don't be long."

"No, just a quick run," Polly said.

"Church at eleven sharp. I don't want you making us late."

"We won't, I promise."

As she passed him, he reached up and ruffled her blond hair, but to Lydia the gesture looked awkward, as if it were something he'd once seen a father do and decided to copy it. Polly's cheeks turned pink, but then she was always nervous around her father and never talked about him, not even in private. Lydia, knowing nothing about fathers, assumed this was normal.

"POLLY, I NEED A FAVOR." LYDIA CLUTCHED HER FRIEND'S arm.

"What is it?"

"A big favor."

Polly's eyes grew bluer and rounder. "I just knew it had to be something really important for you to barge in on Father so early. What is it? Quick, tell me." She twirled Toby's lead in her hand.

They were sitting on a bench in the sunshine, throwing balls for Polly's Tibetan spaniel. They had avoided Victoria Park with its No Dogs. No Chinese notices and opted for Alexandra Gardens, where Toby was allowed to race around, as long as he kept out of the canna flowerbeds and the koi fish pond, where frogs lurked under lily pads and taunted his insatiable nose.

"It's . . . well . . . you see . . . oh Polly, I need to get back into the club."

"What? The Ulysses Club?"

"Yes."

"But why?"

"I just do."

"That's no answer." Polly twisted her pretty face into a scowl, but there was no conviction in it. She was never much good at being cross with Lydia, but tried to keep that fact a secret. "I thought that last night would have put you off that club for life. It would me. To be searched by a ghastly old nurse." She gave a dainty little shudder that rippled through her soft blond hair. "How perfectly disgusting." She leaned closer, eyes fixed on Lydia's. "Was the search very, you know, very sort of . . . intimate?" She held her breath.

"Oh God, yes."

Polly's mouth popped open and she gave a gasp. "Oh Lyd, that's horrible. Poor you." She gave her friend a quick hug.

"So?"

"So what?" Polly asked.

"So will you speak to your father for me?"

"Oh Lyd, I can't."

"You can, you know you can. Please, Polly."

"But why do you want to go back to the club? They searched everyone and every room but didn't find the stolen necklace. So what can you do?" She glanced around quickly and lowered her voice to a bare whisper. "Did you see something? Do you know who took it?"

"No, no, of course not, or I'd have told the police."

"Then why?"

"Because . . . oh, all right, I'll tell you, but you must promise to keep it secret."

Polly nodded eagerly, licked a finger and drew a cross on her throat. "Hope to die."

"Remember the young man who rescued me in the alley on Friday? With his flying *kung fu* kicks . . ."

"Yes?"

"Well, he turned up at the club last night."

"No."

"Yes."

"Did he steal the necklace?"

"Don't be silly," Lydia said quickly, "of course he didn't. He had come especially to speak to me about something. He said it was important. But we were interrupted by all the police running around after they discovered the necklace had gone, so he asked me to come back today . . . I really owe it to him, Polly, and I don't know where else to find him."

To Lydia's horror, she suddenly realized her fingers were tugging at a strand of hair just in front of her right ear. Oh damn. Her mother was right. She dropped it quickly, gave Polly a sideways glance to see if she'd noticed, and bent to pick up Toby's ball.

"But there's something I don't understand, Lyd."

Lydia threw the ball for the dog.

"You say your mother hardly ever scolds you, Lyd, just lets you do what you like. That's why I'm green with envy, you know that. I wish I had the freedom she allows you." She turned and looked quizzically at her friend. "So why all the secrecy? Can't your mother . . . or even her French friend with the Morgan . . . can't they get you in?"

Lydia hated lying to Polly, the one person in the whole world she was honest with, but she had to get back inside the club today if she was to retrieve the rubies from their hiding place in the Reading Room. And now Polly was being stubborn.

Lydia leaped to her feet and tossed her head impatiently. "Neither my mother nor Antoine are members, as you well know. But if you're too scared to ask your father to invite me in there, I'll ask him myself."

"But he'll want to know why."

"That's okay, I'll tell him I lost a brooch or something last night."

"He'll only get annoyed and say if you can't look after something properly, you don't deserve it in the first place."

"Oh, Polly, you are such a baby," Lydia snapped and stalked off toward the park gates.

But Polly came running after her with Toby bouncing around her ankles. "Please, Lyd, don't be angry."

"I'm not."

But she was. Angry with herself. She turned and looked at Polly, at her lovely pale cornflower dress, at her smart patent leather shoes and at her wide blue eyes creased with worry, and hated herself. She had no right to drag this shiny new silver dollar of a person through the dirt. She was so used to it herself, she forgot that others found its smell distressing. She drew Polly's arm through her own and gave her a shaky smile.

"Sorry, Polly, I know I'm too hotheaded sometimes."

"It's the red hair."

They both laughed and felt the friendship slip back in place.

"Okay, I'll ask Father."

"Thanks."

"But it won't work."

"Please try."

"On condition you tell me more about your mystery Chinese rescuer after you see him again." She paused, attached her puppy to the lead once more, ruffled his ears, and, while her face was averted, asked, "You don't think it might be a bit dangerous? I mean, you know nothing about him, do you?"

"Except that he saved me from slavery . . . or worse." Lydia laughed. "Don't fret, you silly. I promise to tell you everything that happens."

"Describe him again to me. What's he like?"

"My flying hawk?"

"Yes."

Lydia was nervous. She was longing to talk about her Chinese protector, to give voice to the images that crowded her thoughts, to talk of the high arc of his eyebrow that rose like a bird's wing and the way he angled his head when he was listening to you, his eyes stealing the thoughts behind your words. She could feel her eagerness to see him again like a hot stone in her chest and she didn't know why. She told herself it was just that she needed to thank him again and to see if he was hurt. That was all. Just politeness.

But she was no better at telling lies to herself than she was at deceiving Polly. And it frightened her, this sudden sense of losing herself in a labyrinth of unknown paths. Frightened and excited her. Something fluttered in the back of her mind and she pushed it away. The barriers between his world and hers were so high, and yet somehow they vanished when she was with him. Polly wouldn't understand.

She didn't even understand it herself, and didn't dare tell Polly the truth of last night.

"Is he handsome?" Polly prompted with a smile.

"I didn't notice much about him," Lydia lied. "His hair is cut short and his eyes are . . . I don't know, they sort of . . . ," *They reach out and see under my skin. Can I say that?* ". . . sort of watch you," she finished lamely.

"And he's strong?"

"He moved fast in the fight, like . . . a hawk."

"Has he got a hawk nose as well?"

"No, of course not. His nose is perfectly straight and when he's not speaking his face is so still it looks like fine porcelain. And his hands are long with fingers that . . .'"

"I thought you said you didn't notice much."

Lydia blushed furiously and stuffed the words back down her throat. "Come on," she said and started to run toward the gate, "let's ask your father."

"All right, but I warn you, he *will* say no."

CHRISTOPHER MASON DID SAY NO. IN NO UNCERTAIN TERMS. As Lydia dolloped a mound of mashed potato onto a plate in St. Saviour's Hall, her cheeks flushed at the memory of the words he used to say it. She had wanted, really wanted, to shut his pompous mouth with a casual mention of seeing it crawling over her mother's breasts last night, to use that knowledge to open doors, but how could she? The thought of Anthea Mason's unfailing kindness to her and of Polly's trusting blue gaze was too much. She couldn't. Just couldn't. So she said nothing and escaped. But now she was desperate.

Another ladle of potato hit the next plate held out to her. She didn't even look at the haggard face behind it as she doled out the food, or the one behind that, because she was too busy searching through the queue of people, seeking out one particular set of broad shoulders and pair of bright black eyes below eyebrows like wings.

"Do pay attention, Lydia," Mrs. Yeoman's voice said cheerily beside her. "You're being a bit overgenerous with the spuds, my dear, and though our good Lord managed to spread five loaves and three fishes among five thousand, we're not quite so handy at it ourselves. I'd hate to run out sooner than we have to."

A merry laugh rearranged the wrinkles on Mrs. Yeoman's face, making her look suddenly younger than her sixty-nine years. She had the leathery skin of a white person who has spent most of her life in the tropics and her eyes were almost colorless, but always smiling. They rested a moment longer on her young companion's face, and then she patted Lydia's arm before resuming the task of issuing bowls of rice gruel to the never-ending line of gaunt faces. It made no difference to Constance Yeoman their color or their creed; all were equal and all were beloved in the sight of her Lord, and what was good enough for Him was good enough for her.

Lydia had been coming to St. Saviour's Hall every Sunday morning for almost a year now. It was a large barn of a place where even whispers echoed up to the high beamed ceiling, and dozens of trestle tables lined up in front of two steaming stoves. Mr. Yeoman had come up one day from the flat below at Mrs. Zarya's and suggested with his usual missionary zeal that they might like to help out occasionally. Needless to say, Valentina had declined and said something about charity beginning at home. But later Lydia had crept downstairs, knocked on their door, breathed in the unique smell of camphor rub and palm of violets that permeated their rooms just as strongly as the hymns and the sad picture of Jesus at the door with a lamp in his hand and the crown of thorns on his head, and offered her services to their charity soup kitchen. At the very least, she reasoned, it meant she would receive one hot meal a week.

Sebastian Yeoman and his wife, Constance, might be retired from the church now, but they worked harder than ever. They begged, borrowed, and browbeat money out of the most unlikely pockets to keep their cauldrons simmering in the big hall behind St. Saviour's Church and every Sunday the poor, the sick, and even the criminal flocked through its open doors for a mouthful of food, a warm smile, and a few words of comfort offered in an astonishing variety of languages and dialects. To Lydia the Yeomans were the real version of Jesus's lamp. A bright light in a dark world.

"Thank you, missy. *Xie xie*. You kind."

For once Lydia let herself look more closely at the young Chinese woman in front of her. She was all sharp bones and matted hair and was carrying an infant on her hip in a funny kind of sling, while two older children leaned listlessly against her. All were dressed in stinking rags and all had skin as gray and cracked as the dusty floor. The mother had the broad but fleshless face and thick brown fingers of a peasant who had been forced from her farm by starvation and thieving armies who stripped the land barer than a plague of locusts. Lydia had seen such faces over and over again; so many times they marched as skulls through her dreams and made her jerk awake in the middle of the night. So now she didn't look at the faces.

With a quick check to see that the Yeomans were too busy with the stew and the yams to notice, she added an extra spoonful to the woman's wooden bowl. The woman's silent tears of gratitude just made her feel worse.

And then she saw him. Standing apart from the others, a lithe and vibrant creature in the midst of this room of death and despair. He was too proud to come begging.

HE WAS WAITING FOR HER WHEN SHE CAME OUT. SHE KNEW he would be. His back was toward her as he stood staring out at the small graveyard that lay behind the church, and yet he seemed to sense the moment she was there because he said without turning his head, "How do the spirits of your dead find their way home?"

"What?"

He turned, smiled at her, and bowed. So polite. So correct. Lydia felt a sharp spike of disappointment. He was putting a distance between them that hadn't been there before, his mouth unsmiling, as though she were a stranger in the street. Surely she was more than that. Wasn't she?

She lifted her chin and gave him the kind of cool smile that Mr. Theo gave to Polly when he was being sarcastic.

"You came," she said and glanced casually away at St. Saviour's bell tower.

"Of course I came."

Something in his voice made her look back. He'd moved closer, so silent she'd heard no footsteps, yet here he was, near enough to touch. And his long black eyes were talking to her, even though his mouth was silent. His face was turned slightly away, but his gaze was fixed on hers. She smiled at him, a real smile this time, and saw him blink in that slow way a cat does when the sunlight is too bright.

"How are you?" she asked.

"I am well."

But the look he gave her said otherwise, and as though he were perched on a cliff edge, his nerves seemed to tighten, his muscles tense under the thin black tunic. It was as if he were about to jump off. Then he gave a strange little sigh, and with no more than a flicker of a shy smile he turned his head. For the first time she saw the right side of it.

"Your face . . . ," she gasped, then stopped. She knew that the Chinese regarded personal comments as rude. "Is it painful?"

"No," he said.

But he had to be lying. That side of his head was split and swollen. A livid black bruise, shot through with dried blood, ran along his hairline from his forehead down to his ear. The sight of it made Lydia furious.

"That policeman," she said angrily. "I'll report him for . . ."

"Doing his duty?" He did not smile this time, his black eyes serious. "I think it would not be wise."

"But you need treatment," Lydia insisted. "I'll fetch Mrs. Yeoman, she'll know what to do." She swung back in the direction of the hall, in a hurry to bring help.

"Please, no." His voice was soft but insistent.

She stopped, looked at him. Looked at him hard, this figure she knew and yet didn't know. He stood very still. Holding something in. What? What more was he keeping from her? His stillness was as elegant as his movements had been in the alley, his shoulders muscular but his hips narrower than her own. Horrible black rubber shoes on his feet.

In the hall earlier, and even when he greeted her, she had not seen the damaged side of his face, and she realized now that he had kept it turned away from her. What if her reaction was all wrong in his eyes? To him it implied . . . what? That he was weak? Or unable to care for himself? She shook her head, knowing this was a strange and delicate world she was entering, as unfamiliar to her as his language. She had to tread carefully. She nodded to indicate acceptance of his wishes, then turned her face toward the tombstones, neat and orderly with carnations in little vases. This world she understood.

"Their spirits go straight to heaven," she said with a gesture at the rectangles of grass. "It doesn't matter where they die, if they are Christians, but if they're wicked, they go to hell. That's what the priests tell us, anyway." She glanced over at him. Instead of looking at the graves, he was watching her. She stared right back at him and said, "As for me, I'll be going straight to hell." And she laughed.

For a moment he looked shocked, and then he gave her his shy smile. "You are mocking me, I think."

Oh God, she'd got it wrong again. How do you talk to someone so different? In all her life in Junchow the only Chinese people she'd ever spoken to were shopkeepers and servants, but conversations like "How much?" and "A pound of soybeans, please," didn't really count. Her dealings with Mr. Liu at the pawnshop were the nearest she'd come to communicating properly with a Chinese native, and even those were spiced with danger. She must start again.

Very formally, hands together and eyes on the ground, she gave a little bow. "No, I'm not mocking you. I wish to thank you. You saved me in the alleyway and I am grateful. I owe you thanks."

He did not move, not a muscle shifted in his face or his body, but something changed somewhere deep inside him and she could see it. Though she didn't know exactly what it was. Just that it was as if a closed place had opened, and she felt a warmth flow from him that took her by surprise.

"No," he said, eyes fixed intently on hers. "You do not owe me your thanks." He came one step closer to her, so close she could see tiny secret flecks of purple in his eyes. "They would have cut your throat when they were done with you. You owe me your life."

"My life is my own. It belongs to no one but me."

"And I owe you mine. Without you I would be dead. A bullet would be in my head now if you had not come out of the night when you did." He bowed once more, very low this time. "I owe you my life."

"Then we're even." She laughed, uncertain how serious this was meant to be. "A life for a life."

He looked at her, but she couldn't fathom the emotion in his eyes this time, it was so still and dark. He said nothing and she wasn't sure how much he'd understood, especially when he asked, "Does your Mrs. Yeoman own a needle and thread?"

"Oh, I expect so. Do you want me to fetch it?"

"Yes, please. It would be kind."

Her eyes scanned his clothes, a V-necked tunic and loose trousers, but could see no holes in them, so maybe it was for some sort of blood-brother ritual, to sew their lives together. The idea sent a flare of heat racing up her spine, and for the first time since she'd been herded into the concert room last night by Commissioner Lacock himself, the tight ball inside her lungs loosened and she could breathe.

10

"My name is Lydia Ivanova."

She held out a hand to him and he knew what she was expecting. He'd seen them do it, the foreigners. Seizing each other's hands in greeting. A disgusting habit. No self-respecting Chinese would be so rude as to touch another, especially someone he didn't know. Who would want to hold a hand that may have just come from gutting a pig or stroking a wife's private parts? Barbarians were such filthy creatures.

Yet the sight of her small hand, pale as a lily and waiting for him, was curiously inviting. He wanted to touch it. To learn the feel of it.

He shook hands. "I am called Chang An Lo."

It was like holding a bird in his hand, warm and soft. With one squeeze he could have crushed its fragile bones. But he didn't want to. He experienced an unfamiliar need to protect this wild fluttering little creature in his hand.

She withdrew it as easily as she had given it and looked around her. He had led her out of the settlement along the back of the American sector and down a dirt track out to Lizard Creek, a small wooded inlet to the west of town. Here the morning sun lazed on the surface of the water and the birch trees offered dappled shade to the flat gray rocks. Lizards flicked and flashed over them like leaves in a breeze. Beyond the creek the land stretched flat and boggy after last night's rain all the way north to the distant mountains. They shimmered blue in the summer heat, but Chang knew that somewhere hidden deep within the crouching tiger was a Red heart that was beating stronger every day. One day soon it would flood the country with its blood.

"This place is beautiful," the fox girl said. "I had no idea it existed."

She was smiling. She was pleased. And that created a strange contentment in his chest. He watched the way she dipped a hand into the gently flowing creek and laughed at a swallow that flashed its wings as it skimmed the water. Insects hummed in the heat and two crickets bickered somewhere in the reeds.

"I come here because the water is clean," he explained to her. "See how clear it is, it lives and sings. Look at that fish." A silver swirl and it was gone. "But when this water joins the great Peiho River, the spirits leave it."

"Why?" She sounded puzzled. Did she know so little?

"Because it fills up with black oil from the foreigners' gunboats and poisons from their factories. The spirits would die in the brown filth of the Peiho."

She gave him a look but said nothing, just sat down on a rock and tossed a stone into the shallows. She stretched out her legs, bare and slender, toward the water and he noticed a hole in the bottom of one of her shoes. The fiery hair was hidden away under a straw hat, and he was sorry for that. The hat looked old, battered, like her shoes. Her hair always looked new and he wanted to see its flames again. She was watching a small brown bird tugging at a grub in a dead branch at her feet.

"Your English is excellent, you know."

She spoke softly and he wasn't sure if it was not to disturb the bird or because she was suddenly nervous alone with a man in this isolated spot. She had shown courage in coming here with him. No Chinese girl would ever take a risk like this. They'd sooner feed their pet turtles to a cobra. Yet she didn't look nervous at all. Her eyes shone with expectation.

He moved to the edge of the water, keeping his distance from her so that she wouldn't become alarmed, and squatted down on a patch of grass. It was still damp.

"I am honored that you think my English acceptable," he said.

While her attention was on the brown bird, he eased the rubber shoe off his right foot. Pain crashed around inside his skull. He began to unwind the blood-soaked cloth that was holding the flesh of his foot together.

"I had an English tutor for many years," he told her. "When I was young. He taught me well." The putrid smell on the cloth rose to his nostrils. "And my uncle went to university at Harvard. That's in America. He always insisted that English is the language of the future and would speak nothing else to me."

"Really? Just like my mother. She speaks God knows how many languages."

"Except Mandarin?"

She laughed, a bright ripple of sound that sent the bird up into a tree, but for Chang the sound of her laughter merged with the song of the river and soothed the burning in his foot.

"My mother is always telling me that English is the only language worth . . ." She stopped. A tight gasp reached his ears.

He turned his head and found her staring, mouth open, at his foot. Her gaze rose to his face and for a long moment their eyes met and held. He looked away. When he lifted his foot off the sodden rags and placed it into the swirling flow of the river, she said nothing. Just watched in silence. He started to rub his hands over the wounds under the water, massaging the poisons out and the life back in. Clots of dried blood drifted on the surface and were instantly snapped up by hungry mouths from below. A steady trail of bright blood drew a darting shoal of tiny fish that flashed green against the yellow stones of the riverbed. The water was cool. His foot seemed to drink in the coolness.

He heard a noise and swung around. She was kneeling on the grass beside him, her face white under the fraying hat. In her hand lay the needle and thread. The presence of her so close made the air between them flutter like doves' wings on his cheek, and his fingertips longed to touch her creamy European skin.

"You'll need these," she said and held them out to him.

He nodded. But as he reached for them, she swayed away from him and shook her head.

"Would it help if I did it?" she asked.

He nodded again. He saw her swallow. Her soft pale throat seemed to quiver in a brief spasm, then settle.

"You need a doctor."

"A doctor costs dollars."

She said nothing more, but threw off her hat, letting loose the wonderful fox spirit of her hair, the way he'd once loosed the fox from the snare. She leaned over his foot. Not touching. Just looking. He could hear her breathing, in and out, feel it brush the jagged edges of his damaged flesh like the kiss of the river god.

He emptied his mind of the hot pain. Instead he filled it with the sight of the smooth arch of her high forehead and the copper glow of one lock of her hair that curled on the white skin of her neck. Perfection. Not pain. He closed his eyes and she started to sew. How could he tell her he loved her courage?

"THAT'S BETTER," SHE SAID, AND HE HEARD THE RELIEF IN her voice.

She had removed her underskirt, quickly and without embarrassment, cut it into strips with his knife, and bound his foot into a stiff white bundle that would no longer fit inside his shoe. Without asking, she cut the shoe's rubber sides, then tied it over the bandage with two more strips of cloth. It looked clean and professional. The pain was still there but at last the blood had stopped.

"Thank you." He gave her a small bow with his head.

"You need sulfur powder or something. I've seen Mrs. Yeoman use it to dry up sores. I could ask her to . . ."

"No, it is not needed. I know someone who has herbs. Thank you again."

She turned her face away and trailed her hands through the water, fingers splayed out. She watched their movement as if they belonged to someone else, as if she were surprised by what they had done today.

"Don't thank me," she said. "If we go around saving each other's lives, then that makes us responsible for each other. Don't you think?"

Chang was stunned. She had robbed his tongue of words. How could a barbarian know such things, such Chinese things? Know that this was the reason he had followed her, watched over her. Because he was responsible for her. How could this girl know that? What kind of mind did she possess that could see so clearly?

He felt the loss of her from his side when she rose to her feet, kicked off her sandals, and waded into the shallows. A golden-headed duck, startled from its slumber in the reeds, paddled off downstream as fast as if a stoat were on its tail, but she scarcely seemed to notice, her hands busy splashing water over the hem of her dress. It was a shapeless garment, washed too many times, and for the first time he saw the blood on it. His blood. Entwined in the fibers of her clothes. In the fibers of her. As she was entwined in the fibers of him.

She was silent. Preoccupied. He studied her as she stood in the creek, her skin rippling with silver stars reflected from the water, the sunlight on her hair making it alive and molten. Her full lips were slightly open as if she would say something, and he wondered what it might be. A heart-shaped face, finely arched brows, and those wide amber eyes, a tiger's eyes. They pierced deep inside you and hunted out your heart. It was a face no Chinese would find alluring, the nose too long, the mouth too big, the chin too strong. Yet somehow it drew his gaze again and again, and satisfied his eyes in ways he didn't understand but in ways that contented his heart. But he could see secrets in her face. Secrets made shadows, and her face was full of pale breathless shadows.

He lay back on the warm grass, resting on his elbows.

"Lydia Ivanova," he said quietly. "What is it that is such trouble to you?"

She lifted her gaze to his and in that second when their eyes fixed on each other, he felt something tangible form between them. A thread. Silver and bright and woven by the gods. Shimmering between them, as elusive as a ripple in the river, yet as strong as one of the steel cables that held the new bridge over the Peiho.

He lifted a hand and stretched it out to her, as if he would draw her to him. "Tell me, Lydia, what lies so heavy on your heart?"

She stood up straight in the water, letting go of the edge of her dress so that it floated around her legs like a fisherman's net. He saw a decision form in her eyes.

"Chang An Lo," she said, "I need your help."

A BREEZE SWEPT IN OFF THE PEIHO RIVER. IT CARRIED WITH it the stench of rotting fish guts. It came from the hundreds of sampans that crowded around the flimsy jetties and pontoons that clogged the banks, but Chang was used to it. It was the stink of boiled cowhide from the tannery behind the godowns around the harbor.

He moved quickly. Shut his mind to the knives in his foot and slipped silently past the noisy, shouting, clattering world of the riverside, where tribes of beggars and boatmen made their homes. The sampans bobbed and jostled each other with their rattan shelters and swaying walkways, while cormorants perched, tethered and starved, on the prows of the fishermen's boats. Chang knew not to linger. Not here. A blade between ribs, and a body to add to the filth thrown daily into the Peiho, was not unheard of for no more than a pair of shoes.

Out where the great Peiho flowed wider than forty fields, British and French gunboats rode at anchor, their white and red and blue flags fluttering a warning. At the sight of them Chang spat on the ground and trampled it into the dirt. He could see that half a dozen big steamers had docked in the harbor, and near-naked coolies bent double as they struggled up and down the gangplanks under loads that would break the back of an ox. He kept clear of the overseer who strutted with a heavy black stick in his hand and a curse on his tongue, but everywhere men shouted, bells rang, engines roared, camels screamed, and all the time in and out of the chaos wove the rickshaws, as numerous as the black flies that settled over everything.

Chang kept moving. Skirted the quayside. Ducked down an alleyway where a severed hand lay in the dust. On to the godowns. These were huge warehouses that were well guarded by more blue devils, but behind them a row of lean-to shacks had sprung up. Not shacks so much as pig houses, no higher than a man's waist and built of rotting scraps of driftwood. They looked as if a moth's wings could blow them away. He approached the third one. Its door was a flap of oilcloth. He pulled it aside.

"Greetings to you, Tan Wah," he murmured softly.

"May the river snakes seize your miserable tongue," came the sharp reply. "You have stolen away my soft maidens, skin as sweet as honey on my lips. Whoever you are, I curse you."

"Open your eyes, Tan Wah, leave your dreams. Join me in the world where the taste of honey is a rich man's pleasure and a maiden's smile a million *li* away from this dung heap."

"Chang An Lo, you young son of a wolf. My friend, forgive the poison of my words. I ask the gods to lift my curse and I invite you to enter my fine palace."

Chang crouched down, slipped inside the foul-smelling hovel, and sat cross-legged on a bamboo mat that looked as if it had been chewed by rats. In the dim interior he could make out a figure wrapped in layers of newspaper lying on the damp earth floor, his head propped on an old car seat cushion as a pillow.

"My humble apologies for disturbing your dreams, Tan Wah, but I need some information from you."

The man in the cocoon of newspaper struggled to sit up. Chang could see he was little more than a handful of bones, his skin the telltale yellow of the opium addict. Beside him lay a long-stemmed clay pipe, which was the source of the sickly smell that choked the airless hut.

"Information costs money, my friend," he said, his eyes barely open. "I am sorry but it is so."

"Who has money these days?" Chang demanded. "Here, I bring you this instead." He placed a large salmon on the ground between them, its scales bright as a rainbow in the dingy kennel. "It swam from the creek straight into my arms this morning when it knew I was coming to see you."

Tan Wah did not touch it. But the narrow slits of his eyes were already calculating its weight in the black paste that would bring the moon and the stars into his home. "Ask what you will, Chang An Lo, and I will kick my worthless brain until it finds what you wish to know."

"You have a cousin who works at the *fanqui*'s big club."

"At the Ulysses?"

"That is the one."

"Yes, my stupid cousin, Yuen Dun, a cub still with his milk teeth, yet he is growing fat on the foreigners' dollars while I . . ." He closed his mouth and his eyes.

"My friend, if you would eat the fish instead of trading it for dreams, you might also grow fat."

The man said nothing but lay back on the floor, picked up the pipe, and cradled it on his chest like a child.

"Tell me, Tan Wah, where does this stupid cousin of yours live?"

There was a silence, filled only by the sound of fingers stroking the clay stem. Chang waited patiently.

"In the Street of the Five Frogs." It was a faint murmur. "Next to the rope maker."

"A thousand thanks for your words. I wish you good health, Tan Wah." In one swift movement he was crouching on his feet ready to leave. "A thousand deaths," he said with a smile.

"A thousand deaths," came the response.

"To the piss-drinking general from Nanking."

A chuckle, more like a rattle, issued from the newspapers. "And to the donkey-fucking Foreign Devils on our shore."

"Stay alive, friend. China needs its people."

But as Chang pushed away the cloth flap, Tan Wah whispered urgently, "They are hunting you, Chang An Lo. Do not turn your back."

"I know."

"It is not good to cross the Black Snake brotherhood. You look as if they have already fed your face to their chow-chows to chew on. I hear that you stole a girl from them and crushed the life out of one of their guardians."

"I bruised his ribs. No more."

A sigh drifted through the heavy air. "Foolish one. Why risk so much for a miserable slug of a white girl?"

Chang let the cloth fall back in place behind him and slipped away.

HE LET HIS KNIFE DO THE TALKING. IT PRESSED HARD against the young boy's throat.

"Your badge?" Chang demanded.

"It's . . . in . . . in my belt."

The boy's face was gray with fear. Already he had pissed himself when dragged into the dark doorway. Chang could feel the thick flesh on his bones as he removed the identity badge and see the sleek sheen on his skin like a well-fed concubine.

"What part of the club do you work in?"

"The kitchens."

"Ah. So you steal food for your family?"

"No, no. Never."

The knife tightened and a trickle of blood mingled with the boy's sweat.

"Yes," he screamed, "yes, I admit, sometimes I do."

"Then next time, you dog-faced turd, take some to your cousin, Tan Wah, or his spirit will come and feed on your fat stomach and burrow into your liver, where it will suck out all the thick rich oil and you will die."

The boy's whole body started to shake and when Chang released him, he vomited over his smart leather boots.

11

"You know, Theo, he was extraordinarily foolish, that Russian last night. Leaving it in his overcoat pocket like that."

"The necklace?"

"Yes."

Theo Willoughby and Alfred Parker were playing chess on the terrace at the Ulysses Club. Theo would have preferred cards, a sharp game of poker, but it was Sunday and Alfred was strict about things like that. No gambling on the Sabbath. Theo thought it absurd. Why not no umbrellas on the Sabbath, or no teeth picking? It made as much sense. Or as little. He moved his bishop and took out one of the pawns from Alfred's defensive triangle.

Alfred frowned. He removed his spectacles and cleaned them meticulously on a starched white handkerchief. He had a round, good-humored face with thoughtful brown eyes, a solid fellow who took his time about things, which was surprising, really, in a journalist. But there was a certain tightness around the mouth that always made Theo suspect that his friend was on the verge of panic. Maybe China wasn't quite what he expected it to be. Above them a fierce blue sky was leeching the energy out of the day. Even the feathery leaves on the wisteria seemed to hang in exhausted indolence, but over on the tennis court two young women in delightful tennis whites were scampering after a ball. Theo watched them with only casual interest.

"It serves him right," he said, "that Russian, I mean. I honestly don't give a damn about it. I know old Lacock and Sir Edward are incandescent with fury that it should happen right under their noses, but really . . ." He shrugged and lit a cigarette. "I have other things on my mind."

Parker lifted his eyes from the board, stared at his companion, and then nodded and moved his queen's knight.

"There are rumors," he said, "that the Russian was an agent sent by Stalin to negotiate with General Chiang Kai-shek. The general has come up from Nanking and is reported to be in Peking at the moment."

"There are always rumors in this place."

"The necklace was supposed to be a gift for Mai-ling, Chiang Kai-shek's wife. Rubies from the dead tsarina's collection of fabulous jewels, they say."

"Is that so? You are remarkably well informed, Alfred." Theo gave a rough laugh. "Fitting that it should pass from one despot's wife to another, I suppose, but whoever has it now will find it worthless."

"How so?"

"Well, no one, not even a Chinese fence, would risk handling that piece now. It's more of a noose than a necklace. It's too well known, too dangerous. So the thief can't sell it. Word is out, and he will find his head up in one of those bamboo cages hanging from the lamp-posts if he so much as breathes a whisper about rubies."

"Barbaric practice," Parker shuddered.

"You have a lot to learn."

THEY PLAYED IN SILENCE FOR THE NEXT HALF HOUR. JUST the chime of a grandfather clock somewhere inside and the alarm cry of a goldfinch disturbed their thoughts. Then Theo, on edge and tired of the game, sprang his trap and Parker's king fell.

"Well done, old boy. You got me fair and square." Parker leaned back in the cane chair, untroubled by the loss, and took his time lighting up his beloved briar pipe. "So why have you called me over here today? I know you hate this place. It's not just for chess, is it?"

"No."

"Well?"

"I'm having a spot of trouble with Mason."

"The education department johnny? The one with the loud mouth and the quiet wife."

"That's the one."

"What of him?"

"Alfred, listen to me. I need to find out something about him, something dirty in his past. Something I can use to get the swine off my back. You're a journalist, you have contacts and know how to dig around."

Parker looked shocked. He drew on his pipe and slowly exhaled a cloud of smoke that caught a passing butterfly. "Sounds bad, old chap. What's he up to?"

Theo kept it short. "I owe Courtney Bank a fair sum. For the expansion of my school last year. Mason is a director of the bank—you know how he puts himself about—and he's threatening to call in the loan unless . . ."

"Unless what?"

"Unless I oblige him."

Parker coughed awkwardly. "Good God, man, what does that mean?"

Theo stubbed out his cigarette, grinding it into dust. "It means he wants to make use of Li Mei."

Alfred Parker turned bright red, even the tip of his nose. "I say, Theo, that's not on, old chap. I don't think I want to hear any more." He glanced away and his eyes followed a native servant in white tunic as he approached the veranda with a small tray in his hand.

Theo leaned forward and tapped Parker's knee sharply. "Don't be a fool, Alfred. That's not what I mean. What do you take me for? Li Mei is my . . ." He stopped when Parker's gaze turned accusingly on him.

"Your what, Theo? Your partner in adultery? Your whore?"

Theo became very still, only the whiteness of his lips betraying him. "That is an insult to Li Mei, Alfred. I ask you to withdraw it."

"I can't. It's true."

Theo stood up with a jerky motion. "The sooner England abandons the racist and religious straitjackets that paralyze men like you and Sir Edward and all the other damned social misfits that cram into this club, the sooner our people and the people of China will be free. Free to think. Free to live. Free to . . ."

"Whoa, my friend. We are all out here to do our duty by king and country. Just because you've gone native doesn't mean you can suddenly assume that the rest of us should forget the laws of God, the need for clearly defined lines of good and evil, of right and wrong. God knows, in this cruel and heathen country His Word is their only hope. His Word and the British Army."

"China was civilized hundreds of years before Britain was even thought of."

"You can't call this civilized."

Theo said nothing. Stood stiffly. Eyes directed at, but not seeing, the two couples who had just taken to the lawn for a game of croquet.

"Sit down, Theo," Parker said quietly.

He disguised the awkwardness of the moment by digging around in his pipe and rapping its bowl with his forefinger. From the lawn came the crack of one ball against another and a cry of "I say, Corky, that's a bit rum."

Suddenly Theo shook himself. Like a dog shakes off water. His eyes half closed, he looked down at his companion. "Alfred, if I believed you were right, I'd leave Junchow tomorrow. But I have faith in these people, in what you call this 'cruel and heathen country.'" He sat down again, stretching out his long legs in an imitation of relaxation, and waved a hand at the Chinese servant with the tray. In perfect Mandarin he said, "A whisky, please." He turned back to Alfred and smiled. "Let us agree to differ. You know I'm what Mason calls a Chink lover."

Alfred was meant to laugh. But he didn't.

"You can't have it both ways, Theo. Neither fish nor fowl. You want the Establishment to send you their children to educate, yet you go out of your way to parade your disdain for their parents. How can it . . . ?" He stopped. Stared at the retreating figure of the servant as he crossed the veranda. "Boy, come back here immediately."

"What's up, Alfred?"

But Parker was on his feet.

The servant was standing looking at them but came no nearer. Alfred strode over to him.

"What do you think you're doing here?" he demanded.

The Chinese said nothing.

Theo went over to them. What the hell had got into Alfred?

"Something is not right here," Parker said, prodding his pipe toward the servant. "Look at him."

Theo looked. Neat white tunic and tray in hand. "Seems fine to me."

"Don't talk rubbish. His face is beaten up."

"So?"

"And his trousers are all wrong. Black but not the regulation uniform. And the bandaged foot, shoes a mess. The club would never let someone looking like that serve the members here. This boy is an intruder."

"I work." The servant held up the tray. "Drinks."

But now that Theo considered it, he could see what Alfred meant. He was right, this boy was not like the others. His eyes were not a servant's eyes. They stared straight back at you, as if he wanted to strike out at you, to hang your head in one of those cursed bamboo cages.

"Who are you?" Theo asked in Mandarin.

But Alfred was pointing at the boy's trouser pocket, which bulged at his side. "Empty that out. Right now."

The boy flicked his gaze insolently from Parker's panama hat to his polished brogue shoes and didn't move.

"Do as you are told," Theo said in Mandarin. "Empty your pockets or you'll be whipped like a gutter dog."

"Fetch the security guards," Parker shouted. "We had a robbery here last night. This person is . . ."

"Empty your pockets," Theo repeated sharply.

For a moment he thought the boy was going to strike. Something in his eyes seemed to struggle free, something wild and angry, but then it was caged once more and the boy lowered his gaze. Without a word he tipped his pocket inside out, spilling its contents onto the tiled floor of the veranda. A large handful of salted peanuts skidded around their feet.

Theo laughed. "So much for your jewel thief, Alfred. The boy's just hungry."

But Parker was not ready to let go so easily. "And your other pockets."

The boy did as he was told. A length of bamboo twine, a fishing hook wrapped in clay, and a folded sheet of paper covered in Chinese character writing. Theo picked it up and scanned it briefly.

"What is it?" Parker asked.

"Nothing much. A poster for a gathering of some sort."

But as the boy bent to retrieve his belongings, Theo caught a glimpse of the bone handle of a knife tucked into his belt, and suddenly he was frightened for his friend.

"Let him go, Alfred. This is nothing to us. The boy was hungry. Most of China is hungry."

"A thief is a thief, Theo. Be it peanuts or jewels. *Thou shalt not steal*, remember?" But he was no longer angry. His face looked sad, his spectacles sliding halfway down his nose. "We owe them that much, Theo. To teach them right from wrong, not just how to lay rail tracks and build factories."

He reached out to take hold of the boy's arm, but Theo intervened. He seized Parker's wrist.

"Don't, Alfred. Not this time." He turned to the silent figure with the black eyes full of hatred. "Go," he said quickly in Chinese. "And don't come back."

The boy set off around the lawn, loping with an uneven stride into the trees that skirted the grounds, then he was gone. To Theo the image was of a creature returning to its jungle, and he wondered what had tempted it out into the open. Certainly not peanuts.

"You might regret that," Parker said with an annoyed little shake of his head.

"Mercy droppeth like the gentle rain from heaven," Theo said cynically and glanced again at the sheet of paper still in his hand. It was actually a Communist pamphlet.

"Sha! Sha!" it said. "Kill! Kill! Kill the hated imperialists. Kill the traitor Chiang Kai-shek. Long live the Chinese people."

The words worried Theo more than he cared to admit. Chiang Kai-shek and his Kuomintang Nationalists had seized control and deserved now to be given a chance, if only the Western powers would back him against these troublemakers. The Communists would only do to China what Stalin was doing to Russia—turn it into a barren wasteland. China possessed too much beauty and too much soul to be stripped bare like a common whore. *God preserve us from Communists. God and Chiang Kai-shek's army.*

"DID HE SAY YES?"

"Yes."

Li Mei kissed the nape of his neck. "I am happy for you, Tiyo. Parker is a good friend to you."

She laid her cheek against his naked back, but her fingers did not cease their firm circular motion on each side of his spine, digging deep into the muscles. Theo was facedown flat on the floor in the bedroom while Li Mei massaged the tension from his body. He was always amazed at the strength of her fingers and how she knew just where to press the heel of her hand to release another demon from under his skin.

"Yes, Alfred is a good friend, though some of his views are so narrow they would sit well on Oliver Cromwell."

"Oliver Cromwell? Tell me, who is this Oliver? Another friend?"

Theo laughed and felt her pound his shoulder blade with her knuckles.

"You joke at me, Tiyo."

"No, my love, I am in awe of you."

"Now you lie. Bad Tiyo." She pummeled his buttocks with tight little fists that sent the blood surging to his loins. He rolled over and held her wrists, then stood and scooped her naked body up into his arms. She smelled of sandalwood and somehow of ice cream. He started to carry her down the stairs.

"Alfred was furious that Mason is so corrupt. Appalled that he was trying to force me to help him break into the opium cartel. I swore to Alfred that just because your father runs it, it doesn't mean I'm involved in any way. You know how I feel about drugs."

"An abomination, that's what you call opium."

He smiled and kissed her dark head. "Yes, my sweet one. An abomination. So he's agreed to dig around in the bastard's past and see if he can find anything that I can use to twist his arm."

He entered the empty schoolroom, cradling her in his arms.

"It is good it is Sunday." She laughed.

He lifted her higher and sat her, facing him, on his own tall desk in front of the rows of seats.

"Now," he said, "when I stand here and talk to my pupils about Vesuvius tomorrow, I shall think of this." He leaned forward and kissed her left breast. "And this when I describe an equilateral triangle." His lips clung to the nipple of her right breast. "And this when I tell the numbskulls about the moist dark heart of Africa." He lowered his head and kissed the black bush that rose at the base of her flat stomach.

"Tiyo," she crooned into his hair, "Tiyo. Take care. This Mason, he is a man of power."

"He is not the only one with power," he said, and laughed. Gently he laid her down on the floor.

12

"WHAT IS THIS?"

Valentina was standing in the middle of the room, pointing a rigid finger at a cardboard box on the floor. Lydia had just come home to find the attic even stuffier than usual. The windows were closed. It smelled different too. She couldn't work out why.

"You," Valentina said loudly, "should be ashamed of yourself."

Lydia shuffled uncomfortably on the carpet, her mind spinning through answers. Ashamed. Of what? Of Chang? No, not him. So here she was again, back to the lies. Which lie?

"Mama, I . . ."

She stared at her mother. Two high spots of color burned on Valentina's pale cheeks and her eyes were very dark, her pupils huge, her lashes heavy.

"Antoine came over," Valentina declared, as if it were Lydia's fault. "Look." The pointing finger flicked again in the direction of the box. "Look in there."

Lydia approached carelessly. It was a striped hatbox with a bright red bow wrapped around it. She could not imagine why on earth her mother would be cross and making a ridiculous fuss about being given a hat. She loved hats. The bigger the better.

"Is it a small one?" she asked as she bent to lift the lid.

"Oh, yes."

"With a feather?"

"No feathers."

Lydia removed the lid. Inside crouched a white rabbit.

★ ★ ★

"Sun Yat-sen."

"What?"

"Sun Yat-sen."

"What kind of name is that for a rabbit?" Polly exclaimed.

"He was the father of the Republic. He opened the door to a whole new kind of life for the people of China in 1911," Lydia said.

"Who told you that?"

"Chang An Lo."

"While you were sewing up his foot?"

"Afterward."

"You are so brave, Lydia. I'd have died before I could stick a needle into someone's flesh."

"No, you wouldn't, Polly. You'd do it if you had to. There's a lot of things we can do if we have to."

"But why not call the rabbit Flopsy or Sugar or even Lewis after Lewis Carroll? Something nice."

"No. Sun Yat-sen he is."

"But why?"

"Because he's opening the door to a whole new kind of life for me."

"Don't be silly, Lyd. He's only a rabbit. You'll just sit and cuddle him, like I cuddle Toby."

"That's what I mean, Polly."

It was one-thirty in the morning. Lydia abandoned her chair at the window. He wasn't coming.

But he might. Still he might. He could be in hiding somewhere, waiting for the night to . . .

No. He wasn't coming.

Her tongue was thick and dry in her mouth. She'd been arguing with herself for hours, eyes glazed with tiredness. No amount of wanting was going to make him come. *Chang An Lo, I trusted you. How could I have been so stupid?*

In the pitch darkness of the room she made her way across to the sink and splashed cold water into her mouth. A low groan crawled out of her because the pain in her chest was more than she could bear. Chang An Lo had betrayed her. Just thinking the words hurt. Long ago she learned that the only person you can trust is yourself but she'd thought he was different, that they had a bond. They'd saved each other's lives and she was so sure they had a . . . a connection between them. Yet it seemed that his promises were worth no more than monkey shit.

He knew that the necklace was her one chance to start again, a bright new life, in London or even in America where they said everyone was equal. A shining life. One without dark corners. Her chance to give back to her mother at least some of what the Reds had stolen from her. A grand piano with ivory keys that sang like angels and the finest mink coat, not one from Mr. Liu's, not secondhand, but gleaming and new. Everything new. Everything. New.

She closed her eyes. Standing in the darkness, in bare feet and an old torn petticoat that had once belonged to someone else, she made herself accept that he was gone. And the ruby necklace with him. The shiny new life. With all its happiness. Gone.

She felt her throat tighten. Started to choke. No air inside her. Blindly she felt for the door. It caught her toe, scraped off the skin, but she pulled it open and raced down the two flights of stairs. To the back of the house. A door to the yard. She yanked at the bolt, again and again until at last it rattled free and she burst out into the cool night air. She took a mouthful of it. And another. She forced her lungs to work, to go on working, in and out. But it was hard. She tried to empty her head of the anger and despair and disappointment and fear and fury and all the wanting and needing and longing. And that was harder.

At last the panic passed. Her body was trembling, her skin prickling with sweat, but she could breathe again. And think straight. That was important, the thinking straight.

The yard was very dark, crammed into a space only a few paces wide by high walls, and it smelled of mildew and things that were old. Mrs. Zarya kept discarded furniture there that slowly decayed and mingled with the piles of rusty pans and ancient shoes. She was a woman who couldn't bring herself to throw her things away. Lydia went up to a battered old tea chest that was lying on its side on top of a broken table, with wire mesh stretched across the opening. She put her face close to the wire.

"Sun Yat-sen," she whispered. "Are you asleep?"

A shuffling, a snuffling, and then a soft pink nose pressed against hers. She unhooked the mesh and lifted the wriggling little body into her arms, where it settled down contentedly against her ribs, its nose pushed into the crook of her elbow. She stood there, cradling the small sleepy animal. An almost forgotten Russian lullaby from her childhood drifted from her lips and she gazed up at the dozen stars glittering far above her head.

Chang An Lo was gone. She had hidden the necklace in the club and believed him when he said he would bring it to her. But the temptation had been too much for him. She'd made a mistake. She wouldn't make one again.

SHE TIPTOED BACK UP THE STAIRS. NO SOUND THIS TIME, her feet finding their way silently through the dark house, the warm bundle still tucked into her arm and her fingertips caressing the silky fur of its long ears and bony little body, its breath like feathers on her skin. She pushed open the attic door and was surprised to see the dim glow of her mother's candle flickering behind the bedroom curtain. She scuttled over to her own end of the room, eager to hide Sun Yat-sen out of sight, but when she ducked round her curtain she stopped dead.

"Mama," she said. Nothing more.

Her mother was standing there. Her nightdress askew, she was staring wide-eyed at Lydia's empty bed. Her hair was a wild tangle around her shoulders and silent tears were pouring down her face. Her thin arms were wrapped tightly around her body as if she were trying to hold all the parts of it together.

"Mama?" Lydia whispered again.

Valentina's head turned. Her mouth fell open. "Lydia," she cried out, "*dochenka*. I thought they had taken you."

"Who? The police?"

"The soldiers. They came with guns."

Lydia's heart was racing. "Here? Tonight?"

"They tore you from your bed and you screamed and screamed and hit one in the face. He pushed a gun into your mouth and knocked your teeth out and they dragged you outside into the snow and . . ."

"Mama, Mama." Lydia rushed to wrap an arm around her mother's trembling shoulders and held her close. "Hush, Mama, it was a dream. Just a horrible dream."

Her mother's body was ice cold and Lydia could feel the spasms that shook it, as though something were cracking up deep inside.

"Mama," she breathed into the sweat-soaked hair. "Look at me, I'm here, I'm safe. We're both safe." She drew back her lips. "See, I have all my teeth."

Valentina stared at her daughter's mouth, her eyes struggling to make sense of the images that crowded her brain.

"It was a nightmare, Mama. Not real. This is real." Lydia kissed her mother's cheek.

Valentina shook her head, trying to banish the confusion. She touched Lydia's hair. "I thought you were dead."

"I'm here. I'm alive. We're still together in this stinking rat hole with Mrs. Zarya still counting her dollars downstairs and the Yeomans' place still smelling of camphor oil. Nothing has changed." She pictured the rubies passing between Chinese hands. "Nothing."

Valentina took a deep breath. Then another.

Lydia led her back to her own bed where the candle burned up the night with an uneven spitting flame. She tucked her between the sheets and gently kissed her forehead. Sun Yat-sen was still huddled against her, and his eyes, pink as a sugar mouse, were huge with alarm, so she kissed his head too, but Valentina did not even notice him.

"I'll leave the candle alight for you," Lydia murmured. It was a waste. One they could ill afford. But her mother needed it.

"Stay."

"Stay?"

"Yes. Stay with me." Valentina lifted the sheet.

Without a word Lydia slipped in and lay on her back, her mother on one side, her rabbit on the other. She kept very still in case Valentina changed her mind but watched the smoky shadows dance on the ceiling.

"Your feet are like ice," Valentina said. She was calmer now and leaned her head against her daughter's. "You know, I can't remember the last time we were in bed together."

"It was when you were sick. You'd caught an ear infection and had that fever."

"Was it? That must be three or four years ago, the time when Constance Yeoman told you I might die."

"Yes."

"Stupid old witch. It takes more than a fever or even an army of Bolsheviks to kill me off." She squeezed her daughter's hand under the sheets and Lydia held on to it.

"Tell me about St. Petersburg, Mama. About when the tsar came to visit your school."

"No, not again."

"But I haven't heard that story since I was eleven."

"What a strange memory for dates you have, Lydochka."

Lydia said nothing. The moment too fragile. Her mother's guard could come up any minute and then she would be out of reach. Valentina sighed and hummed a snatch of Chopin's Nocturne in E Flat. Lydia relaxed and felt Sun Yat-sen stretch out against her and rest his tiny chin on her breast. It tickled.

"It was snowing," Valentina began. "Madame Irena made us all polish the floor till it gleamed like the ice on the windows and we could see our faces in it. That was instead of our French lesson. We were so excited. My fingers shook so much, I was frightened I couldn't play. Tatyana Sharapova was sick at her desk and was sent to bed for the day."

"Poor Tatyana."

"Yes, she missed everything."

"But you were the one who should have been sick," Lydia prompted.

"That's right. I was the one chosen to play for him. The Father of Russia, Tsar Nicholas II. It was a great honor, the greatest honor a fifteen-year-old girl could dream of in those days. He chose us because our school was the Ekaterininsky Institute, the finest in all Russia, even finer than the ones in Kharkov or Moscow. We were the best and we knew it. Proud as princesses we were and carried our heads somewhere up near the clouds."

"Did he speak to you?"

"Of course. He sat down on a big carved chair in the middle of the hall and told me to begin. I'd heard that Chopin was his favorite composer, so I played the Nocturne and poured my heart into it that day. And at the end he made no secret of the tears on his face."

A tear trickled down Lydia's cheek and she wasn't sure who it belonged to.

"We were all standing in our white capes and pinafores," Valentina continued, "and he came over to me and kissed my forehead. I remember his beard was bristly on my face and he smelled of hair wax, but the medals on his chest shone so bright I thought they'd been touched by the finger of God."

"Tell me what he said."

"He said, 'Valentina Ivanova, you are a great pianist. One day you shall play the piano at court in the Winter Palace for me and the Dowager Empress, and you shall be the toast of St. Petersburg.'"

A contented silence filled the room and Lydia feared her mother might stop there.

"Did the tsar bring anyone with him?" she asked, as if she did not know.

"Yes, an entourage of elite courtiers. They stood over by the door and applauded when I finished."

"And was there anyone special among them?"

Valentina took a deep breath. "Yes. There was a young man."

"What did he look like?"

"He looked like a Viking warrior. Hair that burned brighter than the sun, it lit up the room, and shoulders that could have carried Thor's great ax." Valentina laughed, a light swaying sound that made Lydia think of the sea and Viking longboats.

"You fell in love?"

"Yes," Valentina answered, her voice soft and low. "I fell in love the moment I set eyes on Jens Friis."

Lydia shivered with pleasure. It blunted the sharp ache inside her. She closed her eyes and imagined her father's big smile and his strong arms folded across his broad chest. She tried to remember it, not just imagine it. But couldn't.

"There was someone else there too," Valentina said.

Lydia snapped open her eyes. This wasn't part of the story. It ended with her mother falling in love at first sight.

"Someone you've met." Valentina was determined to tell more.

"Who?"

"Countess Natalia Serova was there. The one who had the nerve to tell you last night that you should speak Russian. But where did speaking Russian get her, I'd like to know? Nowhere. When the Red dogs started biting, she was first in line on the trains out of Russia, her jewels intact, on the Trans-Siberian Railway, and didn't even wait to learn whether her Muscovite husband was dead or alive before she wedded a French mining engineer here in Junchow. Though he's off somewhere up north now."

"So *she* has a passport?"

"Oh yes. A French one, by marriage. One of these days she'll be in Paris on the Champs-Elysées, sipping champagne and parading her poodles while I rot and die in this miserable hellhole."

The story was spoiled. Lydia felt the moment of happiness fade. She lay still for a further minute watching the shadows dance, then said, "I think I'll go back to my own bed now, if you're all right."

Her mother made no comment.

"Are you all right now, Mama?"

"I'm as all right as I'll ever be."

Lydia kissed her cheek and bundled the sleeping little rabbit into her arms as she slid from the bed.

"Thank you, darling." Valentina's eyes were closed, the shadows flickering over her face. "Thank you. Put out the candle on your way."

Lydia drew a deep breath and blew out the light.

"Lydia." The word hung in the darkness.

"Yes?"

"Don't bring that vermin into my bed again."

THE NEXT FIVE DAYS WERE HARD. EVERYWHERE LYDIA WENT she could not stop herself from looking for Chang An Lo. Among a sea of Chinese faces, she constantly sought one with an alert way of holding his head and a livid bruise. Any movement at her shoulder made her head turn in expectation. A shout across the street or a shadow in a doorway was all it took. But at the end of five days of staring out of her classroom window in search of a dark figure lingering at the school gates, the hope died.

She had filled her head with excuses for him—that he was ill, the foot infection raging in his blood, or he was hiding out somewhere until the search died down. Or even that he had failed to retrieve the necklace at all and was too worried about loss of face to admit it. But she knew he'd have sent word, somehow. He'd have made sure she wasn't left in the dark. He knew what the necklace meant to her. Just as she knew what it could mean to him. The image of him whipped and fettered in jail raced through her dreams at night.

And worse. Much worse. In just the same way that her father had protected her and had died for it in the snows of Russia, so now she'd been protected by Chang and he'd died for it. She saw his limp body tossed into a black and raging river, and she woke up moaning. But by daylight she knew better. The International Settlement was a hotbed of gossip and rumor, so if the jewel thief had been caught and the necklace reclaimed, she'd have heard.

He was a thief, damn it. Plain and simple. He'd taken the jewels and gone. So much for honor among thieves. So much for saving someone's life. She was so angry with him, she wanted to scratch his eyes out and stomp on the foot she'd sewn up with such care, just to see him in pain as she was in pain. Her head was full of a harsh raw buzzing sound like the teeth of a saw biting into metal and she wasn't sure whether that was rage or starvation. Repeatedly she was told off by Mr. Theo for not paying attention in class.

"A hundred lines, Lydia—*I must not dream*. Stay in and do them at break time."

I must not dream.
I must not dream.
I must   dream.
I   dream.
I must

The words messed up her thoughts and took on colors of their own on the white ruled paper, so that *dream* seemed sometimes red and sometimes purple, swirling over the page. But *not* remained black as a mineshaft and she left it out all the way down the rows, making a deep drop for it, until right at the end when Mr. Theo was holding out his hand for the paper. Quickly she scribbled in the missing *nots*. His mouth twitched with amusement, which only made the buzzing louder in her head, so she refused to look at him and stared instead at the ink stain the pen had made on her left forefinger. As black as Chang's heart.

AFTER SCHOOL SHE THREW OFF HER UNIFORM AND HER hat, pulled on an old dress—not the one with the bloodstains, she couldn't bear to touch that one—and went in search of food for Sun Yat-sen. The park was the place. Any weeds that drew breath in the street were instantly torn up by hungry scavengers, but she'd found a rough bank in Victoria Park, where dandelions had taken over and remained untouched because no Chinese were allowed inside the railings. Sun Yat-sen loved the raggedy leaves and would hop in a flurry of white onto her lap while she fed them to him one by one. She worried about his food more than her own.

When she had filled her crumpled brown paper bag with leaves and grass, she headed over to the vegetable market in the Strand in the hope of picking up a few scraps under the stalls. The day was hot and humid, the pavement scorching the soles of her feet through her thin sandals, so she kept to the shade wherever she could and watched other girls twirling their dainty parasols or disappearing into La Fontaine Café for ice cream or to the Buckingham Tearoom for cool sherbets and cucumber sandwiches without crusts.

Lydia turned her head away. Averted her eyes and her thoughts. Things were not good at home at the moment. Not good at all. Valentina had not left the attic all week, not since the aborted concert, and seemed to be living on nothing but vodka and cigarettes. The musky smell of Antoine's hair oil hung in the room but he was never there when Lydia came home, just the cushions in a mess on the floor and her mother in various stages of despair.

"Darling," she'd murmured the day before, "it is time I joined Frau Helga's, if she'll have me."

"Don't talk like that, Mama. Frau Helga's is a brothel."

"So?"

"It's full of prostitutes."

"I tell you, little one, if no one will pay me for running my fingers over piano keys anymore, then I must earn money by putting my fingers to work elsewhere. That's all they're fit for now." She had held up her fingers, curled over like broken fans, for her daughter to inspect.

"Mama, if you put them to work scrubbing the floor and hanging up your clothes, at least this place wouldn't be such a pigsty."

"Poof!" Valentina had dragged both hands through her wild hair and flounced back to bed, leaving Lydia reading in a chair by the window.

Sun Yat-sen was asleep bonelessly on her shoulder, his nose whispering his dreams into her ear. The book was one from the library, Hardy's *Jude the Obscure*, and it was the third time she'd read it. Its abject misery brought her comfort. The room was a mess around her but she ignored it. She had arrived home from school yesterday to find Valentina's clothes hurled across the floor and left there to be walked over. Signs of another row with Antoine. But this time Lydia refused to pick them up and carefully walked around them instead. It was like walking around dead bodies. And no food in the house. The few things she'd bought to eat with the watch money were long gone.

Lydia knew she should take her new dress up to Mr. Liu's, the beautiful concert frock with the low apricot satin sash. But she didn't. Each day she told herself she'd do it tomorrow, for certain tomorrow, but the dress continued to hang on a hook on the wall while each day she grew thinner.

THE STRAND WAS EMPTYING BY THE TIME LYDIA ARRIVED. The leaden heat had driven people off the street, but the vegetable market in the big noisy hall at the far end was busier than she'd expected this late in the day. The Strand was the main shopping area in the International Settlement, dominated by the gothic frontage of Churston Department Store where ladies bought their undergarments and gentlemen their humidors and Lydia could browse when it rained.

Today she hurried past it and into the market, in search of a stall closing down for the day, one where broken cabbage leaves or a bruised durian were being thrown into a pig bin as the floor was swept clean. But each time she spotted one, a litter of Chinese street urchins was there before her, squabbling and scrapping over the castoffs like kittens in a sack. After half an hour of patient scouting, she snatched up a corncob that a careless elbow had knocked to the floor and made a quick exit. She bundled the cob inside the paper bag along with the leaves and grass and had just stepped off the curb to cross the road behind a swaying donkey cart when a hand snaked out and yanked the bag from her grasp.

"Give that back," she shouted and grabbed for the scruff of the thief's neck.

But the Chinese boy ducked under her arm and was off. His jet-black hair stood up like a scrubbing brush as he wove through the traffic, and though he could be no more than seven or eight years old he nipped in and out with the speed of a weasel. Diving, ducking, twisting. Lydia raced after him, barged around a corner, knocking into a juggler and sending his hoops flying, never taking her eyes off the scrubbing-brush head. Her lungs were pounding but she pushed harder, her legs stretching out in strides twice as long as the weasel's. She was not going to let Sun Yat-sen go hungry tonight.

Abruptly the boy skidded to a halt. Twenty feet ahead, he turned and faced her. He was small, skin filthy, legs like twigs and an abscess under one eye, but he was very sure of himself. He held up the paper bag for a second, staring at her with his black unblinking eyes, and then opened his fingers and dropped the bag on the ground before backing off a dozen paces.

Only then did Lydia stop and look around. The street was quiet but not empty. A small maroon car with a dented fender was parked halfway down on her side, while two Englishmen were fiddling with a motorbike's engine across the road. One was telling the other in a loud voice a joke about a mother-in-law and a parrot. This was an English street. It had net curtains. Not an alleyway in old Junchow. This was safe. So why did she feel unease claw its way into her mind? She approached slowly.

"You filthy thieving devil," she yelled at him.

No answer.

Eyes fixed on him, she bent quickly, scooped up the bag from the ground, and held it tight to her chest, feeling the knobbly vegetable with her finger. But before she could work out what was going on, a hand came from behind, clamped over her mouth, and strong arms bundled her into the back of the small car with the dented fender. It all happened in the blink of an eye. But her own eye couldn't blink. A knife blade was pushed against the top of the socket of her right eye and a harsh voice snarled something in Chinese.

She couldn't open her mouth because of the hand. Her blood was thundering in her ears and her heart knocking holes in her ribs, but she kicked out a foot and connected with a shinbone.

"Be still."

This voice was smoother. Spoke English. His face was smoother too. There were two men, Chinese roughnecks, one broad-faced and reeking of garlic, the other with hard eyes and small smooth features. He was the one holding the knife and twitching its blade on her eyelid.

"You lose eye. No trouble." He spoke softly and she could hear the two Englishmen laughing at their stupid joke across the road.

"Understand?"

She blinked her left eye.

The other man removed his stinking hand from her mouth.

"What do you want?" she breathed. "I have no money."

"Not money." The smooth one shook his head. "Where Chang An Lo?"

Lydia felt sweat slide down her back.

"I don't know any Chang An Lo."

The knife point snicked open her skin. She felt her eyelid sting.

"Where he?"

"I don't know. But don't cut me again. This is the truth. He's gone. I don't know where."

"You lie."

"No. It's true." She held up a finger. "Cut it off and you'll get the same answer. I don't know where he is."

The two faces hesitated and glanced at each other. It was then she saw the coiled black snake tattooed on the side of each neck. The last time she'd seen a snake it was in the alleyway in the old town and that one was black.

"I can guess, though," she added and spat in his face.

The rough face spat back at her and the smooth face leaned closer. "Where?"

"In jail."

An angry frown. "Why jail?"

"He stole something. From the Ulysses Club. They've caught him and chucked him in a cell. They'll probably send him to prison in Tientsin, that's what the English usually do anyway. You won't see him again for a long time."

A fierce exchange burst out between the two men, and then the rough one's eyes grew wide with understanding and he screamed something at her, seized her arm, and hurled her out of the car onto the pavement. The back of her head cracked on the stone, but she barely felt it. The car drove off and the boy had vanished. Relief was so sweet, it flooded her mouth. She scrambled to her feet and was noticed for the first time by one of the Englishmen, who called out, "You all right, miss?"

She nodded and hurried back down the street, the brown paper bag still in her hand.

13

Damn him, damn him, damn him.

Damn Chang An Lo. She had saved his worthless skin for a second time. But what did she get out of it? A bump on the head and a sore eye. No necklace. No Erard grand.

Once back on the Strand, Lydia was shocked to find she was shaking. She was hot, sticky, and annoyed. Her mouth tasted as if it were packed full of sand and she longed for a tall cool drink, one with ice and a slice of mango floating in it. She had had ice only once in her life and that was when Antoine bought her a raspberry juice in an ice cream parlor in the French part of town while waiting for her mother to choose a hat. She had sucked the frozen cubes until her tongue went numb.

She pushed open the glass doors of Churston Department Store and flicked the weight of her hair off her neck for a moment. At least it would be cooler here. The giant brass fans on the ceiling were not ice, but they helped chill the skin. Inside, the counters were busy. At one, an American woman with hair bobbed short was buying Guerlain perfume; at another, a man was holding up a pair of jet earrings to his wife's face and smiling. Probably his mistress, Lydia decided.

Above their heads small wooden canisters whizzed across the room on wires, carrying cash and receipts to and from the little cage in the corner. That was where a woman with a face like a nanny goat and a hair growing out of the mole on her chin hoarded the money and wrote down in tiny writing the sums of each transaction. Normally Lydia liked to watch her busy hands, never still, but today she was not in the mood. In fact she wasn't in the mood for any of this.

Looking at the displays of snakeskin handbags and mother-of-pearl jewelry boxes just made her feel worse.

She turned to leave. And almost stumbled over a man she recognized. It was the cream jacket and panama hat from the Chinese market last week, the watch man, the Englishman with the liking for porcelain. She swerved away, but not before seeing him slide his wallet into the side pocket of his jacket and head for the exit door. Under his arm was tucked a small purchase wrapped in white tissue paper.

The decision was instant. She recalled how easy he'd been. How soft. Unguarded. Anyway, only a fool would carry his wallet so casually. By the time he reached the door, she was there. He held it open for her, touching his fingers to the brim of his hat in a courteous manner and she smiled her thanks as she brushed past him.

In the street, in the heat, she took two steps. No more. A hand seized her wrist and didn't let go.

"Young lady, I want my wallet back." He didn't shout but the rage in his voice flared in her face.

"Pardon?"

"Don't make things worse for yourself. My wallet. Now."

She fought to pull her wrist free, twisted and turned, but his grip was locked solid. This was only the third time since the death of her father that she'd been touched by a man's hand. The first was in the alleyway and then a few minutes ago in the dented car, and now this. She was astonished at how strong they were. She stopped struggling.

"My wallet."

She held up the brown paper bag in her free hand and he lifted his possession out of it, replacing it in his pocket, the inside one this time. But he didn't release her wrist. She lowered her head. What else did he want from her?

"I'm sorry," she offered.

"*Sorry* is not enough. You need to be taught a lesson, my girl. I'm taking you straight to the police station."

"No."

"I warn you, if you make any trouble, I will summon a couple of the traffic police off the street to assist me. That won't be very dignified for you, I assure you."

He marched off, dragging her beside him. A few heads turned, but no one was interested enough to interfere. Lydia's thoughts panicked. She could go limp, sit down on the pavement. But where would that get her?

Neither spoke. They strode on in silence.

"Sir?"

"My name is Mr. Parker."

"Mr. Parker, I won't do it again."

"Indeed you won't. I intend to make sure of that."

"What will the police do to me?"

"Throw you in prison. That's what a thief deserves."

"Even though I'm only sixteen."

Without slackening his pace, he stared at her as a man would stare at a scorpion. She stared back.

"Exactly a week ago I was robbed," he said stiffly. "Most likely some native beggar no older than you. He was probably poor and hungry. But that does not excuse thieving. Nothing does. It is against the Word of God and against the fabric of our society. If he'd asked, I'd have given. That's charity. But not my watch. For heaven's sake, not that."

"If I'd asked, Mr. Parker, would you have given?"

He looked at her and a flicker of confusion crossed his face. "No, I would not."

"But I am poor."

"You're white. You should know better."

She said nothing more. She had to think. Keep her mind working. Then St. Augustine's Church loomed, gray and uninviting, on their right and an idea came to her, so tempting it sent adrenaline skidding to her fingertips.

"Mr. Parker."

He wouldn't turn his head.

"Mr. Parker, I need to go in there."

"What?"

"Into the church."

This time he looked at her, startled. "Why?"

"If I am to go to prison like you say, I need to seek God's peace first."

He jerked to a halt. "Are you making fun of me, young lady? Do you take me for a fool?"

"No, sir." She lowered her eyes demurely. "I know what I did was wrong and I need to ask for the Lord's forgiveness. Please, it won't take long, I promise." She saw him hesitate. "To cleanse my soul."

A silence followed. The noises in the street seemed to recede, as if only she and this man existed in the whole of China. She held her breath.

He adjusted his spectacles on his nose. "Very well. I suppose I can't deny you that. But don't think you can escape in there."

He led her up the stone steps, his fingers still clamped around her wrist, and pushed open the heavy oak door.

She froze.

He stopped and studied her face impatiently. "What now?"

She shook her head. She had never been inside a church before. What if God struck her dead?

He seemed to sense her fear. "God will forgive you, child, even if I cannot."

With fists clenched, she stepped inside. She was not prepared for the drop in temperature, nor the high vaulted ceiling that towered above her the way human beings tower over ants. It made her shiver. Parker nodded to himself, as if pleased with her reaction. The place smelled a bit like Mrs. Zarya's backyard, thick musty air in her nostrils, but its windows made her heart thump with excitement. The light and blaze of colors were so intense, the Virgin Mary's gown more vivid than a peacock's breast and Christ's blood the exact shade of the ruby necklace Chang had stolen from her.

"Sit down."

She sat. In a long pew near the back. She stared up at a man-sized figure of Christ above the altar and expected blood to bubble from its side at any moment. A few people were sitting quietly in other pews, heads bowed, lips moving in prayer, but mainly the church was full of emptiness and Lydia could see why people came here. To feed off the emptiness. It slowed her heartbeat and quieted the panic in her head. Here she could think.

"Let us pray," Parker said and rested his head on his hands, bowing forward against the back of the bench in front.

Lydia did the same.

"Lord," Parker murmured, "pardon us all, sinners that we are. Especially forgive this young girl her transgression and bring her the peace that passeth understanding. Dear Lord, guide her with thy Almighty hand, by the grace of Jesus Christ our Savior, Amen."

Lydia watched between her fingers as a wood louse crawled toward Parker's shiny brogue shoe. There was a long silence and she considered making a run for it now that he'd released her hand. But she didn't. He'd be quick to seize hold of her the moment she moved a muscle from the absurd prayer position, and anyway, she liked it here. The emptiness and the silence. When she closed her eyes she felt as if she were floating up in it. Looking down. Waving good-bye to the rats and the hunger below. Is this what angels feel like? Weightless and carefree and . . .

She snapped open her eyes. So who on earth would look after her mother and Sun Yat-sen if she drifted away on a fluffy white cloud? God didn't seem to have done much of a job with the millions of Chinese starving to death out there, so why should she think He would bother with Valentina and a scrawny white rabbit?

She let the silence settle around her again, eyes only half closed.

"Mr. Parker."

"Yes?"

"May I say a prayer too?"

"Of course. That's what we're here for."

She took a deep breath. "Please, Lord, forgive me. Forgive my wicked sin, and make my Mama better from her illness, and while I'm in prison, please don't let her die, like Papa did." She remembered something she had heard Mrs. Yeoman say. "And bless all Your children in China."

"Amen to that."

After a moment they sat up straight. Parker was looking at her with concern blunting the anger in his brown eyes and placed a hand on her shoulder. "Where is it that you live?"

"WHAT IS YOUR NAME?"

"Lydia Ivanova."

"You say your mother is ill?"

"Yes, she's sick in bed. That's why I had to come into town on my own and why I had to take your wallet, you see. To pay for medicine."

"Tell me truly, Lydia, have you ever stolen before?"

Lydia turned a shocked face to his as they rode into the Russian Quarter in a rickshaw. "No, Mr. Parker, never. Cut my tongue out if I lie."

He nodded at her with a slight smile, his head making her think of an owl. Round glasses, round face, and a small beak of a nose. But clearly nowhere near as wise as an owl. She was confident that once he'd seen her mother comatose on the bed and their dismal room looking like a bear pit, his heart would melt and he'd let her go. He'd forget about the blasted police and maybe even give her a few dollars for a meal. She sneaked a sideways glance at him. He did have a heart. Didn't he?

"Was the watch that was stolen from you very valuable?" she asked as the rickshaw rattled into her street. It looked desperately shabby even to her eyes.

"Yes, it was. But that's not the point. It belonged to my father. He gave it to me before he left for India, where he was killed, and I've carried it with me ever since. The thought of it all those years in his waistcoat pocket and then in mine meant something special to me. Now it's gone."

Lydia looked away. To hell with him.

SHE FLEW UP THE TWO FLIGHTS OF STAIRS. SHE COULD hear Parker's footsteps right behind her. That surprised her. He must be fitter than he looked. She pushed open the door to the attic, darted into the room . . .

And stopped.

She did not feel Parker bump into her but caught his gasp of surprise.

"Mama," she said, "you're . . . better."

"Darling, what on earth do you mean? There was never anything wrong with me. Nothing at all."

Nothing at all. Valentina was standing in the middle of the room and despite the darkness of her hair and of her dress, she managed to make the place brighter. Her hair gleamed, soft and perfumed, around her shoulders and she was wearing a navy silk dress with a wide white collar, cut low to emphasize the curve of her breasts. It fitted snugly at her hips but was designed to hang loose elsewhere, cleverly hiding the lack of flesh on her bones. Lydia had never seen it before. She thought her mother looked wonderful. Shining and glossy.

But why now? Why did she have to choose this moment to transform into a bird of paradise? Why, why?

Parker coughed awkwardly.

"And who is our visitor, Lydia? Aren't you going to introduce us?"

"This is Mr. Parker, Mama. He wants to meet you."

Valentina's smile enveloped him and drew him into her world. She held out her hand, the movement elegant and inviting. He took it in his. "Charmed to make your acquaintance, Mr. Parker." She laughed and it was just for him. "Please excuse our sad little abode."

For the first time Lydia noticed the room. It had changed. It sparkled. Windows thrown open, every surface polished, each cushion in place. A room full of gold and bronze and amber lights, with no trace of a dead body on the floor or a discarded shoe under the table. The air smelled of lavender, and not an ashtray in sight.

This was not what Lydia had planned for him.

"Mrs. Ivanova, it's a pleasure to meet you. But I'm afraid to say I am not here with good news."

Valentina's hands fluttered. "Mr. Parker, you alarm me."

"I apologize for bringing you cause for concern, but your daughter is in trouble." Despite his words, his glance at Lydia was remarkably benign, and she began to feel on surer ground. Maybe he would pass over the wallet episode.

"Lydia?" Valentina shook her head indulgently, making her dark mane dance. "What has she been up to now? Not swimming in the river again."

"No. She stole my wallet."

There was a long silence. Lydia waited for the explosion, but it didn't come.

"I apologize for my daughter's behavior. I will have words with her, I promise you." Valentina spoke in a low, tight voice.

"She told me that you were ill. That she needed money for medicine."

"Do I look ill?"

"Not at all."

"Then she lied."

"I'm considering going to the police."

"Please, don't. Please allow her this one mistake. It won't happen again." She swung around to face her daughter. "Will it, *dochenka*?"

"No, Mama."

"Apologize to Mr. Parker, Lydia."

"Don't worry, she has already done so. And more importantly, she has asked God for forgiveness too."

Valentina raised one eyebrow. "Has she indeed? I'm so glad to hear it. I know just how much she cares about the state of her young soul."

Lydia's cheeks were burning and she scowled at her mother. "Mr. Parker," she said quietly, "I do apologize for lying to you, as well as stealing. It was wrong of me, but when I left here, my mother was . . ."

"Lydia, darling, why not make Mr. Parker a nice cup of tea?"

". . . my mother was out and I was very hungry. I didn't think straight. I lied because I was frightened. I'm sorry."

"Nicely said. I accept your apology, Miss Ivanova. We will forget the matter."

"Mr. Parker, you are the kindest man in all the world. Isn't he, Lydia?"

Lydia tried not to laugh and went over to the corner to make tea. She had seen this before, the way a man left his brains on the doorstep the moment he set foot in a room that contained her mother. One flutter of her dark lustrous eyes was all it took. Men were such idiots. Couldn't they see when they were being plucked and trussed? Or didn't they care?

"Come and sit down, Mr. Parker," Valentina invited with a smooth shift of subject, "and tell me what brings you to this extraordinary country."

He took a seat on the sofa and she placed herself beside him. Not too close, but close enough.

"I'm a journalist," he said, "and journalists are always attracted to anything extraordinary." He gazed at Valentina and laughed self-consciously.

Lydia watched him from her corner, the way his whole body was drawn toward her mother; even his spectacles seemed to lean forward. He might be a fool for a petticoat but he had a nice laugh. She listened idly to their chatter, but her thoughts were a jumble.

What exactly had happened here?

Why was her mother all done up in new finery? Where had it come from?

Antoine? It was possible. But it didn't explain the shine on the room or the lavender in the air.

She placed the tea in their single remaining cup in front of Mr. Parker and slipped him a smile. "I'm sorry we have no milk."

He looked mildly taken aback.

"You must drink it black," Valentina laughed, "like we Russians do. Much more exotic. You will like it."

"Or I could go out and buy some milk for you," Lydia offered. "But I would need some money."

"Lydia!"

But Parker studied Lydia. His gaze traveled over her washed-out dress and her patched sandals and her thin wrists. It was as if he'd only just realized that when she'd said *poor*, it meant having *nothing*. Not even milk. From his wallet he pulled two twenty-dollar notes and handed them to her.

"Yes, go and buy some milk, please. And something to eat. For yourself."

"Thank you." She left before he changed his mind.

It took no more than ten minutes to get hold of milk and half a pound of Marie biscuits, but when she returned, Valentina and Parker were on their feet ready to leave. Valentina was pulling on a pair of new gloves.

"Lydochka, if I don't go now, I will be late for my new job."

"Job?"

"Yes, I start today."

"What job?"

"As a dance hostess."

"A dance hostess?"

"That's right. Don't look so surprised."

"Where?"

"At the Mayfair Hotel."

"But you've always said that dance hostesses were no better than . . ."

"Hush, Lydia, don't be a silly. I love dancing."

"You can't bear men with two left feet. You say it's like being trampled by a moose."

"I shall be protected from that fate this evening because Mr. Parker has kindly offered to accompany me and make sure I do not sit like a wallflower on my first night."

"No chance of that," Parker put in gallantly.

"Do you dance well, Mr. Parker?" Lydia asked.

"Passably."

"Well, then you are in luck, Mama."

Her mother gave her a look that was hard to read, then left on Parker's arm. When they reached the lower landing, Lydia heard Valentina exclaim, "Oh dear, I have forgotten something. Would you be an angel and just wait downstairs for me? I won't be a moment." The sound of her footsteps running back up the stairs. The door opened, then slammed shut.

"You stupid, stupid little fool." Valentina's hand swung out. The slap made Lydia's head whip back. "You could be lying in a police cell right this minute. Among rats and rapists. Don't you leave this house," she hissed, "not till I come back."

And she was gone.

In all her life her mother had never raised a hand to her. Never. The shock of it was still ricocheting through Lydia's body, making it jump and tremble. She put a hand to her stinging cheek and let out a low guttural moan. She roamed around the room, seeking relief in movement, as if she could outpace her thoughts, and then she spotted the package in the Churston Department Store tissue paper that Parker had left behind in his eagerness to escort her mother. She picked it up, opened it, and found a silver cigarette case inlaid with lapis lazuli and jade.

She started to laugh. The laugh wouldn't stop; it just kept ripping its way up from her lungs over and over until she was suffocating on her own sense of the absurd. First the necklace and now the cigarette case, both in her grasp but both beyond her reach. Just as Chang An

Lo was now. *Chang, where are you, what are you doing?* Everything she wanted had slipped from her grasp.

When the laughter finally ceased, she felt so empty, she started stuffing biscuits into her mouth, one, then another and another until all the biscuits were gone. Except one. She crushed up the last one, mixed it with the grass and leaves in her paper bag, and went down to Sun Yat-sen.

14

THE WALL WAS HIGH AND LIME-WASHED, THE GATE BUILT OF black oak and carved with the spirit of Men-shen. To guard against evil. A lion prowled on each gatepost. Theo Willoughby stared into their eyes of stone and felt nothing but hatred for them. When an oil-black crow settled on the head of one, he wanted its talons to tear out the lion's stone heart. The way his own hands wanted to tear out the heart of Feng Tu Hong.

He summoned the gatekeeper.

"Mr. Willoughby to see Feng Tu Hong." He chose not to speak in Mandarin.

The gatekeeper, in gray tunic and straw shoes, bowed low. "Feng Tu Hong expect you," he said.

The keeper's wife led Theo through the courtyards. Her pace was pitiful, her feet no longer than a man's thumb, bound and rebound until they stank of putrefaction under their bandages. Like this hellish country, rotten and secretive. Theo's eyes were blind to China's beauty today despite the fact that he was surrounded by it. Each courtyard he passed through brought new delights to caress the senses, cool fountains that soothed the heat from the blood, wind chimes that sang to the soul, statues and strutting peacocks to charm the eye, and everywhere in the dusky evening light stood ghost-white lilies to remind the visitor of his own mortality. In case he should be rash enough to forget it.

"You devil-sucking gutter-whore!" The words sliced through the darkness.

Theo halted abruptly. Off to his right in an ornate pavilion, lanterns in the shape of butterflies cast a soft glow over the dark heads of two young women. They were playing mah-jongg. Each one was gilded and groomed and dressed in fine silks, but one was cheating and the other was swearing like a deckhand. In China it is easy to be fooled.

"You come," his guide murmured.

Theo followed. The courtyards were intended to show wealth. The more courtyards, the more silver taels the owner could boast, and as Theo knew only too well, Feng Tu Hong was the kind of man who loved to boast. As he passed under an ornately carved archway strung with dragon lanterns and into the final and grandest courtyard, a figure stepped out of the shadows. He was a man of about thirty with too much of the fire of youth still in his eyes. His hand was on the knife at his belt.

"I search you," he said bluntly.

He was broad and stocky with soft skin, and Theo recognized him immediately.

"You will have to use that blade on me first, Po Chu." Theo spoke in Mandarin. "I have not come to be treated like a dog's whelp. I am here to speak with your father."

He stepped around the man in his path and marched toward the elegant low building that lay ahead of him, but before he came anywhere near its steps, a blade fashioned like a tiger's claw was pressing between his shoulder blades.

"I search," the voice said again, harsher this time.

Theo did not care for it. He had no intention of losing face, not here. He swung around so that the knife was now directly over his heart.

"Kill me," he growled.

"Gladly."

"Po Chu, put down that knife at once and beg forgiveness of our guest." It was Feng Tu Hong. His deep voice roared around the courtyard and stamped out the faint murmur of voices from the other courtyards.

The blade dropped. Po Chu fell to his knees and bowed his head to the ground.

"A thousand pardons, my father. I meant only to keep you safe."

"It is my honor you must keep safe, you mindless mound of mule dung. Ask forgiveness of our guest."

"Honorable father, do not order this. I would tear out my bowels and watch the rats devour them, rather than ask it of this son of a devil."

Feng took a step closer. Under his loose scarlet robe he had squat powerful legs that could kick a man to death and the shoulders of an ox. He towered over his son, whose forehead was still pressed tight to the tiled floor.

"Ask," he commanded.

A long intake of breath. "A thousand pardons, Tiyo Willbee."

Theo tipped his head in scornful acknowledgment. "Don't make that mistake again, Po Chu, not if you want to live." He drew a short horn-handled knife from inside his sleeve and tossed it to the ground.

A hiss escaped from the hunched figure.

His father folded his arms across his broad chest with a grunt of satisfaction. In the swirling shadows of the cat-gray twilight Feng Tu Hong looked like Lei Kung, the great god of thunder, but instead of a bloody hammer in his massive hand, he carried a snake. It was small and black and had eyes as pale as death. It coiled around his wrist and tasted the air for prey.

"I EXPECTED NEVER TO SEE YOU IN THIS HOUSE AGAIN, TIYO Willbee. Not while I live and have strength to slice open your throat."

"Neither did I expect to stand once more on this carpet." It was an exquisite cream silk floor covering from the finest hand weavers in Tientsin, a gift four years ago from Theo to Feng Tu Hong. "But the world changes, Feng. We never know what lies in store for us."

"My hatred of you does not change."

Theo gave him a thin smile. "Nor mine of you. But let us put that aside. I am here to speak of business."

"What business can a schoolteacher know?"

"A business that will fill your pockets and open up your heart."

Feng uttered a snort of disdain. Both knew that when it came to business, he had no heart. "Just because you dress like a Chinese"—he stabbed a thick finger toward Theo's long maroon gown, felt waistcoat, and silk slippers—"and speak our language and study the words of Confucius, don't imagine that it means you can think like a Chinese or do business like a Chinese. You cannot."

"I choose to dress in Chinese clothes for the simple reason that they are cooler in summer and warmer in winter, and they do not choke off the blood to my mind like a tie and collar. So my mind is as free to take the winding path as any Chinese. And I think like a Chinese enough to know that this business I bring to you today is sufficiently important to both of us to bridge the black seas that divide us."

Feng laughed, a big sound that held no joy. "Well spoken, Englishman. But what makes you think I need your business?" His black eyes flicked around the room and fixed back on Theo's.

Theo took his meaning. The room could not have been more opulent if it had belonged to Emperor T'ai Tsu himself, but its crass gaudiness grated on Theo's love of Chinese perfection of line. Everything here was gold and carved and inlaid with precious jewels; even the songbirds in their gilded cage wore pearl collars and drank out of Ming bowls encrusted with emeralds. The chair Theo was sitting in was gold-leafed, with dragons of jade for armrests and diamonds as big as his thumbnail for each eye.

This room was Feng Tu Hong's boast to the world, as well as his warning. For on each side of the doorway stood two reminders of what he had come from. One was a suit of armor. It was made of thousands of overlapping metal and leather scales, like the skin of a lizard, and its gauntlet grasped a sharpened spear that could rip your heart out. On the other side stood a bear. It was a black Asian bear with a white slash on its chest, rearing up on its hind legs, its jaws gaping to tear your throat to shreds. It was dead. Stuffed and posed. But a reminder nonetheless.

Theo nodded his understanding. At that moment a young girl, no more than twelve or thirteen, came into the room carrying a silver tray.

"Ah, Kwailin brings us tea," Feng said, then sat back in silence and gazed at the girl as she served each of them with a tiny cup of green tea and a fragrant sweetmeat. She moved gracefully even though her limbs were plump and small, her eyes heavy-lidded as if she spent her days lying in bed eating apricots and sugared dates. Theo knew at once that she was Feng's new concubine.

He drank his tea. But it did not wash away the sour taste in his mouth.

"Feng Tu Hong," he said, "time slides away with the tide."

Instantly Feng waved the girl away. She slipped Theo a shy smile as she left, and he wondered if she would be whipped for it later.

"So, Englishman, what is this business of yours?"

"I am meeting with a man of importance, a great mandarin in the International Settlement, who wants to trade with you."

"What does he trade, this mandarin?"

"Information."

Feng's narrow eyes sharpened. Theo felt his own breath come faster.

"Information in return for what?" Feng demanded.

"In exchange he wants a percentage."

"No percentage. A straight fee."

"Feng Tu Hong, you do not bargain with this man."

Feng balled his fists and slammed them together. "*I* am the one who decides the trade."

"But *he* is the one who has the knowledge to sweep away the foreign gunboats from your tail."

Feng fixed Theo with his black stare and for a long moment neither spoke.

"One percent," Feng offered finally.

"You insult me. And you insult my mandarin."

"Two percent."

"Ten percent."

"Wah!" roared Feng. "He thinks he can rob me."

"Eight percent of each shipment."

"What's in it for you?"

"My handling fee is two percent on top."

Feng leaned forward, his heavy dark jaw thrust out hungrily, reminding Theo of the Asian bear. "Five percent for the mandarin. One percent for you."

Theo was careful to show no pleasure. "Done."

★ ★ ★

"HE SAID YES?" LI MEI ASKED.

"He said yes. And he didn't kill me."

It was meant as a joke but Li Mei turned her head away, swinging her curtain of silken hair between them, and wouldn't look at him.

"My love," Theo whispered, "I am safe."

"So far." She stared out at the fog that was crawling up from the river, blanking out the street lamps and swallowing the stars. "Did you see my cousins?" she asked softly. "Or my brother?"

"Yes."

"And?"

"Your cousins were playing mah-jongg in the pavilion."

"Did they look well?" She turned to him at last, her dark eyes shining with an eagerness she could not hide. "Did they laugh and smile and look happy?"

Theo wound an arm around her slender waist and brushed her hair with his lips. Just the scent of her tightened his loins. "Yes, my sweet, they looked very lovely, with combs of silver in their hair and cheongsams of jade and saffron, pearls in their ears and smiles on their faces. Carefree as birds in springtime. Yes, they looked happy."

His words pleased her. She lifted his fingers to her lips and kissed their tips one by one.

"And Po Chu?"

"We spoke. Neither he nor I were pleased to see each other."

"I knew it would be so."

He shrugged.

"And my father? Did you give him my message?"

"Yes."

"What did he say?"

This time Theo did not lie. He pulled her closer to him. "He said, 'I no longer have a daughter called Mei. She is dead to me.'"

Li Mei pushed her face against Theo's chest, so hard that he was frightened she couldn't breathe, but he said nothing, just held her trembling body in his arms.

15

CHANG AN LO TRAVELED BY NIGHT. IT WAS SAFER. HIS foot still pained him, and in the mountains his progress was slow. His return journey took too long. They almost caught him.

He heard their breath. The sigh of their horses. The patter of the rain on their goatskin capes. He stilled his heart and lay facedown in the mud, their hooves only inches from his head, but the darkness saved him. He gave thanks to Ch'ang O, goddess of the moon, for turning her face away that night. After that he stole a mule from an unguarded barn in a village at the bottom of the valley, but he left a cupful of silver in its place.

It was just after dawn, when the wind off the great northern plain was driving the yellow loess dust into his nostrils and under his tongue, that the sprawl of houses that made up Junchow came into sight. From this distance Junchow looked disjointed. The Oriental jumbled alongside the Western, the soaring rooftops of the old town next to the solid blocks and straight lines of the International Settlement. Chang tried not to think of *her* in there or of what she must be thinking of him. Instead he tried to spit on the barren earth, but the dust had robbed his mouth of moisture, so instead he muttered, "A thousand curses on the *fanqui* invaders. China will soon piss on the Foreign Devils."

Yet despite all his curses and his hatred of them, one Foreign Devil had invaded him and he didn't want to drive her out any more than he would drive out his own soul. As he crouched in the depths of a spinney, his shadow merging with the trees, he ached for her, though he knew he was risking more than he had the right to lose.

Above him the red streaks in the sky looked like blood being spilled.

THE WATER WAS COLD. HE WAS A STRONG SWIMMER, BUT the river currents were fierce and wrapped around his legs like tentacles, so he had to kick hard to be free of them. The foot that the fox girl had sewn up served him well, and he thanked the gods for her steady hands. The river meant that he avoided the sentries and the many eyes that watched the roads into Junchow. He had waited until dark. The sampans and junks that skittered downstream with black sails and no bow lights swept past him to their furtive assignations, and above him the clouds stole the stars from the sky. The river kept its secrets.

When he reached the far bank, he stood silent and motionless beside the rotting hull of an upturned boat, listening for sounds in the darkness, looking for shifting patterns of shadows. He was back in Junchow, near *her* once more. He felt his spirits lift, and after some time spent with only the rustle of rats for company, he slipped away, up into the town.

"AI! MY EYES ARE GLAD TO SEE YOU." THE YOUNG MAN WITH the long scar down one side of his face greeted Chang with a rush of relief. "To have you back, alive and still cursing, my friend, it means I shall sleep tonight. Here, drink this, you look as if you need it."

The light flickered as the torch flames hissed and spat like live creatures on the wall.

"Yuesheng, I thank you. They came close, this time, the gray scorpions of Chiang Kai-shek. Someone had whispered in their ear." Chang drank the small glass of rice wine in one swallow and felt it burn life back into his chilled bones. He helped himself to another.

"Whoever it was will have his tongue cut out."

They were in a cellar. The stone walls dripped with water and were covered in vivid-colored lichen, but it was large and the sounds of the printing press were deadened by the thick walls and the heavy ceiling. Above them stood a textile factory where machines rattled all day, but only the foreman knew of the machine under his workers' feet. He was a trade union man, a Communist, a fighter for the cause, and he supplied oil and ink and buckets of raw rice wine to the nighttime activists. Since the Kuomintang Nationalists had swept into power and Chiang Kai-shek swore to wipe the Communist threat off the face of China, each breath was a danger, each pamphlet an invitation to the executioner's sword. Half a dozen determined young faces clustered around the presses, half a dozen young lives on a thread.

Yuesheng pulled a strip of dried fish from his bag and handed it to Chang. "Eat, my friend. You will need your strength."

Chang ate, his first food in more than three days. "The latest posters are good, the ones demanding new laws on child labor," he said. "I saw several on my way here, one even on the council chamber's door."

"Yes." Yuesheng laughed. "That one was Kuan's doing."

At the mention of her name a slender young woman glanced up from where she was stacking pamphlets into sacks and gave Chang a nod.

"Tell me, Kuan, how do you always manage to find the most insulting places to stick your posters, right under Feng Tu Hong's nose?" Chang called above the clattering noise of the press. "Do you fly with the night spirits, unseen by human eye?"

Kuan walked over. She was wearing the loose blue jacket and trousers of a peasant farmer, though she had recently graduated from Peking University with a degree in law. She had serious black eyes. She did not believe in the soft smiles that most Junchow women offered to the world. When her parents threw her out of the family home because she humiliated them by cutting her hair short and taking a job in a factory, it only sharpened her desire to fight for women, so that they would no longer be owned like dogs by fathers or by husbands, to be kicked at will. She possessed the fearlessness of the fox girl but inside her there was no flame, no light that burned so bright it lit up a room, no heat so fierce that lizards scurried to be near her.

Where was Lydia now? Cursing him, he had no doubt. The image of her fox eyes, narrowed and waiting for him full of fury, sent a laugh through him and Kuan mistook his pleasure. She gave Chang one of her rare smiles.

"That camel-faced chairman of the council, Feng Tu Hong, deserves such special treatment," she said.

"Tell me. What is new while I've been gone?"

The smile faded. "Yesterday he ordered a purge of the metalworkers in the iron foundry, those who were asking for safer conditions at the furnaces."

"Twelve were beheaded in the yard. As a warning to others," Yuesheng spat out and ran a hand down the sword scar on his own face. It seemed to pulsate and darken.

A surge of rage tore through Chang. He closed his eyes and focused his mind. Now was not the time. This moment was surrounded by fire. He needed control, with danger so close.

"Feng Tu Hong's time will come," he said quietly. "I promise you that. And this will bring it faster." He pulled a piece of paper from a leather pouch that hung from his neck.

Yuesheng snatched it up, read it through, and nodded with satisfaction. "It's a promissory note," he announced to the others. "For rifles, Winchesters. A hundred of them."

Six faces found smiles and one young man punched an ink-stained fist into the air in salute.

"You have done well," Yuesheng said, pride in his voice.

Chang was pleased. He and Yuesheng were almost brothers in their friendship. It was the rock on which they stood. He placed a hand on Yuesheng's shoulder and their eyes met in understanding. Each breath was one they earned.

"The news from the south is good," Chang told him.

"Mao Tse-tung? Is our leader still evading the gray bellies' snares?"

"He narrowly escaped capture last month. But his military camp in Jiangxi is expanding every day, where they come like bees to a hive from all over the country. Some with no more than a hoe in their hand and belief in their heart. The time is coming closer when Chiang Kai-shek will discover that his treachery and betrayal of our country have signed his own death warrant."

"Is it true there was another skirmish near Canton last week?" Kuan asked.

"Yes," Chang said. "A train full of Kuomintang troops was blown up and . . ."

A loud crash drowned out his voice and the sound of the press as the metal door burst open at the top of the stairs and a boy hurled himself into the cellar, eyes huge with panic.

"They're here," he screamed. "The troops are . . ."

A shot cracked through the cellar and the boy collapsed facedown on the earthen floor, a bright red stain etched on the back of his jacket.

Instantly the cellar was full of movement. Each knew what to do. Yuesheng had prepared for this moment. Torches were doused. In the darkness enemy boots pounded down the stairs, voices raised, commands thrown at shadows, and two more shots made the walls sing. But in the far corner a ladder was ready. Well-oiled bolts slid back. A hatch was thrown open. But the square of night sky was paler, leaving the figures silhouetted against the opening as they started to slip through it one by one.

Standing last at the base of the ladder beside Yuesheng, Chang saw the dim outline of a soldier approach from the stairs, and with a lightning kick he tore the man's jaw from its socket and heard a high whinny of pain. In a flash Chang had seized his rifle and was sending a blast of bullets screaming around the cellar.

"Go," he shouted at Yuesheng.

"No. You leave first."

Chang touched his friend's arm. "Go."

Yuesheng delayed no longer and sped up the ladder. Chang fired once more and felt a Kuomintang bullet whistle through his hair in reply, and then he leaped up the rungs right on Yuesheng's heels. Bullets tore into the hatch opening from below and suddenly Chang felt a dead weight crash down on him. It was as if his own heart had been torn out.

He seized Yuesheng's body on his shoulder, sprang through the hatch, and raced away into the darkness.

16

"MORE WINE, LYDIA?"

"Thank you, Mr. Parker."

"Do you think she should, Alfred? She's only sixteen."

"Oh, Mama, I'm grown up now."

"Not as grown up as you think, darling."

Alfred Parker smiled indulgently, his spectacles sparkling at Lydia in the candlelight. "I think just this once. Tonight is special, after all."

"Special?" Valentina raised an elegant eyebrow. "In what way?"

"Because this is our first meal together like this. The first of many, I trust, when I am honored to be in the company of two such beautiful women." He lifted his glass briefly to Lydia and then to Valentina.

Valentina lowered her eyes for a moment, ran a finger slowly down the pale skin of her throat as if considering the suggestion, and then flashed her gaze up to his face. Like springing a trap, Lydia thought as she watched with interest the effect it had on Alfred Parker. He turned quite pink with pleasure. Her mother's sensuous dark eyes and parted lips were churning up his brain and robbing him of far more than Lydia had ever tried to take from him.

"*Garçon,*" he called. "Another bottle of Burgundy, please."

They were in a restaurant in the French Quarter and Lydia had ordered *steak au poivre.* The French maitre d' had bowed to her as if she were someone important, someone who could afford a meal like this. In a restaurant like this. She was wearing the dress, of course, her apricot one from the concert, and she made a point of looking around the room at the other diners as indifferently as if she did this every day.

No one could guess this was a series of firsts. First time in a restaurant. First time eating steak. First time drinking wine.

"Trust you to choose something fiery, darling," Valentina had laughed.

Lydia watched Parker closely, copied his table etiquette when it came to the startling array of silver cutlery on the stiff white tablecloth, and noticed the way he dabbed genteelly at the corner of his mouth with his napkin. She'd been surprised when her mother told her Alfred had invited her to join them for supper. Another first. No other man friend had ever included Lydia in their arrangements, and it sent alarm bells clanging through her head, but her desire to eat in a restaurant outweighed her instinct to keep as far away from Mr. Parker as possible.

"Very well," she'd said to her mother, "I'll come. But only if he doesn't lecture me."

"He won't lecture you." She took Lydia's chin in her hand and gave it an urgent little shake. "But be good. Be nice. Sugar and spice, even if it kills you. This is important to me, darling."

"But what about Antoine?"

"Bugger Antoine."

Everything had gone well so far. Only one little slipup. It happened when Parker kindly offered her one of his snails to taste and she had said without thinking, "No, thanks. I've eaten enough snails to last me a lifetime."

Valentina had glared at Lydia. A sharp kick under the table.

"Really?" Parked looked surprised.

"Oh yes," Lydia said quickly, "at my friend Polly's house. Her mother is mad about them."

"I don't blame her. Smothered in garlic and butter?"

"Mmm, delicious." She laughed wickedly. "Aren't they, Mama?"

Valentina rolled her eyes to the ceiling. She didn't want to be reminded of the times they'd spent scrabbling around in the rain, rooting snails out from under bushes and off back lawns at night. Even the occasional worm or frog. The stink of them all in the cooking pot.

Lydia turned a sugar-and-spice smile on Alfred Parker. "Mama tells me you are a newspaperman, Mr. Parker. That must be very interesting."

She heard her mother's little sigh of approval.

"A journalist, yes, on the *Daily Herald*. This is a very disturbed period in China's history but a very crucial one, with Chiang Kai-shek at last bringing some kind of sanity and order to this unhappy country, thank God. So yes, it is extremely interesting work." He beamed at her.

She beamed back.

"Tell me, Lydia, do you read the newspaper?"

Lydia blinked. Didn't this man realize that for the price of a newspaper you could buy two *baos* and have a full stomach?

"I'm usually too busy doing my homework."

"Ah yes, of course, highly commendable. But it would do you good to read a newspaper now and then, to know what's going on in this place. Broaden your young mind, you know, and give you the facts."

"My mind is broad enough, thank you. And I learn facts every day."

Another kick.

"Lydia is at the Willoughby Academy," Valentina said with a glare at her daughter. "She won a scholarship there."

Parker looked impressed. "She must be very bright indeed." He turned back to Lydia. "I know your headmaster well. I shall mention you to him."

"No need."

He laughed and patted her hand. "Don't look so alarmed. I won't mention how we met."

Lydia picked up her glass, buried her nose in it, and wished him dead.

Valentina came to her rescue. "I think you are right about the newspaper, Alfred. It would do her good to widen her knowledge, and anyway," she gave him a slow smile, "it would amuse me to read what you write."

"Then I shall definitely make sure you receive the *Daily Herald* every day without fail, Valentina." He leaned closer to her, and Lydia was sure he was breathing in her perfume. "Nothing would give me greater pleasure."

"Mr. Parker?"

Reluctantly he drew his gaze away from Valentina. "Yes, Lydia?"

"Maybe I know more about what goes on in this place than you do."

Parker sat back in his chair and studied her with a precision that made her wonder if she was underestimating him. "I am aware that your mother allows you a degree of freedom that means you get about more than most girls your age, but even so, that's quite an assumption, Lydia, don't you think? For a girl of sixteen."

She should leave it there, she knew she should. Take another sip of the wonderful wine and let him carry on making sheep's eyes at her mother. But she didn't.

"One thing I know is that your precious Chiang Kai-shek has tricked his followers," she said, "and betrayed the three principles on which the Republic of China was built by Sun Yat-sen."

"*Chyort vosmi!* Lydia!"

"That's absurd." Parker frowned at her. "Who's been filling your head with such ridiculous lies?"

"A friend." *Was she out of her mind?* "He's Chinese."

Valentina sat forward abruptly, her fingernails clicking on the stem of her glass. "And who exactly is this Chinese friend?" Her voice was icy.

"He saved my life."

There was a shocked silence at the table, and then Valentina burst out laughing. "Darling, you are such a liar. Where did you really meet him?"

"In the library."

"Ah, I see," Parker said. "That explains it. A left-wing intellectual. All talk and no action."

"You must stay away from him, darling. Look what the intellectuals did to Russia. Ideas are dangerous." She rapped her knuckles sharply on the table. "I absolutely forbid you to see this Chinese again."

"Oh, don't fret, Mama. You needn't worry. He might as well be dead for all I care."

"MISS IVANOVA, I DO BELIEVE. HOW VERY INTERESTING TO find you here of all places."

Lydia had just left the ladies' powder room and was threading her way back through the tables and the chatter when she heard the woman's voice behind her. She turned and looked up into an amused cool pale blue stare.

"Countess Serova," she said with surprise.

"Still wearing that dress, I see."

"I like this dress."

"My dear, I like chocolate but I don't eat it all the time. Let me introduce you to my son."

She stepped to one side to give Lydia a full view of the young man behind her. He had a long face and was tall like his mother with her thick curling brown hair and the same haughty manner that made one side of his mouth curl up and his eyes half closed, as if the world weren't worth the effort of opening them fully.

"Alexei, this is young Lydia Ivanova. From St. Petersburg also. Her mother is a piano player."

"A concert pianist, actually," Lydia corrected.

The countess conceded a smile.

"Good evening, Miss Ivanova." His voice was crisp. He gave a fractional nod of his head and fixed his gaze somewhere around her hairline. "I hope you are enjoying a pleasant evening."

"I'm having a simply wonderful time, thank you. The food is so good here, don't you think?" It was the sort of thing she thought her mother might say, all light and gay and too good to be true.

But his reply was brief. "Yes."

They hovered on the edge of an awkward silence.

"Must dash," Lydia said quickly.

She turned back to the countess and caught her staring across the room directly at Valentina, who had her head bent close to Alfred Parker's, talking softly. Lydia thought her mother looked more beautiful than ever tonight, so vivid in the navy and white dress, hair almost black in the soft lighting and piled on top of her head, her lips a carmine red. It was a surprise to Lydia that the whole restaurant wasn't staring.

"Nice to meet you again, Countess. Good evening. *Do svidania.*"

"Ah, so tonight you can speak Russian, it seems."

Lydia had no intention of stepping into that trap, so she just smiled and headed back to her table, remembering Miss Roland's instructions at school. *"Lead with your hips, girls, at all times. If you want to walk like a lady, you must lead with your hips."* As she sat down, Valentina looked up and noticed Countess Natalia Serova and her son across the room. Lydia saw her mother's eyes widen and then turn abruptly away, and when the Serovas passed their table a few moments later, neither woman acknowledged the other.

Lydia picked up one of the mint chocolates that came with the coffee. She decided she could definitely get used to this.

THEY LEFT HER OUTSIDE THE FRONT DOOR.

"Sleep well, darling."

Valentina's fingers waved through the front passenger window of Parker's car as if they were trying to escape and then disappeared from view. The black Armstrong Siddeley trundled up to the corner, too big and boisterous for the narrow confines of the street, flashed its brake light at Lydia, and was gone. Off to a nightclub, they said. The Silver Slipper. She stood alone in the dark. The church clock struck eleven. She counted each stroke. The Silver Slipper. If you dance there after midnight, do you turn into a pumpkin? Or even a countess?

She pushed aside such strange thoughts, unlocked the door, and started up the stairs. Her legs felt lifeless now, as if she'd left it all behind in the restaurant, and there was a dull ache somewhere inside her head. She wasn't sure if it was the heavy humid night air or the wine settling under her scalp like a layer of lead. She knew she should feel happy. She'd had an exciting evening, hadn't she? Alfred Parker had been attentive and courteous. More to the point, he was generous. Exactly what they needed. Life was looking up. So why did she still feel so bad? What the hell was wrong with her? Why was there this sick weight in her stomach, there all the time as if she had influenza?

She pushed open the door to the attic. Parker wasn't doing it for her, she knew that. He'd caught her thieving and he'd caught her lying. He was the kind of man who had principles the way their attic had cockroaches, and an unshakable grip on his belief in what was right and what was wrong. All that backbone-of-England stuff, for God and King Harry. A straight bat, isn't that what the English called it? A good egg. She gave a sharp little huff of annoyance. A man like Parker romped around on the moral high ground because he could indulge himself, as thoughtlessly as he could indulge himself in a posh French restaurant. He wouldn't bend.

Until now. Now he had met Valentina.

She struck a match in the dark, lit the solitary candle on the table, and instantly was surrounded by writhing shadows leaping up the wall and stalking the small circle of light. It was unbearably hot in the room. The window was partly open but she could hardly breathe. She yanked the dress impatiently over her head to let the sultry air touch her skin and maybe ease the hollow ache.

"Don't do that."

Lydia gasped at the sound of the voice. Though it was soft, she knew it instantly and her heart tightened in her chest. She spun around but could make out no one in the room.

"Who's there?" she shouted, her heart thumping. "Don't skulk in the dark."

"I'm here." The curtain to her own bedroom area twitched.

She strode over and swept the curtain aside. It was Chang An Lo. He was sitting on her bed.

"GET OUT."

"Listen to me, Lydia Ivanova. Listen to what I tell you."

"I *have* listened. You stole *my* ruby necklace, sold it down south somewhere, and gave the money away. I heard all right. And you expect me to believe you?"

"Yes."

"You are a lying, thieving, rotten, conniving, unscrupulous, filthy rat." She was storming up and down the room, completely indifferent to the fact she was wearing only her underwear. "And I wish I'd let that policeman put a bullet through your black heart when I had the chance."

"I came to tell you . . ."

"To tell me you robbed me. Well, thanks very much. Now leave." She pointed a finger at the door.

". . . to tell you why I did it."

The false-hearted toad was still standing in the center of the room, as calm and cool as if he had brought her flowers instead of lies, and that just made her want to choke him. She'd trusted him, that's how stupid she was, she'd trusted him, she who trusted no one. And what had he done? Just trailed her trust through the sewer and torn a raw hole in her insides.

"Get out," she yelled. "Go on, get out of here. I know why you did it and I don't want to hear a bunch of lies from you, so . . ."

A loud knock on the door stopped her. A voice called out, "Are you all right, Lydia?"

It was Mr. Yeoman from downstairs.

Lydia's eyes met Chang's, and for the first time she saw danger in them. He was up on his toes, ready to strike.

"No," she whispered harshly to him. "No."

"Are you having a spot of bother, dear? Do you need any help?"

Mr. Yeoman was an old man, no match for Chang. Lydia rushed to the door and opened it a crack. He was standing on the landing, his white hair bristling, a brass poker in his hand.

"I'm okay, Mr. Yeoman, thanks. Really. Just . . . arguing with a . . . a friend. Sorry we disturbed you."

His bright bird eyes peered at her, unconvinced. "Are you sure I can't help?"

"Sure. Thanks anyway."

She closed the door and leaned against it, breathing hard. Chang had not moved.

"You have good neighbors," he said in a quiet voice.

"Yes," she said more calmly, "neighbors who don't trick me with sly words." By the teasing light of the candle she could see the skin of his face grow taut across his high cheekbones and he started to speak, but she hurried on, "And if my mother should walk in now and find you here, she'd skin you alive, with or without your *kung fu* kicks. So . . . ," she reached for her dress and slipped it on, "we will go out into the street, you can tell me what it is you came to say, and then I never want to see you again. Understand?"

She heard his intake of breath, and it seemed to suck the air from her lungs.

"I understand."

★ ★ ★

SHE LED HIM TO A HOUSE TWO STREETS AWAY. IT WAS MORE of a shell than a house because it had burned down nine months ago but still lay like a blackened tooth stump in the middle of the brick terrace, and it had become home to bats and rats and the occasional feral dog. Much of what remained had been scavenged, but the outer walls still stood and gave a sense of privacy despite the lack of a roof. Rain had started to fall, a soft gloomy drizzle that sweetened the air and made Lydia's skin twitch.

"So?" She stood and faced him.

Chang took his time. In silence he made himself a part of the darkness and seemed to glide through the ruined rooms, no more solid than the wind that rippled up from the river and cooled Lydia's bare arms. When he was satisfied no others had taken refuge behind the black piles of rubble, he came back to her.

"Now we talk," he said. "I came to see you so that we would talk."

The faintest remnants from the street lamp on the far corner trickled into the space between them, and Lydia looked at Chang carefully. There was a change in him. She couldn't see how or what, but it was there. She could feel it. As she could feel the rain on her face. There was a new sadness at the corners of his mouth that tugged at her and made her want to listen to his heart, to learn why it was beating so slow. But instead she tossed her head and reminded herself that he'd used her, that all his concern for her was worth nothing. Just lies and rat droppings.

"So talk," she said.

"It would have killed you."

"What?"

"The necklace."

"You're crazy." She had visions of it throttling her as she tried it on.

"No, my words are true. You would have taken it to Junchow old town, to one of those snake holes that ask no questions. They rob the thieves that come to their doors but keep their hands white and clean. But no one would touch this necklace, no one would take that risk."

"Why?"

"Because already it was known that it was meant as a gift for Madame Chiang Kai-shek. So you would have returned empty-handed and before you reached home you would be dead in a gutter, the necklace gone."

"You're trying to frighten me."

"If I wanted to frighten you, Lydia Ivanova, there are many more things I could say."

Again his mouth revealed a sorrow that the rest of his face denied. She studied his lips with care and believed them. Standing in the rain in the middle of the filthy ruin under a night sky as black as death, she felt a cold rush of relief. She breathed deeply.

"It seems I owe you my life yet again," she said with a shiver.

"We are involved, you and I." His hand moved through the gap of yellow streetlight that lay between them and touched her arm, a faint brush of skin, no more than a moth's wing in the darkness. "Our fates are sewn together as surely as you stitched the flesh of my foot together."

His voice was as soft as his touch. Lydia felt the solid ball of anger inside her tremble and start to melt; she could feel it trickling through her veins and out through the pores of her skin into the rain where it was washed away. But what if these were lies too? More lies from those lips of his that could make her believe his words. She wrapped her arms around her body and refused to let the small hard core of her anger escape. She needed it. It was her armor.

"Involvement means sharing, doesn't it?" she said. "And it doesn't alter the fact that the necklace *was* mine. If you sold it somewhere in the south where they don't know the importance of it, then at least we should share the money. That sounds fair to me. Fifty-fifty." She held out a hand.

He laughed. It was the first time she'd heard him laugh and it did something strange to her. It made her mind uncurl. For that one fleeting moment she forgot the endless struggle.

"You are like a she-fox, Lydia Ivanova, you sink your teeth in and never let go."

She wasn't sure if that was an insult or a compliment but didn't stop to find out. "How much did you get for it?"

His black eyes watched her face, and still the laugh lingered on his lips. "Thirty-eight thousand dollars."

She sat down abruptly. On a low ragged wall. Put her head in her hands. "Thirty-eight thousand dollars. A fortune," she whispered. "My fortune."

The silence was broken only by something scuttling across the floor and making a dash for the doorway. Chang stamped on it. It was a weasel.

"Thirty-eight thousand," Lydia repeated slowly, rolling the words around her tongue like honey.

"As many lives were taken in Shanghai and Canton."

Canton? What was he talking about? What on earth did Canton have to do with her thirty-eight thousand dollars . . . ? Her mind felt clumsy, but then something clicked inside it. A massacre last year. She remembered everyone talking of it. And then there was the time in Shanghai when, on Chiang Kai-shek's orders, the Kuomintang Nationalists ambushed the Communists and wiped them out in bloody street fighting. A purge, they called it. But in China that was nothing new. Not remarkable. There was always some warlord or other, like General Zhang Xueliang or Wu Peifu, making pacts with another and then betraying each other in savage warfare. So what was it about Canton? Why did Chang bring up that particular incident?

She looked up at him. He had stepped deeper into the shadows, but his voice had given him away. It was so full of rage.

Suddenly it all made sense to her. She leaped to her feet.

"You're a Communist, aren't you?"

He said nothing.

"It's dangerous," she warned. "They behead Communists."

"And they jail thieves."

They stared at each other in the darkness. Silent accusations unspoken on their tongues. She shivered, but this time he did not touch her.

"I steal to survive," Lydia pointed out stiffly. "Not to indulge some intellectual ideal." She moved away from him. "I cannot afford ideals."

She did not hear his footfalls, but suddenly his dark figure was in front of her again. Rain glistened in his cropped hair and turned his skin silver.

"Look, Lydia Ivanova, look at this."

She looked. He was holding up something small and thin, hanging from his fingers. She peered closer at the object. It was the dead weasel.

"This," he said, "is my meal tonight. I am not the one who eats my food in a restaurant using sweet lies and false smiles. So do not offer words about the price of ideals. Not to me."

Lydia's cheeks burned.

"Settle this business now," she said more sharply than she intended. "I want my share of the money."

"You are always hungry like the fox. Here. Feed on this."

He held out a leather pouch to her. She took it. It felt light. Too light. She moved over to where the street lamp's glow was stronger, stepping over crumbling bricks and finding the open rectangle that had once been a window. In a rush her fingers opened the pouch and tipped out its contents, the same way they had trickled the ruby necklace into her palm not so long ago, but this time there were only a few coins. Did he think a handful of dollars would keep her quiet? She felt them smooth and warm against her skin, the price of his betrayal. Was she worth so little to him? She spun around and in three quick strides she was in front of him again. She pulled back her arm and hurled the pieces of silver into his face.

"Go to hell, Chang An Lo. What is the point of saving my life, if you destroy it?"

SHE DIDN'T GO HOME. THE THOUGHT OF BEING ALONE IN that miserable room was more than she could take right now. So she walked. Hard and fast. As if she could walk the heat from her blood.

Walking at this hour was not safe. Tales of kidnap and rape were always rife in the International Settlement, but it didn't stop her tonight. She wanted to rush down to the river where she could escape from the thousands of people all fighting for their square inch of air and space in Junchow, and maybe there she could breathe easier. But not even Lydia was that reckless. She knew about the river rats, the men with knives and a habit to feed, so she headed uphill, up Tennyson Road and Wordsworth Avenue where the houses were safe and respectable and where dogs in kennels kept watch for any stealthy tread.

She was angry with Chang An Lo. But worse, she was angry with herself. She'd let him get under her skin and make her feel . . . oh hell, . . . feel what? She tried to snatch at the swirling knot of emotions that was making her chest all blocked and tight, but they were jumbled together, snagged on one another, and when she pulled they dragged through her lungs and caught at the back of her throat like barbed wire. She kicked at a stone and heard it ricochet off the hubcap of a parked car. Somewhere a dog barked. A car, a house, a dog. With thirty-eight thousand dollars she could have had them all. There were twelve Chinese dollars to the English pound, that's what Parker had told her tonight, more than enough for what she wanted. Two passports, two steamer tickets to England, and a small redbrick house, one that had a bathroom and a parquet floor for dancing. A patch of lawn too for Sun Yat-sen. He'd like that.

Her thoughts shut down. It was too much. She pushed the images out of her mind, but she couldn't push away so easily the images of Chang's intent eyes and the whisper of his touch on her arm. It echoed through her, spreading over her skin from limb to limb.

She tried to work out what it was about him that was different tonight. He was thinner, yes, but it wasn't that. He'd always been lean. No, it was something about his face. In his eyes, in the set of his mouth. She had seen that same kind of expression once before, on Polly's face when her beloved cat Benji was run over. A look of constant pain. Not pain like when she'd sewn up Chang's foot. Something deeper. She longed to know what had happened to him to cause such a change since that day at Lizard Creek, but at the same time she swore to herself she would never ever speak to him again. Tonight he'd made her feel . . . what? What? What?

Bad. He'd made her feel bad about herself.

She turned in through a pair of stone pillars and wrought-iron gates—easy to climb over—and keeping in the deep shadow of the high box hedge that surrounded the property, she ran swiftly through the rain toward the back of the house.

"LYDIA! YOU'RE ALL WET." POLLY'S BLUE EYES WERE WIDE and startled, but her face was still soft with the mists of sleep.

"Sorry to wake you. I just had to come and tell you about . . ."

Polly was pulling at her, dragging the wet dress over Lydia's head and shaking it out with a sorrowful little moan of displeasure. "I hope it's not ruined."

"Oh Polly, never mind the dress. It got soaked when I wore it before but dried out fine. Well, almost fine. One or two water stains on the satin bit, that's all, so a few more won't hurt."

Polly placed the dress with care on a hanger. "Here, wear this."

She threw Lydia a dressing gown. It was white with small pink elephants round the hem and cuffs. Lydia thought it childish but put it on anyway to cover up her fleshless bones. Polly's body was all soft and full of curves, her breasts already full and mobile, while Lydia's were little more than upturned saucers. "When you get some food inside you, darling, they'll fill out, don't fret," her mother had told her. But Lydia wasn't so sure.

Polly sat down on her bed and patted the spot beside her. "Sit down and tell all."

That was one of the things Lydia loved about Polly. She was adaptable. She didn't mind in the least being woken in the middle of the night by a rap at her window and was happy to throw it open to her drenched nocturnal visitor. It was a simple climb up to the second floor, one Lydia had often done before, up the trellis, across the veranda roof, and an easy jump up to the windowsill. Fortunately Christopher Mason was so besotted by his dogs that they were allowed to sleep in the scullery whenever it rained, so there was no risk of losing a chunk of leg to sharp teeth.

"How did it go?" Polly demanded, excitement making her face look younger than her sixteen years. "Did you like him?"

"Like who?"

"Alfred Parker. Who else? Isn't that what you've come to tell me about?"

"Oh yes. Yes, of course. The dinner at La Licorne."

"So what happened?"

Lydia had to search a long way back in her mind. "It was fun. I had prawns in garlic sauce," she breathed heavily into Polly's face to offer proof, "and *steak au poivre* and . . ."

"No, no. Not the food. What was *he* like?"

"Mr. Parker?"

"Yes, silly."

"He was . . . kind." The word surprised Lydia, but when she thought about it she decided it was true.

"How dull!"

"Oh, yes, he's as dull as a Latin lesson. He thinks he knows everything and wants you to think the same. I got the feeling he likes to be admired."

Polly giggled. "Don't be such a dunce, Lyd, all men love to be admired. It's what they're about."

"Really?"

"Yes, really. Haven't you noticed? That's what your mother is so good at and why men flock round her."

"I thought it was because she's beautiful."

"Being beautiful isn't enough. You have to be smart." She shook her tousled blond hair with an affectionate smile. "My mother is absolutely useless at it."

"But I like your mother just as she is."

Polly grinned. "So do I."

"Are your parents in bed?"

"No, they're out at some party at General Stowbridge's place. They won't be back for hours yet." Polly jumped off the bed. "Nobody's here except the servants, but they're off in their own quarters, so shall we go down and make some cocoa?"

Lydia leaped at the offer. "Yes, please."

They hurried out of the room, down the stairs, and into the kitchen. Lydia felt more comfortable here. If she was honest with herself, she didn't actually like Polly's bedroom; it made her tense. It was Polly's behavior in it that unsettled her. Lydia had quickly learned to touch nothing. Absolutely nothing. If she picked up a hairbrush from the dressing table or a book from the bookcase, Polly got all twitchy and rushed to put it back in exactly the right spot and at exactly the right angle. Worse were the dolls. She had a whole row of twenty-three beautiful dolls lined up on a shelf, with china faces and hand-embroidered dresses. If any of them moved as much as a finger or a lock of hair, Polly noticed and felt compelled to strip the whole shelf and set them up again. It took forever.

Lydia steered well clear of them. The odd thing was that these weird obsessions fell away as soon as Polly left her room, and her desk at school was far more scatterbrained than Lydia's own. It was as if in the privacy of her own room she could indulge her anxieties and fears, but elsewhere she hid them away and smiled at the world. Lydia was always careful to make sure no one upset Polly, not even Mr. Theo.

"I'll just go and check on Toby," Polly said. "Won't be long." She disappeared into the scullery.

Lydia wandered into the hall, sliding her feet along the polished floor till they squeaked, and peeked into the drawing room just to catch a glimpse of the gramophone and its shiny brass horn in the hope that their aroma of luxury would drag her mind away from Chang. But they only made her feel worse. Next to the drawing room was the door to Polly's father's study, which was always kept firmly shut. For the hell of it, Lydia tried the handle. It turned.

The room was dark, but she didn't dare turn the light on. A bright yellow rectangle tumbled into the study from the doorway and lay across the big oak desk that sat squarely in the middle of the floor with a row of dark wooden filing cabinets behind it. On the wall opposite was a painting of a tall gray horse with one black hoof and beside it a portrait in oils of a nervous-looking young boy. Presumably Christopher Mason in earlier days. But Lydia's attention was not on the walls. It was on a large leather-bound book that lay on the desktop. With a rapid glance over her shoulder to see if Polly was anywhere near, she stepped into the gloomy room and leaned over the book. On its tan cover was the one word in gold-embossed letters. *DIARY.* She opened it. Quickly she flicked through until she came to the page that showed the date of the concert, July the fourteenth, Saturday.

His writing was large and hurried, a scribble of black ink that was difficult to read, but she made out enough. *Six a.m.—riding with Timberley. Eight-thirty—breakfast meeting with Sir Edward at the Residence.* Below it was something written in and scratched out again by heavy black lines followed by *Tiffin with MacKenzie* and then *Willoughby 7:30.* Finally, written in small letters at the bottom of the page, was *V.I. at Club.* It was underlined.

V.I.

Valentina Ivanova.

So the meeting had not been accidental.

"Lydia?" Polly's voice from the kitchen.

"Coming," Lydia called out. She skimmed through the previous pages. *V.I. V.I. V.I. V.I. V.I. V.I.* One in each month. From January to July. She flicked ahead. One scheduled for August the eighteenth.

"Lyd?" Polly's voice was closer.

She slammed the diary shut and made it to the door just as Polly was pushing it farther open.

"What are you doing in here?" The blue eyes were horrified. "No one is allowed in here, not even Mother."

Lydia shrugged but didn't reply. Her mouth was too dry.

BOTH GIRLS WERE STANDING IN THE KITCHEN BLOWING steam off their cocoa and Polly was laughing as Lydia told her about the way Alfred Parker's spectacles slid down his pink nose when Valentina invited him to remove a wayward crumb from her neck. There was the sound of a key in the front door. Polly froze. But Lydia moved fast. She tossed the last of her drink down the sink, pushed the cup inside a cupboard, and slipped behind the open kitchen door, where she was hidden from sight. She had no time for more than a glance at her friend, who was looking panicked. *Please, please, Polly, use your head.*

"So I really don't think the old boy should . . ." Christopher Mason stopped in midflow. His footsteps rang out crisply on the wooden floor, nearer now. "Polly? Is that you in there?"

For a sickening moment Lydia feared Polly was going to stand there like a rabbit pinned in speeding headlamps, but just in time she got her feet moving and walked out into the hall to greet him.

"Hello, Father. Did you have a nice time at the party?"

"Never mind that. What in blazes are you doing up at this hour?"

"Couldn't sleep. It's so hot and I was thirsty."

To Lydia her friend's voice sounded distinctly odd, but Mason didn't seem to notice. She could hear the evening's brandies blurring the edge of his words.

"Oh, my poor girl," Anthea Mason murmured. "Let me fetch you some cool lemonade. That will help to . . ."

"No, thanks, I've had a drink."

"Well, I'll fetch some for myself anyway. I have a splitting headache." The click of high heels heading Lydia's way.

"Mummy."

"Yes?"

"Let's sit down in the drawing room. I want you to tell me all about the party and what Mrs. Lieberstein wore this time. Did she . . . ?"

"It's much too late for that kind of nonsense now." It was Mason again. "You should be in bed, my girl."

"Oh, please."

"No. I won't say it twice. Upstairs with you."

"But . . ."

"Do as your father says, Polly, there's a good girl. We'll chat about the party tomorrow, I promise."

A pause. Then the sound of bare feet scampering across the hall.

Lydia held her breath.

Polly's door closed upstairs and the sound of it was like a signal to the pair standing in the hall.

"You're too soft on that girl, Anthea."

"No, I . . ."

"You are. You'd let her get away with bloody murder if I weren't here. I won't stand for it. You're letting me down, don't you realize that? It's your job to see she learns how to behave properly."

"Like you did tonight, you mean?"

"What exactly are you implying by that?"

A silence.

"Come on, I demand to know what you're implying?"

For a moment there was no answer, then a long sigh filled the silence. "You know precisely what I'm talking about, Christopher."

"Good God, woman, I'm not a damned mind reader."

"The American woman. Tonight at the party. Is that the way you'd like Polly to behave?"

"For Christ's sake, is that what this is all about and the reason you made me come home early? Don't be so absurd, Anthea. She was just being friendly and so was I, that's all. Her husband is a business contact of mine and if only you would be a bit more outgoing, a bit more fun at these . . ."

"I saw you both being *friendly* on the terrace."

It was said quietly. But the slap that followed it echoed around the hall, and Anthea's sharp gasp of pain drew Lydia from her hiding place. She stepped forward into the kitchen doorway, but the couple in the hall were too intent on each other to notice her. Mason was hunched forward like a bull, his neck sunk into the shoulders of his rumpled dinner jacket, one arm outstretched and ready to swing again. His wife was leaning back, away from him, one hand to her cheek where a red mark was flaring outward to her ear. The earring was missing.

Her blue eyes were huge and round, just like Polly's, but full of such despair that Lydia could hold back no longer. She darted forward but too late. Another slap sent Anthea Mason spinning around. She staggered, caught herself on the umbrella stand, and ran into the drawing room, slamming the door after her. Mason stormed into the dining room, where Lydia knew the brandy was kept, and kicked the door shut behind him. Lydia stood there in the middle of the hall, shaking with fury. From inside the drawing room she could hear the muffled sound of crying and she longed to rush in there, but she had enough sense to know she would not be welcome. So she walked back up the stairs, indifferent to how much noise she made, and returned to Polly's room.

One glance at her friend's face and Lydia knew Polly had heard enough of what had gone on downstairs. More than enough. Her mouth was pulled so tight it was almost bloodless, and she wouldn't look at Lydia. She was sitting on the edge of her bed, a doll clutched fiercely against her chest, her breath coming in quick little puffs. Lydia went over, sat down beside her and took one of Polly's hands in her own. She held it tight. Polly leaned against her and said nothing.

17

Chang was still there when the fox girl came back into the burned-out house. He'd waited for her alone in the darkness, knowing she'd return before she knew it herself. The rain had stopped and a thin sliver of moon shimmered on the wet bricks around him and caught the edge of one of the coins she had discarded so readily. He knew how much money meant to her, but he also knew it would not be the money that drew her back. As soon as she stepped over the threshold, he could see she no longer carried her anger with her or wanted to drive a sword through his heart. He thanked the gods for that. But her limbs seemed to weigh heavy on her and the line of her shoulders was curved down like a camel's back. It pained him to see it.

She stood by the empty doorway, letting her eyes adjust. "Chang An Lo," she called out. "I can't see you but I know you are here."

How did she know? Could she sense his presence as keenly as he sensed hers? He moved away from the wall and into the moonlight.

"I am honored by your return, Lydia Ivanova." He gave a deep bow to show her that he wanted no more harsh words between them.

"Why a Communist?" she asked and slumped down onto a block of concrete that had once been part of a chimney. "What makes you crazy enough to want to be a Communist?"

"Because I believe in equality."

"That makes it sound so simple."

"It *is* simple. It is only men with their greed who make it complicated."

She gave a strange snort of scorn that took him by surprise. No

Chinese woman would ever make such a noise in front of a man. "Nothing is ever that simple," she said.

"It can be."

The mandarins in her Western world had crowded her mind with untruths and blinded her eyes with the mist of deceit, so that she was seeing what they told her to see instead of what was in front of her. Her tongue was quick, but it tasted only the salt of lies. She knew nothing of China, nothing that was true. He moved around to squat down beside the wall again, the bricks solid at his back, and leaned forward to see her face more clearly. He had never known her so still or heard her voice so empty.

"Do you know," he asked in a gentle tone not meant to anger her, "that women and children are still sold as slaves? That absent landlords rob the peasants of the food on their tables and the crops in their fields? That villages are stripped of men, seized by the army, leaving the weak and the old to starve in the streets? Do you know these things?"

She looked at him, but her face gave nothing away tonight.

"China is not going to change," she said. "It's too big and too old. I've learned at school how emperors have ruled as gods for thousands of years. You can't . . ."

"We can." He felt the heat rising in his chest when he thought of what must yet be done. He wanted her to know it. "We can make people free, free to think, free to work for an equal wage. Free to own land. The workers of China are treated worse than pigs. They are stamped into the dung like beetles. But the rich eat from gold plates and study in the scrolls of Confucius how to be a Virtuous Man." He spat on the ground. "Let the Virtuous Man try a day on his hands and knees in the fields. See which matters more to him then, a perfect word in one of Po Chu-i's poems or a bowl of rice in his belly." He picked up a piece of broken brick at his side and crushed it against the wall. "Let him eat his poem."

"But Chang An Lo, you have eaten poems." She spoke quietly, but he could hear the impatience under her words. "You are an educated person and know it is the only way forward. You said yourself you came from a wealthy family with tutors and . . ."

"That was before my eyes were opened. I saw my family riding on the broken backs of slaves and I was ashamed. Education must be for all. For women as well as men. Not just the rich. It opens the mind to the future, as well as the past."

He thought of Kuan with her degree in law, so fierce in her determination to open the minds of the workers that she was prepared to work sixteen hours a day on a filthy factory floor where ten employees died each week from machine accidents and exhaustion. This fox girl knew nothing of any of this. She was one of the privileged greedy *fanqui* who had taken great bites out of his country with their warships and their well-oiled rifles. What was he doing with her? To ask her to change the patterns of her mind would be like asking a tiger to give up its stripes.

He stood up. He would leave her to her scattered coins and her thieving ways. One day she would be caught, one day she would grow careless, however closely he guarded her steps.

"You're going?"

"Yes." He bowed to her, low and respectful, and felt something split in his chest.

"Don't go."

He shut his ears and turned his back on her.

"Then say good-bye to me." Her voice seemed to grow emptier, as if she knew he would not return this time, and a small noise escaped from her throat. She held out her hand as the foreigners did.

He walked over to where she sat on the concrete, bent down to take her small hand in his, and as his face came closer to hers, he smelled the rain on her hair. He breathed it in and inhaled it deep into his lungs until the scent of her seemed to fill his mind, the way the river mists fill the night sky. Her hand lay in his and he could not make his fingers release it. The moon stepped back behind a cloud, so that her face was hidden from him but her skin felt warm against his own.

"And the foreigners?" Her voice was barely a whisper in the darkness. "Tell me, Chang An Lo, what do the Communists aim to do to the *fanqui*?"

"Death to the *fanqui*," he said, but he did not wish for her death any more than he wished for his own.

"Then I must put my faith in Chiang Kai-shek," she said.

She was smiling; he could hear it in her voice though he could not see it with his eyes, but he did not want her to say such words, not even in jest. He felt a fleck of anger land on his tongue like ash.

"The Communists will one day win, Lydia Ivanova, I warn you of that. You Westerners do not see that Chiang Kai-shek is an old tyrant under a new name." He spat again to the ground as the devil's name passed his lips. "He has a lust for nothing but power. He proclaimed that he will lead our country to freedom, but he lies. And the Kuomintang Central Committee is a dog that jumps when he cracks the whip. He will destroy China. He strangles at birth all signs of change, yet the foreigners feed him with dollars to make him grow wise, the way an emperor feeds his pet tiger with songbirds to make him sing."

His hand was gripping her fingers too hard and he could feel her bones fighting each other, but she gave no sign.

"It will never happen," he finished.

"But the Communists are cold killers," she said without withdrawing her hand. "They cut out their enemies' tongues and pour kerosene down their throats. They bring China's new industries to a halt with their strikes and sabotage. That's what Mr. Parker told me tonight. So why did you give them my necklace money?"

"For guns. Your Mr. Parker is twisting the tail of truth."

"No, he's a journalist." She shook her head and he felt a trickle of spray from her wet hair. It flicked on his cheek and set his skin alive. "He must know what's going on, that's his job," she insisted. "And he believes Chiang Kai-shek will be the savior of China."

"He is wrong. Your journalist must be deaf and blind."

"And he says the foreigners are China's only hope for the future if this country is to come out of the Dark Ages and modernize."

Chang dropped her hand. A surge of anger at the arrogance of the Foreign Devils rose in his throat and he cursed them for their greed and for their ignorance and for their vengeful god who would devour all others. Her golden eyes stared at him in confusion. She didn't understand and would never understand. What was he doing? He stepped back quickly, leaving her Mr. Parker's lies in her lap, but his fingers did not listen to his head and felt as empty as a river without fish.

"Did he not tell you, Lydia Ivanova, that the foreigners are cutting off China's limbs? They demand reparation payments for past rebellions. They cripple our economy and strip us naked."

"No."

"Nor that the foreigners rub China's bleeding face in the pig dung by their rule of extraterritorial rights in the cities they stole from us? With these rights the *fanqui* ignores the laws of China and makes up his own to please himself."

"No."

"Nor that he wrapped his fist around our customs office and controls our imports. His warships swarm in our seas and our rivers like wasps in a crate of mangoes."

"No, Chang An Lo. No, he did not." For the first time she seemed to gather fire into her words. "But this he did say, that until the people of China break free from their addiction to opium, they will never be anything but a weak feudal nation, always subservient to some kind of overlord's whim."

Chang laughed, loud and harsh, the sound raking across the broken walls.

She said nothing, just stared at him, shadows stealing her face from his eyes. Some night creature flitted silently over their heads, but neither looked up.

"That's something else your Parker forgot to tell you." His voice was so low she had to lean forward to hear, and again he breathed in the scent of her damp hair.

"What?"

"That it was the British who first brought opium to China."

"I don't believe you."

"It's true. Ask your journalist man. They brought it in their ships from India. Traded the black paste for our silks and our teas and spices. They brought death to China, not only with their guns. As surely as they brought their God to trample on ours."

"I didn't know."

"There is much you don't know." He heard the sorrow in his own voice.

In the long silence that followed, he knew he should leave. This girl was not good for him. She would twist his thoughts with a *fanqui's* cunning and bring him dishonor. Yet how could he walk away without tearing the stitching from his soul?

"Tell me, Chang An Lo," she said just as the headlamps of a car swept into their brick shell, revealing the tight grip of her fingers on a coin she must have picked up from the floor, "tell me what I don't know."

So he knelt down in front of her and started to talk.

THAT NIGHT YUESHENG CAME TO CHANG IN A DREAM. THE bullet that had smashed through his ribs and torn into his heart was no longer there, but the open hole remained and his face was well fed in the way Chang remembered from before the bad times.

"Greetings, brother of my heart," Yuesheng said through lips that didn't move. He was dressed in a fine gown with a round embroidered cap on his head and a hooded hunting hawk on his arm.

"You do me great honor to come to me before your bones are even in the earth. I mourn the loss of my friend and pray you are at peace now."

"Yes, I walk with my ancestors in fields thick with corn."

"That pleases me."

"But my tongue is sour with acid words and I cannot eat or drink till I have emptied them from my mouth."

"I wish to hear the words."

"Your ears will burn."

"Let them burn."

"You are Chinese, Chang An Lo. You come from the great and ancient city of Peking. Do not dishonor the spirit of your parents and bring shame on your venerable family name. She is *fanqui*. She is evil. Each *fanqui* brings death and sorrow to our people and yet she is bewitching your eyes. You must see clear and straight in this time of danger. Death is coming. It must be hers, not yours."

Suddenly, with a wet gushing sound, the hole in Yuesheng's body was filled with boiling black blood that smelled like burned brick, and a high-pitched noise issued from him. It was the sound of a weasel screaming.

THEO STOOD ON THE BANK AND SWORE. THE RIVER LAY flat as if it had just been ironed and the moonlight stretched long fingers over its surface, ruining all his hopes. The boat wouldn't come. Not on a night like this.

It was one o'clock in the morning and he had been waiting among the reeds for more than an hour. The earlier rain and heavy clouds had provided the perfect cover, a black soulless night with only the solitary light of an occasional flimsy fishing sampan burning holes in the darkness. But no boat came. Not then. Not now. His eyes were tired of peering into nothingness. He tried to distract himself with thoughts about what was taking place just a mile upriver in Junchow's harbor. Coastal patrol boats cruised in and out throughout the night, and once he heard the crack of gunfire. It gave him a quick pump of adrenaline.

He was hidden under the drooping boughs of a weeping willow that trailed its leaves in the water among the reeds, and he worried that he was too invisible. What if they couldn't find him? Damn it, life was always choked with *what ifs*.

What if he'd said no? *No* to Mason. *No* to Feng Tu Hong. What if . . . ?

"Master come?"

The faint whisper made him jump, but he didn't hesitate. He accepted the offered hand from the tiny wizened man in the rowboat and climbed in. It was a risk, but Theo was too deeply in to turn back now. In silence, except for the faintest sigh of oars through water, they traveled farther downriver, hugging the bank and seeking out the shadows of the trees. He wasn't sure what distance they rowed or how long it took, for every now and again the little Chinese river-jack shot the boat deep into the reeds and hung in there until whatever danger it was that startled him had passed.

Theo didn't speak. Noise carried over water in the still night air and he had no wish for a sudden bullet in the brain, so he sat immobile, one hand on each side of the rickety craft, and waited. With the moonlight camped possessively on the center of the river, he didn't see how they could possibly make the planned rendezvous, but this was the first run and he didn't want it to go wrong. He could taste the anticipation like a shot of brandy in his stomach and however much he tried to feel disgusted, he couldn't manage it. Too much rested on tonight. He trailed one hand in the water to cool his impatience.

And suddenly it loomed right there in front of him, the curved sweep of a large junk with the long pole to steer at the stern and black sails half furled. It lay in deep shadow in the mouth of an unexpected creek, invisible until you could reach out and touch it. Theo tossed a coin to the Chinese river-jack and leaped aboard.

"Look, Englishman." The master of the junk spoke Mandarin but with a strange guttural accent Theo could barely understand. "Watch."

He grinned at Theo, a wide predatory grin with sharp pointed teeth, then scooped up two fried prawns on the tip of his dagger, flicked them up into the air in a high arc, and caught them both in the cavern that was his mouth.

He offered Theo the knife. "Now you."

The man was wearing a padded jacket, as if the night were cold, and stank like a water buffalo. Theo separated out two good fat prawns from the pile in the wooden dish in front of him, balanced them on the blade of the knife, and tossed them into the air. One fell neatly into his mouth, but the second hit his cheek and skidded onto the floor. Instantly a gray shape darted out from a coil of rope, devoured the prawn, and slunk back to its rope bed. It was a cat. Theo stared. It was a rare sight these days. He assumed it must live permanently on the boat because if it set foot on dry land, it would be skinned and eaten before its paws were even dirty.

His host roared with laughter, unpleasant and insulting, then slammed a fist on the low table between them and emptied the contents of his horn beaker down his throat. Theo did the same. It was an evil-tasting liquid that had the bite of a snake, but he felt it squeeze the life out of his nerves, so he downed a second beaker and grinned back at the junk master.

"I will ask Feng Tu Hong for your worthless ears on a plate as payment for tonight's work if you do not show me respect," he said in Mandarin and watched the man's narrow eyes grow dull with fear.

Theo stuck the knife point into the table and left it swaying there. A hooded oil lamp that was slung from a hook just above their heads sent the crucifix shadow of the dagger sliding into Theo's lap. He reminded himself he didn't believe in omens.

"How long before we meet up with the ship?" he asked.

"Soon."

"When does the tide turn?"

"Soon."

Theo shrugged. "The moon is high now. The river's secrets are there for all to view."

"So, Englishman, that means tonight we will learn whether your word is worth its weight in silver taels."

"And if it's not?"

The man leaned forward and plucked out the knife. "If your word is worth no more than a *hutong* whore's promises, then this blade will make a journey of its own." He laughed again, his breath ripe in Theo's face. "From here," he jabbed the blade toward Theo's left ear, "to there." It came to rest under Theo's right ear.

"There will be no patrol tonight. I have it on good authority."

"May your tongue not lie, Englishman. Or neither of us will be alive to watch the sky grow pale." He drank another beaker of rotgut, rose heavily from his stump of a seat, and went out on deck in silence.

Except there was no silence here. The vessel creaked and flexed and groaned softly at every touch of a wave as it made good progress downriver. Theo could smell the salt water of the Gulf of Chihli and feel its clean breath sweeping away the stench of rotting fish and kerosene that filled the rattan hut in which he was sitting. The hut had a low curved roof, and the woven material was infested with insects that dropped at intervals into his hair or into the dish of fried prawns. He spied a fat millipede crawling on his shirt, picked it off with disgust, and dropped it in his host's beaker.

"You eat more?" It was the master's woman. She was small and timid, her eyes never rising to his.

"Thank you, but no. The sea turns my stomach into a mewling brat that cannot keep down good food. Maybe later, when this is over."

She nodded but didn't leave. Theo wondered why. She stood there, plump and greasy in a shapeless tunic, her black hair pulled back from her face and twined up into a loose coil, and she stared in silence at the cat. Theo waited, but no more words came from her. He tried to think what she might want. Food? Unlikely. She cooked fish and rice in a cauldron under another rattan shelter at the stern where, by the look of her, she fed herself well. She would never sit down to eat with the men because the act of eating was regarded by Chinese as ugly in a woman, so it was something she did in private, like pissing in a pot.

No, this was not about food.

"What is it?" he asked gently. He saw her swallow hard as if she had a fish bone in her throat. "Are you fearful that the guns will come tonight? Because I have promised that they will not attack us while we . . ."

She was shaking her head and her stubby fingers were twisting the amber beads round her neck into a tight knot. "No. Only the gods know what will be tonight."

"Then what is troubling you?"

A shout sounded on deck and feet raced past the hut. Quickly she turned to Theo. For the first time her small black eyes flicked up to his and he was shocked by the distress in them.

"It's Yeewai," she said. "It's not safe for her here among these men. They are brutal. Please take her to the International Settlement where she will be safe. Please, I beg you, master." She came so close to him he could smell the grease in her hair and held out a fist to him. When she opened it, four gold sovereigns lay on her palm. "Take this. To care for her. Please. It is all I have."

She glanced nervously in the direction of the opening to the hut, frightened her man would return, and Theo's eyes followed hers. He was expecting to see a young girl-child standing there, and already he was shaking his head in refusal.

"Please." She took his hand and thrust the gold into it, then turned and seized the cat. She crushed the animal's battered old face against her own and Theo heard a brief harsh sound issue from the creature's mouth that he assumed was meant to be a purr, before she threw it into a bamboo box and twisted a length of twine around to hold down the lid. She thrust the box into Theo's arms.

"Thank you, master," she said in a choked voice, tears flowing down her cheeks.

"No," Theo said and started to push it back at her, but she was gone. He was alone in the hut with a bad-tempered creature called Yeewai. "Oh, Christ! Not now. I don't need this now." He placed the bamboo box down on the planks next to the rope and gave it a kick. A growl like the sound of a blast furnace shot back at him and a claw raked his shoe.

THE WIND BLEW STRONGER NOW AND THE DECK SWAYED alarmingly under his feet, so that he felt the need to hold on to the wooden rail but would not allow himself that luxury. Beside him the master of the junk stood as solid and steady as one of the rocks that threatened to tear a hole in them if they dared to venture too close to shore. They were watching the mouth of the river, the waves etched in silver as the moon picked out a two-masted schooner with a long dark prow. It had tacked smoothly out of the bay and was gliding up toward them, its white sails spread wide like the wings of a black-necked crane against the night sky.

"Now," Theo muttered under his breath. "Now you shall measure the weight of my word."

"My life is on your word, Englishman," the Chinese skipper snarled.

"And my life depends on your seamanship."

The wind carried away his response. Suddenly the crew were readying a small craft to slide into the river, and fifty yards off Theo could see men on the schooner doing the same. Dark figures spoke in urgent whispers, and then the two scows pulled fast through the water toward each other until their port sides rubbed together like dogs greeting one another and a crate passed over their bows. It took no more than ten minutes for the boats to be back aboard the mother vessels and the crate to be hauled away from thieving hands into the rattan hut.

Theo could not bring himself to look at it, so he stayed on deck, but he could hear the junk master slapping his broad thighs and laughing like a hyena. Theo stood in the bows as they skimmed back upriver and was tempted to light a cigarette but thought better of it. Now that they were carrying the contraband they were in real danger, and a glowing cigarette end might be all it took. He was aware that the oil lamp in the hut had been extinguished and they were traveling across the water like a dark shadow, with only the moon's cold glare to betray them. He stuck a Turkish cheroot in his mouth and left it there, unlit.

He was trusting Mason. And deep in his heart he knew that was a mistake. If that bastard hadn't done his part, then the skipper was right. Neither of them would see the dawn. Damn him. With an uneasy growl he sucked on the cheroot, tasted its bitter dregs, and then tossed it down into the waves. Self-interest was Mason's bible. On that Theo had to rely.

But every breath of the way, he prayed for clouds.

THE PATROL BOAT CAME FROM NOWHERE. OUT OF THE night. Its engine roared into life and raced at them out of a narrow inlet, pinning the junk in its powerful searchlight and circling it with a fierce surge of bow wave. The junk rocked perilously. Two men leaped overboard. Theo didn't see them but he heard the splash. In a moment's madness it occurred to him to do the same, but already it was too late. A rifle in the patrol boat was fired into the air as a warning and the customs officers in their dark uniforms looked ready to back it up with more.

Theo ducked into the hut and before his eyes grew accustomed to the deeper level of darkness, he felt a knife at his back. No words were said. They were not necessary. To hell with Mason and his sworn oath. "No patrols tonight, old boy. You'll be safe, I swear it. They want you there on the boat."

"As a hostage to their own safety, I assume."

Mason had laughed as if Theo had made a joke. "Can you blame them?"

No, Theo couldn't blame them.

A match was struck and the kerosene lamp hissed into life, drenching the air with the stink of it. To Theo's surprise it was the junk master at the lamp. The knife was in the hand of the woman. Her man was growling something so rough and coarse that Theo couldn't understand, but he had no need to. The long curved blade in the skipper's right hand was not there to open the crate at his feet.

"*Sha!*" he shouted to the woman. *Kill.*

"The cat," Theo said quickly over his shoulder. "Yeewai. I'll take her."

The woman hesitated for only the beat of a wing but it was enough. Theo had his revolver out of his pocket and pointing straight at the junk master's heart.

"Put down the knives. Both of you."

The skipper froze for a moment, and Theo could see the black eyes calculating the distance across the hut to the Englishman's throat. That was when he knew he would have to fire. One of them would die right now and it wasn't going to be him.

"Master, come quick." It was one of the deckhands. "Master, come see. The river spirits have driven away the patrol boat."

It was true. The sound of the engine was fading, the fierce searchlight gone. Blackness seeped back into the hut. Theo lowered the gun and the junk master instantly leaped out on deck.

"They were bluffing," Theo muttered. "The patrol boat officers just wanted to let us know."

"Know what?" the woman whispered.

"That they are aware of what we're doing."

"Is that good?"

"Good or bad, it makes no difference. Tonight we win."

She smiled. Her front teeth were missing but for the first time she looked happy.

THE SHACK ON THE RIVERBANK WAS FOUL AND AIRLESS, BUT Theo barely noticed. The night was almost over. He was off the water and would soon be in his own bath with Li Mei's sweet fingers washing the sweat off his back. Relief thundered into his brain and suddenly made him want to kick Feng Tu Hong in the balls. Instead he bowed.

"It went well?" Feng asked.

"Like clockwork."

"So the moon did not steal your blood tonight."

"As you see, I am here. Your ship and crew are safe to run another night, another collection." He rested a foot on the crate that stood between them on the floor, as if it were his to give or take away at whim. It was an illusion. They both knew that. Outside, a cart stood ready.

"Your government mandarin is indeed a great man," Feng bowed courteously.

"So great that he talks to the gods themselves," Theo said and held out his hand.

Feng let his lips spread in what was meant to be a smile, and from a leather satchel on his hip he drew two pouches. He handed them to Theo. Both clinked with coins, but one was heavier than the other.

"Do not forget which is yours," Feng said softly.

Theo nodded with satisfaction. "No, Feng Tu Hong, I will not forget what I owe this mandarin, you may be sure of that."

"Don't be angry."

"I am not."

But she was standing stiff and silent by the window. Theo had not expected this.

"Please, Mei."

"It is only fit for the stewing pot."

"Don't be so brutal."

"Look at it, Tiyo, it's a disgusting creature."

"It will catch mice."

"So will a trap, and a trap doesn't stink like a camel's backside."

"I'll bathe it."

"But why?"

"I promised the woman."

"You promised her you'd take it. That doesn't mean you can't eat it."

"For heaven's sake, Mei, that's barbaric."

"What good is it? It will do nothing but eat and sleep and sharpen its claws on you. It's just ugly and nasty."

Theo looked at the gray cat hunched under a chair, its yellow eyes full of pus and hatred. It was certainly ugly, with half one ear missing and its face battered and scarred. Its fur was patchy and looked as if it had not been washed in months.

Theo sighed, exhaustion taking over. "Maybe I'm hoping that when I'm old and ugly and crochety, someone will do the same for me."

He caught her smiling at him.

"Oh, Tiyo, you are so . . . English."

HE LAY IN BED BUT HE DIDN'T SLEEP. LI MEI'S BREATH WAS sweet and warm on his neck and he wondered what dreams made her eyelids flicker so fast, but his own anger at what he had done tonight was too cold and hard in his chest to allow sleep to come. Drug trafficking.

He reminded himself of the reason why he'd risked his life out there on the river in a matchstick boat. His school. He would not give up his Willoughby Academy. Would not. Could not. What difference did it make?

But they would be over soon, these night excursions. He promised himself that.

19

LYDIA WAS AT HER SCHOOL DESK WHEN THE POLICE CAME for her. She was in the middle of writing into her exercise book a list of the mineral wealth of Australia. There seemed to be a lot of gold down there. Miss Ainsley escorted the English officer into the classroom, and Lydia knew before he even opened his mouth that she was the one he'd come to arrest. They'd found out about the necklace. But how? The fear that, because of her, Chang might also be cornered by police made her feel ill.

"How can I help you, Sergeant?" Theo asked. He looked almost as shocked by the intrusion as she was herself.

"I'd like a word with Miss Lydia Ivanova, if I may." The policeman in his dark uniform overpowered the classroom; his broad shoulders and big feet seemed to fill the space between the floor and the ceiling. His manner was polite but curt.

Mr. Theo walked over to Lydia and rested a hand on her shoulder. She was surprised by his support.

"What is this about?" he asked the sergeant.

"I'm sorry, sir, I can't discuss that. I just need to take her down to the police station for a few questions."

Lydia was so panicked by his words that she even thought of making a run for it, but she knew she didn't stand a chance. Anyway her legs were trembling too much. She'd just have to lie, and lie well. She stood up and gave the sergeant a confident smile that made the muscles of her cheeks hurt.

"Certainly, sir. I'm happy to help."

Mr. Theo patted her back and Polly gave her a grin. Somehow

Lydia made her legs move, one foot in front of the other, heel-toe, heel-toe, heel-toe, and wondered if anyone else could hear the banging in her chest.

"Miss Ivanova, you were at the Ulysses Club the night the ruby necklace was stolen."

"Yes."

"You were searched."

"Yes."

"Nothing was found."

"No."

"I'd like to apologize for the indignity."

Lydia remained silent. She watched warily. He was laying a trap for her, she was certain, but she couldn't yet see how or where.

It was Commissioner Lacock himself, so she knew she was in real trouble. Just being in the police station at all was bad enough, but to be escorted into the commissioner's office and told to sit down in front of his big glossy desk made her hear the clang of the prison cell door in her head. Shut in. Four bare walls. Cockroaches and fleas and lice. No air. No life. She was frightened she would blurt it out, confess everything, just to get away from this man.

"You gave me a statement that night."

She wished he'd sit down. He was standing behind his desk with a sheet of paper in his hand—what was on it?—and was studying her with gray eyes so sharp she could feel them piercing through each layer of her lies. The monocle just made it worse. His uniform was very dark, almost black, full of gold braid and bright silver bits that she felt were designed to intimidate. Oh yes, she was intimidated all right but had no intention of letting him know it. She concentrated on the tufts of hair poking out of his ears and the ugly liver spots on his hands. The weak bits.

"Commissioner Lacock, has my mother been informed I'm here?" She made it haughty. Like Countess Serova and her son Alexei.

He frowned and rubbed an impatient hand across his thinning hair. "Is that necessary at the moment?"

"Yes. I want her here."

"Then we shall fetch her." He gave a nod to a young policeman positioned by the door, who promptly disappeared. One down, one more to go.

"And do I need a lawyer?"

He placed the sheet of paper on top of a pile on his desk. She wanted to read it upside down but didn't dare take her eyes from his. He was staring at her with what looked like an amused expression. Cat and mouse. Play before you pounce. Her hands were sweating.

"I hardly think so, my dear. We've only asked you down here to pick a man out of a lineup."

"What?"

"Yes, the man you described in your statement. The prowler you saw through the library window of the Ulysses Club. Remember him?"

He was waiting for a reply. Relief had robbed her of breath. She nodded.

"Good, then let's go and take a look at them, shall we?"

He walked over to the door and to Lydia's amazement her own legs followed as if it were easy.

I⊤ WAS A PLAIN ROOM WITH GREEN WALLS AND BROWN linoleum on the floor. Six men stood in a row and each one of them turned hostile brown eyes on her as she entered, flanked by two policemen. The policemen were burly and big, but the men in the lineup were bigger, shoulders as wide as a shed and fists like slabs of meat at their sides. Where had they found them all?

"Take your time, Miss Ivanova, and remember what I told you," Lacock said and led her to one end of the row. "Eyes front," he ordered sharply and it took her a moment to realize it was addressed to the six men.

What had he told her? She tried to recall but the sight of the row of silent men had jammed her mind. She couldn't take her eyes off them. All the same, yet all so different. Some were taller or broader or older. Some were mean and arrogant, others were bowed and broken. But all had black bushy beards and wild hair, and were dressed in rough tunics and long boots. Two had a dark leather patch over one eye and one had a gold tooth that glinted like an accusing eye at her.

"Don't be nervous," Lacock encouraged. "Just walk slowly down the line, looking at each face carefully."

Yes, that's right, she was remembering his instructions now, walk along the row, say nothing, then walk the row a second time. Yes. She could do it. And then she'd say it was none of these men. Easy. She took a deep breath.

The first face was cruel. Hard cold eyes, a twisted lip. The second and third were sad with gaunt faces and a hopeless air, as if they expected nothing except death. The fourth was proud. He wore an eye patch and held himself well, sticking out his barrel chest, his oily curls unable to hide the long scar on his forehead. This one looked her straight in the eye and she knew him at once, the big bear of a man she'd seen down in her street the day before the concert. The one with the howling wolf on his boots. He was the man she'd described to the police in the hope of distracting their attention from herself. She kept her own face blank and moved on to the last two, but she barely saw them. An impression of bulk and muscle and a crooked nose. Number Six wore an eye patch, she noticed that. Stiffly she walked back to the beginning and put herself through it once more.

"Take your time," Lacock murmured again in her ear.

She was going too fast, slowed her pace, made herself stare into each grim dark face. This time Number Four, the one with the wolf boots, raised an eyebrow at her, which made the commissioner rest his baton heavily on the man's shoulder.

"No liberties," he said in a voice accustomed to instant obedience, "or you'll spend the night in jug."

Just when Lydia thought it was all over and she could escape this dismal green room, it got worse. The last man spoke. He was smaller than the rest but still big and wore the eye patch. "No say it's me, miss. Please not. I got wife and . . ."

A baton in the hand of the sergeant slammed into the side of his head. Blood spurted out of his nose and over Lydia's arm. The sleeve of her white school blouse turned red. She was bundled out of the room before she could open her mouth, but the moment she was back in Commissioner Lacock's office she started to complain.

"That was brutal. Why did . . . ?"

"Believe me, it was necessary," Lacock said smoothly. "Please leave the policing to us. If you give those Russkies—excuse the expression—an inch, they'll take a mile. He was told to say nothing and he disobeyed."

"Were they all Russians?"

"Yes, Russians and Hungarians."

"Would you have treated an Englishman like that?"

Lacock frowned heavily and looked as if he were about to say something sharp to her, but instead asked, "Did you recognize any of them as the face of the prowler you saw at the Ulysses Club?"

She shook her head. "No."

"Are you sure?"

"Yes. Absolutely certain."

His shrewd eyes studied her carefully, and then he leaned back in his chair, removed his monocle, and spoke in a concerned voice. "Don't be nervous of telling the truth, Lydia. We won't let any of those men come anywhere near you, so you needn't be afraid. Just speak out. It's the Russki with the scar on his forehead, isn't it? I can tell you've seen that one before."

Abruptly the room was spinning around her and the commissioner's face was receding into a tunnel. There was a booming in her ears.

"Burford," Lacock ordered, "bring the girl a glass of water. She's as white as a sheet."

A hand touched her shoulder, steadied her swaying body; a voice was saying something in her ear but she couldn't make it out. A cup was pressed to her lips. She took a sip, tasting hot sweet tea, and gradually something began to penetrate the mists that fogged her brain. It was a smell. A perfume. Her mother's eau de toilette. She opened her eyes. She hadn't even realized they were closed, but the first thing they saw was her mother's face, so close she could have kissed it.

"Darling," Valentina said and smiled. "What a silly you are."

"Mama." She wanted to cry with relief.

Her mother held her close and Lydia breathed in her perfume till it cleared her head, so that when Valentina released her she was able to sit up straight and accept the cup of tea with a steady hand. She looked directly at Commissioner Lacock.

"Commissioner, there was no face at the window the night the necklace was stolen."

"What are you saying, young lady?"

"I made it up."

"Now look here, there's no need to back out just because you've seen a roomful of rough rogues who have put the fear of the devil into you. Tell the truth and shame the devil, that's . . ."

"Mama, tell him."

Valentina looked at her and made a little grimace with her mouth that Lydia knew meant she was annoyed.

"As you wish, *dochenka*." She lifted her head, sending her hair rippling in a dark wave around her shoulders, then turned serious eyes on the chief of police. "My daughter is a lying little minx who should be whipped for wasting police time. She saw no face at the window. She makes up such stories to get attention. I apologize for her misbehavior and promise to punish her severely when I get her home. I had no idea her stupid tale would be taken so seriously or I would have come and told you before now not to believe a word of it."

She lowered her eyelashes for a moment in a display of maternal distress, then looked up slowly and fixed her eyes on Lacock's. "You know," she said softly, "how silly adolescent girls can be. Please excuse her this time, she meant no harm." She turned her dark gaze on her daughter. "Did you, Lydia?"

"No, Mama," Lydia murmured and had to bite back a smile.

"I MEAN IT. I'LL GIVE YOU A GOOD WHIPPING WITH MR. YEO- man's horsewhip tonight."

"Yes, Mama."

"You are a disgrace to me."

"I know, Mama. I'm sorry."

"Where in God's name did I go wrong? You are a wild thing and deserve to be locked up in a cage. You know that's true, don't you?"

"Yes, Mama."

"So." She stood in the middle of the pavement with her hands on her hips and stared at her daughter. "What am I to do with you?" She was wearing an old but stylish linen suit the color of ice cream, and it made her pale skin look like silk. "I'm so pleased the commissioner gave you such a telling off. Good for him. He had every reason to. Don't you agree?"

"Yes, Mama."

Suddenly Valentina burst out laughing and gave Lydia a quick kiss on her forehead. "You are wicked, *dochenka*," she said and rapped her daughter's knuckles with her clutch bag. "Take yourself off back to school now and don't you ever give them reason to drag me to that police station again. You hear me?"

"Yes, Mama."

"Be good, my sweet." Valentina laughed and stuck out a hand for a rickshaw. "The offices of the *Daily Herald*," she called to the coolie as she jumped in, leaving Lydia to walk up the hill to school.

SHE DIDN'T GO BACK TO SCHOOL. SHE WENT HOME IN-stead. She was too rattled. It frightened her that she had so nearly pointed to Number One, the man with the hard eyes, and said, *He's the one. That's the face I saw at the window. He's the thief.* It would have made everything so easy, and Commissioner Lacock would have been happy rather than angry.

She sat in the shade on the paving stones in the little backyard and fed Sun Yat-sen strips of a cabbage leaf she had scrounged from Mrs. Zarya. She scratched the bony top of his head where he liked to be rubbed and ran her hand over the silky fur of his long ears. She envied him the ability to find total happiness in a cabbage leaf. Though she did understand it. Valentina had brought home a box of Lindt chocolates last night, a big white and gold one, and they had eaten pralines and truffle cones for breakfast. It had felt like heaven. Alfred was certainly generous.

She tucked her legs up tight against her chest and sank her chin onto her knees. Sun Yat-sen stood up on his hind legs, rested a soft front paw on her shin, and twitched his nose in her hair while she traced a finger down the long line of his spine and wondered how far a person would go to have someone to love. Alfred was in love with her mother. Oh, any fool could see that. But how did Valentina feel about Alfred? It was hard to say, because she was always so bloody private about what went on in her head, but surely she couldn't love him. Could she?

Lydia thought about that till the sun had disappeared completely behind the roof ridge, about exactly what it meant to be loved and protected. Then she wrapped her arms round the rabbit and held him close, her cheek tight against his little white face. He never seemed to mind how much she squeezed him; it was one of the things she adored about him, his squashiness. She kissed his pink nose and decided to let him roam loose in the yard and hope Mrs. Zarya wouldn't notice, before she ran up to the attic and snatched a knotted handkerchief from under her mattress.

The handkerchief lay heavy in her pocket as she made her way across to the old Chinese town, and her footsteps quickened at the thought that she might bump into Chang somewhere in its narrow cobbled streets. But all she encountered were cold hostile stares and the hiss of words that made her want Chang at her side. It annoyed her that she had no idea where he lived, but she'd never yet felt able to ask him outright, to tear aside that strange cloak of secrecy he hid under. But next time she would. Next time? Her heart gave a little clatter under her ribs.

GLASS LAY SCATTERED ACROSS THE COBBLES OF COPPER Street and no one was doing anything about it. A young man carrying a yoke pole around his neck hobbled past Lydia, leaving an imprint in blood at every step, but most people scuttled against the opposite wall and kept their eyes averted. Only the rickshaw runners were forced to cross the glass. Those wearing straw sandals were lucky; those with bare feet were not.

Lydia stood and stared in horror at Mr. Liu's shop front. At where it had been. It was now a naked gaping hole. Everything was smashed into thousands of pieces; his glass window, his red latticework, his printed signs and scrolls, even the door and its frame lay twisted on the ground. The shops of the candlemaker and the charm seller on each side of it were untouched, open for business as usual, so whatever or whoever had done this had aimed it just at him. At Mr. Liu. She stepped inside what was left of the pawnbroker's, but it was no longer dark and secretive. Sunlight strode in, exposed the packed shelves to any passing gaze, and Lydia felt a sharp tug of sympathy for the place. She knew the value of secrets. In the center of the room Mr. Liu sat still as stone on one of his bamboo stools, while across his knees lay the long blade of the Boxer sword that used to hang on the wall. There was blood on it.

"Mr. Liu," she said softly, "what happened?"

He raised his eyes to her face, and they were older, much older. "Greetings to you, Missy." His voice was like a faint scratching on a door. "I apologize that I am not open for business today."

"Tell me what happened here?"

"The devils came. They wanted more than I could give."

Around his feet the jewelry display cases were crushed and empty. Lydia felt a lurch of alarm. The shelves didn't look as if they had been touched, but the really valuable stuff was gone.

"Who are these devils, Mr. Liu?"

He shrugged his thin shoulders and shut his eyes. The world blocked out. She wondered what inner spirits he was calling on. But what she couldn't understand was why nothing was being done to clear up the mess, so she went over to where the inlaid screen used to stand, now trampled into the floor, and set his kettle on the little stove at the back. She made them both a cup of jasmine tea on a tray and carried it over to him and his sword. His eyes were still closed.

"Mr. Liu, something to cool your blood."

A faint flicker of a smile moved his lips and he opened his eyes.

"Thank you, Missy. You are generous, and respectful to an old man."

Only then did she realize the oiled queue that used to hang down his back had been chopped off and was lying on the floor, and his long tufty beard had been hacked back to gray stubble. The indignity of such an act overwhelmed her for a moment. Worse than the attack on the shop. Far, far worse.

She pulled up the other stool and sat down on it. "Why doesn't anybody come to help?" People were passing in full view of them, but their faces looked the other way.

"They are afraid," he said and sipped the scalding liquid with indifference. "I cannot blame them."

Lydia stared at the sword, at the blood turning brown. The attack must have happened only shortly before she arrived because part of it still glistened on the blade.

"Who are these devils?"

A long silence settled in the shop alongside the dust and the shattered glass while Mr. Liu started to breathe deeply in and out, long and slow.

"You don't want to know such things," he said at last.

"I do."

"Then you are a fool, Missy."

"Was it the Communists? They need money for guns, I hear."

He turned his black eyes on her, surprised. "No, it was not the Communists. Where does a foreigner such as you hear of those people?"

"Oh, around. Word spreads."

His eyes were sharp. "Take care, Missy. China is not a place like others. Here different rules apply."

"So who are the devils who make up the rules that say they can destroy your shop and take your money? Where are the police? Why don't they . . . ?"

"No police. They will not come."

"Why not?"

"Because they are paid not to come."

Lydia felt cold, despite the tea. Mr. Liu was right; this was not her world. Chinese police were not like Commissioner Lacock. The chief of police in the International Settlement, whom she had loathed so passionately only a couple of hours ago, suddenly appeared to be a reasonable and honorable figure. Respected and reassuring. She wanted his monocle and his authoritative voice to storm up here and sort out this mess. But this was not in his jurisdiction. This was Chinese Junchow. She sat in silence. Nothing was said for so long that it came as a slight shock when Mr. Liu lifted up the sword in one hand, pointing it straight out in front of him, and said, "I cut one."

"Badly?"

"Bad enough."

"Where?"

"I sliced the tattoo off his neck." He said it with quiet pride.

"Tattoo? What kind of tattoo?"

"What is it to you?"

"Was it a snake? A black snake?"

"Maybe."

But she knew she was right. "I've seen one."

"Then look away or the black snake will bite out your heart."

"It's a gang, isn't it? One of the triads. I've heard about these brotherhoods that extort money from . . ."

He held a hooked finger to his lips. "Don't even speak of them. Not if you want to keep your pretty eyes."

She slowly placed her tiny cup on the enameled tray on the floor. She didn't want him to see her face. He had frightened her.

"What will you do?" she asked.

He brought the sword crashing down onto the tray, slicing it neatly in half and making Lydia leap to her feet.

"I will pay them," he said in a whisper. "I will find the dollars somewhere and pay them. It is the only way to put food on my family's table. This was just a warning."

"Can I help you sweep up the glass and . . . ?"

"No." It was harsh the way he said it, as if she'd offered to chop off his feet. "No. But thank you, Missy."

She nodded. But did not leave.

"What is it, Missy?"

"I came to do business."

He spat viciously on the floor. "I have no business today."

"I came to buy, not to sell."

It was as if a key turned. His dull eyes brightened and he found his shopkeeper's smile. "How can I help you? I'm sorry so much is damaged but . . . ," he glanced to the rail at the back of the shop, "the furs are still in excellent condition. You always liked the furs."

"No furs. Not today. What I want is to redeem the silver watch I brought last time." She slid her hand into her pocket where the handkerchief lay. "I have money."

"So sorry, it is already sold."

Her small cry of dismay surprised him. He studied her face carefully.

"Missy, today you have been good to an old man when no one of his own kind would even look at him. So today you have earned a kindness in return." He walked over to the black stove and lifted down a brown glazed pot from the shelf that held the lacquered tea caddies. He opened it and took out a small felt package.

"Here," he said. "How much did I pay you for the watch?"

Not for one moment did she think he had forgotten.

"Four hundred Chinese dollars."

He held out his frail bird-claw hand.

From her pocket she lifted out the handkerchief containing the money and placed it in his palm. His fingers closed quickly around it. She took the felt package and, without even looking at it, put it in her pocket.

He was pleased. "You bring the breath of fire spirits with you, Missy." He watched her for a moment, and she tucked a copper strand of hair behind her ear self-consciously. "You take risks coming here, but the fire spirits seem to guard you. You are one of them. But a snake has no fear of fire, he loves its warmth, so tread carefully."

"I will." As she picked her way out through the debris, she looked back over her shoulder. "Fire can devour snakes," she said. "You watch."

"Stay away from them, Missy. And from the Communists."

The mention surprised her. On impulse she asked, "Are you a Communist, Mr. Liu?"

His face barely changed, but she felt the door slam down between them.

"If I were foolish enough to be a supporter of Communism and of Mao Tse-tung," he said in a louder voice, as if talking to someone out in the street, "I would deserve to have my head rammed on a stake on the town wall for all the world to throw filth at."

"Of course," she said.

He bowed to her, but not before she saw the smile.

20

HE COULD BE DEAD. FOR ALL SHE KNEW. CHANG COULD BE dead already. The words clanged in Lydia's head like one of their god-damn brass bells, its vibration chipping pieces out of her. They could have hunted him down and struck. Like Mr. Liu. But worse.

She raced back through the old town, her eyes scouring this time for the brand of the Black Snake among the noisy crowds that tramped the narrow streets. On one corner she stumbled across a storyteller in his booth with his audience perching, entranced, on wooden benches around him, and one of them looked up at her with narrow eyes that seemed to know her. She had never seen him before, she was certain. His neck was wrapped in a loose black scarf and she wanted to tear it off to look underneath. Would she find a snake? Or blood from Mr. Liu's sword? His silent gaze seemed to follow her down the street. She ran faster. Out under the ancient arch and up the Strand into the Settlement.

The library. Cool in there. Safe in there. No Chinese allowed inside.

She was out of breath by the time she reached the ornate stone building with its gothic windows and arched entrance. It stood right in the center of the International Settlement, straddling the main square, and she only just remembered to say a polite "Good after-noon" to Mrs. Barker at the desk. She dashed into one of the dozens of long and dim aisles lined with shelf after shelf of books right up to the ceiling, and she hurried down to its far end, like a fox going to earth.

She breathed deeply. It was a struggle. Everything out of control. Her lungs didn't want to fill up and her knees were shaking in time to the racketing of her heart. *Chang An Lo, where are you?*

This was panic. Blind panic. Just the thought annoyed her. That helped. Annoyance. It began to elbow out the frantic thoughts of snakes and swords whirling around her brain and she felt clear air open up in there, so that she could think straight.

Of course he wasn't dead. Of course not. She would feel it if he were. She was sure she would. But she must find him, warn him.

Of course the man listening to the storyteller wasn't one of them. Of course not. He'd stared at her just because he didn't like Foreign Devils in the Chinese town. That's all.

Of course. Of course. Don't be absurd.

She sank down to the cool tiled floor, her head leaning against the good solid English rack of books stacked behind her. She had no idea which ones they were but liked the contact with them. They comforted her in some strange way she didn't understand. She shut her eyes.

"TIME TO GO, LYDIA."

Lydia opened her eyes. She blinked in the overhead light and jumped to her feet.

"Dozed off, did you, dear? I expect you've been working too hard." Mrs. Barker's face was kindly with big freckles like raindrops on her nose, and she sometimes saved a toffee in her desk for Lydia. "We're closing in ten minutes."

"I'll be quick," Lydia said and hurried into another aisle.

Her head felt like lead. Her thoughts were still snatching jerkily at scraps of violent dreams that had haunted her brief sleep, but she recognized the man in front of her instantly. He was reaching for a book on a high shelf, unaware of her presence, and she caught sight of the title. *Photography: The Nude Figure: Female.*

"Hello, Mr. Mason. I didn't know you were interested in photography."

He jumped; she saw his fingers nearly slide off the book, but he gathered himself well and turned his head casually. His expression was friendly, but his dark suit made him look authoritative and remote.

"Well I'm blowed, I didn't expect to find you here, Lydia. Shouldn't you be at home doing homework?"

"I'm just finding some books."

"Run along, then. Mrs. Barker wants to close."

"Yes, I will." But she twiddled a finger idly over the spines of a row of poetry volumes in front of her and waited to see if he would put the book back. He did.

"Do you know what I would like, Mr. Mason?" She didn't even bother to look at him.

"What's that?"

"An ice cream."

He actually managed to smile at her as he said, "Then let me buy you one, Lydia."

THE RAIN HAD STARTED UP AGAIN, SHARP AND STINGING, BY the time she hurried home. In the attic she found her mother preparing to go out for the evening and she felt a kick of disappointment. Oh yes, the job. For a moment she had forgotten, the dance hostess job. It paid the rent and that's what she wanted, wasn't it? So she mustn't complain, but she didn't want to be on her own, not tonight. Valentina was artfully twisting her hair up on top of her head and her eyes were bright with anticipation.

Not just the job then.

"Is Alfred joining you again tonight?" She picked up one of her mother's hairpins lying on the floor and detached two long dark hairs from it. She twined them around her finger.

Valentina was humming a snatch of Beethoven's Fifth but silenced herself to apply the vivid carmine lipstick that Lydia loved.

"Yes, he's picking me up, darling." She turned her head sideways in the mirror to study the effect. "He comes to the hotel every night I work and buys all my dances. He's a dream."

"What dull dreams you have, Mama."

"Poof, don't be so ridiculous," Valentina snapped. "He's helping us. Where do you think your supper came from?" She gestured to a large slice of veal pie on a plate with melon and a French baguette. "You should be grateful."

Lydia said nothing but sat down at the table and opened one of the poetry books she had brought home from the library. She flicked through the pages and said as if it had only just occurred to her, "Why don't you invite him up here for a minute, so I can thank him myself?"

Valentina stopped powdering her throat. She was wearing the navy silk dress again, the one Alfred Parker said he admired, but Lydia was quite sure that to Alfred even sackcloth and ashes would look heavenly if Valentina was wearing it.

"Why?" her mother said warily. "What are you up to?"

"Nothing."

"You are never up to nothing, *dochenka*. Look at this afternoon with the commissioner. I meant it when I said you are too wild and deserve a whipping."

"I know, Mama."

Valentina fastened a cloisonné necklace around her throat.

"That's pretty, Mama. Is it new?"

"Mmm."

"I'll behave better, you'll see. So will you invite Mr. Parker up here before you leave? Please."

Valentina ran a hand along her jawline as if searching out any flaws. "I suppose so."

ALFRED PARKER BEAMED AT LYDIA. "THIS IS NICE."

He was wearing an elegant charcoal suit and had put something shiny on his brown hair so that it gleamed, and to Lydia he did look quite decent for once. Shame about the spectacles though. He was drinking the little shot of vodka she had poured him and didn't even mention that it was in a cup. Lydia was back at the table with her book.

"Busy with homework, eh?"

"Yes."

He stepped closer and peered at her book. His waistcoat smelled of tobacco. "Wordsworth, I see."

"Yes."

"Do you like poetry?"

"Yes."

"Ah."

"Lydochka," Valentina said in a voice that was much too polite, "I believe you wanted to say something to Alfred."

"Yes."

Alfred beamed at her again.

She took a deep breath. "I am sorry I behaved badly toward you and I want to thank you for your kindness to me." She glanced at her mother's necklace. "To us. And so I would like to give you this."

The words had come out faster than when she'd rehearsed them in her head. She held out the small felt package tied up in the red ribbon that had been on Sun Yat-sen's hatbox. Alfred looked impressed.

"Lydia, my dear, no need for gifts, I assure you."

"I want you to have it."

Even her mother was looking pleased.

"Thank you, how nice," he said as he accepted the present and placed an embarrassed kiss on Lydia's cheek. His jaw was rough against her skin. Carefully he unwrapped the bow and the felt, clearly expecting a homemade trinket of some sort. When he saw the silver hunter watch gleaming in his palm, his face drained till it was paper white, and he sat down heavily on the sofa.

Valentina was the one to speak. "Good God, little one, where on earth did you find that? It's beautiful."

"In a pawnshop."

Alfred Parker was fingering the watch, opening its case, winding its spring, adjusting its hands, as if his own hands couldn't get enough of it. Without for one second taking his eyes off it, he said in an amazed tone, "It's mine."

"Yes."

"How did you know which pawnshop to find it in?"

"Because I put it there."

Valentina glared at Lydia over Alfred's head and made a savage twisting gesture with her two hands, as if she wanted to wring her daughter's neck.

Slowly Alfred looked up and stared at Lydia, comprehension seeping in. "You stole it?"

"Yes."

He shook his head. "You mean you stole my father's watch from me?"

"Yes."

He rubbed a hand across his mouth, holding in the words. "No wonder you asked if it was valuable."

Lydia was feeling worse than she'd expected. He'd gotten the watch back, so why didn't he go now? Go and dance.

But he stood up and walked over to her until he was standing right next to the table and she could see the hairs in his nose.

"You are a very wicked girl," he said and his voice sounded all tight, as though he were in physical pain. "I will pray for your soul." One hand held the watch, the other was clenched on the table, and she knew there was a lot more he wanted to say but didn't.

"You have it back now," Lydia mumbled, her eyes refusing to back down from his. "Your father's watch. I thought you'd be pleased."

He said nothing, just turned and walked out of the room.

"*Dochenka*, you little fool," Valentina hissed at her, "what have you done?"

IT WAS AFTER MIDNIGHT WHEN LYDIA HEARD HER MOTHER return. Her footsteps in the black and silent room sounded loud, her high heels click-clacking on the floorboards, but Lydia lay in bed, face to the wall, pretending she was asleep. She refused to open her eyes, even when Valentina pulled aside her curtain and sat down on the end of Lydia's bed. She sat there for a long time. Without speaking. Lydia could hear her uneven breathing and the rustle of her skirt, as if her fingers were as busy as her thoughts. The church clock struck twelve-thirty and, after what seemed an age, one o'clock, and only then did Valentina speak.

"You are lucky you are still alive, Lydia Ivanova. Maybe he didn't skin you alive, but I nearly did. You frighten me."

Lydia wanted to cover her ears but didn't dare move.

"I calmed him down." Her mother gave a long sigh. "But I didn't need this. Twice in one day. First the police station and now the watch. I think you have gone crazy, Lydia."

For a while there were no more words and Lydia began to hope she had finished. But she was wrong.

"It's all been lies, hasn't it?"

Valentina waited for an answer but when none came, she continued, "Lies about where money came from. When I think back, I see lots of them. All the times you said Mrs. Yeoman paid you to run errands for her or that you found a purse in the street or had helped someone out with their homework for a fee. And there was no job with Mr. Willoughby at the school, was there? That money came from Alfred's watch. You are a wicked thief."

Valentina took a deep breath. But Lydia was suffocating.

"You must stop. Stop now. Or you will end up in prison. I won't allow that. You must never steal. Not again. Not ever. I forbid it."

Her words were becoming jerky. Abruptly the weight lifted off the bed and Lydia heard the heels again and a candle flickered into life at her mother's end of the room. The chink of a bottle against the rim of a cup made Lydia feel sick. She curled up in a tight ball under the sheet and pressed her knuckles against her mouth, so hard it hurt. Her mother hated her. Said she was wicked. But if she hadn't been wicked, they would have starved in the gutter long ago. So what was right? Or wrong?

Helping Communists. Was that right or wrong?

Silently she started to recite the Wordsworth poem she had been learning for homework that evening. To drown out the words in her head. *I wandered lonely as a cloud* . . . But what did a cloud know about loneliness?

21

CHANG BARELY HEARD HER FOOTSTEP BEHIND HIM, SHE was so quiet. The stealth of a fox. Yet he knew it was her, as surely as he knew the beat of his own heart. He ceased watching the river and faced her. Her appearance trickled pleasure, sweet as honey, into his veins. She wore no hat and her hair was a tumble of rippling copper in the sunlight, but her eyes were full of shadows. She looked more fragile than he'd ever seen her.

"I hoped I would find you here," she said shyly. She gestured toward the creek and the narrow strip of sand where she had sewn up his foot. "It's so quiet, it's beautiful. But if you came here to be private . . ."

"No, please." He bowed to her and spread out a hand to entice her to stay. "This place was a drab desert before you walked into it."

She bowed in return. "I am honored."

She was learning Chinese ways. The deep sense of contentment it gave him took him by surprise.

She sat down on the big flat rock, stroked its gray surface, warm in the sun, and watched a lizard that scurried out of a crack. It was dusty and gray with long spiky claws.

"I need to warn you, Chang An Lo. That's why I've come."

"Warn me?"

"Yes. You're in danger."

The weight of the word pressed tight against his ribs. "What danger do you see?"

He crouched quietly down by the water's edge but turned his head so that he could still look at her. She was wearing a light brown dress and it merged with the trees. Her eyes fixed on his.

"Danger from the Black Snake brotherhood."

He hissed, a hard and angry sound. "Thank you for the warning. They threaten me, I know. But how do you hear of the Black Snakes?"

She gave him a lopsided smile. "I had a chat with two men who had black snake tattoos on their necks. They dragged me into a car and demanded to know where you were."

She made light of it, but his heartbeat trailed away to nothing. He dipped his hand into the water to hide the sudden tremble. He must rule the anger, not let it rule him. His dark eyes looked into hers.

"Lydia Ivanova, listen to me. You must stay out of the Chinese town. Never go near it, and be watchful even in your own settlement. The Black Snakes carry poison in their bite and they are powerful. They kill slowly and savagely, and . . ."

"It's all right. They let me go. Don't look so fierce."

She was smiling at him, and his heartbeat returned. She dragged a hand through her hair as if plucking thoughts from her head, and he could feel in the tips of his fingers her desire to talk of other things.

"Where do you live, Chang An Lo?"

He shook his head. "It's better you do not know."

"Oh."

"It is safer for you. To know nothing of me."

"Not even what job you do?"

"No."

She released a little huff of annoyance, puffing out her cheeks as a lizard will sometimes do, then tilted her head and gave him an enticing grin.

"Will you at least tell me your age? That can do no harm, can it?"

"No, of course not. I am nineteen."

Her questions were rude, far too personal, but he knew she did not mean them to be and he took no offense. It was her way. She was a *fanqui* and to expect subtlety in a Foreign Devil was like expecting toads to bring forth the song of a lark.

"And your family? Do you have brothers and sisters?"

"My family is dead. All dead."

"Oh, Chang, I'm sorry."

He took his hands from the water and drew a bullfrog from the mud. "Are you hungry, Lydia Ivanova?"

★ ★ ★

HE LIT A FIRE. HE BAKED THE FROG AND ALSO TWO SMALL fish from the river, all wrapped in leaves, and she ate her share in front of him with relish. He whittled four sticks into rudimentary chopsticks and enjoyed teaching her to use them, touching her fingers, curling them around the sticks. Her laughter when she dropped the fish from them made the branches of the willow trees whisper above their heads and even Lo-shen, the river goddess, must have stopped to listen.

She relaxed, in a way he'd never seen before. Her limbs grew loose; her eyes emerged from their shadows and abandoned that wary look that was as much a part of her as her flaming hair. And he knew what it meant: she felt safe. Safe enough to tell him a tale of when she was eight years old and broke her arm trying to imitate one of the backflips of the street acrobats. A Chinese girl had tied two bamboo chopsticks tight on each side of the break to keep it safe until she reached home. Her mother scolded her but as soon as it was well again, she had arranged for a Russian ballet dancer to teach her daughter the correct way to do a backflip. To demonstrate, Lydia Ivanova jumped to her feet, leaped into the air, and performed a neat flip that sent her skirt flying over her head for a moment in a most undecorous manner. She sat down again and grinned at him. He loved her grin.

He laughed and applauded her. "You are Empress of Lizard Creek," he said and bowed his head low.

"I didn't think Communists approved of empresses," she said with a smile and stretched out on her back on the sand, her bare feet trailing in the cool water.

He thought she was teasing him but he was not sure, so he said nothing, just watched her where she lay in the shade, the tip of her tongue between her lips as if tasting the fresh breeze that flickered off the water. Her body was slight and her breasts small, but her feet were too big for Chinese taste. She was so unlike any other he'd ever known. So alien, so fiery, a creature that broke all the rules, yet she brought a strange warmth to his chest that made it hard for him to leave her.

"I must go," he said softly.

She rolled her head to face him. "Must you?"

"Yes. I am to go to a funeral."

Her amber eyes grew wide. "Can I come too?"

"That is not possible," he said curtly.

Her audacity would test the patience of the gods themselves.

THEY STOOD AT THE BACK OF THE PROCESSION. TRUMPETS blared out. He could feel the fox girl behind him, sense her excitement as she clung close. She was small and slight like a Chinese youth, and the clothes he'd borrowed for her—white tunic, loose trousers, felt sandals, and wide straw conical hat—made her invisible. But her presence here worried Chang.

Would Yuesheng object? Would the appearance of a *fanqui* at his funeral give power to the evil spirits that the drums and cymbals and trumpets were driving away? *Oh, Yuesheng, my friend, I am indeed bedeviled.*

Even the sky was white, the color of mourning, displaying its grief for Yuesheng. The coffin carriage at the head of the solemn procession was draped in swathes of white silk and drawn by four men all in white, declaring their sorrow. Buddhist priests in saffron robes beat their drums and scattered white petals along the winding route to the temple. Chang felt the girl's cheek brush his shoulder as the crowd crushed around them.

"The man in the long white gown and *ma-gua*," he murmured, "the one prostrate on the ground behind the coffin, he is Yuesheng's brother."

"Who is the big man in the . . . ?"

"*Hsst!* Do not speak. Keep your head down." He looked over his shoulder but could see no one paying any attention to them. "The big man is Yuesheng's father."

The chanting of the priests drowned out their words.

"What are those people throwing in the air?"

"It is artificial paper money. To appease the spirits."

"Shame it's not real," she whispered as a fifty-dollar note floated past her nose.

"*Hsst!*"

She did not speak again. It was good to know the fox could hold its tongue. During the slow progress to the temple, Chang filled his mind with his memories of Yuesheng and the bond they had shared. It had always weighed heavy on Chang's heart that Yuesheng had not seen or spoken to his father for three years because of the anger he carried against him. Three long years. The ancestors would be displeased that he had hardened his face against his duty of filial respect, but Yuesheng's father was not a man easy to honor.

In the temple, in front of the bronze statues of Buddha and Kuan Yin, the coffin was placed at the altar. Incense scented the air. Prayers were chanted by monks. White banners, white flowers, delicate food, fruit and sweetmeats, all laid out for Yuesheng. The mourners kowtowed to the ground like a blanket of snow on the temple floor. Then the burning began. In a large bronze urn the monks laced their prayers with the smoke of burned paper objects for Yuesheng to use in the next life: a house, tools and furniture, a sword and rifle, even a car and a set of mah-jongg tiles, and most important of all, foil ingots of gold and silver. Everything devoured by the flames.

Chang watched as the smoke rose to become the breath of the gods, and he felt the beginning of a sense of peace. The knife pain of loss grew less. Yuesheng had died bravely. Now his friend was safe and well cared for, his part in the work was over, but as Chang's eyes sought out the heavy figure at the front of the mourners, he knew his own work had barely begun.

"You are the one who brought me my son's body, and for that I owe you a great debt. Ask what you will."

The father wore a white headband. His white embroidered padded jacket and trousers made his shoulders and thighs look even broader than they were. The sash at his thick waist was decorated with pearls sewn into the shape of a dragon.

Chang bowed. "It was an honor to serve my friend."

The big man studied him. His mouth was hard and his eyes shrewd. Chang could see no grief in them, but this man did not reveal his emotions lightly.

"They would have cut off his limbs and scattered them, if you had not carried his body away to me. The Kuomintang does that to frighten others. It could have taken my son's spirit many years to find them all before returning whole to our ancestors. For that gift, I thank you." He bowed his head to Chang.

"My heart is happy for your son. His spirit will be pleased to know you offer a gift in return."

The black eyes tightened. "Name the gift and it shall be yours."

Chang took a deliberate step closer and kept his voice low. "Your son gave his life for what he believed in, to open the minds of the people of China to the words of Mao Tse . . ."

"Do not speak to me of that." The father turned his head away in a dismissive gesture, the muscle at the top of his jaw bunched and hard. "Just name the gift."

"A printing press."

A harsh intake of breath.

"Your son's press was destroyed by the Kuomintang."

"My word is given. The printing machine shall be yours."

Chang bowed, no more than a dip of his head. "You do great honor to your son's memory, Feng Tu Hong."

Yuesheng's father turned his broad back on Chang and strode away to the funeral banquet.

HE MUST TAKE THE FOX HOME. SHE HAD SEEN ENOUGH. IF SHE stayed, she would be discovered. The guests were no longer bowing their heads in grief but were tipping them back to drink *maotai*, chattering like pigeons. She would be noticed. He glanced over his shoulder to where she was tucked close behind him and wondered what would happen if he lifted off her wide straw hat. Would the fire spirits of her hair sweep through the great crowd of guests and burn the truth from their tongues: that they had offered no kindness to Yuesheng while he lived?

"Did you ask him?"

It was Kuan, his companion from the cellar. She appeared suddenly in front of him, dressed in black instead of white and carrying a satchel on her back. He had not expected her to come to the funeral, as her work in the factory gave no time off. He moved a few paces away from the fox girl.

"Yes, I asked for the gift. He agreed."

Kuan's dark slanted eyes widened in disbelief. "You are fortunate you still carry your head on your shoulders instead of in a bucket." She leaned close. "Did he warn you? Against printing more pamphlets and posters?"

"No. There was no point. He despises us, as he despised his son."

She smiled gently. "Don't grieve so, Chang An Lo. Yuesheng died doing what was right and he is happy now."

"He will be happier when we bring freedom to this shackled country of China," Chang whispered fiercely. He drew in a deep breath of scented air. "And Yuesheng's father will help us bring that day nearer. Whether he wants to or not."

22

"You look tired, old sport," Alfred Parker said, pausing to dig around in the murk of tobacco at the bottom of the bowl of his pipe. "A bit gray round the gills."

Theo ran a hand over his eyes. They felt gritty and raw. "Yes, I'm feeling a bit rough actually. Not sleeping well these days."

"Not fretting over the spot of bother with that Mason chappie, are you? I thought you said you'd sorted it out."

"Yes, I have. No problems there. It's the end-of-term examinations, so I'm up marking papers till all hours."

Plus the fact that he'd spent much of the last three nights in wafer-thin boats bobbing around on the river. Staring out endlessly into blackness. Last night it had sheeted down with rain, but nevertheless the nighttime collections were going smoothly and Theo was surprised at how quickly his own share of silver at the end of each run was growing heavier. That could only mean one thing. They were growing bolder, trafficking in ever-larger cargoes, taking greater risks. They relied on his word. And he relied on Mason's.

No wonder he was looking gray round the gills.

He and Parker were in Theo's favorite teahouse in Junchow. Parker had wanted a meeting and agreed to join him there, overcoming his scruples about hygiene and correctness. Tea without milk was not Alfred's idea of tea at all, but he said he was interested in experiencing a traditional Chinese teahouse to broaden his understanding of the natives. Theo had laughed. Alfred might be an excellent journalist on European matters in China, but he would never have an understanding of the natives. When the slender young girl in her high-necked cheongsam brought over the plain earthenware teapot and poured the red brew into their tiny cups, Alfred smiled at her so warmly that she shook her head and pointed upstairs. Theo knew it didn't enter his friend's head that she thought he wanted sex with her and was telling him the singsong girls were in rooms above, ready to offer the moon and the stars. For a fistful of dollars, of course.

Around them the low bamboo tables buzzed with the erratic tones of Chinese merchants and bankers, even a few Japanese diplomats, well dressed and well fed, all men who were on the right side of the food shortages. The place was bright and colorful, fooling customers into a sense of good fortune. Crimson lanterns and golden lions and bright songbirds in elaborate cages soothed away irritations, while a girl with hair like a raven's wing plucked a soft tune on the *chin*. The clack of mah-jongg tiles never ceased. Normally Theo found it peaceful here, but not today. Somehow he seemed to have lost the knack. *Peaceful* felt a long way away right now.

"So, Alfred, why the urgency? What is it you are so keen to discuss?"

"You asked me to dig around in Christopher Mason's past, remember? I know you said you've settled whatever your differences were with him, but even so . . ."

Theo leaned forward. "Found any skeletons?"

"Not exactly."

"Then what?"

"Just a few irregularities."

"Such as?"

"He's not quite what he seems, for a start. His parents owned a small hardware shop in Beckenham, Kent. Not the import-export business he claims."

"Well, well, so Mason's *pater* was in a brown-apron job. Interesting."

"There's more."

Theo grinned. "Alfred, you are a first-class diamond."

Parker took a moment to relight his pipe. "His first job was in the customs and excise department in London. And word has it that he wasn't above marketing some of the contraband goods he confiscated—French brandy and perfume, stuff like that."

"Now why doesn't that surprise me?"

"He eventually moved over to the planning applications department but only after there was a whiff of scandal about him and his boss's wife. Seems she liked rough treatment . . . and he provided it." Parker was frowning uncomfortably. "Not the sort of thing a decent chap would do."

Theo was touched by his friend's naïveté. There was something so defenseless about it. His own innocence had been swallowed up by a gunshot in an office in Kensington ten years earlier, and since then he had always expected to bump up against the bad in people. It just seemed to happen that way. Invariably. That's why he liked teaching. Children were raw material; there was still a chance for them. And there was Li Mei, of course. Li Mei gave him hope. But Parker was an odd sort of fellow because the shiny edges were still intact, not dulled or chipped away by reality. Rare thing these days. Quite refreshing in its way. And there was something different about him today, something exuberant.

"And," Parker lowered his voice, "he resigned from Planning after only eighteen months."

"Enlighten me."

"Rumors. Nothing definite, you understand."

"Get on with it, man."

"Kickbacks."

"Ah!"

"Money under the table. Buildings going up where they shouldn't. That sort of thing. Resigned in the nick of time and shipped out to Junchow. Lord only knows how he wangled a berth in the education department over here, but apparently he's good at what he does, though not well liked by those under him. They wouldn't say more. Frightened for their jobs, I suppose."

"Wouldn't you be?"

Parker looked startled. "Of course not. Not if I saw corruption."

The girl came just then with another pot of steaming tea, and she poured them both a cup.

"*Xie xie*," Parker said. *Thank you.*

Theo almost choked on the hot liquid. "Well spoken, Alfred."

"Well, I thought I'd learn some of the lingo while I'm here.

Comes in useful in my line of work and anyway, you see, old chap, there's someone I want to impress."

Theo watched his friend turn quite pink.

"Alfred, you sly dog. Who's the lucky lady? Anyone I know?"

"Yes, as a matter of fact, she is. The mother of one of your pupils."

"Not Anthea Mason, surely."

Parker looked put out. "Of course not. The lady is called Valentina Ivanova." Just the mention of her name painted a shy smile on his lips.

"For heaven's sake, Alfred," Theo said sharply, "you must be mad. You're asking for trouble."

Parker blinked behind his spectacles, taken aback by the unexpected heat of the response. "What do you mean, Theo? She's a wonderful woman."

"Oh, she's beautiful, I grant you that. But she's a White Russian."

"So? What's wrong with that?"

Theo sighed. "Oh, Alfred, everyone knows those women are desperate to marry a European. Any European. The poor creatures are stuck here, no papers, no money, no jobs for them. It must be hell. That's why half the prostitutes in the brothels of Junchow are White Russian women. Don't look so shocked, it's a fact." He softened his tone. "I'm sorry to burst your bubble, my friend, but she's just using you."

Parker shook his head, but Theo could see his confidence draining away. The journalist removed his spectacles and started to clean them thoroughly with a virginal white handkerchief. "I thought you'd understand," he said gruffly without looking up. "You of all people. About all this love business. The way it makes a chap feel quite . . ." He paused.

"Ill?"

Parker attempted a smile. "Yes, I feel ill." He replaced his spectacles and stared, immobile, at the carefully refolded handkerchief between his fingers. "I see her face everywhere," he said softly. "In the mirror when I shave, on the blank page when I type up my pieces, even on old Gallifrey's desk blotter—he's my editor—during deadline conferences."

"You've got it bad, old fellow. She has certainly hooked you."

"I thought you'd understand," he said again.

"Because I'm with Li Mei, you mean? No, Li Mei is not with me for my money, I promise you that. For a start I haven't got any, more's the pity, and anyway she comes from a wealthy Chinese family that has turned its back on her because of me. So it's a very different situation. I warn you, steer well clear of Valentina Ivanova. She'll just walk away the moment you take her back to England."

Parker's mouth was taut. He pushed aside his cup untouched. "I did wonder what a beautiful and accomplished woman like that would see in a chap like me."

"Oh, Alfred, get a grip on yourself. Like I said, you're a first-class diamond."

Parker shrugged stiffly.

"Look, why not just enjoy her company? Take her to bed for a few months and get her perfume out of your blood, then you don't . . ."

"Theo, you may possess a heartless heathen soul," Parker said without rancor, "but I do not. I am a Christian, you see, and as such I try to follow His commandments. So no, I won't bed her and then abandon her."

"More fool you, my friend."

There was a silence between them. A girl came offering sugared dumplings on a tray, but they both waved her away. Behind them a man shouted in triumph as he won his game of mah-jongg. Theo lit a cigarette. His throat ached; he'd smoked too many recently.

"Leave her now," he said quietly, "before you get in too deep. I'm saying this for your own good. And don't forget there's the daughter as well. Not easy, that one."

Parker ran an uncertain hand over his high forehead, trying to hold his thoughts together. "I don't know, Theo, maybe you're right. It seems to me that love is such a destructive force. Love of a person, love of an ideal, love of a country. It just wipes out everything else and causes havoc. And as for the daughter, don't even mention her to me. That girl is beyond help."

23

CHANG STOOD IN THE DARK. STILL AS STONE. THEY WERE there, all around him. He could hear them. The rustle of a sleeve, the brush of thigh against wall, the scrape of shoe on gravel. It had been a risk. To show himself at the funeral. It meant they would track him down, he knew that. But it would have brought dishonor on him if he had shunned Yuesheng's final moment. Yuesheng was his blood companion and he owed him respect, especially as it could so easily have been Chang's own body lying dead in the cellar that night when the Kuomintang attacked. So now the Black Snakes were here. Death lay in the shadows, awaiting its feast.

He was in a cobbled square in the old town, his back pressed to a studded oak door, inset under an arch. Black figures flicked from one street to another, crouched and coming fast from all directions. Movement in doorways. Sharp eyes seeking him. No moon to highlight the blades in their fists but he had no doubt that they were there, hungry for blood.

He counted six of them in all, but could hear more. One was standing tight against a wall no more than ten paces to his right, guarding the entrance to a narrow *hutong*, an alleyway that led deep into the maze of back streets. He had a harsh way of breathing. With a silent leap and an upward slam of his heel, Chang put an end to it, but before the body had even touched the ground, he was into the *hutong* and running, low and lithe. Above him in an upstairs window a light flooded on and a shout sounded from behind, but he didn't turn.

He moved faster. Ducked into deeper darkness. Feet skidding on rotting filth. He led them on through the alleys, stringing them out as they fought for speed, so that when the fastest man found himself at a crossroads twenty feet ahead of his companions, he had no idea what flew out of the shadows and thudded into his chest, snapping ribs like twigs, until it was too late and he couldn't breathe.

Chang swept through the darkness. Winding and twisting. Ambushing. One man lost the use of a leg and another the sight in one eye. But a nighttime honey wagon, the cart piled high with human manure and the stench enough to choke a man, blocked his path and he was forced to swerve left down a slope that led nowhere.

A death trap.

Sheer walls on three sides of a rough courtyard. One way in. One way out. Six men spread behind him, breathing hard and spitting venom. Three of them carried knives, two wielded swords, but one held a gun and it was pointed straight at Chang's chest. He said something guttural and a sword carrier stepped forward. He came at Chang and the long blade sang through the air. Chang stilled his breathing, drew on the energy racing through his blood, and in one fluid movement swept a leg under his attacker. A sting of pain skittered down his side, but he took three rapid steps and leaped into the air at the back wall, struggled for a fingerhold, slipped, caught again, and then swung his heels over his head in a full arc. On the roof but not safe. A bullet tore past his ear.

A howl of anger down in the courtyard and the man with the gun seized the swordsman's weapon and sliced it down in a blow that disemboweled the sword's owner. The wounded man fell forward to his knees, clutching at his writhing innards as they spilled from his body, a high wailing scream rising from his mouth. A second blow from the sword silenced the scream and sent his head rolling into the gutter. The gun pointed once more at the roof. But Chang was gone.

LYDIA HAD TIME TO THINK. THE STRETCH OF TWENTY-TWO yards at the center of the pitch was wearing thin, but around it the turf spread out like a shimmering lake of green. The grass was trimmed with precision and treated with a respect that baffled her because the men seemed to pay more attention to its welfare than they did to their children's. But she loved to watch cricket. She liked to imagine this same scene taking place on the other side of the world in England. At this very moment in every town and village the weekend was being besieged by men in white flannels strutting around with pads and bats, knocking hell out of a small hard ball. It was so wonderfully pointless. Especially in this heat. Only people with nothing to do all day could think up a game so bizarre.

Men in white.

To one nation it means a game. To another it means death. Worlds apart. Oceans adrift. But what happens to someone caught in the middle? Do they drown?

"More tea, dear? You look miles away."

"Thank you, Mrs. Mason." Lydia accepted the tea, drew her thoughts away from Chang An Lo, and helped herself to another cucumber sandwich, which she added to the plate balanced on the arm of her deckchair.

Polly's mother was wearing heavy sunglasses and a wide-brimmed hat trimmed with roses from her garden, but neither quite hid the bruise around her left eye or the swelling on her cheekbone. "I tripped over Achilles, Christopher's lazy old cat, and banged into a door, silly me," Lydia had heard her laugh to the other wives, but it was obvious from their expressions that no one believed the lie. Lydia looked at her with new respect. To come here today for the match and face up to this humiliation with such a firm smile and a steady hand as she dispensed tea, that took courage.

"Mrs. Mason," she said in a loud voice, "that is such a pretty dress, it really suits you." It was frilly and floral, the kind of dress only an Englishwoman would wear.

"Why, thank you, Lydia," Anthea Mason said, and for one ghastly moment Lydia thought she was going to cry, but instead she popped a smile on her face and an extra sandwich on Lydia's plate.

Out on the field Christopher Mason hit another four, but Lydia refused to join in the ripple of applause. Beside her Polly beamed with delight and fondled her puppy's head to cheer him up. He was sulking at being kept on a lead when the ball was just asking to be fetched.

"Isn't Daddy clever, Toby? He'll be in such a good mood today."

Lydia wouldn't look at her.

★ ★ ★

"YOU'LL GET YOURSELF KILLED, LYD."

"Don't talk such poppycock. It was only a funeral."

"But why? No one goes to Chinese functions. The natives here keep to themselves and we do the same. That way everyone stays happy. You've got to accept that they don't like us, Lyd, and they're different from us. Mixing together. It can't be done."

"How do you know?"

"Because it can't. Everyone knows that."

"You're wrong. Chang and I are . . . ," Lydia sought for a word that wouldn't shock Polly, ". . . friends. We talk about . . . well, about things, and I see no reason why we can't mix. Look at all the children who have *amahs* as nannies to look after them when they're little and they really love them. So why does it have to change just because the children grow up?"

"Because they have different rules from us."

"So you're saying it only works when they adopt our rules and live as we live."

"Yes."

"But they're just people, Polly. Like us. You should have seen and heard their grief at the funeral. They were hurting just like we do. Cut them and they bleed. So what do rules matter?"

"Oh, Lyd, this Chang An Lo is getting you all muddled up. You must forget about him. Though I must admit Mr. Theo seems to make it work with his beautiful Chinese woman."

"But he hasn't married her, has he?"

"Exactly."

"And when Anna Calpin was young she used to love her *amah*, but now she makes her sit on the toilet seat for ten minutes when it's cold in winter to warm it up before Anna uses it."

"I know. But you've never had Chinese servants, Lyd. You don't understand."

"No, Polly. I don't."

THE STREET SEEMED NORMAL. A CHINESE VENDOR STOOD on the corner trying to sell sunflower seeds and hot water, a boy was playing marbles in the gutter, and an old Russian *babushka* was sitting in a rocking chair in her doorway, plucking a guinea fowl. At her feet two filthy street urchins were snatching at feathers as they fell and stuffing them into a pillowcase. The big wheels of a rickshaw rattled down the road kicking up grit.

Lydia tried to work out what had made her halt. It was the street where she lived. She'd walked it a million times. It was hot, she was dusty, and her dress was sticking to her skin. She needed a cold drink. Only twenty yards to her own front door. So what was it? What made her hesitate?

Be watchful, Lydia Ivanova. Don't sleep while you walk. They let you go once but not a second time. Chang's words to her. Well, she was being watchful all right, keeping alert, yet she could see nothing to be nervous about. Oh hell, maybe Polly was right. Maybe he was getting her head all muddled over nothing. She hurried down the street, impatient with herself, and it was as she was unlocking the front door that she sensed the movement behind her. Not that she saw or heard anything. More a sudden shifting of the air at her back. She didn't turn. Just threw herself over the threshold and slammed the door behind her. She leaned heavily against it, not breathing. Listening.

Nothing. A car's Klaxon, a child's laugh, the savage shriek of a gull overhead.

She took a deep breath. Had she imagined it?

She waited while the minutes ticked by, and still her pulse thudded in her ears.

"Lydia, *moi vorobushek*, come here, come." It was Mrs. Zarya beckoning at the end of the hall. She was wearing a bright pink kimono, and her hair was wrapped up in wire curlers. "I have a piece of yam for your Mr. Sun Yat-sen. Here, take it."

Lydia moved, but her feet felt heavy. "That's kind, Mrs. Zarya. Sun Yat-sen will like that." She remembered the clutch of grass that she'd sneaked from the cricket club. It was scrunched tight in her hand. "Going somewhere special tonight?"

"*Da*, yes. To a soirée." Mrs. Zarya said it proudly. "A poetry reading at General Manlikov's villa. He was a friend of my husband and he is a fine man who has not forgotten his old comrade's widow."

"Have a good time." Lydia scampered up the stairs. "Thanks for the yam. *Spasibo.*"

★ ★ ★

IT WAS WHEN SHE REACHED THE LAST FLIGHT OF STAIRS that she heard the voices coming from the attic. They seemed to strike her upturned face. She stood still. One was her mother's, low and intense; the other was a man's, raised in what sounded like anger. They were speaking Russian. She opened the door quietly. Two figures were together on the sofa, talking fast, hands gesturing through the air between them. Lydia felt a shiver of dismay and wanted to leave, but it was too late. It was the man from the police lineup, the big bearded bear with the black oily curls and the eye patch, the one with the wolf boots. Beside him Valentina looked like a tiny exotic creature perched on the edge of the seat. The man was staring straight at Lydia with his one dark eye and it was enough to turn her cheeks a fiery red.

"Look, I'm sorry," she said at once. "I didn't mean to make the police come after you like that, I just . . ."

"Lydia," her mother said quickly, "Liev Popkov speaks no English."

"Oh . . . well, tell him I apologize, Mama."

Valentina spoke in rapid Russian.

He nodded slowly and rose to his feet, filling the attic room with his massive shoulders, ducking his head to avoid the low ceiling, and still he stared at Lydia. She wasn't sure whether it was hostility or curiosity, but either way it made her uncomfortable. But what confused her was how on earth he had discovered where she lived. *Chyort!* She was jumpy as hell.

He walked over to the door where she was standing, and up close she feared he would tear off her head with one of his great paws.

"I'm sorry," she said once more before he had the chance to unsheath his claws, and she held out her hand.

To her surprise he took it, swallowed it up inside his own, and shook it gently. But his single black eye seemed to stare at her in disgust.

"Do svidania," she said politely. Good-bye.

He grunted and shambled out of the room.

"MAMA, WHAT DID HE WANT?"

But Valentina wasn't listening. She was pouring herself a drink. Into a glass, not a cup, Lydia noticed, another sign of Alfred's generosity.

Her mother walked over to the replaced mirror on the wall and stared at her reflection as she took a first taste of the vodka.

"I am old," she murmured and ran a hand down her cheek and throat, over the rise of her breasts and hip. "Old and scrawny as a sewer dog with worms."

"Don't, Mama. Don't start that. You are beautiful, everyone says so, and you are only thirty-five."

"This stinking climate is destroying my skin." She put her face right up close to the mirror and ran a finger slowly around her eyes.

"Vodka ruins your skin faster."

Her mother said nothing, just tipped her head back and emptied the alcohol down her throat, and then for a brief moment she closed her eyes.

Lydia turned away and looked out the window instead. The old woman in the rocking chair had fallen asleep and the two urchins were trying to slide the half-plucked bird from her grasp, but even in sleep her fingers clung on. Lydia leaned out and shouted at them. They stopped their thieving and ran off down the street with their pillowcase of feathers. Above the rooftops the sky was streaked with lilac tendrils as the sun started to slide away from China, but Lydia was not to be distracted.

"What did that man want, Mama?"

Valentina was at the table, refilling her glass. "Money. Isn't that what everyone wants?"

"You didn't give him any."

"How could I give him money when I don't have any?"

Lydia considered snatching the vodka bottle away and pouring it out the window, but she'd tried that once and knew it didn't work. It was like pushing a stick into a wasp's nest. It only made her worse.

"I thought you were going to work at the hotel this evening."

Valentina gave her a look that made it quite clear what she thought of work and hotels. "Not tonight, darling. They can stuff their work up their own fat backsides. I'm sick of it. Sick to bloody death of their groping hands and their thrashing hips. I want to chop them all up into tiny pieces, like *steak tartare*."

"It's just a job, Mama. You don't really hate it."

"I do. It's true. They sweat. They stink. They put their hands where they shouldn't and where they wouldn't if I were one of their own kind. They want to fuck me."

"Mama!"

"And Alfred too. That's what he wants to do."

"I thought he came and bought all your dances to protect you from the others."

"When he can." She sipped her drink. The glass was fuller this time. "But often he has to work late for deadlines at his newspaper office." She fluttered her fingers in the air. "Such rubbish they all write. As if this colony were the center of the universe."

"How did that Russian man find me here?"

Her mother shrugged eloquently. "How the hell should I know, darling? Use your head. From the police, I suppose."

Valentina was wearing an old cotton dress that she hated but deigned to put on in the house to save her few other clothes for best. It always put her in a bad mood, and Lydia swore that tomorrow she would throw it in the trash. For now, she went over to the stove and started chopping up the piece of yam.

"*Dochenka*, something occurred to me today."

"That vodka can kill you?"

"Don't be so impudent. No, it occurred to me to wonder where the money came from to redeem Alfred's watch from the pawnbroker. Tell me."

The knife hesitated in Lydia's hand.

"The truth, Lydia. No more lies."

Lydia put down the knife and turned to face her mother, but she was back in front of the mirror staring at her reflection. It seemed to give her no pleasure.

"It happened when I was walking past the burned-out house in Melidan Road," Lydia said casually. "Two people were shouting at each other in there, a man and a woman."

"So? Are you saying these people gave you the money?"

"Sort of. The woman threw a handful of silver at the man and then they both shouted some more and left. So I went in and picked up the money from the floor. It wasn't stealing. It was just lying there for anyone to find."

Valentina narrowed her eyes suspiciously. "Is that the truth?"

"Honestly."

"Very well. But it was wicked of you to steal the watch in the first place."

"I know, Mama. I'm sorry."

Valentina turned and studied her daughter critically for a minute. She shook her head. "You look an awful mess. Quite horrible. What on earth have you been up to today?"

"I went to a funeral."

"Looking like that!"

"No, I borrowed some clothes."

"Whose funeral?" She was turning back to the mirror, losing interest.

"A friend of a friend. No one you know."

Lydia finished chopping the yam and wrapped it in a scrap of old greaseproof paper, then took a large bowl of water into her bedroom and proceeded to strip off her damp dress and grimy shoes. She washed herself all over and brushed her hair till every last morsel of dirt and dust was out of it. She must make more effort with her appearance or Chang An Lo would never look at her the way he'd looked at the Chinese girl with the fine features and the short black hair at the funeral today. Their heads close together. Like lovers.

"BETTER?"

"My darling, you look adorable."

Lydia had put on the concert dress and shoes. She wasn't sure why.

"I don't look horrible anymore, do I, Mama?"

"No, sweetheart, you look like peaches and cream." Valentina was wearing only her oyster-silk slip now, her long hair loose around her bare shoulders. She placed her empty glass on the table and came to stand in front of Lydia. Even half drunk she moved gracefully. But her eyes looked suspiciously red at the rims, as if she might have been crying silently while Lydia was behind her curtain, or it could just be the vodka talking. She cupped Lydia's face in her hands and studied her daughter intently, a slight frown placing a crease between the finely arched eyebrows.

"One day soon you will be truly beautiful."

"Don't be silly, Mama. You will always be the beautiful one in this family."

Valentina smiled, and Lydia knew she had said the right thing.

"You will be pleased to hear, little one, that I have tonight decided to create a new me. A modern me."

Her mother released her face and headed for the drawer beside the blackened stove. Lydia experienced a sudden unease. It was where the knives were kept. But it wasn't a knife her mother picked out, but a pair of long-bladed scissors.

"No, Mama, don't, please don't. You'll see everything differently in the morning. It's only the drink that's . . ."

Valentina stood in front of the mirror, seized a great handful of her dark hair, and sliced it off at jaw level.

Neither spoke. Both were shocked by the image in the mirror. It was brutal. Lopsided and bewildered. The reflection of a woman who was lost between two worlds.

Lydia recovered first. "Let me finish it for you or you won't get it straight. I'll make it look smart, really chic."

She gently took the scissors from her mother's rigid hand and proceeded to cut. Each snip of the blades felt like treachery to her father. Valentina had always told her how he'd adored her long hair and described how he used to stand behind her each night before going to bed and brush it into a silky smooth curtain with long, slow strokes that set it crackling full of sparks. Like shooting stars in a night sky, he used to say. Now the soft waves lay like dead birds at her feet. When the act was finished, Lydia picked them up, wrapped them in a white scarf of her mother's, and laid the slender bundle under her pillow. It deserved a proper funeral.

To her surprise, her mother was smiling. "Better," she said.

Valentina shook her head from side to side and her hair bounced and swung playfully, curving into the nape of her neck and emphasizing her long white throat.

"Much better," she said again. "And this is just the beginning of the new me."

She lifted the half-empty bottle of Russian vodka off the table, walked over to the open window where the evening sky looked as if it were now on fire above the gray slate roofs, and stuck out her arm, tipping the clear liquid into the street without even a glance below.

Lydia watched.

"Happy now?" her mother asked.

"Yes."

"Good. And no more dance hostess for me either."

"But we need that money for our rent. Don't . . ."

"No. I have decided."

Lydia began to panic. "Perhaps I could do it instead. Become a dance hostess, I mean."

"Don't be absurd, *dochenka*. You are too young."

"I could say I'm older than sixteen. And you know I dance well, you taught me."

"No. I am not having men touch you."

"Oh, Mama, don't be silly. I know how to look after myself."

Valentina gave a sharp high laugh. She dropped the bottle onto the floor and seized her daughter's arm. She shook it hard.

"You know nothing of men, Lydia Ivanova, nothing, and that's the way I intend to keep it. So don't even think about such a job." Her eyes were angry, and Lydia could not quite understand why.

"All right, Mama, all right, calm down." She pulled her arm free and said carefully, "But maybe I could find some other job."

"No. We agreed a long time ago. You must get yourself an education."

"I know, and I will. But . . ."

"No buts."

"Listen, Mama, I know we said the only way for us to climb out of this stinking hole is for me eventually to get a decent job, a proper career, but until then how are we going to . . . ?"

"It is *not* the only way."

"What do you mean?"

"I mean there's another way."

"How?"

"Alfred Parker."

Lydia blinked and felt a rush of sour saliva in her mouth. "No." It was no more than a whisper.

"Yes." Her mother tossed her newly bobbed hair. "I have decided."

"No, Mama, please don't." Lydia's throat was dry. "He's not good enough for you."

"Don't be silly, my sweet. I'm sure his friends will say I'm not good enough for him."

"That's rubbish."

"Is it? Listen to me, Lydia. He's a good man. You never minded about Antoine, so why object to Alfred?"

"You were never serious about Antoine."

"Well, I'm glad you realize I intend to be serious about Alfred." She said it gently and lifted a strand of her daughter's shining hair between her fingers, as if to remember what long hair felt like. "I want you to be nice to him."

"Mama," Lydia shook her head, "I can't . . . because . . . ."

"Because what?"

Lydia scraped the tip of one of her new shoes along the floor. "Because he's not Papa."

A strange little moan escaped Valentina's lips. "Don't, Lydia, don't. That time is over. This is now."

Lydia seized her mother's arm. "I'll get a job," she said urgently. "I'll get us out of this mess, I promise, you don't need Alfred, I don't want him in our house. He's pompous and silly and fiddles with his ears and rams his bible down our throats and . . ." She took a breath.

"Don't stop now, *dochenka*. Let's hear it all."

"He wears spectacles but still he can't see how you twist him around your finger like a wisp of straw."

Valentina gave an elegant shrug. "Hush now, my sweet. Give him time. You'll get used to him."

"I don't want to get used to him."

"Don't you want to see me happy?"

"You know I do, Mama, but not with him."

"He's a fine Englishman."

"No, he's too . . . ordinary for you. And he'll change everything, he'll make us as ordinary as he is."

Valentina drew herself up to her full height. "That is insulting, Lydia, and I . . ."

"Don't you see," Lydia rushed on, "I only gave him back his stupid watch to get rid of him." Her voice was rising. "I used up all that precious money because I thought it would make him hate me so much, he'd go away and never ever come back. Don't you see?"

Valentina stood very still. Her face drained bone white as she stared at her daughter. The air in the room was too brittle to breathe.

"You underestimate me," her mother said at last. "He won't leave."

"Don't, Mama. Don't do this to us."

"I have decided, Lydia."

Suddenly Lydia could not bear to be in the same room with this *new* Valentina Ivanova. She snatched up the greaseproof package, rushed out of the room, and kicked the door savagely behind her.

"Little sparrow, what are you doing out here in the dark?"

It was Mrs. Zarya. She was wrapped in a long velvet cloak and wore an elaborate hat with a black ostrich feather curling around its crown. Diamond drop earrings caught the light from her window and sparkled like fireflies. This was not a Mrs. Zarya that Lydia recognized.

"Just feeding Sun Yat-sen," she muttered.

"You have been feeding him for a very long time."

Lydia said nothing. The rabbit was cradled in her arms and she could feel its rapid heartbeat against her chest.

"Did he like the yam?"

"Yes, thank you."

There was a silence, neither quite sure where to go next. Somewhere in the street a pig started to squeal. It sounded like a night demon.

"You look nice," Lydia said.

"Thank you. I am off to General Manlikov's soirée now."

A soirée. A Russian soirée. It would be better than the room upstairs.

"May I come with you, Mrs. Zarya?" Lydia asked politely. "I am wearing my smart dress."

The Russian woman's stiff and lonely old face softened into a delighted smile. "*Da.* Yes. You must come. You might learn something of the great country that bore you. *Da.*"

"*Spasibo,*" Lydia said. *Thank you.*

24

LYDIA WAS DETERMINED TO ENJOY THE EVENING. HER FIRST soirée. It was held in one of the big villas in the avenue that formed the border between the Russian and British Quarters, where Lydia sometimes came to admire what a pocketful of tsarist jewelry had bought for the few lucky ones. But tonight the music only made her feel worse. It flowed like floodwater under her defenses and loosened everything inside her. Her words to her mother and her fears for Chang jostled inside her head until she couldn't think straight.

The piece was a romantic extract from *Prince Igor* by Borodin, one of the Russian *moguchaya kuchka*, played well enough but not as well as her mother would have performed it. Lydia concentrated on the pianist's fingers, caressing the keys the way her own fingers caressed her rabbit's fur. Intimate and needy.

"Now we dance," Mrs. Zarya declared, "before someone starts to sing one of the sad Georgian laments."

The rows of chairs were swept aside to the edges of the ballroom and couples began to take to the floor. Mrs. Zarya sat herself down heavily next to Lydia against the wall, rustling her voluminous taffeta evening dress. It smelled seriously of mothballs and had a tiny mend in one sleeve that was probably where she'd caught it on something, but Lydia toyed with the idea that it might be a bullet hole from a Bolshevik rifle.

"You enjoy so far?" Mrs. Zarya asked.

"Very much. *Spasibo*."

"Excellent. *Otlichno!*"

Oddly, it was the hour of poetry reading at the beginning of the evening that Lydia liked best. She hadn't understood a word of it, of course, but that didn't matter. It was the sounds. The voice of Russia. The full-bodied vowels and complicated combinations that rolled around the speakers' mouths and somehow seemed to resonate. Her ears found a strange satisfaction in them. That surprised her.

"I liked the poetry," she said, "and I like the chandeliers."

Mrs. Zarya laughed and patted her hand. "Of course you do, little sparrow." Her large bosom quivered with amusement.

"Do you think someone will ask me to dance?" Lydia's eyes followed the swirling dancers enviously. She didn't care who asked. Even one of the old men with the tsarist medals on their chests and the sadness in their eyes, just as long as it was someone. Someone male.

"*Nyet*. No. Of course you cannot dance."

"Oh, but I can, I'm good at it. I know . . ."

"No. *Nyet*." Mrs. Zarya tapped Lydia's knee sharply with her folded fan. "You are too young. It would not be fitting. A child, you are. A child does not dance with a man."

At that moment General Manlikov, a square and impressive figure with curly white hair and a very upright way of walking, bowed to them both and offered his arm to Mrs. Zarya. She inclined her head and accompanied him onto the dance floor. Lydia watched. It annoyed her to be called a child, but most of the fifty or more people here were old, some well dressed, others showing signs of patch and mend like Mrs. Zarya, and all bound together by the same consciousness of class and country. They were in a grand ballroom with tall gilt mirrors ranging all the way down one long wall and elegantly arched windows on the other, opening onto what looked like a terrace and gardens. It was dark out there, moonless and godless. But the bright lights and laughter in the ballroom made Lydia bold.

She rose and stood in the doorway of the French windows, staring out into the blackness. Nothing moved. Not even a bat or a branch. She could see no one, but that didn't mean they couldn't see her. Nevertheless she stepped out on the terrace and started to dance, a Chopin waltz floating softly through the open windows. The damp air felt cool on her cheeks and her bare arms shivered with secret pleasure as she spun and swayed on her own to the music. For one inward moment everything else was washed away, leaving her head clear and clean at last.

"How quaint."

She stopped and swung around. A young man in his early twenties was leaning languorously against the door frame, observing her. Slowly and deliberately he started to applaud. It was almost an insult.

"Enchanting."

"It is impolite to spy on a person," Lydia said sharply.

He shrugged indifferently. "I had no idea this terrace was reserved for just you."

"You should have made your presence known."

"The dancing display was too . . . entertaining." He spoke English with a slight Russian accent and his mouth curled up at one side.

"General Manlikov's entertainment is provided in the ballroom, not out here. A gentleman would respect a lady's privacy." It was meant to be cutting, the way Valentina sometimes spoke to Antoine.

He drew a silver cigar case from his breast pocket, took his time lighting a cheroot, first tapping its end on the back of the case, and then regarded her with a lazy mocking expression. He clicked his heels together and tipped his head in a curt bow.

"I apologize for not being a gentleman, Miss Ivanova."

The fact that he knew her name came as a shock. "Have we met?" she demanded.

But as the words came out of her mouth, she realized who she was talking to. It was Alexei Serov, the son of Countess Natalia Serova. She barely recognized him now. Except for his manner. That was as haughty as ever. But his thick brown hair had been cropped very short and he was wearing an elegant white evening jacket with finely tapered black trousers that emphasized his long limbs. He looked every inch the son of a Russian count.

"I seem to remember we were introduced in a restaurant. La Licorne, I do believe."

"I don't recall," she said in an offhand manner and moved away from him to lean against the stone balustrade that edged the terrace. "I'm surprised you do."

"As if I could forget that dress."

"I like this dress."

"Clearly."

The music ceased and suddenly the night air was full of silence. She made no effort to break it. Faintly she could smell wood smoke mingling with the aroma of his tobacco. It struck her as a very male smell. It made her think of Chang. Not that he smelled of smoke; no, his was more of a clean river smell, or was it of the sea? For a brief second she wondered if his skin would taste salty on her tongue, and instantly felt herself blush, which irritated her.

"You're the Russian girl who doesn't know how to speak Russian, aren't you?" said Alexei Serov.

"And you're the Russian who doesn't know how to speak English politely."

Their eyes fixed on each other and she became aware that his were green and very intense, despite the air of casual indifference he assumed.

"The music was excellent," he commented.

"Rather average, I thought. The bass was too heavy and the tempo uneven."

His mouth curved again in that arrogant way of his. "I bow to your superior knowledge."

She felt the urge to demonstrate that she knew more of the world than just music. "It is peaceful here now in the International Settlement for pleasant soirées like this." She gestured toward the brightly lit room. "But everything in China is changing."

"Do enlighten me, Miss Ivanova."

"The Communists are demanding equality for workers instead of feudalism, and a fair distribution of land."

"Forget the Communists." He said it dismissively. "They will be stamped out within the next few weeks. Right here in Junchow."

"No, you're wrong. They're . . ."

"They are finished. General Chiang Kai-shek has ordered an elite division of his Kuomintang troops to be sent here to rid us of their flea bites. So you are quite safe with your soirées, don't worry."

"I'm not worried."

But she was.

Suddenly a quickstep struck up in the ballroom, a surge of music full of life and energy.

On impulse Lydia said, "Would you like to dance?"

"With you?"

"Yes."

"Out here?"

"Yes."

His face looked as if she'd just asked him to jump into the honey wagon. "I think not. You are too young."

She was stung. "Or is it that you are too old?" she retorted and started to dance on her own again as if oblivious to his presence.

Round and round in dizzying circles, but it annoyed her that Alexei Serov didn't have the courtesy to leave. She kept her eyes half closed and would not look at him, blanking him out and letting Chang take her into his arms instead, as she floated on the faint breeze and her body swayed and twirled from one end of the terrace to the other. The rhythm of the music seemed to beat inside her blood. Her breath came fast and she could feel her skin so alive it seemed to be aware of every touch of the night dew and each shiver of a moth's wings as it fluttered toward the circle of light.

"*Ya tebya iskala,* Alexei."

Lydia stopped, her mind still spinning. A young woman was standing beside Alexei Serov, holding a glass of red wine in each hand and speaking words Lydia could not understand. Her straight blond hair was shaped into a neat corn-colored cap and she wore a modern dress that stopped just below the knee like Lydia's own, but this young woman's was beaded all over in vivid blues, a Paris dress, a fashion-house dress. It emphasized the blue of her eyes, which right now were focused with surprise on Lydia. The moment was over. Lydia treated the pair to what was meant to be a gracious nod of the head and walked past them with chin high. They were murmuring to each other in Russian but as Lydia re-entered the ballroom, she heard Alexei Serov slip deliberately into English.

"That girl is just like her father. He had a temper too. I once saw him throw his violin on the fire because he could not get the note he wanted from it."

Lydia's ears were burning. But she kept walking.

CHANG AN LO WATCHED HER. FROM THE DAMP DARKNESS of a sprawling weeping willow tree. Watched her on the terrace the way he would a long-tailed swallow, swooping and diving through the sky for the pure joy of it. The air around her seemed to vibrate and her hair set the night on fire. He could feel its heat and hear the crackle of its flames.

He breathed lightly and felt a sharp unmistakable flicker of anger rise up in him. The dance and the music were strange to his senses, but Lydia Ivanova's actions were clear. She was moving the way a young female cat moves in front of a likely male when she's ready to mate, swaying and seductive, seeking out his advances, rubbing and purring and twitching her flanks.

The man was acting uninterested, his body soft and boneless in the strip of yellow light from the window, but he didn't leave. His eyes hooked into the dancing girl in such a way that it made Chang want to skewer him on the tip of a fishing spear and watch him writhe. It was not only the Black Snakes that slithered toward her. The boneless man's hands forgot to smoke the cheroot between his fingers, but his half-closed eyes did not forget to watch each graceful dip and rise of her hips. He stayed there.

Like the shadow stayed. The one by the steps up to the terrace, the one merging with the bulk of a water butt, deeper black against black. The one whose breath would end. A gleam from a window glinted on the metal of a *shuriken* in a poised hand.

Chang drew his knife. He watched over her.

25

"Mama, is it true my father played the violin?"

"Where did you hear that?"

"At the soirée. Is it true?"

"Yes, it's true."

"Why did you never tell me?"

"Because he played it so badly."

"Did he once throw a violin into a fire in anger?"

Valentina laughed softly to herself. "Ah yes, more than once."

"So he had a temper?"

"*Da.* Yes."

"Am I like him?"

Valentina turned back to painting her nails. Her glossy new bob swung over her cheek, hiding her expression from Lydia's sharp gaze. "Every time I look at you, I see his face."

"Get out of bed."

"No."

"Darling, you drive me crazy. You've been lying in bed all week."

"So?"

"I don't understand you. Usually you're in such a rush to be out and doing things but now . . . Oh *dochenka*, you make me spit, you really do. Just because the school term is finished and you've got yourself a mountain of books there, it doesn't mean you can read the rest of your life away."

"Why not? I like reading."

"Don't be so wretched. What is that big fat book anyway?"

"*War and Peace.*"

"*Oh gospodi!* For God's sake, make it Shakespeare or Dickens or even that imperialist pig Kipling, but please not Tolstoy. Not Russian."

"I like Russian."

"Don't be silly, you know nothing Russian."

"Exactly. Time I did, don't you think?"

"No, I do not. It's time you got out of bed and went over to Polly's to eat some of her lily-white mother's plum pie that you always sing the praises of. Go out. Do something."

"No."

"Yes."

"No."

"You must."

"Why do you want me out of here? Because you want to jump into bed with Antoine?"

"Lydia!"

"Or is it Alfred now?"

"Lydia, you are a rude and impertinent child. I just want you to be normal, that's all."

"What is normal, Mama?"

"Anyway, I've finished with Antoine."

"Poor Antoine."

"Poof, he deserved no better."

"And Alfred? What have you decided the Englishman deserves?"

"Alfred is a very kind man with a generous heart, and I would remind you that God says the meek shall inherit the earth."

"I thought you didn't believe in God."

"That's got nothing to do with it. Now come on, tell me why you lie here in this stifling pit and won't go out anymore."

"Because I don't want to."

"You're odd, Lydia Ivanova. Do you know that? Any girl who lies in bed day after day with a white rabbit on her chest and reading about war is odd."

"Better odd than dead."

"What?"

"Nothing."

"Oh darling, you make me spit."

SHE KNEW. THE MOMENT THEY INVITED HER TO COME WITH them to the restaurant, she knew why. She washed her hair, put on her apricot dress and satin shoes, as instructed. The restaurant was not La Licorne this time. It was Italian and had little private booths with leather-padded banquettes and low lighting from candles overflowing the necks of stubby wine bottles wrapped in raffia. Lydia pushed the strips of something called linguini around her plate and waited for Alfred and Valentina to get to the point.

Alfred was smiling a lot, so much she thought his cheeks must ache. As if he'd swallowed a smile machine.

He poured her a glass of wine and said cheerfully, "This is jolly, isn't it, Lydia?"

"Mmm." She wouldn't meet her mother's eye.

"I hear you're still studying hard even though school is over for the summer. That's excellent, my dear. What is it you are concentrating on?"

"Russia and Russian."

She saw a slight flicker of surprise at the back of his eyes, but his smile didn't waver. "How interesting for you. After all, it is your heritage, isn't it? But Josef Stalin is doing brutal things to his people now in the name of freedom, distorting the very meaning of that word, so the world you are reading about in your books no longer exists in Soviet Russia, my dear. It's barbarous what's going on there. The *kulak* farmers and peasants are starving to death under this new Communist regime."

"Like they did under the tsar, you mean?"

A faint groan escaped from Valentina.

"Come now, Lydia," Alfred said with quiet determination, "let's not get into that discussion this evening. Tonight is a time for celebration." He glanced almost shyly in Valentina's direction. "Your mother and I have some news that we hope will make you very happy."

Valentina made no comment. Just looked at her daughter with watchful eyes.

Lydia started to talk. Somehow it seemed to her that if she could fill their little booth with her own words, stuff them into every spare corner, there would be no room for Alfred to squeeze in his news.

"Mr. Parker," Lydia said with a show of concern, "I think you said my headmaster, Mr. Theo, is a friend of yours, didn't you? Well, I need some advice because he was acting very strangely toward the end of term. You see, he would set us all some work to do in class and he'd put his head in his hands on his desk and stay like that for absolutely ages, as if he were asleep, but he wasn't because sometimes I caught his eyes staring straight at us behind his fingers, and Maria Allen thinks he must be having trouble with his beautiful Chinese mistress and is suffering from a broken heart but . . ."

"Lydia." It was Valentina.

". . . but Anna says her father behaves like that when he has a hangover, and one day Mr. Mason burst into the classroom all red in the face and dragged Mr. Theo out of . . ."

"Lydia!" Sharper this time. "Stop it."

For the first time Lydia looked at her mother's face. She uttered no more words, but her eyes pleaded.

Valentina turned away. "Tell her, Alfred. Tell her our good news."

Alfred beamed at her. "You see, Lydia, your mother has done me the great honor of agreeing to become my wife. We are going to be married."

They waited expectantly for her response.

Lydia made a huge effort. She forced a smile, though her teeth stuck to her lips. "Congratulations," she said. "I hope you'll be very happy."

Her mother leaned forward and kissed her briefly on her cheek.

26

CHANG AN LO FOUND THE NOTE. HE KNEW IT WAS FROM her before he opened it and he delicately fingered the paper to seek out the touch of her skin on it. The note was crammed into a small gherkin jar and placed on the flat rock at Lizard Creek, the one she liked to sun herself on. A leafy branch had been placed over the jar to make it less obvious to any eyes but his, and the thin silver leaves of the birch tree had curled and dried in the heat. She had been careful. No names. Just a warning.

"Kuomintang elite troops on their way to Junchow," it read. *"To wipe out Communists. Leave now. Urgent. You and your friends. Go."*

The word *Go* was underlined in red. At the bottom of the folded piece of paper she had added a sketch of a snake with its head sliced off and blood dripping from the wound.

THE NIGHT WAS DEMON BLACK. NO MOON. JUST UNRELENTING drizzle that deadened any sound. The house was grand and well guarded. Sentries almost invisible under the upturned eaves. High outer walls with no windows, and each courtyard lit by colored lanterns even in the middle of the night. In every doorway that faced the court-yards wind chimes tinkled ceaselessly, warding off evil spirits and evil-minded intruders alike, but the main threat to Chang came from the broad-headed chow chow dog that roamed the innermost courtyard. Its sharp ears picked up what human ears missed.

Chang's footsteps on the roof tiles were muffled. His felt shoes moved with slow patience, edging nearer, one silent step at a time. It was not the large inner courtyard that was his aim, but the previous one, the one with the fountain spurting from the dolphin's gaping mouth, the carp moving like white ghosts in the ornamental pond at its base and in the corner the plum tree laden with ripe fruit. The tree was old and its branches leaned against the house the way an old man leans on his stick. Chang was all in black, waiting, crouched in the shadows on the roof. Eyes and mind focused on one window.

The patrol guard did his job thoroughly, jabbing his heavy cane into the shrubs and under the delicately carved benches. Chang heard the *thwack* of the stick as it skewered some night reptile on the marble floor, and a low growl came from not far away. The lantern on the veranda threw light down one side of the guard's face, keen eyed and alert, hungry for something or someone to relieve the tedium of his nightly routine. Chang had no intention of doing so. Not yet.

Eventually the guard strode away to the shadows of the next courtyard where the dog offered a servile whimper of welcome, and while the animal was distracted, Chang moved fast. Wet tiles, slick under his feet. Along the top ridge. More tiles, moss-covered and treacherous. The tree, as easy as stepping stones. Over the veranda. The open window. A low light glimmered behind the curtain. Chang stepped over the sill.

IT WAS A LARGE ROOM. IN THE CENTER STOOD A MASSIVE black-oak bed, silk canopied and deeply carved with the shapes of bats with wings spread wide and fangs bared and long-necked birds devouring scorpions and frogs. To one side of the bed a candle burned in a jade holder and around it lay a confusion of fallen glasses and bottles, leather thongs, pools of spilled beer and a small brass burner. A long-stemmed pipe of stained ivory had been thrown on top of it all. The air smelled sweet and sickly.

Chang stood in the fold of the curtain for just long enough to make out three figures on the sheets. Two lay still and silent, eyes wide with fear. Staring at the knife in his hand. They were two young concubines, wrists bound with cords of leather to a hook attached to the headboard, and both were naked. Their smooth skin glistened with fragrant oil. One had what looked like a whip mark across her small breasts. Between the young concubines a large male figure lay sprawled on his back, slack-jawed and snoring, a yellow trail of vomit on the side of his face and the pillow. He wore nothing but a belt of snake teeth around his waist, which was thick and muscular, and his stomach was covered in dense wiry hair.

Chang fixed his eyes on the girls. It was a long time since he'd had a woman. The one with the whip mark was very beautiful, eyes like sloes and breasts that swelled soft and inviting, tilting upward with pink bud nipples. He moved closer, slowing his breathing, and stood at the foot of the bed. In one swift leap he was kneeling on it, between the man's naked legs. The man's closed eyes were quivering behind his eyelids but otherwise he did not move a muscle, unaware of anything except the drugged chaos of dreams beyond control. Chang reached over and removed a pair of chopsticks from the bedside table, sending both girls scurrying into a tight huddle on the pillows, the thongs pulled taut around their wrists. They were trembling, their long black hair flickering in the candlelight.

"A demon of the night," one whispered.

"Don't kill us."

He paid them no heed. Using the chopsticks in his left hand, he took hold of the man's limp penis and raised it until it was pulled taut and upright. A groan came from the sleeper's mouth, and one heavy hand crept down to his groin but then lay still. Chang slipped the sharp tip of his knife through the tangle of black hairs till it found the base of the penis and with a small twist of his wrist he snicked the fragile flesh.

A screech like the whinny of a horse rang out and made Chang expect the guard's return.

"Silence," he hissed.

The man's mouth shut and his teeth ground together. Whether in fear or pain was not clear. To Chang it made no difference.

"Silence," he ordered again.

The man's eyes were narrowed to slits, and they were staring with hatred at Chang. For one moment they sought out the sword, slender and delicately engraved, that hung on the wall above a small shrine, but Chang increased the pressure of his blade.

"What is it you want?" the man growled. His body was rigid and still as stone.

"I want your balls on a plate."

* * *

CHANG WAS IN CONTROL. A DANGEROUS POSITION TO BE in. In this great dragon of a house with all its bowing servants and well-tended courtyards only one man held power. Only one man breathed fire. That man was Feng Tu Hong.

Chang made his way through the archway. Across the final court-yard, the finest one where even in the darkness and the rain the gilded jaws of bronze lions glinted and threatened from their plinths. Guards and servants scurried forward, then backed away in alarm. Petals swirled across the marble floor, wet and fraying. The dog growled low in its throat and stood stiff-legged with hackles raised but did not attack.

Because ahead of Chang shuffled the hunched figure of Po Chu. The rain streamed off the strong curve of his back and down between his naked buttocks. He still wore only the belt of snake fangs but a leather thong now bound his wrists to his ankles in front of him, so that he was bent almost double, and another shackled his feet no more than two hand-spans apart. His progress like a crippled turtle was slow and humiliating, while the knife point on his testicles encour-aged him to keep edging forward. From his mouth came a stream of obscenities that Chang ignored.

"Feng Tu Hong," Chang called out, "I have your camel-humping son sitting on the point of my blade. If you ever wish to have him seed grandsons for you, open your doors and let him crawl on his belly to your feet."

The wind snatched at his words and the night sky swallowed them. Around him he could hear swords being drawn and the hiss of sharp breath, but none dared approach too close, and a callused hand had the sense to seize the dog by the scruff. Chang felt the power of the moment. It rose in him like a typhoon, racing through his veins and driving all fear before it. He must enjoy this moment, taste its sweetness. It could be his last.

THE ORNATE DOORS BURST OPEN AT THE TOP OF THE STEPS and Feng Tu Hong stood there, almost as broad as the archway itself. His powerful frame was wrapped in an embroidered robe of bright scarlet, though he still wore the white headband of mourning for Yuesheng. He disdained any weapon, but behind him hovered two broad-faced bodyguards with Lugers in their hands. The guns were pointed at Chang.

"You crave death," Feng stated.

His slanted eyes were black and very still. They gave no sign of the fury behind them. He folded his arms across his barrel chest.

"This is the second time I bring you a son, Feng Tu Hong. But this time this one is not dead." He stared steadily at the leader of the Black Snake triad. "Not yet."

Feng lowered his gaze to the dark head of his son, his only surviving son. It was disgracefully close to the floor.

"Po Chu, you dishonor me again," he said, words heavy with scorn. "I should let him slice you into worthless strips, no more use to me than a monkey's fingernails."

"Let us talk inside," Chang said swiftly, "where there are fewer ears and no rain to wash away our words."

Feng jutted out his heavy jaw and took a long shuddering breath that shook his whole body, then abruptly turned on his heel and swept back inside. Chang waited for the bodyguards to scuttle after him, then followed with Po Chu, who was still bent double and hopping sideways up the steps, his breath coming in short, savage grunts. The tethered man had nothing to say now, as if the weight of his father's words had crushed what was left of his spirit. Only the silent hatred remained, as naked and exposed as his own buttocks.

Inside the hall to the right was a wall of shrines with pictures of ancestors and other dead kin, full of fresh offerings of food and drink and incense sticks arranged in front of each one. The photograph of Yuesheng among them took Chang by surprise, though it shouldn't have. He studied it. The young confident face. A sensation like spikes driven through the pressure points of his feet made a blinding ball of light dart erratically behind Chang's eyes. He turned away but a memory followed him. It was of Po Chu beating his younger brother to a bloody pulp because of his political allegiance to Mao Tse Tung, and Yuesheng refusing to raise a hand to defend himself. Chang elicited a high moan from Po Chu by increasing the pressure of his knife in the soft sagging flesh between his legs, the knife that was a gift from Yuesheng. It possessed a fine blue-steel edge and a hilt of buffalo horn with the image of a Chinese unicorn, Chi Lin, carved on each side for good fortune. Now it was thrust in Yuesheng's worthless brother's greasy balls.

That would have made Yuesheng laugh.

Chang felt his friend's spirit very close at this moment. His voice rustling in the air. Maybe because Yuesheng knew they were about to be reunited. He'd come to show the way. But Chang shook his head, a sharp little flick.

"Not yet, Yuesheng," he murmured.

"So." FENG HAD POSITIONED HIMSELF IN THE CENTER OF A magnificent room, bright with gold and jade decoration and elegant scrolls on the walls, as if to remind Chang exactly who was in charge here. He stood with legs apart, arms folded, his head thrust forward on his broad neck and his face a cold blank mask. "So. What is the price this time? Another printing press? I believe that is the price for a son. Even a shameful one."

"No."

Chang jabbed the side of his hand down onto the back of Po Chu's neck, sending him sprawling to his knees, then seized a handful of black hair and yanked hard. He slid the knife up under his chin. Po Chu was sweating heavily, his tethered hands quivering as if both wrists were broken, his skin slick and gleaming as he gulped for air and raised panicked eyes to his father.

"Honorable and wise parent," he gasped in a hoarse voice, "I beg you to grant what this devil asks."

Feng spat.

"You are nothing to me."

"Very well," Chang said easily, "if he is worth nothing, he is of no use to me either. Prepare to meet your ancestors, Feng Po Chu."

He gripped the hair, tightened his hold on the hilt, and saw the Lugers rise in readiness. The sudden foul stench of feces soiled the room as Po Chu lost control of his bowels. Blood trickled down the blade of the knife onto Chang's fingers.

"Take him," Feng said to Chang through tight lips. "Take away my son. He is nothing but poison in my heart."

Chang uttered a loud cry that rocked the focus of the room, commended his own spirit to his ancestors, and prepared for the stillness of the end, but even as he did so, a band of sorrow tightened around his chest. His heart turned to lead at the knowledge that he wouldn't see her again in this lifetime and that the thread that bound them would be cut. He had failed her, his fox girl. His last moment on this earth had come and she was still in danger.

Po Chu screamed.

Chang stretched his prisoner's throat so taut, the tendons stood out like teeth. He tensed his muscles for the final cut.

"Stop."

It was Feng. His eyes no more than black lines on a face of stone.

"What is your price this time?"

Silent tears were running down Po Chu's cheeks.

"A life."

"Your own life?"

"No."

"Speak. Whose life?"

"The girl I stole from your Black Snakes in the *hutong*. Your men are pursuing her."

"Because she lied." Feng's voice was flecked with anger. "She told them she didn't know you or where you were hiding, but she was seen with you later. She lied. It is a matter of honor."

"Feng Tu Hong, she is a barbarian and like all barbarians she does not understand about honor. The girl is not worth the spittle from your mouth, but I give you your son, your only surviving son now that Yuesheng is gone, in exchange for her feeble existence. A fair bargain, I think."

"You insult me. And you insult my son. If you want the barbarian whore's life so much, why did you not ask for it when I promised you any gift you wanted when you brought me Yuesheng's body to be buried? Why not then?"

"My reasons are my own."

Feng glared at him. Somewhere behind an inlaid screen a male laugh drifted out and the sound of slippers brushed over the thick silk carpet as a tall figure stepped out into the room, a lazy cigarette in his hand.

"Only ask questions, Feng, if you are sure you will receive answers. This young colt is outrunning you." The voice was soft and pleasant.

It belonged to the Englishman. Chang recognized him instantly from the Ulysses Club. The one who spoke Mandarin as if his tongue were born to it. He was wearing a long loose gray gown and an embroidered cap on his head, a man trying to be something he was not. Chang could make out the effort of it in his pale gray eyes, but there was something else in them too. Something in pain. Something that wanted to claw itself to death.

Feng Tu Hong gave him a warning look that would have silenced most men, but the Englishman merely shrugged, gave a slight smile and asked Chang in Mandarin, "So who is this barbarian girl you bargain for so persuasively?"

"A Russian chit, *fanqui*," Feng growled. "Not one worth having."

"Her name?"

Chang saw his interest, though the Englishman tried to hide it.

"Ivanova," Chang told him. "Lydia Ivanova. One with fire on her tongue as well as in her hair."

"Ah." The Englishman nodded silently, ran a hand thoughtfully over his forehead, and turned to Feng. "I'll buy her from you." He said it casually, as he would for a bag of chestnuts from a street trader. He pulled a drawstring pouch from his pocket. It looked heavy. "Tonight's share. For the chit." He tossed it across to Feng, but the Chinese made no attempt to catch it and it fell with a dull thump on the carpet at his feet.

"The girl is not for sale," Feng said and stepped over the pouch. "She is to die. As an example to others who lie to us." His black eyes were fixed on the knife blade at his son's throat. "But in exchange for that dung-stinking cur on his knees there, I offer you your own life, Chang An Lo. And my word of protection. You will need it. Or Po Chu will drain the lifeblood from your body as slowly and painfully as a boar roasts on a spit over a fire. Do you accept?"

There was a long silence. Outside a dog's howl split the darkness.

"I accept." Chang withdrew the knife.

Instantly a guard leaped forward and sliced the thongs that bound Po Chu. He struggled to his feet, his body stiff and shaking with shame. The feces slithered down his legs. He looked ready to sink his teeth into Chang.

"Po Chu," Feng snarled. "I have given my word."

Po Chu did not move. He remained only inches from Chang, breathing hatred into his face.

Chang shut him out. His usefulness was over. His father would have let him die rather than swallow his own words. But Chang could not have asked for the girl's life in payment for Yuesheng's body because it would have dishonored Yuesheng's spirit. To be bargained for a *fanqui*. That brought shame. But the printing press was vital to China's future and was something that Yuesheng had died for. It was a fitting price.

"And the girl?" the tall Englishman asked.

Feng looked over at him, saw his concern, and gave a small cruel smile. "Ah, you see, Tiyo Willbee, I have ordered her bowels to be twisted around her neck until she can no longer breathe and then her breasts to be cut off."

The Englishman closed his eyes.

Chang doubted that it was true. Ordered her death, yes. But the manner in which she should die, no. The leader of the Black Snakes would leave such things to the inventiveness of his followers. He had spoken the words only to spit venom at his English guest. Chang wondered why.

"Feng Tu Hong, I thank you for the honorable exchange we have made," Chang said with formal politeness. "A life for a life. Now I offer you something more important than a life."

Feng had been striding toward the door, eager to rid himself of the sight and smell of his son. He halted.

"What," he demanded, "is more important than life?"

"Information. From General Chiang Kai-shek himself."

"*Ai-aiee!* For a toothless cub, you speak boldly."

"I speak truly. I have information of value to you."

"And I have men who know how to drag it from you with tortures you have never even dreamed of. So why should I bargain for it?" He turned away.

The Englishman stepped forward. "Show some sense, Feng. Exacting information by such methods takes time." He gestured idly at Chang, leaving a trail of cigarette smoke in the air. "In this case,

I suspect quite a lot of time. And maybe this is urgent. Where's the harm in striking a deal?" He laughed, soft and low. "After all, it's what we did, you and I, and look where it's got us."

Feng frowned, impatience catching up with him. "So. What is this new bargain you offer?"

"I will give you secret information. From Chiang Kai-shek's office in Peking. In return you give me the flame-haired Russian."

Feng laughed, a rich, strong sound that loosened his tight jaws and made the others in the room breathe easier. "You will have this chit? Whatever the cost?"

"No. I will have her. For this cost."

"Very well. Agreed."

"Word has come from Chiang Kai-shek before he returns to his capital in Nanking. Elite troops are coming to Junchow. They are approaching as I speak. To destroy all Communists, spike their heads on the town's walls, and dig out corruption in the government of Junchow. As honored chairman of our Chinese Council, it seems to me this information is of value to you in advance of their arrival." He gave a low bow and heard Po Chu groan.

Feng remained still and silent for a long moment. His face had grown pale, in fierce contrast to his scarlet robe, and his broad hands clenched and unclenched. Suddenly he strode across the room.

"The girl is yours," he called without turning. "Take her for yourself. But don't expect any good to come of it. To mix barbarians with our civilized people is always a first step to death." A servant on his knees held open the door, and the leader of the Black Snakes was gone.

Chang gave the Englishman a nod. An acknowledgment of his help. Neither spoke. Po Chu spat on the floor with an incoherent curse, then disappeared into the night, so Chang left the room and made his way out into the courtyard once more. It was when he was crossing the shadows of the second courtyard that he saw a black uniformed guard trudging through the drizzle with drooping shoulders and a burden in each hand. In one was the severed head of the chow chow dog, its black tongue hanging out like a scorched snake. In the other was the head of the guard with the hungry face, his filmy eyes no longer alert. The price of failure in the household of Feng Tu Hong was high.

As Chang's attention was distracted for a split second by this bloody sight, the full weight of a gun slammed into the side of his head and he slid into the blackness of hell.

27

SEPTEMBER, AND HOT. STILL HOT.

A brass fan whirred on the ceiling. All it did was take bites out of the leaden air and chew it up a bit. Lydia was sick of standing here with her arms stretched out while Madame Camellia stuck pins in her. She was sick of the satisfied private smile on her mother's face as she draped herself in the client's chair and watched. Most of all she was sick of the silence from Chang. It roared in her ears and made her long for news of him.

No word for a month. A whole desperate month of not knowing.

He must have taken heed of her warning. Left Junchow. That had to be the reason for his silence. Had to be. Which meant he was at least safe. She clung to that thought, warmed her hands on it, and murmured again and again as she lay wide-eyed in bed at night, "He's safe, he's safe, he's safe." If she said it often enough, she could make it true. Couldn't she?

He was tucked away now in one of the Red Army training camps; she pictured him there, taking potshots at targets and marching up and down, polishing his boots and his buckles, doing scary things on the end of ropes. Isn't that what soldiers did in camps? So he was safe. Surely. Please let him be safe. Please, let all his strange gods protect him. He was one of their own, wasn't he? They'd care for him. But she took deep breaths to quiet her racing heart, because she didn't trust them, neither his gods nor hers.

"Darling, do stop fidgeting. How can Madame Camellia work properly when you won't keep still?"

Lydia scowled at her mother. Valentina was looking extremely cool and elegant in an exquisite cream linen suit made by Madame Camellia, Junchow's most coveted dressmaker. Her salon copied the very latest Paris fashions and had a long waiting list of clients, so it was an honor to be allowed to cut in line, all because of Alfred, who had pulled a few strings. Valentina's heart was set on having the very best for her wedding.

"Doesn't she look adorable in it, Madame Camellia?"

The Chinese owner of the salon glanced up at Lydia's face and studied it for a while in silence. Lydia was standing on a small round padded platform in the middle of the room while Madame Camellia touched and tugged and twitched the soft green silk, which was as pale as her songbird's throat. A bird sat in a pavilion cage in the corner of the room and sang with a constant burst of trills and spiraling notes that grated on Lydia's taut nerves.

"She looks lovely," Madame Camellia said with a sweet smile. "The *eau de nil* color with her hair is just perfect."

"You see, Lydia, I told you you'd adore it."

Lydia said nothing. Stared at the jade pins in the dressmaker's hair.

"Mrs. Ivanova, some swatches of the new tweeds from Tientsin arrived this morning. In readiness for winter. I thought you might like one for your honeymoon costume. Would you care to view them?" It was spoken as if conferring a special privilege.

"Yes, I'd be delighted."

Madame Camellia nodded to her young assistant, and Valentina was escorted out of the room. The walls were pale and soothing with rose-pink drapes, but splashes of color were provided by a bowl of orchids and the bird's golden cage.

"Miss Lydia." She spoke softly. "Would you like to tell me what it is about the dress that displeases you?"

The dress? As if she cared about the dress. She dragged her thoughts back into the room and looked down at the satin-smooth hair that was coiled up on top of the dressmaker's head. A delicate camellia, made of the finest white silk, nestled in its ebony folds. She looked like a little black-crested bird, bright and quick, her tiny figure encased in a tight turquoise cheongsam with a side slit to show off one slender leg, but Valentina had mentioned that at night Madame dressed in stylish Western fashions while she did the rounds of the nightclubs on the arm of her latest American lover. She had made herself into a wealthy woman and could pick and choose.

She looked at Lydia with intelligent eyes.

"Tell me how you'd like it to be."

"It's my bridesmaid dress. Mama is the person deciding on it."

"Yes, I know. But what style would you prefer?"

"I'd like it more . . . well, more . . ." She thought of Chang's bright eyes. What would make them shine?

"More what?"

"More revealing."

Madame Camellia did not laugh. Or say, *What have you got to reveal?* She nodded to herself and reached up to shift a piece of material here and unpick some stitches there.

"Better?"

Lydia gazed into the long mirror in front of her. The demure high neck her mother had chosen was transformed into a fluid scoop that showed soft white skin.

"Much better. Thank you."

Madame Camellia started to adjust the sleeves, to shorten and tighten them.

"Madame, you live in the Chinese old town, don't you?"

"Mmm." Her mouth was full of pins.

"Are the soldiers still there?"

Skillful fingers were tucking the pins round the armholes. "The stinking gray bellies, you mean?"

"The ones with the yellow armbands. From Peking. The Kuomintang troops."

"*Ai!* They are devils."

"So they're still in Junchow?"

Madame Camellia dropped her charming smile, and abruptly her face looked its age. "They sweep through like a sandstorm, each day a different street. Tearing workers from their stools and scribes from their offices. They go anywhere a finger is pointed. Beheadings and executions at sunset, till our streets run red. They claim they are wiping out Communism and corruption, but it seems to me that many old scores are being settled."

Lydia's mouth went dry. "Are any young people being killed?"

Madame Camellia looked at the Russian girl more carefully. "Some. Students and their like. Communist ideals are fierce among the young." She lowered her voice. "Do you know one?"

Lydia almost spoke his name, she was so desperate for news.

"No," she said quickly. "I am concerned for them all."

"I see." The dressmaker gently touched her hand. "Many escape. There is always hope."

Lydia's throat tightened, and she wanted to scratch out the eyes of his callous gods. She looked away and saw her reflection in the mirror.

"Do you think, Madame, that I could have green beads over the dress?"

THEY DIDN'T TALK. NOT ABOUT THE WEDDING. LYDIA WAS aware that preparations for it were being made. She heard mention of a date in January, but she didn't ask and she wasn't told. Letters started to arrive by each post in thick embossed envelopes but she passed no comment, and even when Valentina was out she made a point of not looking inside the lovely rosewood box where they were all tucked away. The box was an engagement present from Alfred. The box and the ring. A solitaire diamond. It radiated light even in their dingy room and Lydia couldn't help thinking that Mr. Liu would give "plenty dollar" for a ring like that.

The days grew cooler. Still no word from Chang. But black shadows no longer hung around her in the streets and a sudden movement on the edge of her sight lost its power to set her pulse pounding. It took her a while to be certain, and she was never quite sure how she knew. But she did. They were gone, the snakes. They had crawled back into their fetid holes. She didn't know why this should be so but she was convinced it was something to do with Chang. Even from afar he protected her.

Nothing else had changed in the attic. Lydia struggled to concentrate on her schoolwork in the evenings, chewing on the end of her pencil and casting sideways glances out the window, scanning the street for a quick light step, or sometimes staring at her mother on the sofa. At the bottle and the glass. They were always at Valentina's side despite the absurd display of abstinence the day she cut her hair. Only the height of the liquid inside them varied. She would sit there with a music score on her lap and hum a Bach fugue softly to herself until she reached some point in her head that was unbearable, and then she'd hurl the pages across the room. For hours after that she'd stare blankly at the space in front of her, seeing things that her daughter could only guess at.

Lydia tried talking, but the only solace Valentina sought at such times was in the bottle. Lydia was a fine judge of the moment when she could half lift her mother off the sofa and roll her into bed. Too soon and she became aggressive. Too late and she was unable to stay upright. Her slender body never seemed to grow heavier despite the food that now appeared regularly on the table. Neither Valentina nor Lydia ate much of it. Only Sun Yat-sen grew fatter and more contented.

"Would you like a proper hutch for your rabbit?" Alfred asked one Saturday when he'd come to take Valentina to the races. She had always loved horses.

"Yes." Lydia had meant to say no.

"Well, my dear, I'll be delighted to buy one. Let's go and choose it now while your mother," he smiled indulgently at Valentina, "does whatever it is your mother does."

Out in the marketplace Lydia chose the biggest and brashest rabbit hutch she could find. One with separate compartments and special zinc drinking and feeding bowls and funny little curling decorations on top like a pagoda. She knew Alfred was bribing her. He knew. And she knew.

"Lydia, I'm confident we can make this work. Us, I mean. You and I as part of the same family. I'd like us to try."

Lydia bit her tongue. Today she had let him buy her and she felt dirty, her skin all gritty. Is that how Mama felt each day? Bought and dirty. Is that why she's drinking so much when he's not around, to flush away the grit? Lydia looked at his shiny spectacles and his polished cheeks and wondered if he had even a grain of an idea how much he was hurting them both. No, she decided, Alfred Parker's eyes were blind behind their ugly thick lenses and his mind was a gray colorless box of self-righteousness. How could he possibly think she would ever want to be part of the same family?

"Thank you for the hutch," she said coolly and walked up the stairs.

THE BROWN FISH SLIPPED THROUGH THE COLD CLEAR CUR-rent of the river, rippling its wide body smoothly over the gravel. This time, Lydia told herself. This time. She held her breath. Tense and still.

Her spear sliced down through the water. And missed. The fish fled. She cursed it and waded back onto the narrow strip of sand at Lizard Creek, where she squatted down under the dazzling blue sky of autumn and waited for the flurry of panic in the river to subside. Just being here in this place brought her closer to Chang. She remembered the feel of his damaged foot in her hand, the weight of it on her palm, and the tension in his skin as she'd threaded the needle back and forth through its ragged edges. The intimate warmth of his blood on her fingers. Marking her. As she was marking him.

When finally the stitching was over he'd sighed and she'd wondered if it was with relief or . . . and she knew this was stupid . . . because he missed the touch of her hands. She brushed her fingers over the empty sand now, seeking out any faint traces of his blood. In her head she could hear as clear as the sound of the river itself the strange little laugh he gave when she asked him to find a way into the Ulysses Club and retrieve the rubies. When she recalled it, she felt sick. How could she have thought of putting him in such danger?

"You would turn me into a thief," he'd said sternly.

"We can split the money between us."

"Can we split the prison sentence between us too?"

"Don't get caught and there'll be no prison," she'd scoffed.

But even then her cheeks had started to burn. She'd turned them to the breeze off the silvery surface of the river and wanted to tell him not to take the risk after all. Forget the necklace. But her tongue wouldn't find the words. When she looked back at him his mouth was curved in a smile that somehow soothed the fretting of her soul. It was a strange feeling, one that was new to her. To be with someone and not have to hide things. He saw what was inside her and understood.

Unlike Alfred Parker. He wanted her to be somebody she would never be and would never want to be, the perfect rose-pink English miss. His dull little soul was eager to snatch her mother away from her and give her a rabbit hutch in exchange. What kind of bargain was that?

Oh Chang An Lo, I need you here. I need your clear eyes and your calm tongue.

She rose to her feet, trying to move smoothly, and stared hard at the water. She had to catch a fish to present to Mrs. Zarya, so she took from her pocket a penknife she'd pinched from a boy at school and proceeded to whittle the tip of her spear to an even sharper point, the way she'd seen Chang do. The stripped willow branch didn't need it, but it made her feel better. To be cutting something.

"My great heavens, *MOI VOROBUSHEK,* where did that hideous thing come from?" Mrs. Zarya flapped her hands in a flurry of astonishment and eyed Lydia with sudden suspicion. "You not offering it instead of rent, are you? This month is now time."

Lydia shook her head. "No. It's a gift. I caught it for you."

Mrs. Zarya smiled broadly. "Clever little sparrow. Come."

Lydia was relieved that instead of waddling back into the living room with its oversized furniture and the accusing eye of General Zarya, her landlady led her farther down the corridor to a narrow kitchen. She had never been in it before. It was small and brown. Two chairs, a table, a stove, a sink, and a cabinet. Everything brown. But it smelled clean and soapy. In one corner stood a well-polished samovar with its little teapot keeping warm on top.

"Now," Mrs. Zarya said, "let us look on this sea monster you bring me."

Lydia placed her gift on the table. It was a large wide-winged flatfish, as brown as the wood it lay on but spattered with tiny yellow flecks on its broad back.

"You catch this?"

"Yes."

Mrs. Zarya nodded appreciatively and prodded it with one finger. "That is good. So now I cook it. You eat with me too?"

Lydia grinned. "*Spasibo.* You are kind, *dobraya. Ya plohaya povariha.* I am not a good cook."

"Ah, so you speak Russian at last. *Otlichno!* That is good."

"No, I'm learning it from a book but it's hard that way."

"Tell that lazy nothing mother of yours to put off the bottle and teach her daughter *russkiy yazik.*"

"She won't."

"Ah." Mrs. Zarya opened her arms wide and swept Lydia to her overflowing bosom in a warm suffocating hug before Lydia saw it coming. The huge black bosom smelled of mothballs and talcum powder, and she could feel a whalebone digging into her cheek.

"Help," she mumbled.

The Russian woman released her with a look of concern.

"I need help," Lydia said. "To learn Russian, I mean."

Mrs. Zarya thumped a heavy hand against her own bosom. It vibrated disturbingly. "I, Olga Petrovna Zarya," she said in triumph, "teach you your mother tongue. Yes?"

"*Da.*" Yes.

"But first I grill fish."

LYDIA HAUNTED THE PLACES CHANG MIGHT BE. AFTER school each day she clambered first down to Lizard Creek, always expecting that this time at last she would push her way through the tangle of bushes and see his dark head bent over the beginnings of a fire or his knife swiftly flashing through the flesh of a fish or the bark of a willow twig. Everything he did, he did smoothly. Cleanly. Not messy like herself. She pictured it as she lay in bed at night, saw him raise his eyes from whatever task he was doing and look at her in that intense way of his. With a smile and a gleam that told her he was pleased she had found him.

Because she wasn't sure how he felt about her. Maybe he was staying away because he'd had enough of her and her crazy *fanqui* arguments. She tried to think back. Had she insulted him? Going to the funeral. Was that the problem?

Not the gray bellies. Don't let it be because of the gray bellies.

Chills whipped through her body whenever she thought of their swords or their rifles pointed at his head. She saw the soldiers. With their armbands and the sun on their caps as if they owned the world. Strutting around the old town. It was madness but she went there, couldn't stay away. She steered clear of the *hutongs* but scanned the crowds in the main streets, again and again and again, and found nothing but hostile eyes and jostling poles and mouths that shouted unimaginable words at her. Once she even spotted a neck with a Black Snake tattoo. But the man showed no interest in her. She didn't run. Any more than she ran from the beggars who reached out at her with skeletal fingers or from the well-clad Chinese businessman who offered her a ride in his big black Cadillac. The chance of finding Chang among all this teeming humanity was . . .

She refused even to think the word.

"AH, MISSY, MY EYES ARE BRIGHT WITH THE PLEASURE OF seeing you again. It has been a long time." Mr. Liu waved her to a seat and spread his hands to indicate his shop. "I hope my miserable premises are not too disgusting to you."

Lydia smiled. "It looks different. Very modern. Your customers must come here just for the delight of viewing such a grand place, Mr. Liu."

Mr. Liu's stick-dry figure seemed to swell with pride, and he scuttled away to the stove where the teapot was waiting. It was a new one. Plain cream porcelain. In fact everything was new. Shelves, cabinets, door, window, even the stool she was sitting on. Gone was the bamboo one and the ebony table. In its place was a modern chrome and plastic one. The shelves and counter were the same: modern, clean and horrible. Only the black stove remained of what used to be. And the jasmine tea. That hadn't changed.

"I'm impressed, Mr. Liu. Business must be very good indeed."

"Times are hard, Missy, but there is always someone who needs something. The trick is to provide it." His face was older, the dry walnut skin thinner than tissue, and his hair was short and white now, but the wispy beard was coming back. He fingered it constantly like an old friend.

She wondered what it was he had learned the trick of providing. Guns? Drugs? Information?

"Mr. Liu, if I wanted to find someone in old Junchow, how should I go about it?"

His eyes narrowed. Settled on her face.

"You have this person's address?"

"No."

"Place of work?"

"No."

"His family?"

"No." She didn't notice the *his* slipped in there.

"Friends?"

She hesitated. "I know one friend. By sight only."

"So." He folded his hands into his sleeves and considered her for so long she started to grow uncomfortable. "So," he said again. "This someone. He could be in trouble?"

"It's possible."

"In hiding?"

"Maybe."

"I see."

She waited what seemed an age while he considered again.

"The place to search, Missy, is the docks. Down by the harbor. There the world is lawless and nameless. The dollar is the only language that they speak. The dollar and the knife."

"Mr. Liu, you are generous with your words. Thank you."

"Be careful, Missy. It is a dangerous place. Life there is worth less than a hair from your copper head."

"Thank you for the warning, I will remember it." She sipped her tea and looked around at the many objects on display. The metal leg by the door had gone but in its place stood a giant turtle shell. "I have something small you may find of interest."

He drank his tea impassively.

Lydia pulled out an object wrapped up in a cloth. It was a handbag. Alfred had bought it as a present for Valentina and earned himself a kiss in return, but after he'd gone, Valentina had shuddered and thrown it under her bed.

"Red!" she'd exclaimed. "As if I'd ever be seen holding a *red* handbag."

But it looked expensive. Satin covered, with tiny white pearls along the top. Lydia laid it on the new table. Mr. Liu glanced at it but didn't pick it up. His mouth pulled tight into a straight line.

"Thirty dollars," he offered.

Lydia gaped at him. It was more than she'd expected. She certainly wasn't going to argue. She nodded. He drew a roll of notes from inside his gown and counted six of them into her hand. His fingernails were long and clean.

"Thank you, Mr. Liu. You are generous." She rose to leave.

"Take care, Missy. This life only comes once. Don't throw it away."

SHE BURIED IT. THE THIRTY DOLLARS.

In a jar at the base of the big flat rock. Each time she went to Lizard Creek she used a pebble to scratch a line on the side of the big rock, just so that he'd realize she'd been there. Now she arranged pebbles in a small mound over the top of the spot where she'd buried the glass jar, like a cairn.

"You'll know, Chang An Lo. I'm certain you'll know. It isn't much, thirty dollars, but it's something. I'll bring more, I promise. It'll help if you're in need."

She rested a hand on the top stone of the cairn and curled her fingers around it as if she could curl her fingers around Chang himself.

"Don't let him be in need," she whispered to his gods. "Except in need of me."

28

THEO OPENED HIS EYES ABRUPTLY, BREAKING FREE FROM the fierce grip of his dreams. He was suffocating. His lungs would barely move, blackness was creeping into his head, a needle point of pain at his throat was . . .

His eyes finally registered what was in front of them.

The cat. For God's sake, it was just the bloody cat. Yeewai was crouched on his chest, her evil yellow eyes no more than inches from his own and her talons kneading the soft skin between his collarbones. A noise like a steam engine was coming from her mouth but Theo had no idea whether it was a purr or a growl.

He pushed the animal down onto the eiderdown and instantly realized the warm body of Li Mei was no longer beside him in the bed. Oh Christ, what time was it? He sat up. His head exploded into ten thousand pieces, each one of them embedding into his brain, and the cat's claw raked his hand in protest. Theo groaned, rolled his legs over the side of the bed, and let his hands do the work of holding his head together.

It was morning and his mouth tasted like the inside of a rat's ass.

Another day. Sweet Christ.

HE FELT COLD. REALLY COLD. THE AIR IN THE CLASSROOM was so chilly Theo expected to see his own breath rise like smoke from his mouth. He shivered. His limbs ached.

He was seated in his usual place at his high desk in front of the class, but there was a stove behind him and he was near enough to reach behind to feel it. The blasted caretaker must have forgotten it again. To his surprise the stove was hot and when he thought about it, the condensation on the windows meant the room must be warm, fighting off the northerly blasts outside. The pupils looked comfortable, not chilled. The pupils. Rows of them. Unruly creatures. Today they felt like leeches on his skin, sucking him dry, draining all the knowledge from his head into theirs. He shivered again and tried to concentrate on the pile of papers in front of him, but the writing kept blurring and his eyes lost focus. He had arrived late and set the class a history exercise to do while he tried to mark the homework he should have dealt with last evening.

That was the trouble with spending so many nights out on the river. These days he never seemed to be anything but cold and tired, the sort of tiredness that eats into your bones. The Chinese captains of the junks and sampans and the oarsmen in the scows were used to him now and he was used to them. No more scares. No blades. And no cats, thank God. And they knew only too well the way to ease the pain of the wind driving off the river and knifing down your throat where the damp rotted your lungs. So they taught him. How to make the wait seem shorter and the fear lose its edge. Just the thought of the pipe upstairs in the drawer by his bed set his hands shaking.

A shout made him raise his head. He hadn't even realized it had dropped onto his hands. A dark-headed lad was struggling with a girl over the ownership of a pen.

"Philips," Theo said sharply.

"But sir, I . . ."

"Silence, boy."

The culprit glared at the girl. She smirked.

Theo let it pass. Their faces merged into gray patterns in front of his eyes. He blinked to bring them back into sharp outline and looked around at the other young faces. Few appeared to be working. Girls were whispering behind their hands, and one of the boys was folding a sheet of paper with perfect precision into a paper dart. The Russian girl was staring out the window. With an effort he ran a hand over his eyes to wipe away the cobwebs that felt as if they clung there. The Russian girl turned to watch and he felt a touch of unease. There was something about the way that girl looked at you, as if she could see into all the black holes you tried to hide. He wondered if she knew how lucky she was to be still alive after that Black Snake business with Feng Tu Hong.

Alfred was a fool to get involved with that family.

For no reason he suddenly recalled the conversation he'd had with the girl in the Ulysses Club and the ferocity of her desire to mold her life into something she wanted. By sheer force of will. Well, life wasn't that simple. Didn't it ever occur to the silly girl to wonder why she was the only foreigner in the school, the only non-British pupil among all the Taylors and Smiths and Fieldings? Didn't she find that odd? Not that she was much of a mixer. She'd always kept to herself, except for the Mason girl. He looked at Polly's glossy blond head bent over her work. She seemed to be the only one really concentrating on the exercise, and suddenly a bitter anger rose in his throat, so that he felt an urge to strike out at the poor defenseless creature.

Christopher Mason.

A fitting name. A man of stone.

"No," Mason had said over a gin at the club, with a smile that wasn't a smile. "No. It will not end so easily."

"Damn you, man," Theo had retorted. "The debt to the bank will be repaid by early next year and then that's an end to it as far as I'm concerned. No more."

"I must disagree."

"Don't be absurd. You can run the business on your own. You don't need me anymore, neither you nor Feng Tu Hong."

"Oh, but I do, Willoughby. Don't underestimate yourself." Slate gray eyes and a slate gray tongue.

"Why?"

"Because, my dear chap, Feng won't do the deal without you. The old devil wants you in on it or he shuts up shop, God only knows why."

Theo felt chills up his spine. "That's your problem," he said, "not mine." He started to walk away.

"The inside of a jail is not very pleasant, I'm told."

Theo swung round. The urge to crush his fist into this man's grinning face almost blew him over the edge, but some vestige of survival instinct clawed him back from the brink. He leaned over Mason, emphasizing the difference in their height, breathing hard in his face.

"Is that a threat?"

Mason nodded slowly. "Yes."

"You mean you would report me. To customs."

"Exactly that. As a trafficker in opium, Foreign Mud as they call it. I can provide times, dates, black-sail boats, the whole damn lot. Witnesses who saw you. You'd be staring at four filthy walls and ten years in prison before you could even blink." There was savage enjoyment on his face.

"If you shop me, Mason, I'll take you down into that hell with me, you bastard, I swear to God I will."

Mason laughed. "Don't kid yourself, you bloody fool. You have no proof. There's nothing to connect me with your nighttime activities on the river. You don't think any of that money has gone into my bank, do you?" He laughed again, a harsh grating sound that tried Theo's nerves. "You're in a box, Willoughby, and you can't get out, any more than a dead man can crawl out of his coffin. So just enjoy the nice cozy benefits, why don't you?" He stared with amusement at Theo. "It looks to me, old chap, as if you're up to your eyeballs in them already."

Theo knew he was trapped. The rage inside him was burning holes in his belly and only the sweet black paste seemed to blunt the pain. But Li Mei did not understand. She said little. But he saw the look in her eyes each time he went to the drawer.

"Sir?"

Theo blinked hard. Got his brain moving. The class was still there. It was Polly. Pretty Polly.

"Yes?"

"I've finished, sir."

"In which case, Miss Mason, why don't you join me here in front of the class and read it out loud for the benefit of those who lack your speed of mind."

Polly's shoulders hunched down as if she wanted to crawl under her desk. She mumbled something.

"Pardon, Miss Mason, I didn't catch that."

"I said I'd rather not, sir."

Mason's laugh in his ears goaded him on. He didn't normally make Polly read aloud to the class as her academic talents were very mediocre, but to hell with it. Today would be different. She stood in front of the rows of expectant faces and started to read in a halting voice, her cheeks a miserable red. Theo realized with surprise that she was talking about Henry VIII and the Field of the Cloth of Gold. Is that what he'd set them? He'd forgotten already. Her words faltered, stumbled, grew slower and smaller.

"That's enough, Miss Mason. You may sit down."

She threw him a glance of gratitude and escaped back to her seat. *Gratitude.* She should be hating him for that display of petty cruelty, hating him as much as he hated himself.

"I congratulate you, Polly, on your diligence in class. The rest of you," he scowled at his pupils and vaguely registered a tawny gaze glaring at him with fury, "will stay in at break time and write an account of the Diet of Worms. You, Polly," he smiled at her benignly, "you are excused from it because you have worked well."

Her blue eyes widened with pleasure.

It was too easy. To take revenge that way. Mason was the one who deserved the spike through his heart. If he had a heart, that is.

"MR. THEO?"

"What is it, Lydia?"

"Please, would you do some translation for me? Only a few sentences. Into Chinese, I mean."

It was the end of the school day and his head was thrumming. He could barely stop his limbs trembling and twitching, desperate to seek out the pipe and the paste and the little heated spoon, but first he had to steel himself for the ordeal of the parents-at-the-gate ritual. Fortunately the wind was keen and gusting through the yard, so the mothers and *amahs* did not linger over picking up their offspring or stand around making aimless conversation. But now the Russian girl wanted something. What did she say? Translation? She was holding a piece of paper out to him, expecting him to take it. His fingers reached out and he saw her watching the way the tips jumped erratically around the paper before he grasped it. With an effort he read what was on it. There were four short sentences.

1. Do you know someone called . . . ?

2. Can you direct me to . . . ?

3. Where is . . . ?
4. Does he live/work here?

"Ah." He smiled at her. "The young Chinese. You're after him, aren't you?"

He was astonished by the girl's reaction. Her mouth fell open, her lips bleached bone white, and she seemed suddenly painfully young and as vulnerable as eggshell.

"How do you know?" she asked urgently. "Where is he? Have you seen him? Is he well? Do you . . . ?"

"Slow down, Lydia." Her hand was shaking worse than his. "If we're talking about the same person, no, I don't know his name and I don't know where he is. But you needn't worry about him because when I saw him last he was under the protection of Feng Tu Hong, the big boss of the Chinese Council and of the Black Snakes, so he should . . ."

She swayed. He wasn't sure if it was shock or relief.

"When?" she breathed.

"When what?"

"When did you last see him?"

"Oh, some time back . . . I'm not quite sure when it was exactly. He was talking to Feng Tu Hong. About you."

"Why me? What did he say?"

Theo was struck by her need. It reminded him of his own. As if she were bleeding inside.

"Lydia, dear girl, calm down. He asked Feng to tell his Snake brotherhood to leave you alone, though I have no idea what you did to get them so riled up in the first place."

"What did this Feng say?"

"Well, Feng . . . ," he hesitated, somehow unwilling to reveal too much of the sordid truth to this young girl, "Feng agreed to do so, to leave you alone, I mean. Simple really."

"Mr. Theo, please don't treat me as a fool. I know how China works. What was the price?"

"You're right. He gave some information in return. About the troops arriving from Peking. That's all."

Her skin had gone that awful sickly white of someone suffering from TB. Theo started to worry about her. "I think you ought to sit down a minute and . . ." He put out a hand.

"No." She pulled her arm away. "I'm fine. Tell me what happened."

"Nothing. They let him go. That's all there is to it."

"So it's the gray bellies," she whispered.

"Pardon?"

"The translation," she said quickly. "Of my sentences on the paper. You'll do it? Please."

"Of course. By tomorrow."

"Thank you."

She hurried out of the gate, fighting against the ceaseless flow of rickshaws, and started to run, her hat flapping behind her in the wind.

THEO WAS SITTING AT HIS KITCHEN TABLE. IT WAS OLD AND etched with character, the dark mahogany wood imprinted with the life of some unknown Chinese family. But right now the table held no interest for him. It was what was *on* the table. He had set the items in a row.

A pipe, long and slender and made of finest carved ivory with blue metal decorations, was first. Normally he would admire its effortless elegance of line but not today. It wasn't quite like an ordinary pipe because there was no bowl at the far end, but an inch or so from the tip was a hole on top of the pipe and into the hole was screwed a small metal cup, shaped like a pigeon's egg, with a tight wooden cap held in place by a brass band. The cap was decorated in ivory with the Chinese character *xi* for happiness.

Next to the pipe stood a small white jug. It contained water. Theo was having problems with it. The water kept appearing and disappearing like waves and when it disappeared, the inside of the ceramic jug became transparent instead of solid and he could see right though it to the little brass burner beside it on the table.

That wasn't possible.

The part of Theo's mind that was still holding on told him he was hallucinating. But his eyes told him otherwise.

Next to the burner was the dream bringer. It lay inside an ancient malachite box that dated back to the Chin dynasty. He lifted the lid and felt the familiar kick of anticipation at the sight of the black paste. Using a brass spoon he scooped some out, about the size of a pea. His hands shook but he managed to pour a few drops of water from the jug into the spoon with the paste, unaware that he was spilling it all over the table as well, but lighting the wick of the spirit burner was harder. It kept moving. Shifting position. He wrapped one hand tightly around its brass base to stop its antics and finally brought the lighter and wick together.

Now.

He held the spoon over the heat. Watched with impatience as the water evaporated and the paste turned to treacle. This was high-quality merchandise, he could tell, made from the poppy pods themselves, the *Papaver somniferum*, not from the dross of the stems or the leaves. That rubbish gave you nothing more than a mild heat in your blood and a violent desire to vomit. When it was ready he tipped the heated paste with painstaking care into the cup on top of the pipe and fitted the lid over it. He could feel his pulse knocking holes in his wrists.

He took a long draw on the pipe. His lungs filled with the pungent vapor, held it down deep inside, and his head started to uncoil, to flatten out all the pain into one long thin line that he could cut and let go. It was like a warm summer wind flowing through his veins, swirling out from the core of his body and into his limbs, cooling and soothing. Soft and sweet and relaxing. He took two more pulls on the pipe, breathed it deep into his mind and felt a smile of joy spread unbidden to his lips as he started to soar.

Dimly he was aware of Li Mei in the room. She floated toward him, her oval face more perfect than ever as she leaned close and placed a kiss on his lips. She tasted of moonlight. He could feel her behind him, fingers gently massaging the back of his neck.

"I relax you, Tiyo," he heard her whisper. "You do not need that black death."

Then her hair tickled his cheek as she bent over him and her hot tears dropped onto his skin and felt like warm kisses.

"Li Mei, I love you with all my heart, my beloved," he murmured, his eyes closing.

Her arms wrapped around him, hard and urgent, squeezing the breath from him. Very faintly he heard her voice, as if from a long way in the distance.

"Tiyo, oh my Tiyo, my father has you in his grip. Can't you see? It is his way of seeking revenge on you for leading me away into the *fan-qui* world. You promised me, my Tiyo. That you would never let him lure you into the dragon's mouth. Tiyo, my love, Tiyo."

Somewhere far, far away Theo heard her scream his name.

Dark dreams. Demon dark. Spiked with fire.

They swirled in Chang An Lo's head. So fierce and so relentless that he didn't know if he was awake or asleep. He was floating in blackness. Spinning. Spiraling upward. Then sinking and plunging into the thick slime at the bottom. It sucked at his skin and tried to slide into his mouth. The stench of it was suffocating.

He gasped for air and suddenly he was floating again with clean fresh air filling his lungs and pure cold water soothing his tongue, washing away the filth. His eyes could make out fireflies. Dancing in the darkness that wrapped itself around him as cold as a shroud. He could see them, pinpricks of fire. Moving and swaying. And he could smell the burning.

Scorched meat. Burnt flesh. Just as when he'd cooked the bullfrog on the fire for Lydia. Except this time it was his flesh. He remembered how her hair hung down as she reached for the skewered creature. Hair brighter than the flames.

He could feel her fox-spirit with him now, blunting the fine edge of pain that sliced into his bones and into his sinews with each breath. He could see her tongue, soft and pink, and feel her fingers moist on his raw skin. At times he heard screams and his brain didn't know if they were his or hers. But she was with him. So bright she filled his mind.

29

THERE WERE MORE CARS ON THE STREETS. OR MAYBE IT was just that Lydia was noticing more. In more colors too, it seemed. So Alfred said anyway. He often talked cars, about motors with names like Lanchester and Bean, and it irritated her the way her mother always looked impressed. Once Valentina had even asked what a torque tube was, which had left Lydia open-mouthed. She stood on the pavement outside Tuson's Tearoom, shuffling from foot to foot in an effort to keep from freezing and started counting the maroon ones that drove past.

"Hello, young lady. Punctual, I see. Good show."

"Hello, Mr. Parker."

They hadn't yet worked out a way of greeting each other. A kiss was too intimate—far too intimate—and a handshake too formal. Usually he gave her a little pat on the arm and she nodded a lot. It sort of got them through the awkward moment.

"Let's go in then," he said, bustling up to the teashop door. "It's devilishly nippy out here."

He was swathed in a woolen muffler and a heavy tweed overcoat, and as he held open the door for her she saw him glance at her own coat and she felt acutely conscious of the thinness and smallness of it and of her lack of gloves. But she liked the way the coconut mat went *ding* when she stepped on it, announcing her arrival.

"NOW, LYDIA, WHAT IS THIS ABOUT?"

She was biting into her *tarte au citron*. Its sourness rasped her tongue. Parker's toffee-brown eyes were looking at her closely from behind his round metal spectacles and there was a sharpness to them, an appraising awareness that wasn't there when he was around Valentina. Lydia's stomach gave a little lurch and she put down the tart. This could be harder than she thought.

"Mr. Parker," she said with careful courtesy, "I asked if we could meet today because," she took a deep breath, "I would like to borrow some money from you."

"My dear girl," he laughed lightly, dabbing the crumbs of his éclair from his lips with a napkin, "I am delighted you feel you can come to me with such a request, just like a . . ." He stopped there, cleared his throat, and buffed his spectacles on his spotless handkerchief.

Like a what? A daughter. That's what. He'd wanted to say the word but backed off at the last second. She smiled across the table at him and already he was pulling out his wallet, the one she'd stolen. Without his spectacles he looked almost attractive, though nowhere near as handsome as Antoine, and he drove a lumpy sedan, an Armstrong Siddeley, not a skittish little sportscar, but she pushed all that out of her mind. The money. Concentrate on the money.

He was leaning toward her in a confidential manner, chuckling. "What is it for? A little something for yourself? Or maybe your mother? You can tell me."

"It's for a friend."

"Ah, a birthday gift perhaps."

"Something like that."

"Perfectly understandable. So how much would you like? Twenty dollars enough?"

"Two hundred dollars."

"What!"

"Two hundred dollars."

He said nothing, but his bushy eyebrows drew together and his mouth tightened into a negative line. He looked as if she had insulted him.

"Please, Mr. Parker. Please. I need it for my friend."

He picked up his cup, sipped his tea, and shifted his gaze away from her to the window, to the crowds bustling past with bags from Churston Department Store or Llewellyn's Haberdashery, fur collars pulled up around their ears. She had a feeling he wished he were out there with them. When he turned back to her, she knew his answer before he spoke.

"I am sorry, Lydia. But the answer to your request is no. I can't give you that kind of money. Not unless I know who it is going to and why."

"Please say yes." Her voice was soft and her hand crept halfway toward him, leaving a track on the white tablecloth.

He shook his head.

"It's important to me," she urged.

"Look, Lydia, why can't you just tell me who this friend is and what the money is needed for?"

"Because it's . . ." She was going to say dangerous, but knew that would send him and his wallet skidding out the door. "It's a secret," she said instead.

"Then I can't help you."

"I could lie to you, tell you some story."

"I'd rather you didn't."

"I'm being honest. I've come openly to you, the man who is soon to marry my mother, asking for your help." She swallowed every remaining scrap of her pride and added, "As your daughter."

For a split second she thought she had him. Something like delight flickered in his brown eyes, but then he was gone again.

"No, absolutely not. You must understand, Lydia, that it would be my duty to refuse to hand out that kind of money to any daughter of mine unless I knew the reason for it. Money has to be earned, you know, and I work hard as a journalist to do so, therefore I . . ."

"Then I'll earn it."

He sighed and glanced out the window again as if seeking escape. At the next table two women in feathered hats laughed shrilly when a waitress brought them buttered crumpets, and Parker began polishing his spectacles yet again. Lydia realized it was a sign of stress.

"How," he asked unhappily, "could you possibly earn it?"

"I could help out at the newspaper. I can fetch and carry and make tea and . . ."

"No."

"But . . ."

"No. We have plenty of people to do all those things already and anyway, your mother would be furious with me if I distracted you from your educational studies."

"I'll talk to her. I can get her to . . ."

"No. That's final."

They stared at each other. Neither willing to look away.

"There's another way," Lydia said. "For me to earn two hundred dollars."

Something in the way she said it made him instantly wary. He sat back in his chair and folded his arms across his chest, so that his jacket sleeves puckered and crumpled.

"Let's leave it there. Why don't we just finish our cakes and talk about . . . ," he searched for a subject, ". . . Christmas or the wedding." He gave her an encouraging smile. "Agreed?"

She returned his smile and withdrew her hand. "Certainly. The wedding is set for January, isn't it?"

He nodded and his eyes grew bright at the thought. "Yes, and I hope you're looking forward to it as much as your mother and I are."

She picked up a sugar cube from the bowl and started to suck one corner of it. Parker didn't look pleased, but he passed no comment.

"It seems to me," she said gently, "that the start of a marriage is an important time. You have to learn about each other, don't you, and get used to living together. Accept the other person's little habits and, well, foibles."

"There's some truth in that," he said carefully.

"So it seems to me," she took a tiny bite out of the sugar and crunched it between her teeth, "that having a ready-made daughter around could make the situation twice as . . . hard."

He sat up straight, both hands flat on the table. His expression was stern. "What are you implying here, Lydia?"

"Just that it would be extremely helpful to you if that daughter promised to do exactly as you told her. No arguments. No disobedience for, shall we say, the first three months of your new and, I'm sure, wonderful, married life?"

He closed his eyes. She could see his jaw clicking and unclicking. When he opened his eyes again they did not look as happy as she'd hoped.

"That is extortion, young lady."

"No. It's a bargain."

"And if I don't agree to this bargain?"

She shrugged and bit another piece off the cube.

"Are you threatening me, Lydia?"

"No. No, of course I'm not." She leaned forward and the words tumbled out. "All I'm doing is asking you to give me a chance, a fair chance to earn two hundred dollars. That's all."

He shook his head, and the sugar tasted like ash in her mouth.

"You are a devious child, Lydia Ivanova, but this kind of unholy behavior must cease once your mother and I are married and you become Lydia Parker. I know your poor mother would be appalled at your duplicity." Suddenly he rapped the table hard three times with his silver cake fork. "Three months. With not a word or a look out of place from you. I have your word on it?"

"Yes."

He opened his wallet.

IN A DIMLY LIT YARD MARKED OUT WITH A CIRCLE OF STRAW bales, the dog that looked like a wolf was having its throat torn out. Inch by inch. Strips of fur and flesh flew across the circle. Gobbets of blood spewed out into the eager faces of the men who edged too close, as the pale dog, the one that looked like a ghost, shook its snarling head from side to side and dragged more of the soft gullet into its jaws. One ear was hanging by a thread. Its shoulder was ripped open and dangling down in a loose scarlet flap, but its grip on the wolf-dog's throat was a death grip and the crowd roared its approval.

Lydia took one look at the savagery taking place inside the circle of straw, one glance at the bloodlust in the eyes of the men, and then she walked over to the wall and was quietly sick. She wiped her mouth. She'd come this far and now was not the time to back out. For five days she had scoured the Russian Quarter of Junchow, walked its mean streets after school each day, seeking out Liev Popkov. The bear man. The one with the eye patch and the boots. Five days of rain and wind.

"Vi nye znayetye gdye ya mogu naitee Lva Popkova?" she asked again and again. "Do you know where I can find a man called Liev Popkov?"

They had looked at her with suspicion and narrowed northern eyes. Anyone asking questions meant trouble. *"Nyet,"* they shrugged. "No."

Until tonight. She had plucked up the courage to walk into one of the dark and dingy bars, a *kabak*, that stank of black tobacco and unwashed male bodies. Hers was the only female face, but she stood her ground and finally on payment of a half dollar a toothless old goat told her to try the dog yard behind the stable.

Dog yard. More like death yard.

It was where the men gathered on a Friday night to get their thrills, raw and unadulterated. Dog fighting. It put fire in their bellies and in their veins, wiping out the degradation of a week of hard, miserable labor. Here they bet on who would live and who would die, knowing that a win meant a good night's vodka and maybe a girl as well if their luck held.

Liev Popkov was there. Lydia spotted him easily. Towering above the tight huddle of onlookers whose breath drifted in the icy air like incense around the dark yard. A lantern on the wall behind Popkov threw his broad shadow across the circle and onto the warring dogs. She couldn't see his face clearly but his great body looked motionless and lazy, and when he did shift position it was like the slow lumbering movement of a bear.

She went over and touched his arm.

His head turned, faster than she expected. Though one eye was obscured by the patch and the lower half of his face was covered by the black beard, his single eye registered complete surprise and his mouth fell open, revealing big strong teeth. Tombstone teeth.

"Dobriy vecher. Good evening, Liev Popkov," Lydia said in her carefully rehearsed Russian. "I want to talk to you."

She had to shout above the roar of the crowd and for a moment she wasn't sure if he'd heard her or even understood her, because all he did was blink silently and continue to stare at her with his one dark eye.

"*Seichas,*" she urged. "Now."

He glanced over at the dogs. An artery had been severed and canine blood pumped into the icy night air. His expression gave nothing away, so she had no idea if he was winning or losing, but he effortlessly shouldered a path through the press of men around him to the back wall of the yard. It was in deep shadow and smelled of damp.

"You speak our language," he growled.

"Not well," she replied in Russian.

He leaned against the wall, waiting for more from her, and she had a sudden image of it crumbling under his weight. Up close he was even bigger. She had to tilt her head back to look at him. At first that was all she saw. The bigness of him. That was exactly what she wanted. He was wearing a Cossack hat of moth-eaten fur jammed over his black curls and a long padded overcoat that stank of grease and came right down to the tip of his boots. And he was chewing something. Tobacco? Dog meat? She had no idea.

"I need your help." The Russian words came to her tongue more readily than she expected.

"*Pochemu?*" Why?

"Because I am searching for someone."

He spat whatever was in his mouth onto the yard floor. "You are the *dyevochka* who made trouble for me. With police." He spoke gruffly but slowly. She wasn't sure if this was his normal way or done just for her to understand the language that was still a struggle to her. "Why should I help you? You of all people."

She opened her hand. In it lay Alfred's two hundred Chinese dollars.

30

He didn't speak, Liev Popkov. But neither did she. Yet they kept close, even touching at times. Side by side they hunched forward against the biting wind that whipped up off the Peiho River, and Lydia's lungs ached with the effort.

"Here," he muttered.

He meant the narrow street that twisted away from the quayside to their left. It was gray and cobbled and stank of putrid fish guts. She nodded. His broad shovel of a hand pulled her tight against him, so that not a crack of the thin wintry light sneaked between them and her body became no more than an extension of this great greasy bear. It was weird the effect he had on her mind. She felt big and bold and fearless. The hostile eyes around them no longer sent shivers down her spine, and when one of the Chinese dockhands reached out to touch her as he passed, Liev casually raised an arm and smashed his elbow into the man's face. Broken bone and blood and high-pitched screams. She looked at the mess and felt ill. They kept on walking, no comment. Liev was a man of few words.

In the beginning on their first few forays down around the dockland quays, she had tried to speak to him in her halting Russian, to offer some flow of simple conversation, but all she received in reply were grunts. Or no response at all. She grew used to it. It made it easier for her to concentrate on the faces that swarmed over the congested harbour and in the slippery *hutongs*, easier to avoid the thousands of shoulder poles carrying weighty piles of God-knows-what in their buckets and panniers. Easier to watch where her feet were stepping.

Easier. But not easy. None of this was easy.

* * *

"LYDIA IVANOVA."

Lydia's head jerked up from her desk. Wisps of bright dreams fled her mind and she stared up into Mr. Theo's eyes. Gray eyes that had turned black, the pupils were so huge, and his tongue was sharper than ever.

"Are you with us, Miss Ivanova? Or shall I bring a bed into class for you?"

"No, sir."

"You surprise me, girl. I would have thought the love affair between Philip II of Spain and Mary Tudor of England would be passionate enough to keep your eyes open in class. Isn't that what girls your age like? Love affairs. Even with young Chinese boys."

"No, sir."

He smiled a little. She did not return the smile.

"Detention after school. You can do me an essay on . . ."

"Please, sir, not after school. I'll do detention for a whole week of lunch breaks, but not . . ."

"You'll do detention when I say, young lady."

"It's just that . . ." Her voice trailed away. Everyone was looking and listening. Polly was making signs but Lydia couldn't work out what.

"Lydia." Mr. Theo walked over to her desk. His black headmaster's gown billowed around him and to Lydia's mind he looked like a long-legged crow come to peck her eyes out. "You will do detention today. After school. Understand?"

She wanted to hit him. As Liev Popkov would have done. But she lowered her head. "Yes, sir."

"OH, LYD, YOU SILLY. WHEN WILL YOU LEARN TO GROVEL TO him?" Polly was clucking over her like a mother hen. "All you had to say was 'I'm sorry, Mr. Theo, I promise I won't let it happen again,' and he would have let you off."

"Really?"

"You are so naïve, Lyd. Of course he would."

"But why?"

"Because that's what men like. It makes them feel powerful."

Understanding dawned. Yes. People want to feel powerful. She had seen its effects in the alien world of the docklands when she was linked to Liev Popkov and had learned the way it made you feel good. Powerful men. They made sure they got what they wanted, just as Polly's father knew how to get things he wanted. Or people he desired. It made Lydia's skin crawl. A question occurred to her, but she wasn't sure quite how to put it to Polly.

"Polly, you're much better at handling people than I am. I can't even get my mother to do things I want sometimes." She paused and rubbed the side of a fingernail. "By the way, does she ever come to visit your house?"

"Gosh, no. What an odd question. Why on earth would she?"

"I thought maybe she might come to talk to your mother, you know, like mothers do when their daughters are friends." She shrugged. "I just wondered, that's all."

"You are a strange one sometimes, you know."

"You'd tell me if she did. Come to your house, I mean."

"Of course."

"Promise?"

"I promise."

"Good."

"How's Mr. Parker, by the way?"

"He's still around."

"Oh, you're so lucky. When they're married he'll give you everything you've ever wanted like a house and pretty clothes and holidays and everything." She laughed and poked her friend lightly in the ribs. "Including a nice new school uniform. It's what you need."

"It's not what I need," Lydia snapped. "It's what people with power make you think you need."

"Oh, Lyd, you're hopeless."

LIEV POPKOV WAS STILL STANDING AT THE END OF HER road, waiting for her. He must have been there a long time because snow had built up into epaulettes on his shoulders and his fur hat had turned white like a stoat in winter.

"I'm sorry," she said. "*Prostitye menya*. I'm late because I had to stay longer at school."

He grunted. Moved off with his loose shambling gait, so that Lydia had to scamper to keep up, and headed again for the harbor. It was a dismal but frantic world down there where everything from rhinoceros horns to ten-year-old slaves were bought and sold, but nevertheless Lydia liked the chance to gaze at the sleek liners and the rusting tramp steamers that brought the outside world into the heart of Junchow. It made England seem so close she could almost reach out and grab it in her hand. She watched hard-eyed men and fur-coated women stride down the gangplanks as if they owned the world, while at their feet coolies begged to carry their bags. The snow had stopped falling.

"This one," Liev growled.

He led her down yet another dank and filthy alleyway where native hawkers tried to sell even the rags off their backs. One stall was offering bathroom taps, a whole tea chest of them smuggled out of one of the import warehouses that surrounded the harbor, while farther down was a row of porcelain-faced dolls sitting up like little dead children. Lydia had never possessed a doll in her life and was constantly baffled by whatever it was that drove girls to want one. Even to love the wretched things. Like Polly did. It was so . . .

A moon-faced man broke up her thoughts. He was speaking in rapid Chinese and pointing back down the alleyway. She started to shake her head to indicate she didn't understand but realized he was talking to Liev, not to her. The man kept jabbering louder and louder, throwing his arms around. Liev just swung his great head back and forth. *Nyet. Nyet. Nyet.*

The man drew a knife.

Lydia tried to back away, but two men had placed themselves directly behind her. She felt her breath stop, and start up again too fast. With one hand Liev Popkov seized her wrist; with the other he drew from under his coat a knife that was almost a sword, long and curved and double-edged. Its hilt was heavy black metal and sat firmly in the Russian's fist. He leaped forward with a low growl, dragging Lydia with him. Her feet skidded from under her on a patch of iced-up vegetable pulp, but without even glancing in her direction he yanked her into the air and slashed at the Chinese moon-face at the same time.

It was over before it began. The men vanished. A splash of blood started to freeze on the cobbles. Liev slipped the knife back into his belt and, without releasing her wrist, plodded on down through the crowded *hutong* as if nothing had happened.

"What," Lydia demanded in English, "was that about? Did you really have to use that knife?"

He halted, stared at her with his one good eye, shrugged, and moved on.

She tried again. In Russian this time.

"*O chyom vi rugalyis?*"

"He wanted to buy you."

"Buy me?"

"*Da.*"

She said no more. Knew she was shaking. Damn the bloody bear. She hated him to know she was frightened. She tried to snatch her wrist away, but it was like trying to pull a rivet out of one of the metal ships with your bare fingers. It just didn't happen.

"I didn't know you speak Mandarin," she said.

"He offered good money," he said and uttered a deep growling sound that it took her a moment to recognize as a laugh.

"Damn you," she said in English.

The growl went on and on.

"In here," she said to shut him up.

It was a *kabak*. A bar.

SHE KNEW IT WAS A MISTAKE THE MOMENT SHE WAS INSIDE. Twenty pairs of eyes turned. Stared at them as if a snake had crawled through the door. The air hung solid and lifeless under the low ceiling and was full of odors Lydia did not recognize. A stove in one corner coughed out heat and fumes.

She stared back at the men. Her eyes roamed their faces and their clothes, all gray as ash, and the crazed enamel tables where they sat hunched over some colorless rotgut liquid. The grimy bamboo counter had a chained monkey at one end and the man behind it had no ears. He wore a soiled rag around the top of his head and held another in his hand. He was wiping a glass with it. Without taking his eyes off Liev Popkov for one second, he reached under the counter and brought up a rifle. He thumbed back the hammer with the ease of long practice and pointed the business end straight at Lydia's chest. She felt her ribs contract. The rifle looked ancient, probably a relic from the Boxer Rebellion. But that didn't mean it didn't shoot straight.

Nobody spoke.

Liev nodded. Moving slowly he pulled her behind him and backed out of the bar.

"He wasn't there," she said outside. She was relieved to see her breath coiling in icy vapor from her mouth, in and out, her ribs still working.

Liev nodded again. "There are many bars."

THEY WENT INTO TEN BARS THAT EVENING. SCATTERED over different areas of the harbor. No more rifles were pushed in their faces, but no smiles either. Eyes regarded them with the same loathing and mouths muttered curses and spat hatred on the floor.

Word was spreading. About the giant bear who broke men's faces and the flame-haired girl. When they entered a bar and stood inside the door for no more than two minutes, heads raised because they'd heard of this strange pair who haunted the dockland. Lydia could see it on their faces, as clearly as she could see the desire to slit their *fanqui* throats. Each time she peered through the gloom of some narrow stinking room and heard the silence slide over the tables as drinkers turned to stare, she did not expect to find the one face she sought, the one with the intense and thoughtful eyes that had always observed her so closely and the nose that flared when he was amused though his mouth was slow to smile. She didn't expect to see it. But still she hoped.

In one of the bars a short barrel of a man with oiled hair came and placed himself nervously in front of them. He said something in Chinese.

Liev Popkov fixed his eye on the questioner but grunted to Lydia in Russian. "He says, who are you looking for?"

"Tell him the name is not for his ears. Tell him to say to all his . . . ," she hunted for the Russian word, ". . . *pyanitsam* . . . customers that the girl with red hair was in his bar. She searches for someone."

Liev frowned at her.

"Tell him," she said.

He told him.

Outside in the street once more, the big man took root, indifferent to the snow flurries that were burrowing into his black beard, and put a hand on her shoulder. It felt like a truck had landed on it.

"Why don't you tell his name?"

"Because it is too dangerous for him, *slishkom opasnoye.*"

"A Communist?"

"A person."

"How will you find him if you will not say his name?"

"I am here. People talk. He will hear."

"And he will know it is you?"

"Yes. He'll know."

L YDIA LAY IN BED FULLY CLOTHED. SHIVERING. SHE couldn't get the dockland ice out of her bones. They felt as if they were cracking open, and even though she tucked her fingers under her armpits the chill air still managed to spike needles through them. Her old eiderdown was wrapped around her, tight as a cocoon, with every scrap of clothing she possessed draped on top, but still she was cold. The old black stove spluttered. Not that it was short of kerosene. Not now they had Alfred. But the meager heat coaxed from it was no threat to the breath of the Chinese winter that climbed in through the window each night.

The door to the attic banged open.

"*Blin!* Sorry, darling, I didn't mean to wake you."

Lydia heard the church clock strike two.

"I wasn't asleep."

"I'll just light a candle. Go to sleep now."

Valentina had gone out with Alfred to a party. She'd been drinking. Lydia could tell by her footsteps. There was the flick of a lighter, a faint glow in the darkness, the noise of a chair dragged across the floor, then silence. Lydia knew what her mother was doing. Sitting in front of the stove. Smoking. She could smell it. And drinking. She knew it. Though Valentina could open a bottle and pour a glass of vodka without a single sound. Still, she knew it.

"Mama, I saw something bad today."

"How bad?"

"I saw a dead baby. Naked. It was lying in a gutter and a rat was biting off its lips."

"Ach! Don't, sweetheart. Don't let such things into your head. This God-cursed country is too full of them."

"I can't forget it."

"Come here, little one."

Lydia slid out of bed, still wrapped in her eiderdown, and pushed aside the curtain wall. Her mother was hunched in front of the stove, cigarette in one hand, glass in the other. She was wearing a new fur coat, the dense color of honey, and her cheeks were flushed.

"Here, this will make you forget." She held out the glass to Lydia.

Lydia took it. Never before had she done so. But now . . . now she needed . . . needed something. To help her hold on to the belief that somewhere out there Chang was safe. Her head was drowning. Great suffocating pools of blackness had opened inside it. Faces. They floated to the slimy surface, faces and faces and more faces, Chang's eyes so wide and watchful and so eager to make her understand, and then came a dead baby with no lips, a Chinese jaw smashed to a pulp, Mr. Theo's huge echoing pupils, and all the street faces full of hatred and spite and venom.

She drank the vodka.

A kick in the gut. Then warmth. It seeped up into her chest and made her cough. She drank again. Slower this time. The black pools were turning gray. She sipped again. It tasted foul. How could anyone like this stuff?

Her mother watched her but said nothing.

Lydia sat down on the floor in front of the stove and Valentina stroked her head.

"Better?"

"Mmm."

Valentina took back the empty glass and refilled it for herself. "Do you like my coat?"

"No."

Valentina laughed and ruffled the beautiful soft fur. "I do."

Lydia leaned her head back, rested it on her mother's knee, and closed her eyes.

"Mama, don't marry him."

Slowly and gently Valentina continued to stroke her daughter's hair. "We need him, *dochenka*," she murmured. "In this world when you need something, you have to ask a man. That's the way it is."

"No. Look at us. We've survived all these years without a man. Between us we managed. A woman can . . ."

"That's balderdash, to use one of Alfred's words." Valentina laughed again, but this time there was no humor in it. "It was always through men that I got my concert bookings, never women. Women don't like me. They see me as a threat. *C'est la vie.*"

But Lydia heard the loneliness in the words.

"It is not balderdash, Mama. It's true. We can manage."

"*Dochenka*, don't make me mad at your stupidity. Look at yourself. When it's a rabbit you want, you get it out of Antoine. For a hutch or money, it's Alfred. Oh yes, don't look so surprised. He told me you came to him for a few dollars."

"It was for . . . things."

"Don't worry, I'm not prying. In fact Alfred was quite touched by it because you asked him instead of going out and stealing it."

"That man is easily pleased."

"He said he believed it was a sign of your growing maturity. And of a better sense of morality."

"Did he really say that?"

"Yes."

"But, Mama, I ask women for help too. Like Mrs. Zarya and Mrs. Yeoman, and even Anthea Mason showed me how to bake a cake. You taught me how to dance. And Countess Serova taught me to walk taller."

Valentina snatched her hand away from Lydia's head. "What?"

"She told me to hold my . . ."

"What in the name of all that's holy has it got to do with that witch of a woman?" Valentina threw the vodka down her throat. "How dare she? How dare . . . ?"

"Mama." Lydia twisted around to look at her mother, but her face was swathed in deep shadow from the single candle on the table behind her. Only her eyes glittered. "Don't get upset, Mama. She's not important."

Valentina drew hard on her cigarette, a bright pinprick of fire, and exhaled fiercely as if she were spitting poison.

Lydia rubbed her cheek against the fur-covered knee. "She can't hurt you."

Valentina was silent, then stabbed out her cigarette, lit another, and refilled her glass. Lydia felt her own head swirling gently with a pleasant drowsy slowness that made her eyelids too heavy to raise. Behind them Chang's smile floated in mist.

"Where do you go these days, Lydochka? After school, I mean."

"I go to Polly's house. We're working together on a project for school. I told you."

"I know you did." She drank more of the vodka. "That doesn't mean it's the truth."

Lydia almost told her then. Everything. About Chang and his crazy leaps and his foot and his fierce beliefs and the way his mouth curved into a perfect . . . The drink had loosened her tongue and words were longing to pour out, to tell someone. Someone.

"Mama, what did your parents say when you married a foreigner?"

To her horror she felt her mother's knee start to tremble beneath her cheek and when she looked up, tears were rolling down her mother's face. Lydia gently stroked the knee, over and over, the fur almost as soft as Sun Yat-sen's under her fingers.

"They disowned me."

"Oh, Mama."

"They had the eldest son of a fine Russian family from Moscow all lined up for me. But instead Jens Friis and I eloped and they cursed us. Disowned me." She brushed the tears from her face with the back of the hand that held the cigarette, only just avoiding setting fire to her hair.

"You loved each other, that's all that matters."

"No, *durochka*, you little fool. It's not enough. You need more."

"But you were happy together, you were, you've always said so."

"Yes, we were. But look at me now. The curse of my family has done this to me."

"That's crazy. There are no such things as curses."

"Don't you kid yourself, darling. The one thing that monster Confucius got right among all his claptrap about women is that you should obey your parents." She tapped her glass on the top of Lydia's head. "That's something you need to learn, you little alley cat. Parents really do know what's best for their children."

Lydia began to laugh. She couldn't help it. It just bubbled up from nowhere and burst out regardless. Once she'd started she couldn't stop and lay her face in her mother's lap, howling with laughter.

"It's the drink," Valentina murmured, "you silly thing." But she was starting to laugh herself.

"Do you know," Lydia giggled, "that Confucius said a nursing mother should feed her grandparents from her breast when they can no longer eat solid food."

"Good God!"

"And," Lydia gasped out, "a man should feed his own fingers to his parents in time of famine."

"Well, *dochenka*, it's about time you fed me yours." She picked up one of Lydia's hands and took a bite of her smallest finger.

Lydia went weak with laughter, tears streaking her cheeks and her breath coming in great noisy hiccups.

"Wicked child," Valentina suddenly exclaimed, "look, the vermin is here!"

Lydia rolled her head around and saw the long white ears flicking with concern by her side. Sun Yat-sen had hopped off her bed and come to inspect the noise. She scooped him up into her arms, placed a kiss on the tip of his pink nose, laid her head down on her mother's lap, and was instantly asleep.

31

CHRISTMAS DAY WAS DIFFICULT. LYDIA GOT THROUGH IT. Her mother had a hangover, so hardly spoke, and Alfred was ill at ease playing host in his small and rather gloomy bachelor flat across the road from the French Quarter.

"I should have booked a restaurant," he said for the third time as they sat at the table while his cook presented them with an over-cooked goose.

"No, angel, this is more homey," Valentina assured him. She managed a smile.

Angel? Homey? Lydia cringed. She pulled her Christmas cracker with him and tried to look pleased when he placed a paper hat on her head.

Two high points made the rest almost bearable.

"Here, Lydia," Alfred said as he held out a large flat box wrapped in fancy paper and satin ribbon. "Merry Christmas, my dear."

It was a coat, a soft grayish-blue. Beautifully tailored, heavy and warm, and instantly Lydia knew her mother had chosen it.

"I hope you like it," he said.

"It's lovely. Thank you."

It had a wide wrapover collar and there was a pair of navy gloves in the pocket. She put them all on and felt wonderful. Alfred was beaming at her, expecting more, and it made her want to explain to him, *Just because you gave me a coat, it doesn't make you my father.* Instead she stepped forward, put her arms around his neck, and kissed his cleanly shaven cheek that smelled of sandalwood. But it was the wrong thing to do. She could see in his eyes that he believed things between them had changed.

Did he really think he could buy her that easily?

The other highlight of the day was the electric wireless. Not the cat's whisker kind, but a *real* wireless. It was made of polished oak and had a brown material mesh in the shape of a bird over the speaker at the front. Lydia adored it. She spent most of the afternoon beside it, fiddling with its knobs, flicking between stations, filling the room with the strident voice of Al Jolson or the honey-smooth tones of Noel Coward singing "A Room with a View." She let Alfred's attempts at conversation flow unheeded most of the time, but after an item of news about Prime Minister Baldwin, he started on about the wisdom of signing a tariff agreement and officially recognizing Chiang Kai-shek's government, proud that Britain was one of the first countries to do so.

"But it's Josef Stalin, not us Brits," he said, "who has had the foresight to pour military advisers and money into Chiang's Kuomintang Nationalists. And now Chiang Kai-shek has decided to get rid of the Russkies, more fool him."

"That doesn't make sense," Lydia muttered, one ear still tuned to Adele Astaire and "Fascinating Rhythm." "Stalin is a Communist. Why would he be helping the Kuomintang who are killing off the Communists here in China?"

Alfred polished his spectacles. "You must see, my dear, that he is backing the force he believes will be the victor in this power struggle between Mao Tse-tung's forces and Chiang Kai-shek's government. It may seem a contradictory choice for Stalin to make, but in this case I must say I think he's right."

"He's expelled Leon Trotsky from Russia. How can that be right?"

"Russia, like China, needs a united government and Trotsky was causing factions and divisions, so . . ."

"Shut up," Valentina snapped suddenly. "The pair of you, shut up about Russia. What do either of you know?" She stood up, poured herself another full glass of port. "It's Christmas. Let's be happy."

She glared at them and sipped her drink.

They left early, but didn't speak on the way home. Both had thoughts it was best not to share.

IT WAS ON NEW YEAR'S DAY THAT EVERYTHING CHANGED.

The moment Lydia stepped into the clearing at Lizard Creek, she knew. The money was gone. The sky was a clear-swept blue and the air so cold it seemed to take bites out of her lungs, but wrapped up warm and snug in her new coat and gloves she didn't care. The trees bordering the narrow strip of sand were bare and spiky, their branches white as skeletons, and the water a dazzling surge of energy beneath. Lydia had come intending to add yet another mark to the flat rock, a thin scratched line, to show that she had been here again, however pointless it may seem.

But the cairn was gone.

The mound of pebbles she'd built at the base of the rock. Destroyed. Scattered. Gone. The spot of earth where it had stood looked gray and rumpled. She felt a thud in her chest and tasted a burst of adrenaline on her tongue. She dropped to her knees, tore off her gloves, and scrabbled with her hands in the sandy soil. Though the earth elsewhere was frozen hard, here it was soft and crumbly. Recently disturbed. The glass jar was still there. Ice cold in her fingers. But no money inside. The thirty dollars gone. Relief crashed through her. He was alive. Chang was alive.

Alive.

Here.

He had come.

In a clumsy rush she unscrewed the metal lid of the jar, pushed her hand inside, and withdrew its new contents. A single white feather, soft and perfect as a snowflake. She laid it on the palm of her hand and stared at it. What did it mean?

White. Chinese white. For mourning. Did that mean he was dead? Dying? Her mouth turned dry as dirt.

Or . . .

White. A dove's feather. For peace. For hope. A sign of the future. Which?

Which one?

She remained for a long time kneeling beside the small hole in the earth. The feather lay wrapped between her carefully cupped hands like a baby bird, while the wind knifed in off the river and straight into her face. But she barely noticed and eventually placed the feather in her handkerchief, folded it into a neat package, and tucked it into her blouse. Then she drew the penknife from her pocket, cut a lock of her hair from her head and dropped it into the jar. She screwed the lid up tight and reburied it. Built another cairn.

To her eyes it looked like a grave marker.

A NOISE IN THE UNDERGROWTH BEHIND HER MADE HER swing around as two magpies clattered into the air with a raucous cry of alarm and a flash of blue-black wing. Hairs rose on her neck. A smile and a cry of delight leaped to her lips and she took a step forward to greet him.

It wasn't Chang.

Disappointment tore through her.

A long-fingered hand with yellow nails thrust aside a low holly branch to enter the clearing, and for no more than a split second Lydia glimpsed a tall thin figure clothed in rags.

It wasn't Chang.

Then the figure was gone. Lydia moved fast. She raced after him, charging through the bushes, indifferent to thorns and scratches. The track was little more than an animal run, narrow and winding beneath the birch trees, but patches of dense shrub offered places to hide.

She couldn't see him. She stopped running. Stood still, listening, but could hear nothing but her own heart pounding in her ears. Her breath rasped in the cold air. She waited. A kestrel high overhead hovered and waited with her. Her eyes scoured the stretch of woodland for movement, and then she saw a single branch flutter and grow still. It was over to her left in a thick clump of elder and ivy where a smattering of frozen berries clung to the stalks and a finch hopped from branch to branch.

Did the bird cause the flutter?

She edged forward. Her fingers closed over the penknife in her pocket, eased it out, and flicked open the blade. She moved nearer, watching every tangle of brushwood and hollow of shade, and just

296 · KATE FURNIVALL

when she was thinking she had lost him, a man leaped out from almost under her feet and started to run. But his movement was erratic. He stumbled and swerved. Easily she outpaced him, raced up behind him with her heart thumping, and touched his shoulder, but just that slight extra weight tipped him forward and he sprawled facedown on the hard earth. Instantly she crouched beside him, knife in hand. Whether she could use it was something she didn't care to think about right now.

But the slumped figure offered no resistance. He tipped himself over on his back and raised his hands above his head in surrender, so Lydia was able to take a good look at him. He was painfully thin. Cheekbones like razor blades. With skin that was yellow and eyes that seemed to roll and float loose in his head. She had no idea of his age. Twenty? Thirty? Yet the cracked and peeling skin on his hands looked much older and there were raw lesions on his face.

She seized hold of the cloth of his filthy tunic, ragged and fraying and stinking of stale urine, and wound it tight around her fist in case this fleshless stork should suddenly take it into its head to fly.

"Tell me," she said speaking slowly and clearly, in the hope he could understand English. "Where is Chang An Lo?"

He nodded, eyes fixed on her face. "Chang An Lo." He raised a bony finger and pointed it at her. "Leeja?"

"Yes." Her heart lifted. Only Chang could have told him her name. "I'm Lydia." With a heave she yanked him to his feet, but despite his height his skin-and-bone frame was so light they both almost toppled over. "Chang An Lo?" she asked once more and cursed her lack of Mandarin.

"Tan Wah," he pointed to himself with his yellow fingernail.

"You are Tan Wah? Please, Tan Wah, take me to Chang An Lo." She gestured toward the town.

He bobbed his scruffy black head in understanding and set off at an uneven pace through the undergrowth. Lydia kept one hand on his tunic. Her skin prickled with impatience.

THEY WERE HEADING DOWN TO THE HARBOR. SO IT SEEMED she had been searching in the right place. In the world of no-names. No laws. Where weapons ruled and money talked. Yes, Mr. Liu had been right. Chang was here. Close. She could feel him waiting for her. Breathing in her mind. She tugged at Tan Wah's tunic to hurry him because without Liev at her side she was uneasy down in this world. The risk was high.

She had grown accustomed to the smell of the streets now. The quayside was teeming with people, pushing and jostling each other, dodging around rickshaw wheels, shouting and spitting, heaped wheelbarrows and shoulderpoles barging a path, all a swaying seething mass. Lydia wasn't looking at their faces this time. That's why she didn't see it coming. An old man, bent double under a mound of firewood on his back and with lank sparse hair falling around his face, merged into the gray swirl of humanity around her. She didn't even glance at him. Not until he stopped right in their path. Then she noticed the black eyes looking up at her bright with greed. His head was twisted sideways to peer around the massive bundle on his back.

He made no sound. Just swept out a thin-bladed knife from under his padded tunic and without a word sank it up to the hilt in Tan Wah's stomach.

Lydia screamed.

Tan Wah coughed and sank to his knees, his hands scrabbling at the sudden scarlet stain. Lydia seized his arm to support him, but as his face fell forward the old man sliced the blade expertly across his throat. Blood sprayed in a wide arc. Lydia felt it hit her face, obscenely warm in the cold air.

"Tan Wah," she cried out and knelt on the filthy ground beside his limp body. His bloodshot eyes were still wide open and staring, but already the film of death had settled on them.

"Tan Wah," she gasped.

A hand was tugging at her shoulder. She leaped to her feet, pulling free of the grip, and shouted out to the faces in motion around her.

"Help me. This man is dead, he needs . . . Please, fetch police . . . I . . ."

A woman under a thick headscarf and a coolie hat was the only one to stop. She had a child strapped to her back. She ducked down, tapped Tan Wah's cheek as if that could check whether his spirit had fled, and then started to rifle through the dead man's rags, seeking his pockets. Lydia screamed at her, thrust her aside as rage ripped through her throat, robbing her of words, so that only a primitive animal growl escaped.

The woman melted back into the indifferent crowd. Hands were clutching at Lydia, but her mind was spinning and at first she thought the hands were there to help. To steady her. Then it dawned. The old man with the firewood was undoing her buttons. He was stealing her coat. Her coat. That's what he wanted. *Her coat.* He had killed Tan Wah for a coat.

She spat at him, and from her pocket she yanked out the open penknife. With a separate part of her mind she registered that his blackened hands stank of tar as they tore at her buttons and that he hadn't stabbed *her* because he didn't want to ruin the coat. She drove the penknife with all her strength into the top of his arm and felt it scrape bone. His mouth opened in a high wailing toothless screech, but his hands released the coat.

Lydia threw her weight against the bundle of wood on his back, sending him sprawling onto the cobbles like an upended turtle. Then she turned and ran.

A WHITE FACE. IT LEAPED OUT AT HER. A WESTERN LONG nose. Short blond hair greased flat on his head. A uniform. Among all the black oriental eyes, this pair of round blue ones made Lydia throw herself across the street and hold on to the arm of the man coming down the steps of a rowdy gaming house. She could smell whisky on him.

"I'm sorry," she gasped, breath like fire in her chest. "I'm sorry but I . . ."

"Hey there, little lady, what's got you all rattled? Ease up now."

He was American. A sailor. U.S. Navy. She recognized the uniform. His hands soothed her as he would a fretful mare, stroking her back and patting her shoulder.

"What's up?"

"A man. He killed my . . . my . . . my companion. For nothing. Stabbed him. He wanted my . . ."

"Calm down, you're safe with me, honey."

". . . wanted my coat."

"Fucking bandits. Come on, we'll find a cop and get this mess sorted out. Don't you fret yourself." He started walking her up the street. "Who was this companion of yours? I sure hope it was a guy because I'd hate to think of a pretty lady . . ."

"It was a man. A Chinese."

"What! A goddamn Chink. Well, we'd better take a rethink here."

He stopped walking and, with his arm firmly round her waist, elbowed his way past a goat that was dangling by its feet from a pole and bleating pathetically. He pulled her into an arched doorway where they could talk more easily.

"You've had a fright, miss. But look, if it's just a stinking Chink we're talking about, you'd do better to let the local Chink cops sort this one out." He smiled, his blue eyes reassuring, his teeth white and well-cared for, his soft Southern accent as smooth as syrup.

Abruptly she tried to break away from his grip on her waist.

"Let go of me, please," she said curtly. "If you won't help me, then I'll find a policeman myself."

His mouth crushed down on hers.

Shock and revulsion rocked her. She fought wildly to free herself, dragged her nails down his cheek, but with a curse he pinned her arms behind her back, pressed her tight against the wall where the bricks crushed her wrists, and started to pull and yank at her skirt. She kicked and struggled. Writhed away from his hands. But it was like fighting against one of America's battleships. His fingers were thrusting under the elastic of her underwear, his tongue invading her mouth like a slug.

She bit hard. Tasted blood.

"Bitch," he growled and hit her.

"Bastard," she hissed through the hand clamped over her mouth.

He laughed and snapped the elastic.

"Stop right there." A male voice spoke coldly in the American's ear.

All Lydia could see was the tip of a gun barrel pressed against his temple. The click of the hammer being cocked sounded like a cannon in the sudden silence in the doorway. She seized her chance. Lashed out, kicked hard, caught the American's shin a vicious crack. He grunted and backed off.

"Kneel down," the voice ordered.

The sailor knew better than to argue with a gun. He knelt. Lydia slipped out onto the busy road, ready to take to her heels again, indifferent to her rescuer. Chivalry seemed to come with a high price these days.

"Lydia Ivanova."

She halted. Stared at the man in the heavy green jacket, his face creased with concern. It was familiar. Her mind groped through the rush of blood to her head and the animal urge to flee.

"Alexei Serov," she said at last in astonishment.

"At least you recognize me this time."

Relief came in a warm thick wave. "May I?" She held out her hand for the revolver.

"You're not going to shoot anyone."

"No, I promise."

He released the hammer safely and allowed her to take the gun from his grip. She crunched the heavy metal butt of it down on the American's skull, then returned it to Alexei Serov.

"Thank you." She gave him a wide smile.

He looked at her oddly. His eyes scanned her face, her hair, her clothes. "Come," he said. "I'll see you home." He offered her his arm with extreme politeness. "Hold on to me."

But she backed away. "No. No, thank you. I'll just walk beside you." Even she could hear that her voice was not normal.

"You're very shaken, Miss Ivanova. I don't think you'll manage it on your own."

"I will."

He stared at her again, nodded.

"But there's been a murder," she told him rapidly and pointed back down the street, though she knew it was hopeless.

"There are murders every day in Junchow," Alexei Serov said with a brusque shrug. "Don't concern yourself."

He set off with a long stride and signaled three men waiting quietly behind him to follow. Only then did Lydia notice them. They were Kuomintang soldiers.

He saw her right to her door.

"Is your mother home?" he asked.

"Yes," she lied.

She needed to be alone, needed silence. Chang An Lo had been so close, barely a whisper away, but now . . .

Yet Alexei Serov ignored her protests and escorted her all the way up to the attic, ducking his head to avoid the slope of the roof over the last few stairs. Normally she would have died before taking anyone into their room. Even Polly. But today she didn't care. He sat her down on the sofa and made her cups of tea, one after another, dark and sweet. He talked to her occasionally but not much, and when he sat down in the old chair opposite, she noticed the chipped cup in his hand. Slowly, like climbing up from some deep slimy tunnel underground, her mind was starting to focus again. His gaze was roaming around the room and when he saw her watching him, he smiled.

"The colors are wonderful," he said and gestured to the magenta cushions and the haphazard swathes of material. "It's nice."

Nice? How could anybody in their right mind call this miserable hole *nice*?

She sipped her tea. Studied this man who had invaded her home. He was leaning back in the chair, fully at ease, not like Alfred who always felt edgy up here. She had the strange feeling that Alexei Serov would be at ease wherever he was. Or was it all an act? She couldn't tell. His short brown hair was clean and springy, not brilliantined like most, and his eyes were the shade of green that made her think of the moss on the flat rock at Lizard Creek. He was long and languid all over, his face, his mouth, his body, the way he crossed his legs. Except for his hands. They were broad and muscular and looked as if he had borrowed them from someone else.

"Feeling better?" he asked.

"I'm fine."

He gave a low laugh as if he doubted her words but said, "Good. Then I shall leave you."

She tried to stand but found she was wrapped in her eiderdown. When had he put that there?

He leaned forward, observing her closely. "It is dangerous for a woman to go down to the docks. On her own, it is suicidal."

"I wasn't on my own. I was with a . . . companion. A Chinese companion, but he was . . ." The word wouldn't come.

"Murdered?"

She nodded jerkily. "Stabbed." Her hands started to tremble and she hid them under the quilt. "I have to report it to the police."

"Do you know his name? His address?"

"Tan Wah. That's all I know of him."

"I would leave it there, Lydia Ivanova." He spoke firmly. "The Chinese police will not want to know about it, I assure you. Unless he was rich, of course. That would change their outlook."

Tan Wah's skeletal face, yellow as the loess dust that blew in on the wind, floated before her. "No, he wasn't rich. But he deserves justice."

"Do you know the man who stabbed him? Or where to find this murderer?"

"No."

"Then forget it. He's just one of many dying on the streets of Junchow."

"That is harsh."

"These are harsh times."

She knew he was right, but everything in her cried out against it. "It was for my coat. He wanted my coat. Tan Wah is dead for just a stupid hateful bloody coat . . ."

She threw off the eiderdown and leaped to her feet, tearing at the buttons of her Christmas coat, shaking the foul thing off her shoulders and hurling it to the floor. Alexei Serov rose, picked up the blue coat and very deliberately draped it over the chair he had been sitting in. Then he walked over to the small sink beside the stove and returned with an enamel bowl of water and a washcloth.

"Here," he said. "Wash your face."

"What?"

"Your face." He put the wet cloth in her hand. "I must go now, but only if you're sure you're . . ."

Lydia gasped. She had moved over to the mirror on the wall by the door and looked at herself. It was a shock. No wonder he had stared at her oddly. Her skin was paper white except for a fine smattering of blood spray all over her face and neck like dark brown freckles. One cheek was swollen where the American had slapped her, and there was a long scratch just in front of her left ear, most likely from the dash through the undergrowth in the woods. But worse was her hair. One whole side of it was stiff with dried blood. Tan Wah's blood.

She didn't look at her eyes. She was frightened what she might see there.

Quickly she wiped the cloth over her face, then hurried over to the sink and stuck her head under the tap. The water was ice cold but immediately she felt better. Cleaner. Inside. When she stood up she expected Alexei Serov to be gone, but he was standing behind her holding a towel. She rubbed her hair and her skin with it, fiercely, as if she could rub the images from her mind, but when she dragged a brush through her hair so roughly it snapped the handle, she made herself stop. Took a breath. Forced a laugh. It wasn't much of a laugh.

"Thank you, Alexei Serov. You have been kind."

For the first time he seemed awkward and ill-suited to the room as he clicked his heels and dipped his head in a formal bow. "I am pleased to assist." He marched over to the door and opened it. "I wish you a rapid recovery from your ordeal today."

"Tell me one thing."

He waited. His green eyes grew wary.

"Why do you have Kuomintang soldiers at your beck and call?"

"I work with them."

"Oh."

"I am a military adviser. Trained in Japan."

"I see."

"Is that all?"

"Yes."

"Then good-bye, Lydia Ivanova."

"*Spasibo do svidania,* Alexei Serov. Thank you and good-bye."

He nodded and left.

Before his footsteps had faded on the stairs there was a sharp exclamation on the lower landing. It was her mother's voice. After a brief torrent of Russian that Lydia couldn't catch, Valentina burst into the attic room.

"Lydia, I don't ever want to see that Russian here again, do you hear me? Never. I forbid it. Are you listening? Damn, it's cold in this wretched room. I absolutely will not have that hateful family anywhere near . . . Lydia, I am talking to you."

But Lydia had taken her eiderdown and curled up inside it on her bed. She closed her eyes and shut out the world.

★ ★ ★

CHANG AN LO. I AM SORRY.

It was the middle of the night. Lydia was staring up into the darkness. A pain in her temples was thudding in rhythm with her heartbeat. She had worked it out. For Chang to send Tan Wah to Lizard Creek, he must be ill. Or wounded. It was the only explanation. Otherwise he would have come himself. She was sure of it. Sure as she was of her own life. And now because of her, Tan Wah was dead, which meant she had put Chang in greater danger. Without Tan Wah, Chang An Lo might die. Her throat ached with unshed tears.

"Lydia?"

"Yes, Mama?"

"Tell me, *dochenka*, do you think I am a bad mother?"

The attic room was as dark as death except for a thin slice of moonlight that drew a silver line down the center of the curtain that formed Lydia's bedroom wall. Her mother had drunk steadily all evening and had been muttering to herself in her own bed for some time, never a good sign.

"What is bad, Mama?"

"Don't be foolish. You know perfectly well what bad means."

Lydia made the effort to talk. This would be their last night together in this room. "You have never cooked me plum pie. Nor sewn up holes in my clothes. Or bothered whether I brushed my teeth. Does that make you bad?"

"No."

"Of course not. So there's your answer."

A wind rattled the window. To Lydia it sounded like Chang's fingers on the pane. The noise of a distant car engine grew louder, then faded.

"Tell me what I have done right, *dochenka*."

Lydia chose her words with care. "You kept me. Though you could have abandoned me at any time in St. Mary's Children's Mission. You'd have been free. To do whatever you wanted."

Silence.

"And you've given me music, all my life there's been music. Oh Mama, you've given me kisses. And colorful scarves. And shown me how to use the tongue in my head, even if I've driven you crazy with it. Yes, you did," she insisted. "You taught me to think for myself and, best of all, you let me make my own mistakes."

A cloud passed over the moon and the sliver of light died in the room.

Valentina still said nothing.

"Mama, now it's your turn. Tell me what I have done right."

There was the sound of a deep intake of breath from the other end of the room and a low moan. It took a whole minute before Valentina spoke.

"Just your being alive is right. It is everything."

Her mother's words seemed to burn up the darkness and set fire to something inside Lydia's head. She shut her eyes.

"Now go to sleep, *dochenka*. We have a big day tomorrow."

But an hour later Valentina's voice came again whispering through the darkness. "Be happy for me, darling."

"Happiness is hard."

"I know."

Lydia pressed the heels of her hands against her eyes to scrub away the pictures of Chang, alone and sick, behind her eyelids. Happiness she could get by without. But she was determined to hold on to hope.

32

ACHINGLY BEAUTIFUL.

That's how Theo thought Junchow looked this morning. It had snowed overnight and now the town dazzled. Its drab gray roofs had been transformed into sparkling white slopes with curling eaves like sledges, eager to slip and slide away. Even the solid British mansions were no more than fragile icing. The light from the sky was a strange muted pink that made everything glitter, including the school court-yard below, where the perfect imprint of the paw marks of a night creature trailed through the snow from one end to the other.

"You go now, Tiyo, or you be late."

Reluctantly he abandoned the window. Li Mei was standing be-hind him in a virginal white gown. A snowflake. He took her in his arms and kissed her soft lips but released her when he saw liquid trickle down her cheek. She was melting. He took the top hat she was holding in her hands. It was seal gray and appeared ridiculous to him. He was wearing a morning coat with absurd tails and a stiff white collar. Li Mei touched his cheek, smelled the flower in his lapel, and straightened the hat on his head.

"You look very fine, Tiyo, my love."

"A very fine idiot," he laughed.

She laughed with him.

"Come with me," he said.

"No, my love."

"Why?"

"It would not be fitting."

"Bugger fitting."

"No, I do other things today."

"What things?"

"I go speak with my father."

"With Feng Tu Hong? Damn that devil. You swore you wished never to see him again."

She lowered her head, her black hair swaying in a rippling curtain between them. "I know. I break my oath. I pray the gods will forgive me."

"Don't go to him, sweet one. Please. He might hurt you and I couldn't bear that."

"Or I might hurt him," she said, lifting her almond-shaped eyes to his. Achingly beautiful.

THEO TRIED TO CONCENTRATE. THE WEDDING SERVICE WAS thankfully short. That was the advantage of a civil ceremony over one of those elaborately drawn-out church weddings, full of fluff and flummery that Theo loathed. This was better. Brief and to the point. Shame for Alfred though. He was quite put out by not being allowed to exchange vows in a church before God, but if he insisted on marrying a woman who had been married before, what did he expect? The Church of England was a bit of a stickler about these niceties.

The bride was sparkling. That was Theo's problem. He was sitting in the front row of seats behind the groom, only dimly aware of the other guests around him, of hats and perfumes and neatly tied cravats. It was the bride's cream bolero that was bothering him. It was covered with tiny seed pearls that shimmered and shifted each time she breathed, seizing the light and swirling it around Theo's head, making it difficult for him to think clearly. He focused on the back of her dress instead, on her slender hips under the ivory-colored chiffon, on the soft curves and the sweet rise of her buttocks. Abruptly he wished he were at home with Li Mei. In the bath. His tongue trailing up her buttery thigh.

He shook his head. Blinked hard. Emptied his brain of such thoughts. These days it was impossible to know where his mind would wander off next, and that worried him. He removed his gray gloves and chafed his hands together, oblivious to the noise, but a woman behind him tapped his shoulder pointedly, so he ceased. There were no more than about thirty people present, mainly colleagues of Alfred's from the *Daily Herald*, and Theo recognized one or two chaps from the club as well, but there was a large-bosomed elderly woman in taffeta, very Russian, whom he didn't know and a bright but stringy couple with clouds of white hair who smiled a lot. Vaguely he recalled Alfred mentioning that they were retired missionaries who'd lived in the same house as Valentina.

"Do you, Alfred Frederick Parker, take this woman . . . ?"

No, they'd got it all wrong. It was this woman who was taking Alfred. It was obvious to everyone but the poor blighter himself. This woman and her daughter. Theo brushed a hand over his burning eyes. Where was the daughter?

He recalled noticing her earlier when she walked into the chamber behind her mother, very upright and remote. She knew how to walk, that girl. Like she was queen of the jungle in her leaf-green dress and pelt of shining copper hair. He glanced across the aisle and found her. She was staring stiffly down at the pale green gloves on her lap and picking at their fingers with sharp little tugs. Her hair was draped forward but did not quite hide a long scratch beside her ear. She had clearly been in a fight in that jungle of hers.

Theo leaned back in his seat and risked closing his eyes. Instantly he was swept away in a world of sampans and swaying decks and yellow teeth. As clear as day he could see Christopher Mason adrift on a raft in the wide mouth of the river, covered in snakes devouring his eyes and crawling into his ears.

Theo smiled and started to snore.

"WHAT DO YOU THINK, THEO, OLD CHAP? PRETTY DAMN DEcent I'd say, wouldn't you?"

"Yes, it's a fine house you've rented, Alfred." It was at the eastern end of the British Quarter near St. Sebastian's Church, tucked away in a leafy avenue. "You and your beautiful bride should be very happy here." He didn't mention the daughter.

"I think so too."

They were standing on the terrace looking out over the extensive garden that even in the bleak grip of winter managed to look well cared for. Smoke from their cigars spiraled up into the still air and the brandy snifters were almost empty. Theo was desperate to leave. His eyes ached and his skin prickled painfully. It felt as if a rodent were wriggling around under it, gnawing at the nerve ends. Behind him in the drawing room the buzz of voices enjoying themselves rose steadily as the wedding party made the most of the food and drink. Music drifted out, something by Paul Whiteman's band. The sound of it scraped like razor blades in his ears.

"Off soon?" he asked.

"Anytime now." Alfred checked his pocket watch. "The taxi is coming to take us to the station at three-thirty. Then it's a whole week at Datong. Just the two of us. On honeymoon. Valentina and me." His smile was so broad, Theo thought it would split his face in half.

"You'll love the Huayuan temple."

"I'm really looking forward to seeing it. Valentina too."

"I bet she is. What about the girl?"

"Lydia?"

"Yes. Staying here is she? Or with . . ." Theo's mind went blank. What was the little blond girl's name? Sally? Dolly? Polly, that was it. "Or with Polly?"

For the first time that day Alfred's beaming smile faded a fraction. "She's chosen to stay here. There's the cook and his wife living in, of course, as well as the houseboy and gardener coming in each day, so she won't be on her own."

"No need to worry then."

"Well, I can't say I'm happy about it. She refused to go to stay with the Masons, even though she was invited, and won't hear of my employing a respectable woman to live here with her as a chaperone while we're away." He removed his spectacles and polished them thoroughly. "It's only a week," he muttered to himself. "And she'll be seventeen this year. What trouble can she get into in a week?"

Theo laughed and looked down at the damp gray stone under his shoes to shield from the glare of lights flickering inside his eyes. "Don't fret, dear fellow, that girl knows how to take care of herself."

Alfred looked at him solemnly. "That's what worries me."

"What is it that worries you, my angel?" It was Valentina, come to join them on the terrace.

310 · KATE FURNIVALL

"Ah, I'm worried that it might snow again and make our train late."

"Nonsense, even the weather is on our side today. Nothing will go wrong."

She laughed and stepped up close to her husband, so close she could lean her body against his as she stood beside him. Alfred beamed at her. He slid an arm around her waist and she turned her face up to him in a manner that made Theo think of a flower turning toward the sun. He could see his friend aglow with pride and such naked love that there was something vaguely indecent about it. Theo feared for him.

It was bitterly cold on the terrace and Valentina was wearing only the creamy chiffon dress that floated around her as she moved. He noticed her nipples harden under the flimsy material. Whether from chill or from lust, he had no idea. Theo much preferred the vivid red clothes, red for happiness, that the Chinese wore at weddings instead of the pallid shades of white favored by Westerners, but even so, he had to admit she looked lovely. Dark hair and eyes shining. Around her long neck hung three strands of pearls, as pale as her skin. Aware of his eyes on her, she turned and held his gaze for a beat longer than was strictly polite, then she smiled up at Alfred again.

"Angel, do come back indoors. It's freezing out here and Mr. Willoughby is looking very pale."

"By Jove, she's right, Theo, you are a bit on the peaky side. Trust a woman to notice."

"Indeed," Theo said and headed indoors with the intention of taking his leave.

As the newlywed couple entered the drawing room arm in arm, a cheer went up and everyone joined in singing "For he's a jolly good fellow . . ." and followed it with "For she's a jolly . . ."

Raised voices at the front door broke through. The singing ceased abruptly. A deep roar of anger barged into the room with a native houseboy fluttering with birdlike chirrups in its wake. Theo wondered for a moment if it was one of his hallucinations. It was too bizarre to be real. A huge man, mean and vicious and obviously drunk, had forced his way into the midst of the wedding party with a barrage of Russian curses. He wore a curly black beard and a ragged eye patch,

THE RUSSIAN CONCUBINE • 311

and his clothes looked and smelled as if he hadn't been out of them since the Bolshevik Revolution. But others were also staring in alarm at the intruder. Bizarre or not, it must be real. The room itself seemed to shake and dwindle in size as the massive creature stumbled forward, growling, swaying, and swerving out of control.

"The man's drunk."

"Wish I had my gun with me."

"Call the police."

"Keep back, Johnnie, or someone will get hurt."

Theo stepped into his path. He wasn't quite sure what he intended to do, maybe pull the short knife from his ankle scabbard, which he always carried these days. Or maybe the flashing lights in his head had made him invisible and he could smash his fist into the fellow without being seen himself. That crazy thought did cross Theo's mind. All he knew was that he didn't want his friend Alfred hurt. Not on his wedding day.

The single black eye swept over him and instantly a massive elbow came crashing toward his face. A fierce yank on Theo's arm sent him tumbling to one side, and the blow landed on his shoulder instead of destroying his cheekbone. A pair of amber eyes peered into his and he saw the Russian girl's hands still clutching his arm where she had pulled at him. Then she was gone.

Through the pain that was hammering on his brain and the light blinding his eyes, he tried to make sense of what he saw. The *tu-fei*, the Russian bandit, charged at the wedded pair. Alfred, mild-mannered and calm Alfred, threw himself forward with an animal cry of fury to protect his beloved, but the great paw knocked him aside with barely a flick of a muscle. Alfred was on the floor, blood on his head.

Screaming. Someone was screaming.

Valentina Ivanova—no, Valentina Parker—was yelling at the big man in Russian. She slapped his face. Not once, but three times. She had to reach up high to do so and looked like a kitten playing with a lion's muzzle. Yet he didn't touch her. He growled and roared and shook his great furry head from side to side. He staggered and swayed, too drunk to stand firm, and still she screamed at him.

"*Poshyol von.* Get out of here, you stinking Russian pig. *Ubiraisya otsyuda gryaznaya svinya.*"

"Prodazhnaya shkura," he bellowed and then in English, "You whore."

Theo got himself over to Alfred and helped him to his feet.

"Stop it, stop it. *Prekratyitye.*"

It was the girl. She seized hold of the man's massive arm and pulled him to look at her. His black eye was slow to abandon the bride's face but eventually shifted to the girl at his side.

"Poshli, come," she said urgently. "Come with me. Quickly. *Bistro*. Or you will be shot like a dog."

Then it was over. The shouting stopped. The man was gone. Alfred was rushing to Valentina. The girl disappeared. The last thing Theo could recall was the sight of her small figure dragging the big bandit from the room and the odd thing was that he went quietly, tears rolling down his cheeks into his thick beard. The old woman with the vast bosom was standing, arms outstretched, in the middle of the room, gazing up at the ceiling and declaiming in a heavy Russian accent, "You shall pay for this. God will make you pay for this."

Theo wondered if she meant him.

33

Lydia had to run. Even though he had been drinking, Liev moved fast on his great long legs, as if there were a demon inside him.

"Damn you, Liev Popkov," she swore. "Slow down."

He halted, studied her blearily with his one eye. He seemed surprised to find her at his side.

"What," she demanded, "was all that about? Why did you break up the wedding party? *O chyom vi rugalyis?*"

He shook his head and lumbered on, at an easier pace this time. It was raining now, but cold enough to turn to snow again at any moment. Lydia was in the wrong clothes. The green beaded frock was not meant to keep out the Chinese winter. She had seized her coat from the cupboard in the hall on her way out, the old thin coat, not the bloodied new one—she hated that one—but she was wearing silly satin shoes and no hat. She took hold of his arm and gripped it hard. Her fear that the violent confrontation with her mother would cause him to abandon her made her dig her fingers in tight and concentrate on seeking out the right Russian words.

"Why did you do that to my mother? Tell me. Why? *Pochemu?*"

"A Russian must marry a Russian," he grunted and lowered his head into the rain. He would say no more.

"That is nonsense, Liev Popkov."

But she left it there. Her Russian was not adequate to the emotions she was struggling with. The sight of her mother's beautiful face so twisted with anger and the sound of the Russian words pouring from her mouth too fast for Lydia to grasp had shaken her. It had stolen something solid from her world. Why would Liev barge into the house? None of it made sense.

SHE GUIDED THE BIG BEAR PAST THE RAILWAY STATION AND down to the docks. He seemed to have no care for what direction he took, unaware of where he was going until a singsong girl in a bright yellow short cheongsam that showed off her legs reached out and touched his cheek with a hand whose nails were as green as dragon scales.

"You want jig–jig?"

He brushed her aside. But his head came up and he looked around, saw the tall metal cranes and the gambling dens and the chain gangs of porters. For the first time he noticed the rain. His bloodshot eye turned to Lydia and frowned.

"I have a plan," she said in Russian. "I found a man. He knows my friend, the one I'm searching for. This man I found is . . . dead now. I did not understand his Chinese words but he said the name Calfield. I think it is here. Somewhere."

"Calfield?"

"Da."

She knew she hadn't explained it well, but it was hard to find the words in his language. Her impatience got the better of her. She pulled him toward the buildings overlooking the quayside and pointed to the names up on their frontage. JEPHERSON'S TIMBER YARD and LAMARTIERE AGENCE. Across the road DIRK & GREEN WHEELWRIGHT next to WINKMANN'S CHANDLERY. All jumbled up among the Chinese businesses.

She gestured to Liev. "Calfield? Where is it? You must ask."

Understanding dawned. "Calfield," he echoed.

"Yes."

It had taken her hours. Lying awake last night, trawling through the nightmare of yesterday. Again and again she came back to the knife disappearing into Tan Wah. His soft hoarse cough. The blood. How could there be so much blood in one so thin? She wanted to scream aloud *No, no,* but she had made her mind go back, further back. To the wood. When she first asked Tan Wah about Chang An

Lo. His chatter of words meant nothing to her but she went over them. Remembering. Listening. Seeing his floating eyes. His hairless face, already a skeleton. His teeth, yellow and chipped.

Words. Sounds. Unfamiliar and alien.

Just as the folds of the dividing curtain turned from black to gray, the start of their last morning in that attic room, one word stepped out into the front of her mind from all the meaningless sounds. *Calfield*. Tan Wah had definitely used the word.

Calfield.

She gnawed at it like a bone. He had been taking her to Chang, that much was clear. Then he had waved his bony hand toward the quay and said *Calfield*.

It was a business or trading company of some sort, she was sure of it. Calfield was an English name and no Englishman lived down there at the docks, so it had to be a business. She had planned to seek out Liev Popkov the second her mother and Alfred left for the station, but his intrusion just made it happen earlier. The honeymooners would set off anyway and probably not even notice she wasn't there in all the excitement. They wouldn't miss her.

"Lydia Ivanova." It was the bear. His voice was steadier now, his words less slurred. "*Pochemu?* Why you want this friend so bad?"

She glared at him. "That is my business."

He growled, literally growled. Then he reached into the greasy pocket of his long overcoat and pulled out a stack of banknotes. He took her hand in his great paw and placed the money on her palm, curling her fingers around it to hide it from jealous eyes.

"Two hundred dollar," he said in English.

A wave of sickness hit her stomach. The return of the money was so final. He'd finished with her.

"Don't leave. *Nye ostavlyaitye menya.*"

He said nothing. Just removed the long woolen scarf from around his neck, draped it over her wet head, and wound it around her shoulders. It stank of God-knows-what filth and stale sweat all mixed up with tobacco and garlic, but something in the gesture stilled her fear. He wouldn't leave her. Surely.

But he did.

★ ★ ★

SHE FELT BETRAYED. THERE WAS NO REASON WHY SHE should, but she did. It was a business arrangement, nothing more. Two hundred dollars of protection, that's what she'd bought. Liev had more than earned it already, risked his life time and again during her search in this dangerous place for no more than Alfred probably paid for her new coat. But now he had returned the money. All of it.

She didn't understand.

Nor did she understand why she felt so hurt by it. It was business. Nothing more. She watched him walk into a *kabak* and knew he would not come out this time. He was there to drink. She wanted to shout after him. To beg.

No.

She pulled the scarf as far over her face as it would go and scuttled along close to the wall, keeping her eyes on the ground, seeking no contact of any kind with the faces and bodies that milled around her. She knew she was in danger. She remembered the moon-faced man who had tried to buy her and the American sailor. She fingered the two hundred dollars in her pocket and was tempted to cast it away, knowing it increased her risk, but she couldn't bring herself to do so. To throw money away would feel like slitting her wrists.

What she needed to do was to go into one of the European companies and ask. Simple.

A hand touched her shoulder, a black-eyed smile leaned toward her face. She jumped away and hurried for the first door she could see that bore an English sign above it. E. W. HALLIDAY. Maybe the smile meant well. She would never know. She pushed open the door and was instantly disappointed. The place was nothing like she had been expecting. It was a long and low-ceilinged room that even in daylight remained dim because the window was so small and grimy. A handful of Chinese workers were busy stacking cardboard cartons onto pallets against the wall, but an unpleasant oily smell seeped in from behind large double doors that led to what appeared to be a factory behind.

A Chinese man at a desk near the door raised his head. He wore tiny steel-rimmed glasses and a thin ribbon mustache that made him look almost European, and his desk was littered with thick ledgers. A tall black telephone was ringing, but he ignored it.

"Excuse me," Lydia said, "do you speak English?"

"Yes. How may I help you, miss?"

"I am searching for a company called Calfield. Do you know it?"

"Yes."

"Where is it?"

"In Sweet Candle Yard."

"Could you direct me there, please?"

At that moment the double doors swung open, breathing a gust of hot air into the front office and giving Lydia a brief glimpse of a kind of purgatory taking place behind. Dozens of matchstick figures were leaning over great vats with long paddles, pushing something down into a steaming liquid that scalded their faces a raw and blistered scarlet. As the doors swung shut they disappeared back into their own daily hell.

"You go down Leaping Goat Lane and over to the godowns. Calfield is there."

The man waved a hand in a vague direction, bowed a dismissal, and picked up the telephone to stop its jangling. Lydia left, the oily stink still in her nostrils. Outside she stared at the numerous streets and alleyways running off the quayside. Leaping Goat Lane.

Which one?

All the signs were written in Chinese characters. She could be looking straight at Leaping Goat Lane and not know it. A rickshaw raced past and water splashed from its wheels, drenching her in slime. Her satin shoes were ruined; she was wet through and shivering.

"Leaping Goat Lane," she said aloud and climbed up on the low ledge of a stone trough in front of a water pump where the water had dripped into a frozen tear. At the top of her voice she shouted out, "Can anyone tell me which is Leaping Goat Lane?"

Several of the heads hurrying past turned to stare at her with interest, and she saw two thin men in bamboo hats swerve from their path and shoulder their way toward her. She swallowed. It was a risk, but time was running out for Chang and she was desperate to find him. Suddenly she was whisked off her feet. Something seized her, whirled her into the air, and shook her like a rag doll. Her eyes rattled in her head. She kicked out. Punched the side of a face. Bit something.

"Lydia Ivanova. *Nyet*. No. *Nyet*."

It was Liev Popkov. He shook her again and she wrapped her arms around him with relief.

THEY HURRIED DOWN LEAPING GOAT LANE. THE RAIN WAS falling harder. A mule train carrying great coils of rope trekked past them with much shouting and whip cracking. Liev Popkov kept one hand firmly round Lydia's wrist.

He had been angry with her. For misunderstanding him. For thinking he would go into a bar for anything other than information. He told her off, shouted at her for leaving instead of waiting, and his anger pleased her. She knew she should be frightened of him but she wasn't. No more than her mother had been in the face of his drunken onslaught. That thought jolted her. Even the men at the wedding party had backed off in alarm and talked of guns and police, but not Valentina. It made Lydia wonder for the first time whether her mother knew Liev Popkov better than she was admitting.

"The godowns." Lydia pointed.

Ahead of them stood a group of buildings, large and lifeless, with corrugated roofs and no windows. These were the warehouses where imported and exported goods were stored until the tax inspectors had taken their cut. A few uniformed guards with guns on their hips patrolled in a desultory manner, more interested in keeping dry than watching out for thieves. The yards here were even worse than the streets. They stank of putrefaction. All around were bundles of sodden rags, at the base of walls or hunched tight under a sill or in a gutter.

Lydia knew that there were people under the pathetic scraps of cloth, but which ones were breathing and which ones were dead and rotting where they lay, only their gods knew. The sick fear that one could be Chang An Lo drove her to approach a huddle in a doorway, where she could just make out a dark thatch of wet hair and a high forehead that looked familiar. But when he lifted his face to her, it wasn't Chang. This man's eyes had no fire. No hope. His skin was covered in blackened boils, and foamy crimson blood was trickling from the side of his mouth.

Lydia remembered the two hundred dollars in her pocket. She reached in for it, but before her fingers had freed up a few notes Liev Popkov yanked her away.

"*Chuma*. The plague," he said in English with disgust. In Russian he added, "He'll be dead before nightfall." He took the money from her and replaced it in his own pocket.

Plague.

Just the word sent shivers through her. She'd heard Alfred mention it. He said that it had started in the army and that when the warlords were defeated, the soldiers fled back to their villages, spreading the disease like wildfire. Famine in the scorched fields sent the peasants flocking into the towns for food and work but instead they coughed their lungs into a gutter. Died frozen in their rags. Lydia took off her coat and draped it over the trembling heap of bones.

"Fool, *glupaya dura*," Liev swore.

But she knew he would not take back the coat, not now. It was plague ridden. Her fear for Chang burned in her chest and she hurried onward to the warehouses. Calfield had to be one of them. Had to be.

It was.

CALFIELD & CO., ENGINE MACHINERY. The sign was painted in black on the eighth godown they came across. Liev had removed his own overcoat and placed it on Lydia despite her objections, but underneath he wore an odd assortment of garments, including a thick leather tunic that shrugged off the rain. They searched. Every inch of ground. They paced around the Calfield warehouse and then out farther, circling other warehouses, other storerooms.

"Nothing here," Liev muttered. He looked up at the slate sky and then at her wet face. She clamped her chattering teeth shut. "Home," he said.

Lydia shook her head. "*Nyet*. I search again."

She went around to the back of the row of corrugated buildings once more and scanned the stretch of bare wasteland that lay behind them. Nothing grew there. Even the weeds had been torn up and eaten, but a hundred yards or so in the distance were the bare spikes of a bush that had somehow managed to grub a life for itself. A bank of mist had settled behind it. For no reason other than that there was nowhere else to search, Lydia headed in that direction.

The wasteland was a sea of mud with no roots to hold the soil together. She slipped and skidded at every step, stumbling to her knees, blinking the rain from her eyes, but she finally reached the stubby bush. When she raised her head from watching where she placed her feet, avoiding the trailing coat, she saw what lay behind it. A shallow gully. Five or six feet deep with a sluggish layer of rainwater covering the bottom. That's what caused the mist. A few yards off to her right stood a row of ramshackle shelters, half collapsed by the rain.

"Chang!" she shouted and slithered down the muddy bank.

34

LYDIA FOUND HIM. INSIDE THE THIRD HEAP OF DRIFTWOOD and rags and newspapers that was meant to keep the rain off but failed miserably. She was terrified he was dead, he lay so still. Eyes closed. His skin as gray as the water that swilled over the earth beneath him. She crawled inside the hutch, too low to stand, and knelt beside him in the mud, her heart like a stone in her throat. He was wrapped in old newspaper that was so wet from the rain pouring through the roof and from the water rising underneath that it was disintegrating and freezing at the same time. His eyes were encrusted shut and his face was covered in sores. But not boils. Thank God. Not the plague.

She touched him. Like ice. A cocoon of ice. Her fingers tore fiercely at the paper, stripped it from his body. She gasped. His body. It was barely there. A few rags and a few bones. The sight of them wrenched a cry from her. Her eyes stung with tears. The stench was of rotting flesh and it was the smell of death.

No, no, not dead. Not dead. She wouldn't let him be dead.

She swept Liev's heavy coat from her shoulders and laid it on top of Chang's inert form. "Don't let go, my love," she called out to him but barely recognized the voice as her own. She leaned over him, brushed a hand across his cold forehead, placed her lips on his, and kept them there, willing the warmth of her body and the force of her life into him. His lips, cracked and scabbed, gave the slightest of trembles beneath hers. But it was enough.

"Liev," she shouted, "Liev, come . . ."

There was no need to call. He was there. With an easy nudge of his hand he tore off what little remained of the hutch's roof, bent down, and hoisted Chang onto his shoulder. Lydia quickly wrapped the coat around the still form and pulled it tight against the rain.

"A rickshaw," she said. "We need a rickshaw."

"No rickshaw puller take me. I'm too heavy. Nor touch this sick body."

"Can you carry him as far as the British Quarter?"

His lips unsheathed a grin inside his black beard. "Can a tiger catch a fawn?"

THE BOLT TO THE BACK GATE WAS LOCKED. LIEV JUST leaned against it and it sprang open with a loud crack as the nails left the wood. Lydia checked that the garden of her new home was empty. It was nearly dark and still raining. She was thankful for that. These smart streets were not ones where you could pass unnoticed if you were covered in mud and carrying a strange bundle, but the gray gloom of evening gave them shadows to hide in. A narrow alley ran behind the back gardens of the houses, where the rubbish was put out for collection, and it was to this that she had led Liev.

"Hurry," she whispered and pointed at the shed.

Instantly he was across the corner of the lawn and ducking through the narrow door. Lydia was frantic with fear that Chang might have died on Liev Popkov's shoulder, and she cradled his head tenderly as his limp body was lowered to the dusty floor. She touched his cheek with her fingertips. Shuddered. With relief. With alarm. At the fiery heat of his skin. He was burning up inside. The scabs on his lips had burst open and blood was oozing out, trailing green pus with it. She jumped to her feet.

"Wait here," she said to Liev.

She ran. Down the length of the lawn, across the slick grass, keeping to the dark border under the trees. She tried to think as she ran, to list what she needed—blankets, clothes, food, warm drinks . . . or ice, did he need ice for a fever? . . . bandages and medicines, but what medicines, she didn't know, she needed help, she needed . . . Wait a minute. The lights. They were on in the house. The curtains were closed but still the windows cast yellow bars across the terrace. How could she not have noticed earlier? Did that mean people were still there? Or had the servants left the lights on for her? What did it mean? What?

She didn't know. She just didn't know.

She veered off toward the far side of the house to the kitchen door and tried the handle. It turned. The kitchen was empty. The cook had obviously retired to rest after his exertions for the party. She closed the door quietly behind her and was hit by a wave of dizziness as the warm air enveloped her. She had been cold and wet for so long now that the sudden change in temperature made her teeth ache. She was trailing mud and water over the black and white tiles, so she eased off her shoes and tiptoed out into the hall.

Two things happened.

First, she caught sight of her reflection in the long mirror that hung at the bottom of the stairs and barely recognized herself. A filthy wet scarecrow. Liev's black scarf plastered to her head and shoulders, her green dress no longer green, caked with mud and clinging to her body so tight it was indecent. Blue lips, shaking. Bloodless fingers. Eyes too dark to be hers. It came as a shock.

Second, the voices. From the drawing room. Her mother's. Then Alfred's.

A pulse thumped in her head. Why hadn't they gone? Off on honeymoon. Why weren't they on the train?

"No, Alfred," her mother's voice rushed out at her. "Not till I've seen her. Not till I know she's . . ."

Lydia didn't wait for more. Suitcases stood by the front door, coats and umbrella draped across them.

She raced up the stairs. Silent, she must be silent. In her room, her smart new room, she tore off her dress and underclothes and threw them into the bottom of the wardrobe. Using an old sweater she scrubbed her hair and skin till it tingled. Quick brush. Old dress. Cardigan. Downstairs.

She walked into the drawing room with a ready-made smile. "Hello, Mama, I didn't expect to see you still here."

"Lydia," Alfred exclaimed. "Thank the Lord you're home. Your mother has been worried sick. Where have you been?"

"Out."

"Out? That's no answer, my girl. Apologize to your mother at once."

Valentina was standing staring at Lydia, her limbs very rigid, her back to the fire, a half-smoked cigarette in her hand. There were two high spots of color on her cheeks, as though the heat of the fire were affecting her. But Lydia knew her mother. Knew those telltale spots. They meant fear.

Why? Her mother knew she often roamed the streets of the settlement, had done so for years. Why the sudden fear?

"Lydia," Valentina said slowly, "what's wrong?"

"Nothing."

Valentina took a long draw on her cigarette and exhaled with a little grunt, as if she'd been prodded in the chest. She was still wearing the chiffon dress but had replaced the bolero with a warm suede jacket, and there were dark smudges under her eyes.

"I'm sorry, Mama. I didn't mean to delay you. I thought you'd have gone ages ago. With all those guests to wave you good-bye, I didn't think you'd even notice that I . . ."

"Don't be silly, Lydia," Alfred said. She could see he was trying hard to hang on to his temper and be polite. "Of course we wanted to say good-bye, both of us. Now take this." He held out a brown envelope. "It contains some money in case the need should arise before we're back, but of course Wai, he's the cook, will provide your meals, so you shouldn't need much. A trip to the cinema perhaps?"

Lydia had never been to the cinema in her life. At any other time she'd have jumped at it.

"Thank you."

"You'll be all right here on your own?"

"Yes."

"Anthea Mason said she'd look in now and again to see that you're okay."

"No, I'll be fine. Is there another train tonight? I'm sorry I made you miss yours but there must be another one you can catch if you hurry." She looked over at her mother. "I'd hate you to miss out on your honeymoon because of me."

"Well, actually . . ." Alfred began.

"Yes," Valentina said with an annoyed lift of one eyebrow. "We can change trains at Tientsin. Alfred, be an angel and fetch me a glass of water from the kitchen, would you? I'm finding it hot in here." She ran a wrist across her forehead. "Probably all the tension of . . ." She let her voice trail away.

"Certainly, my dear." He glanced at Lydia. "Put your mother's mind at ease, so she can go off feeling reassured." He left the room.

Immediately Valentina tossed her cigarette into the fire and came to stand right in front of Lydia. "Tell me, quickly. What happened?"

Lydia felt weak with relief. Yes, of course, she could tell her everything, she'd know what to do, where to buy medicines, a doctor, she could . . .

Valentina seized her arm. "Tell me what that dirty great wolf wanted."

"What?"

"Popkov."

"What?"

Valentina shook her. "Liev Popkov. You went off with him. What did he say?"

"Nothing."

"You're lying."

"No. He was just drunk."

Valentina looked closely at her daughter, then gently wrapped her arms around her and pulled her close. Lydia breathed in her musky perfume and held tight, but as she did so she felt her own body start to shake uncontrollably.

"Lydochka, sweetheart, don't." Valentina's hand stroked her damp hair. "I'll only be gone a week. I know we've never been apart before but don't be upset. I'll be back soon." She kissed Lydia's cheek and drew back a step. "What, tears? From my I-never-cry *dochenka*. Don't, sweetheart."

Valentina reached for the silver tray of drinks on the sideboard. With a quick glance to check that the door was still closed, she poured a glass of vodka, drank it straight down, shuddered, and poured another which she carried to her daughter.

"Here. It will help."

Lydia shook her head. No words. No breath.

Valentina shrugged, drank it herself, and replaced the glass. The red spots on her cheeks were fading.

"My sweet darling." She held Lydia's face between her hands. "This marriage is a new future for us. You will grow to like him, I promise. Be happy." She smiled, but there was something not quite right about it. "Please. You and me. Let's learn to be happy."

Lydia hugged her mother close. "Go to Datong, Mama. Go and be happy."

"That's right, ladies, kiss and make up. Don't want to see anyone looking sad, not today of all days." Alfred beamed at them both, handed his wife the water and patted Lydia on the back. "I've telephoned for the car and it should be here any minute. Excited?" he asked his wife.

"Ecstatic."

"Good."

Then there was a fuss with coats and cases and last-minute hugs, but as Alfred and Valentina were walking out the front door, Lydia said, "Is it all right if I buy a padlock for Sun Yat-sen's shed?"

"Of course," Alfred replied airily. "But why do you want to padlock your rabbit in?"

"To keep him safe."

SHE WASHED HIM. SOFTLY. BARELY TOUCHING THE DAMAGED skin with a cloth soaked in warm water and disinfectant. His rags were crawling with lice and she threw them outside into the rain.

His body was a sickening sight. So thin she could count the bones. And it was branded. Burn marks, each one in the shape of an S. Like snakes. Six of them, scorched into his chest. The burns were black and rotting but even they were nothing compared to his hands. As she unwound the foul strips of cloth that were twisted tight around his fingers, she almost gagged on the smell, and however careful she was, chunks of blackened skin and flesh came away with the bandages.

Left behind were the maggots. White squirming creatures devouring Chang An Lo. Dozens of them. Lydia recoiled in horror.

Liev Popkov raised his head from his chest at her cry. He was on the floor, slumped against the wall next to Sun Yat-sen's pagoda cage, the vodka bottle she had brought from the house still in his hand.

"Ah *otlichno!* Maggots," he rumbled. "They are good. Eat away the bad and clean the wound. Leave them."

His head slid forward onto his chest once more and he uttered a deep shuddering snore that Lydia found oddly comforting in the cold shed. She drew the oil lantern nearer to Chang's hands and studied them. It was brutal. The little finger was missing on each hand. They had been hacked off. The wounds had festered until the hands had swollen into rotting melons that had burst open, filled with pus and maggots.

With painstaking care she lifted out each maggot. She kept telling herself they were no worse than cockroaches or worms. Only once was she actually sick and that was when she pulled out one particularly fat white slug and it popped between her fingers. When they were all removed, she sluiced clean water and disinfectant through the wounds and, after a moment's uncertainty, replaced two of the maggots in each hand. Liev Popkov should know. He'd been through bad times, probably seen any number of bullet holes and saber cuts during the revolution, so he should know. But what if the maggots ate their way up to Chang's brain?

She forced that thought out of her head.

Quickly she dabbed something on the gaping wounds. OPODEL-DOC & LAUDANUM. She'd found it in the first-aid kit in the bathroom along with some bandages, and it seemed better than nothing. Slivers of bone glimmered white through the raw flesh, and she swathed them in gauze and clean bandages. Chang An Lo made no sound. Sometimes his eyelids flickered. That was the only way she knew he was alive.

LYDIA HAD NEVER LOOKED AT A NAKED MAN BEFORE. SHE spooned warm water with honey over his lips and eased a dribble of it into his mouth but she was frightened he might choke, so she kept it to only a drop or two every half hour. And all the time she was aware that he was naked.

The sight surprised her. She had no idea his private parts would be so . . . so soft or so loose or so embedded in thick hair, yet oddly, with Chang she felt no embarrassment. When she removed the rags from Chang's loins, Liev Popkov had growled his disapproval from his spot against the wall, but he was too busy combing through the fibers of his overcoat and snapping up stray lice between his thumbnails to care too much. It was obvious he thought the Chinese was dying. And what did it matter to him? Liev was eating a hunk of cheese from the kitchen and swigging from the vodka bottle. No interest in words.

After she had tended Chang's hands as best she could and spread the liniment over his chest as well, she covered his top half with a blanket to keep him warm and set to work on his lower half. She bathed his hips and stomach and it was like bathing a skeleton. Empty bones. When had he last eaten? Days? Weeks? She had thought she knew what hunger was, but not this. Not like this. She squeezed out the wet cloth again and started to wash the mat of black hair at the base of his stomach, but it was deeply encrusted with . . . what? Blood. Feces. Urine. More lice. A wave of crippling pain for him swept up from her own stomach, and it was with gentle, nervous fingers that she lifted his penis.

The softness of it surprised her. It lay still on the palm of one hand while she soaped it with the other, easing off the filth and scabs, delicately patting the skin dry with a towel. There was something so unbearably vulnerable about it. Even the tracery of blue veins left it looking bare and exposed, as if it needed another barrier between it and the world. Is that why men want women so much? As a barrier? A protection?

"I'll protect you, Chang An Lo, I swear," she breathed. "Like you protected me."

She washed his legs, then his feet. She ran a finger over the scarred line that she had sewn with her own hands at Lizard Creek, and finally she took a pair of scissors, returned her attentions to his groin, and cut away the matted pubic hair and lice. It felt like cutting away his secrets.

DURING THAT FIRST NIGHT AT HIS SIDE, SHE STRUGGLED with what was staring her in the face. It was almost dawn before she admitted it to herself. She couldn't take Chang to the Chinese hospital. She couldn't. Neither could she call a doctor.

It was obvious.

The Black Snakes had done this to him, and he had chosen to risk death in Tan Wah's hovel rather than expose himself to recapture by seeking help from any medical people. Or even from friends where he was known among the Communists. Clearly he knew the Snakes had eyes everywhere.

"You could have come to me," she whispered more than once and traced a finger along the sheer edge of his cheekbone.

Now she had to think.

The facts were bad. No adult would permit her to keep Chang here; she knew what they would say. They'd make faces and insist it was not right for a young girl. *Scandalous.* He'd be whisked away to the Chinese hospital, which was exactly where the Black Snakes would be waiting with their knives and their branding irons. No. No well-meaning adults. She was on her own. Her head dropped into her hands and struggled to work out her next step. It was some time before she lifted her face and gazed across the small musty shed at the big bear slumped in a heap. She wasn't alone.

She walked over and thumped his shoulder.

"Liev Popkov," she said urgently. "Wake up."

35

THEO DROVE FAST. HE WAS ANGRY. ANGRY ENOUGH TO leave the black paste in the drawer this morning. His body ached and every pore of his skin sweated for the dream-filled smoke, but he needed his mind sharp. Sharp as a rat. It was still early and the morning mist drifted over the roofs, no wind to shift it, and the day seemed to be holding its breath. Theo parked the Morris Cowley outside the black oak gates and spat in the faces of the stone lions on the gateposts. Lions guard the hearth. Well, not this time.

The gatekeeper bowed submissively, almost scraping the ground with the earflaps of his quilted hat.

"My master Feng Tu Hong not expecting you today, noble professor."

"It is not your honored master I have come to see, Chen. It is his pus-head son, Po Chu."

The gatekeeper didn't exactly smile, but his face, usually so immobile and correct, took on a sly hint of animation. "I send worthless wife to tell Important Son you here and wish to . . ."

Theo did not wait but strode through the gate and up into the courtyards. Behind him the scurrying sound of a woman's bound feet made the hairs on the back of his neck rise.

"PO CHU, YOU PIG-HUMPING PIECE OF DEVIL'S SPIT, IF YOU ever lay a finger on my Li Mei again, I shall personally stick a blade through your eyes and straight down your gullet."

"Wah! You talk like a tiger, Tiyo Willbee, but at night you crawl on your belly like a worm to eat the poppy. I hear from the sampans.

You shiver and you shake the way a whore does on her back with her legs in the air. You talk big but you crawl small."

"What I do out on the river is not your affair. But be glad that the remaining whispers of last night's dream smoke keep me from calling the great war god Kuan Ti down from the skies to ram his spear through your bloodless heart for what you did to her."

"The whore needed it."

"Take care, Po Chu. Li Mei is no whore. She is your honorable sister."

"No sister of mine would bed a *fanqui*. She needed to be told."

"Needed your stinking fist in her face?"

"Yes, by all the gods, she needed it."

"Because she came to make peace with your father?"

"No. Because she thought my venerable father would be fool enough to give her what she wanted without a bargain."

"Bargain? What bargain?"

"*Ai-ay!* The headmaster does not know his whore as well as he thinks."

"Enjoy this breath, Po Chu, because it will be your last if you call my beloved a whore again. Tell me what bargain?"

"She begged. Ah, Tiyo Willbee, how she begged. Tears as big as crocodiles."

"Begged? For what?"

"For our honorable father to release you from the deal with that monkey brain Mason, from the trafficking. Of course the great Feng Tu Hong in his wisdom was not moved by her street girl ways."

"I warned you, scum of the gutter."

"But he offered her a bargain. He agreed to release you from the deal if . . ."

"If what?"

"If she kowtows to him nine times and comes back to this house to live out her life as his dutiful daughter. Hah! But she has brought fields of shame to the honorable name of Feng and needed to be taught the meaning of respect. That was when I hit her. Many times."

"Like this?"

★ ★ ★

"GOOD GOD, OLD FELLOW, WHAT THE DEVIL HAVE YOU BEEN up to?"

Theo rubbed his jaw. A livid bruise was spreading along it, and one corner of his lip was split. Christopher Mason was staring at him with an expression of unease.

"Tripped over my cat," Theo said indifferently. "I came over because your houseboy said you would be here and I need a word with you."

"Now?"

"Yes, now."

Mason glanced across the room at his wife and the two girls. "It's not a good time, Willoughby. Later maybe."

"Now."

The situation struck Theo as rather odd. To be seated with that bastard Mason, all civil and polite, in Alfred Parker's new home the day after the disrupted wedding, with no Alfred around and the stepdaughter prowling by the French window like a dog on guard duty. It all felt strange. The girl looked ragged. Something had hollowed out her amber eyes, set them deep in dull shadows and colored her lips gray. She kept giving each of her guests impatient stares to indicate she would be rid of them, but Anthea Mason was determined to fuss over her.

"Poor Lydia didn't sleep well and who can blame her, alone in an unfamiliar house," she fretted, with a good-natured smile at the girl. "I came over this morning, Mr. Willoughby, and what do I find? Only that she's given the houseboy and the gardener the week off with full pay and told the cook that she just wants him to provide an evening meal and nothing else. Please, tell the dear girl she must accept the fact of servants in her life now that she is living in respectable circumstances like the rest of us. You're her headmaster, so she should listen to you."

"For God's sake, Anthea, just forget it," Mason snapped. "You've seen her, like you promised you would, and she's fine." He turned to Theo. "I'm only here because I'm taking my wife and daughter over to the stables to see my new hunter. He's a splendid bay with the lungs of an elephant and will run the hocks off Sir Edward's dun stallion any day of the week. You see if he doesn't."

"I want to see Sun Yat-sen, your rabbit," Polly suddenly announced, blue eyes wide.

"What a good idea," Anthea smiled. "Where is it?"

"Bloody stupid name for an animal," Mason commented, but he stood up and led the way toward the French windows. "I used to have a black and white lop-eared rabbit when I was a youngster, Polly. Called it Daniel. Nice little animal. So, young lady, let's all take a look at . . ."

"Not today." Lydia stood with her hand holding the French windows shut.

"And why not?"

"He's disturbed. By the move. By everything changing."

"But Lyd, please," Polly pleaded. "You said he was happy in his pagoda in the shed. That's not changed, has it?"

"No, but . . ."

"Excellent." Mason brushed the girl aside. "I like rabbits." He barged out into the bare wintry garden, Polly at his heels as he strode down the path.

Anthea watched them. "He likes all animals," she said to Theo with a sad smile and followed her husband.

"It's human beings he has a problem with," Theo muttered to himself and glanced at the Russian girl. She looked almost as bad as he felt. His head was splitting, as if it had a meat cleaver embedded in it. She was standing very still, both hands pressed flat against the window, her eyes fixed on the timber shed at the bottom of the garden. Polly was opening the door.

"MR. WILLOUGHBY." LYDIA SPOKE SOFTLY.

She was watching her friend's father fondling Sun Yat-sen's long ears. The Mason family were all gathered in a little group on the lawn, admiring the snowy white animal in Polly's arms, oblivious to the cold. Their breath circled them like mist.

"What is it, Lydia?"

The girl was still standing just inside the French windows, but now Theo noticed her gaze had shifted to an untidy pile of rags at the back of the lawn. The gardener should know better than to leave his rubbish in full view of the house. But of course she'd given him a week off.

"Where can I buy Chinese medicines?"

"Are you sick, child?"

"No."

"You don't look well."

Slowly she turned and fixed her eyes on him. "Neither do you."

He laughed as if she'd made a joke, and the effort of it sent a wave of nausea through him. "In the Street of One Hundred Steps there is a Chinese herbalist. But I doubt that he speaks English."

"Will you come with me?"

Theo shook his head but, despite the gaping hole in his mind where the smoke from the pipe needed to be, he said, "I suppose I could." There was just something about the girl. "After I've had my talk with Mason."

"I'll send him in to you."

And she did.

"SO?" MASON WOULDN'T KEEP STILL. IN HIS JODHPURS AND riding boots he paced up and down the carpet. Plainly he was embarrassed. "This isn't the place for this discussion."

Theo knew this was not the way one Englishman should talk to another on a Sunday morning with the family just outside the window. He should be talking about horses or cricket or his motorcar or what the hell the share market was up to back home. Or even the outrageous new law that the PM, Baldwin, had passed to give the vote to women as young as twenty-one, as if flappers of that age knew anything at all about politics. But drugs? No. That was unacceptable.

"Listen to me, Mason. Listen hard. The situation has changed for me. I am severing all connections with Feng. I'm sick of being used as bait by both you and that bastard."

"Damn it, man, fish bait is all you're fit for right now. Look at yourself, you're shaking."

"Forget that. You're not listening to me, Mason. I'm telling you that our arrangement is over. I will have nothing more to do with the Black Snakes and their opium trade. I was a bloody fool to get involved in the first place, I realize that now. You twisted my arm at a time when . . ."

"No, don't give me that. You wanted the money."

"I was protecting my school."

"Don't stick your headmasterly head in the sand, Willoughby. Join the human race. I despise people like you. You're no different from the rest of us, however superior you like to think yourself because you can read this heathen language and understand the pious gibberish of their Confucius and their Buddha. You were just plain greedy."

"Like you, you mean."

Mason laughed, delighted, as if paid a compliment. "Exactly." He smoothed a hand over his slicked-back hair in a self-satisfied manner. "I don't know what has suddenly got you all fired up, but you'd better put a stop to it right now. Pull yourself together, man."

"I'm glad you're getting my point at last. I *am* pulling myself together. No more night trips out on the river. No more black paste for me. It's over. It's a filthy trade."

"God damn you, Willoughby. We both know that the Chinese bastard won't deal with me without you in the middle of it."

"Too bad."

"Don't threaten me."

"I'm not threatening. I'm telling."

"You bloody fool, I'll go straight to the police and you'll be inside a filthy prison cell before you even start your next bout of the shakes."

"Mason, I'm telling you to let this go. You've made more than a good profit from our deal so far. Now it's finished. Just let it go. Find yourself a new enterprise and let us end this now like English gentlemen." He held out his hand and made certain it did not shake.

Mason took his time. He looked from Theo's face to his outstretched hand and back again. "Go to hell," he sneered and walked out through the French windows to the terrace. "Polly, Anthea," he shouted. "Time to go. I want to see what this horse of mine can do." He turned and stared back at Theo through the glass, his gray eyes flat and hard. "I might even have to use the whip on him."

Theo wanted to kill him. There and then. His hand even slid to the short ivory-handled knife he kept up his sleeve, and he had to remind himself that it was the opium talking, warping his thoughts. But if he could only take a few breaths on the pipe, it would still the infernal racket in his head, just this once, just one more time. He swung away in a jerky movement and stepped into the hall but stopped in the doorway when he saw Lydia Ivanova sitting on the bottom step of the stairs. She was watching him. He didn't like the look in her eyes. The concern.

It meant she had heard.

"PLEASE, LYD. GO ON."

"No."

"Why not?"

"Your father is waiting."

"Just a quick look, that's all."

"No. Another day."

"Tomorrow?"

"No."

"Oh, Lydia, for heaven's sake, I'm only asking for a look at your new bedroom, not at the inside of Mr. Parker's safe or anything like that. Why not?"

"Sorry, Polly, but it's not tidy."

"Don't be silly. You've only been in it twenty-four hours."

"No, Polly. Not today. Please."

"What's the matter with you, Lyd? You look . . ."

"I'm fine. Did you like holding Sun Yat-sen?"

"Oh yes, he's utterly gorgeous. Papa liked him too."

"Your father is calling you to the car."

Leaning in the doorway, Theo waited while the girls parted, a slight awkwardness between them. Little chickens. Fluffy and new. No idea how life has a habit of slicing your head off when you're not looking.

36

HIS FACE. IT WAS ALL BRITTLE CHEEKBONES. SKIN STRETched so tight it looked as if it would split. White as the pillow. Dirty purple hollows around his eyes. But it was his mouth that upset Lydia most. Before, when he leaped into her life that first day in the alleyway or later in the burned-out house when he talked of why only the Communists could drag China out of the tyranny of its feudal past, his mouth had been full and curved and brimming with vital energy. Not just energy, she thought, but a kind of inner power. A certainty. That was gone. His lips, more than any other part of him, looked dead.

Quickly she reached out and touched him. Warm. Alive. Not dead.

But too warm. Hot. Too hot.

He was lying in her bed. Again she squeezed out the cloth in the bowl of cool water. It smelled funny. That was the Chinese herbs. To soothe a fever, that's what Mr. Theo said they were for, to cool the blood. Tenderly she bathed Chang An Lo's brow, his temples, his throat, and even the black stubble on his bony scalp. She felt a sense of achievement to see it clear of lice and all the other things that had been crawling around up there, and it pleased her to stroke it. Reassured her.

She sat on a chair beside the bed all day. As the light from the window changed from gray to grayer, she listened to the rain dripping outside. Sudden gusts of it against the glass panes. The colors drained from the room as it grew darker and still she kept bathing his limbs, his chest, and his sharp pelvic bones till she knew his body almost as completely as she knew her own. The texture of his skin and the shape of his toenails. She anointed the infected wounds with strange Chinese unguents, changed bandages, and dripped restorative herbal teas through his cracked lips. All the time talking to him. She talked and she talked. Once she even managed to laugh as she fought to drench his ears with sounds of life and happiness, to give back to him the lost energy.

But his eyes never opened, not a flicker, and his arms and legs lay lifeless, even when she changed the bandages on his hands, and she knew it must hurt horribly on some deeper plane where she couldn't reach him. But sometimes sounds came from his mouth. Whispers. Low and urgent. She leaned over and put her ear close to his mouth, so close she could feel his faint breath hot on her skin, but she could make no sense of the sounds.

But once, when she was spreading a grainy yellow salve over his lips with her forefinger, his mouth suddenly opened just a fraction and his lips closed over her finger. It was an extraordinarily intimate act. The tip of her finger in the soft moist folds of his mouth. More intimate even than when she held his penis in her hand and washed it. She felt a surge of exhilaration and hugged it to herself. She rested her own lips on his forehead.

That moment was enough to carry her through the long night.

THE CHINESE MEDICINES WERE NOT WORKING.

Lydia's throat was closing in a wave of panic. He'd want the Chinese medicines. Not *fanqui* concoctions, she was certain of that. But when would they start to work? When? As each hour crawled past, his skin burned more. Hot and dry as desert sand. In the cold and lonely darkness, she wrapped both her hands around his forearm, just above the bandages on his wrist and she held on tight.

She would not let him go.

Would not.

DAWN FILTERED THROUGH THE CURTAINS AND A SOFT MISTY light slowly filled the room. It was cold. Lydia was wrapped in her coat and she kept the eiderdown, a pretty peach one that was glossy and new, tucked tight around the still figure on the bed. But she was appalled at her own ignorance. Should she light the gas fire that was in the room attached to one wall? Keep the air warm? And place the rubber hot-water bottle at his feet? Or was that all wrong? Maybe she should open the window to allow the icy air in to cool him from the outside.

Which?

She felt cold sweat on her own body and fought back the panic. She was tired, she told herself, too tired. That's what the Chinese man had said to Mr. Theo. The herbalist. He said she looked as if her *chi* had drained away, and he insisted that she buy a mixture of herbs he concocted for her to drink like tea, but she was far more interested in what he prepared for Chang An Lo. For fever, burns, and infected wounds, she told Mr. Theo, that's what she wanted, and he had translated her needs to the herbalist and then translated to her the instructions for use of the treatment.

Lydia had felt reassured the moment she walked into the herbalist's little shop. It smelled wonderful. Its shelves were crammed with glass jars of all shapes and sizes, some blue, some green, some a muddy brown, all full of herbs and leaves and other things Lydia could not even guess at but she had a crazy feeling there might be something like lizards' hearts or porcupine's gallbladder and rhino horn. Great ceramic bowls of seeds and dried flowers and sheets of tree bark stood on the floor and scented the shop with enticing aromas. But best of all was the herbalist himself. He positively gleamed with good health, with teeth so white Lydia found she could not look away from them.

She had handed Alfred's envelope of money over to Mr. Theo for payment. It was more than enough, thank God. Or more accurately, thank Alfred. For this once she did genuinely thank him, a reluctant, grudging kind of thanks that surprised her. But she knew that without him, she wouldn't have found Chang because she couldn't have hired Liev.

Mr. Theo said little. Just asked if it was all for that Chinese friend of hers.

"I'd rather not discuss it, if you don't mind."

He shrugged, his tall frame loose and somehow disjointed, but he didn't seem to mind. She noticed he bought some preparations for himself too and at any other time she'd have been curious, especially after what she'd overheard on the stairs between him and Mr. Mason. But her fear for Chang An Lo was all she had room for right now. So she sat. Watched Chang's face slowly materialize out of the darkness, each moment bringing another detail of it to her hungry gaze, and she was astonished at how familiar it was to her already. As if it were imprinted deep in her brain. The thickness of his eyelashes, the angle of his nose, the exact flare of his nostrils and curve of his ear. She could see them with her eyes shut.

Very gently while she sat in the chair she laid her head on the pillow next to his, her forehead resting against his hot cheekbone. Making a connection. She closed her eyes and asked herself why it was she cared so much, so much it hurt, but she couldn't come up with an answer.

"TELL ME THE SYMPTOMS."

"Fever. A really high fever. Unconsciousness. Infected wounds and burns."

"Overall health? I mean is the patient in good condition otherwise or one of the undernourished mass of the Chinese population of Junchow? It makes a big difference, you know." Mrs. Yeoman was twisting her thick white hair into a bun at the back of her head and sticking clips in it. Lydia had never seen her hair loose before, it was like liquid snow, but then she had never come calling this early before.

"He's very weak. And thin. Very thin."

"I'll happily come and tend to him, you know, if he needs medical help. So tell me where . . ."

"No. Thanks, Mrs. Yeoman, but no. He won't accept European help."

"But he will accept yours?"

"No. I'm just giving the medicines to his family."

"Lydia, my dear, it does my heart good to see you so concerned for the poor people of this country. We are all God's children, yet so many Westerners treat the Chinese worse than dogs. It's shameful to see, especially when they . . ."

"Please, Mrs. Yeoman. I need to hurry."

"Forgive me, dear, you know how I prattle on. Here's the list for the chemist. Mr. Hatton in Glebe Street is very good, always open with the lark, and he will give you first-class advice if you mention my name."

"Thank you. I'm sorry to disturb you so early."

"Don't fret, child. Be good while your mother is away, won't you? Don't do anything she wouldn't like."

"No, of course not. I'm going to write an essay on *Paradise Lost* down at the library today."

"That's my girl. Your mother should be proud of you."

"Ah, little sparrow, what you do back so soon? That stepfather throw you out already?"

"Mrs. Zarya, hello. I just came over for some information from Mrs. Yeoman."

"Hah! And you rush off not even to say *dobroiye utro* to your favorite teacher of Russian. *Nyet, nyet.* I have baked fresh *pirozhki* and you must taste."

"*Spasibo*, thank you. Another time. I promise. Must dash now. Sorry. *Prostitye menya.*"

"Little sparrow, I want you come to party, a *bal*, with me. Big Russian party."

At any other time she'd have jumped at the chance, but right now it was just an unwelcome intrusion.

"I'm too busy at the moment but thank you anyway."

"Busy? Busy? *Blin!* What is this *too busy*? You must see how your people throw grand party. Everyone there, so . . ."

"I must leave now. Sorry. Enjoy the party."

"Is at Countess Serova's villa."

That raised her interest. At the Serov villa. She'd like to see how grandly Russian aristocracy lived.

"Really?"

"*Da.* Next week."

"I'll think about it."

"Good. You come."

"I'll think about it."

He was still breathing.

She had a tight pain in her chest each time she left him, even for a few minutes to fetch water or throw away soiled bandages, which she first wrapped in newspaper and buried at the bottom of the dustbin outside the back door, always keeping an eye out for Wai. The cook lived with his silent wife in a low extension to one side of the house and was more than happy not to bother her, except to present an evening meal of soup, chicken, and trifle in the dining room. It was the same food every day and she knew he was taking advantage of her inexperience but she didn't care. She hardly touched it anyway. Just ate the trifle and took the soup upstairs to spoon a few drops of it into Chang An Lo's mouth.

He always swallowed. She watched nervously each time. Afraid he might not. But the knot of his Adam's apple rose and fell and she licked her own lips with relief.

Sometimes she sang to him. Or read to him by the hour. About Pip, poor Pip the outsider, so ambitious with his *Great Expectations*, yet so full of pain and shame. She knew exactly how he felt.

"Is all this too alien for you, Chang An Lo, this world of Dickens and London society? It's a million miles away from both of us, isn't it?"

So she swapped over to Rikki Tikki Tavi in India and told him he must laugh when the mongoose gobbles up the big snake's eggs.

"You see, snakes, even Black Snakes, can be killed, Chang."

And she hummed a Russian folk song to him, *Ya vstretil vas*, as she bathed his forehead and arms from an enamel bowl into which she had stirred a teaspoon with a few drops of camphor oil. *To promote sweating,* Mr. Hatton had said. *A counterirritant to fever.* And when she'd finished, she laid her forehead on the quilt that covered him and allowed herself a tiny shiver of fear.

Please, Chang An Lo. Please.

THE SOUNDS OF THE TEMPLE. THEY CAME TO CHANG AN LO like the voice of the gods. Through the mists of incense. The tinkle of the small brass bells and the low murmur of incantations.

A river of sound. It drew him. Up from the black mud at the bottom. He felt his face break free from the slime, foul and poisonous slime that was devouring him. It had filled his mouth and his eyes, seeped into the coils of his mind until the wind of life could not reach there anymore and he knew he would soon be looking into the face of Yang Wang Yeh, the final judge of human souls.

He floated.

Swept up on the sound, drifting higher, drawn by the current of it toward the light.

At last he saw her and his heart started to beat once more. She was smiling at him. Her beautiful face. He murmured her name. *Kuan Yin*. Again. *Kuan Yin*. The goddess who understood pain. He remembered with a clear rush of cool blood to his brain that when her father tried to burn her to death, she had put out the fire with her bare hands. Pain. Hands. China's sweet and holy goddess of mercy, Kuan Yin, my pain is nothing to yours.

A bird settled on his chest. It was small and light but covered with coppery feathers. They glowed so bright they burned the slime from his eyes. From his ears. He could hear the bird sing. Just one sound. Over and over, it twirled inside his head.

"Please."

37

SHE WOULD NOT LET HIM SEE HER FACE.

"Li Mei, don't. Please."

But she hid her face in the pillow. Her shame was far worse than her pain.

"My sweetest love," Theo murmured, "let me bathe your swollen cheeks and kiss the black bruises away from your eyes."

She curled up tight, away from him.

Theo bent over the bed and kissed the back of her head, breathing in the sandalwood scent of her raven's-wing hair. "Forgive me, my love. I shall leave you in peace. Here are some medicines from the herbalist; the one in the black pot is for the pain, the other for the damaged skin."

He waited, torn between a fierce desire to sweep her into his arms and the knowledge that more than anything she wanted to hide the evidence of her disgrace from him.

"Li Mei?"

Silence.

"Li Mei, listen to me. You must never return to your father. Whatever happens. We both know he would beat you into the ground and make a slave of you, so you must stay away from him. And from that turd-sucking brother of yours, Po Chu. Promise me that."

Nothing.

He reached out and rested a hand on the slender curve of her hip. "In exchange I promise to have nothing more to do with the dream smoke."

Still no answer. But her shoulders started to shake. She was crying.

* * *

THAT NIGHT THEO DIDN'T GO TO BED. NOR DID HE KEEP THE appointment on the river. He went down to the empty schoolrooms, to the large carved oak chair that stood at the end of the hall, and then he summoned one of the yard boys to come with ropes. The nine-year-old boy was unhappy to do as Theo ordered, but in the end he obeyed because if he lost his job his mother and father and four sisters would starve.

Theo sat there all night.

No one to hear his moans and his cries except the yellow-eyed cat. Most of the time she just sat and watched him but once jumped up on his lap with a loud yowl. His wrists were bound to the wooden arms, where carvings of tigers grinned up at him, mocking his torment, and his ankles tied to the chair's stout legs.

When a faint red glow finally came up over the horizon, Theo knew he was looking into the eyes of the devil himself.

38

Exhaustion finally claimed her. Lydia woke with a start to find herself still in the chair but sprawled forward on the bed, her weight pinning down one side of Chang. She jumped off in alarm. His hand, she mustn't crush his hand.

It was dark and cold and her mind felt thick as treacle. She stood up, stripped off the clothes she had been wearing for the last forty-eight hours, pulled over her head one of the two new embroidered nightdresses that lay in her otherwise empty chest of drawers, and lifted the sheet.

She slid into the bed. Instantly all desire for sleep vanished. She lay on her side, curving her body to fit beside his, aware of his nakedness and the thin cotton of her nightdress between them. She let her arm rest across his waist and her cheek lie against his shoulder, so that she could smell the cooling camphor on his skin. She breathed it in.

"Chang An Lo," she whispered, just to hear his name.

She closed her eyes and experienced a warm bubbling sensation in her chest. Happiness? Was this what happiness felt like?

She dreamed bad dreams.

Her mother was fixing a metal collar around Chang's neck. He was naked and Valentina was dragging him on the end of a heavy chain through great drifts of snow. It was in the heart of a forest with wild winds and the howling of wolves, the sky red and bleeding onto the white snow beneath, like scarlet rain. There was a man on a great horse. A green greatcoat. A rifle. Bullets flying through the air, slamming into the pine trees, into her mother's legs. She screamed. And one bullet tore into Chang's bare chest. Another lodged between two of Lydia's own ribs. She felt no pain but couldn't breathe; she was gasping for air, filling up with ice in her lungs. She tried to shout but no sound came out, she couldn't breathe . . .

She shuddered awake.

The room was full of daylight, sweet and normal daylight that steadied her racing pulse. She turned her head and gasped aloud.

Chang's black eyes were staring right at her, no more than a hand's breadth from her own.

"HELLO." HIS VOICE WAS A WHISPER.

"Hello." She smiled at him, a wide welcoming grin. "You're back."

For a long moment he studied her face, then nodded very faintly and murmured something too low for her to catch. Abruptly she became acutely aware of her leg draped over his, of her arm warm against his skin and her hip tight next to his, and suddenly she was embarrassed. She blushed fiercely and slid out of the bed. When she was on the floor she turned to face him and gave a formal little bow, hands together, a brief lowering of her head.

"I am pleased to see you awake, Chang An Lo."

His lips moved, life returning to them, but no words came out.

"I would like to give you medicine and food," she said softly. "You need to eat."

Again he gave the faint nod, and closed his eyes. But she knew he was not asleep. She felt in a panic. But a totally different kind of panic from before. She told herself it was a kind of fluttery on-the-surface panic because she feared she may have offended Chang An Lo with the forwardness of her actions, made him disgusted with her alley-cat ways, and that he would not want her to nurse him or feed him or even touch his body, that body she knew so well now. But all of this was nothing like the deep-down panic of before when she thought he would die, that he would leave her with just his bones and none of himself, that she would never see again the way his black eyes . . .

Stop it. Stop it.

He was awake. That meant everything. Awake.

"I'll fetch some hot water," she said and scuttled downstairs.

★ ★ ★

Her touch was like sunlight to him. It warmed his skin. Inside, Chang felt cold and empty, like a reptile after a night of frost, and it was the touch of her fingers that brought life flowing back to his limbs. He started to feel again.

With feeling came pain.

He fought to center his mind. To use the pain as a source of energy. He focused on her fingers as she peeled back the bandages. They were not beautiful. The nails were square where they should have been oval and her thumbs were oddly long, but her hands moved with a confidence that was beautiful. He watched. They would heal him, those hands.

But when he saw his own mutilated hands, the pain broke free from his grip on it and exploded in his head. It blew him apart. He tumbled in pieces back down into the slime.

He opened his eyes.

"Lydia."

She didn't look up from where she was bent over a metal bowl stirring something strongly scented inside it. A thin wintry ray of sunlight from the window trickled over her hair and down one side of her face, so that she seemed to shine.

"Lydia."

Still she ignored him.

He closed his eyes and thought about that. It took some time to occur to him that he had not moved his lips. He tried again, this time concentrating on working the muscles of his mouth. They felt stiff, as though they had not been used for a long time.

"Lydia."

Her head shot up. "Hello, again. How are you feeling?"

"Like I'm alive."

She smiled. "Good. Stay that way."

"I will."

"Good."

She stood beside the bed looking down at him, the spoon in her hand frozen above the bowl and dripping a purplish liquid from its edge. He could hear the *ping* of each drop as it hit the bowl. She kept standing there, just staring at him. Hours passed in his head. Her face filled his eyes and floated through the void of his mind. Hers were large round eyes. A long nose. It was the face of a *fanqui*.

"Do you need something for the pain?"

He blinked. She was still there, the spoon dripping in her hand, her gaze fixed on his face. He shook his head.

"Tell me about Tan Wah," he said.

As she told him, her words brought grief to his heart but it was her eyes, not his, that filled with tears.

THIS TIME HE DID NOT OPEN HIS EYES.

If he opened them, she'd stop. She was gently massaging his legs. They were like sticks of dead bamboo, fit for nothing but the fire, but gradually he could feel the heat starting to build in them, the blood creeping back into the wasted muscles. His flesh was waking up.

She was humming. The sound pleased his ears even though it was a foreign tune that had none of the sweet cadences of Chinese music. It flowed from her as effortlessly as from a bird and somehow cooled the fever in his brain.

Thank you, Kuan Yin, dear goddess of mercy. Thank you for bringing me the fox girl.

"WHERE IS YOUR MOTHER?"

The thought slipped into his mind as he awoke. This was the first time it had occurred to him. Until now his sluggish fevered mind had not thought beyond this room. Beyond the girl. But after another night of fitful, broken sleep that was a jagged nightmare of black sorrow in his body and black grief in his heart for Tan Wah, he knew he was more alert.

He started to see dangers.

The girl smiled at him. It was meant to reassure. But behind the smile she was anxious, he could see it.

"She is away in Datong with her new husband. She won't be back until Saturday." As an afterthought she added, "Today is Tuesday."

"And this house?"

"It is our new home. There's no one here but us."

"Servants are not *no one*."

The skin of her cheeks turned a dull red. "The cook lives in an annex but I hardly see him, and I have told the houseboy and gardener not to come for a week. I am not a fool, Chang An Lo. I know it was not a well-wisher who did this to you."

"Forgive me, Lydia Ivanova, the fever makes my tongue foolish."

"I forgive you," she said and laughed.

He did not know why she laughed, but it warmed some cold place inside him and he slept.

"WAKE UP, CHANG, WAKE UP." A HAND WAS SHAKING HIM. "It's all right, shh, don't shout, you're safe. Wake . . ."

He woke.

He was drenched in sweat. His heart was roaring in his chest. Red fury burned the sockets of his eyes and his mouth was as dry as the west wind.

"You were having a nightmare."

She was leaning over him, her hand on his mouth, silencing his lips. He could taste her skin. Slowly his mind clawed its way to the surface. He kicked away the feel of knives at his genitals and the smell of burning flesh in his nostrils.

"Breathe," she murmured.

He dragged air deep into his lungs, again and then again. His head was spinning but his eyes were open. It was dark, with just a whisper of light from a street lamp slinking under the curtains, enough for him to make out shapes in the room, the clothes cupboard, the table with the mirror and the medicine bottles. Her. He could see the slender silhouette of her, hair all rumpled and wild-edged. Her hand had left his mouth and was hovering above his damp forehead, fearful to touch. He breathed once more, picked up a rhythm for it.

"You're shivering," she said.

"I need a bottle."

There was a slight pause. "I'll get it."

She turned on the light. Not the overhead one with the cream shade and silk fringe but the small green lamp that was on the table of medicines. He would have preferred the dark for this task. She came with the wide-necked bottle and lifted the quilt and blankets from his body. He rolled on his side, felt his head swim from just that simple movement, and said nothing while she slid the bottle over his penis. The flow of urine was labored and sporadic; it took time, too long. He was aware of her embarrassment, just as he was aware of the nakedness of his loins where she had clipped away the black hair when he was unconscious. He hated her doing this, but his own hands were bandaged into useless swollen stumps. Neither he nor she were yet used to it, and the sound of the liquid trickling into the glass bottle made his ears burn.

At the end when she held the bottle up to the light and said, "Looks like a good vintage," he had no idea what the girl meant.

"What?"

"A good vintage." She grinned at him. "Like wine."

"Much too dark."

"Less blood in it than last time though."

"The medicines are working."

"All of them." She laughed as she gestured to the colorful row of bottles and potions and packages.

On the table they formed a strange mixture of cultures, Chinese and Western, and yet she seemed totally at ease with both in a way he admired. Her mind was so open and ready to make use of whatever came her way. Just like a fox.

He lay back on the pillow. Sweat trickled from his forehead. "Thank you."

The effort had exhausted him, but he remembered to smile at her. Westerners threw smiles around like chicken feathers, another sharp divide in customs, but he had seen how much a smile mattered to her. He gave her one now.

"I am humbled," he said.

"Don't be."

"Look at me. I am empty. A hawk without wings. You should despise such weakness."

"No, Chang An Lo, don't say that. I'll tell you what I see. I see a brave fighter. One who should be dead by now but isn't because he will never give in."

"You blind your mind with words."

"No. You blind your mind with sickness. Wait, Chang An Lo, wait for me to heal you." She reached out and rested a cool hand on his burning forehead. "Time for more quinine."

THROUGHOUT THE REST OF THE NIGHT SHE DOSED HIM AND bathed him and battled the fever. Sometimes he heard her speaking to him and at others he heard himself speaking to her, but he had no idea what he said or why he said it.

"Spirit of niter and acetate of ammonium with camphor water."

He recalled her voice wrapping around those difficult words as she spooned things into his mouth, but they were just sounds with no meaning.

"Mr. Theo said the herbalist claimed this Chinese brew will work miracles on a fevered brain, so . . . no, please, no, don't spit it out, let's try again, open up, yes, that's it. Good."

More sounds. *Mistertheo.* What is *mistertheo?*

Always the cooling cloth on his skin. The smell of vinegar and herbs. Lemon water on his dry lips. Nightmares stealing his mind. But at dawn he could feel the fire in his blood at last begin to stutter. That was when he started to shiver and shake so violently he bit his tongue and tasted blood. He felt her sit beside him on the bed, felt the pillow dip under her as she rested back against the wooden headboard and wrapped her arms around his shoulders. She held him tight.

THE DOORBELL RANG. THE HAIRS ON HIS NECK ROSE AND he saw Lydia lift her head as though scenting the air. Their eyes met. They both knew he was trapped.

"It'll be Polly," she said in a firm voice. She went over to the door. "I'll get rid of her, don't worry."

He nodded and she left, closing the bedroom door behind her. Whoever this *Polly* person was, he called a thousand curses down on her head.

39

"Good morning, Miss Ivanova. I hope I haven't called too early."

"Alexei Serov. I . . . didn't expect you."

The Russian was standing on the doorstep, tall and languid as ever in his fur-collared coat, but he was the last person she wanted to see right now.

"I was concerned about you," he said.

"Concerned? Why?"

"After our last meeting. You were very upset by the death of your companion in the street."

"Yes, of course. I'm sorry, my mind is . . . Yes, it was unpleasant and you were very kind. Thank you." She took a small step back, preparing to shut the door, but he hadn't finished.

"I called at your previous address and Olga Petrovna Zarya told me you live here now."

"That's right."

"She said your mother has remarried."

"Yes."

"My congratulations to her." He gave her a small bow, and she thought how much more graceful Chang was at that movement.

"Thank you."

He gave her the edge of a smile. "Though your mother wasn't so pleased to see me at your previous house, if I recall correctly."

"No."

An awkward silence settled between them that she did nothing to break.

"Am I disturbing you?" he asked.

"Yes, I'm sorry but I'm in the middle of something at the moment."

"Then I apologize. I won't detain you any longer. I have been very busy myself or I would have called on you before now to make sure you are well."

"Busy?" Her interest sharpened. "With the Kuomintang forces?"

"That's right. Good-bye, Miss Ivanova."

"Wait." She found a smile. "I apologize for keeping you standing on the doorstep like this. How rude of me. Maybe you'd like a cup of tea. Everyone needs a break sometime."

"Thank you. I'd like that."

"Please, do come in."

Now that she had him in a chair with a cup of tea in his hand, a beautiful bone china one with a handle so fine you could see through it, Lydia was having difficulty finding out what she wanted to know. As often as she steered the conversation toward military matters, he sidestepped the subject and talked instead about the Chinese opera he'd seen the previous evening. Even when she asked outright about the numerous Communist posters she'd seen in the town demanding the right of access for the Chinese to the parks in the International Settlement, he just laughed that lazy superior laugh of his.

"They'll be wanting access to our clubs and croquet lawns next," he said.

She had no idea whether he was teasing her or was deadly serious. His tone was amused and languorous but she wasn't fooled. His green eyes were quick and observant, watching her, taking in at a glance her new surroundings. She had the feeling he was playing a game with her. She sipped her tea warily.

"So the Communists are still active in Junchow," she commented, "despite the efforts of the elite Kuomintang troops."

"It would seem so. But driven into holes in the river bank like rats. The Kuomintang flag flies everywhere to remind people who is in charge now." He smiled through half-closed eyes. "At least it's a fine banner to display and cheers the place up a bit with its bright colors."

"But do you know what the flag's colors mean?"

"They're just colors."

"No. In China everything has a meaning."

"So?" He leaned back in his chair, one arm exactly placed on each armrest. He looked to her just like the young tsar must have looked on his throne in the Winter Palace, and she resented his arrogant manner. "Enlighten me, Miss Ivanova."

"The red body of the flag represents China's blood and suffering."

"And the white sun?"

"Purity."

"The blue background?"

"Justice."

"Interesting. You seem to know more than most about China."

"I know that the Black Snakes of Junchow are fighting both the Communists and the Kuomintang for control of the council."

For the first time his green eyes widened. She felt she had scored a point.

"Miss Ivanova, you are a young Russian girl. Where has someone like you heard of the Black Snakes?"

"I listen. I see the tattoo. Just because I am female and not yet seventeen doesn't mean I am unaware of the political situation here. I am not one of the delicate flowers in your salons who sit at home all day doing embroidery or sipping champagne, Alexei Serov. I live in this world."

He leaned forward, and all sign of laughter was gone from his face. "Miss Ivanova, I have seen the way you take risks. I urge you to avoid any contact with the Black Snakes. Right now they are even more dangerous than ever."

"Why is that?"

"Because the father and son at the head of it have split. The father publicly whipped Po Chu for disobedience and now Po Chu is gathering his own tong around him, trying to wheedle his way into an alliance with the Kuomintang. But no one is trusted. Everyone plays off against one another, shifting pieces like a chess game."

"Will the son seize control from the father?"

"I don't know. He is reckless. Already he has acquired the means to create huge problems."

"What do you mean?"

"Explosives. He derailed a train carrying explosives from Funan Province last week, and a captain in the Kuomintang Army told me only yesterday that his spies say all hell is about to break loose."

"Does that mean Chiang Kai-shek will send in more troops?"

"Undoubtedly."

"You will therefore be even busier. *Advising*. That's what you do, isn't it? You advise the Kuomintang on military strategy."

"That is correct."

"Does it never occur to you that they are no better than the savage warlords were? That Chiang rules like a dictator and you are helping him?"

Instantly Alexei Serov assumed that irritating half-smile and leaned back in his chair once more. He picked up his cup but he had forgotten it was already empty, and he placed it back down on the table at his side.

"You may be remarkably well informed about Chinese matters, Miss Ivanova, but it's obvious you are woefully ignorant about one aspect. China, like Russia, is a vast country and is made up of a great diversity of peoples and tribes who would happily cut each other's throats if a strong dictator like Chiang Kai-shek did not hold them together with an iron fist. The Communists are full of fine ideals, but in a country like this they would wreak havoc if they ever got to power. But they will never succeed. Their answers are far too simplistic. So yes, I work hard for the political and military system that will root them out of their holes and destroy them."

Lydia stood up abruptly. "You are obviously very busy. Don't let me detain you."

He blinked, surprised. Then he inclined his head courteously. "Of course. Excuse me. I recall that you said you were in the middle of something when I arrived." He rose to his feet, his long frame moving elegantly inside his immaculate suit, his brown cropped hair at odds with the smoothness of the rest of him.

Lydia became aware of her own rumpled dress and uncombed hair. She was about to run a hand through her mane but stopped herself. What this man thought of her did not matter one bit. He was rude and arrogant and a supporter of a ruthless dictator. To hell with him. Her mother was right.

At the front door she handed him his coat and felt obliged to hold out her hand. "Good-bye, Alexei Serov, and thank you again for your assistance."

He held her hand briefly and studied it as it lay in his own, as if he would discover its secrets.

Lydia withdrew it.

His green eyes, lazy and half-closed once more, settled on hers in a speculative way. "My mother, Countess Natalia Serova, is holding a party next week. Maybe you would like to join us? Monday at eight. Do come." He laughed, a light teasing sound. "We can sit and talk about troop movements."

Behind him in his car on the gravel drive a Chinese chauffeur in military uniform sat patiently behind the steering wheel, and a small Kuomintang flag fluttered on the bonnet in the icy breeze.

"I'll think about it," Lydia said and shut the door.

SHE RAN UP THE STAIRS TWO AT A TIME. THE BEDROOM door was closed, but she opened it in a rush and was already speaking as she entered the room.

"Chang, it's all right, I . . ."

She stopped. The bed was empty. The sheet thrown back and the quilt gone.

"Chang?"

The air was cold. She felt a chill wind brush her cheek. The window was wide open and the curtains billowing.

"No," she breathed and rushed over to the sill. Outside there was no sign of his broken body on the terrace beneath. Her room looked out onto the back garden, which appeared bleak and bare, no movement except a foraging magpie. Empty. A tight pain gripped her chest.

"Chang," she called, but softly.

Something made a noise behind her. She swiveled around and

watched the door swing shut. Behind it, tight against the wall where he had been hidden by the open door, stood Chang An Lo. His face was white. But his body was wrapped in the peach quilt and from his right wrist dangled the unraveled twists of a bandage. In his swollen fingers were the scissors she used on the bandages, the long blades held like a dagger.

40

THEO FELT LIKE DEATH. BUT HE LOOKED VERY MUCH ALIVE. He was wearing his finest suit, the charcoal with the narrow pinstripe, a starched white shirt, and his favorite striped silk tie. A real Foreign Devil. Stiff and upright. Today Feng Tu Hong would see an enemy, but an enemy in control.

He parked the Morris Cowley in a back street in the Chinese part of town, tossed a grubby urchin a couple of coins to watch it, and joined the crush of bodies heading uphill to the square. A sharp wind snatched at hair and jackets and made people duck their heads under their woven bamboo hats. Theo lifted his face to it and felt it numb the sickening ache behind his eyes. He needed his eyes to be clear. He elbowed his way through the chattering crowd and could see no other *fanqui* as he passed under the writhing dragon archway into the wide open square. He paid no attention to the hostile looks. Feng Tu Hong was the only one he had eyes for.

"Excuse me, honorable sir, but it is unwise for you to be here today."

It was a small elegant man speaking at his shoulder. He was wearing the saffron robe of a monk, and his shaven head gleamed as if freshly oiled. He smelled strongly of juniper and his smile was as peaceful as a sunflower's.

Theo bowed. "I am here to speak with the president of the council. At his command."

"Ah, then you are in safe hands."

"That is debatable."

"All things are debatable. But those who have faith in truth and are determined on the path, they will find awakening."

"Thank you, holy one. I will hold that thought."

QING QUI GUANG CHANG. OPEN HAND SQUARE. IT WAS the wrong name for it, Theo decided. The hands that were soon to be in front of him would be closed. In fear.

The square was cobbled and surrounded by teahouses and shops with vivid red banners waving in the wind. A startling gold-painted elephant's tusk arched over the doorway of the colorful theater that dominated one side. Everything was bright and decorated and seemed to sway with movement under the curling eaves of the roofs, flicking up strange carved talismans to the gods. The usual market of caged birds and sacks of spices from the southern provinces was banished today and in its place a small wooden platform, six feet square and two feet high, had been erected in front of the grand theater entrance. On it stood a large ebony chair. On the chair sat Feng Tu Hong.

At his side stood Theo.

Eager faces full of anticipation lined the square, leaving the central area empty. They had trekked in from the fields and over from their offices or kitchens to be entertained, to have their daily drudgery relieved for one brief and dramatic moment. It was the display of power that drew them. It reassured them. In this changing and slippery world, some things remained the same. The good old ways. Theo could see it in their faces, and his heart sickened for them.

Feng raised one finger. Immediately the far corner of the crowd parted and a long column of gray uniforms and badly polished boots marched into the square. The Kuomintang. They acknowledged the president of the council, then formed an inner square and faced outward into the crowd. Their rifles bristled in their hands. Theo studied their blank young faces because it was preferable to thinking about why they were there, and he focused on one very upright soldier in particular who was having difficulty hiding his sense of pride. He looked all shiny and new, as if he had come fresh from Chiang Kaishek's military academy in Whampoa.

Soldiering was traditionally regarded as a lowly occupation in China, unlike in the West, but Theo had noticed a great change in

Chiang Kai-shek's latest recruits. These had their minds trained and indoctrinated, as well as their bodies, so that they believed in the task they were doing. And they were paid a decent wage for the job. Chiang Kai-shek was no fool. Theo admired him. But he feared that development for China would be slow. Chiang was fundamentally a conservative. He liked things the way they were, despite his posturing and promises of revolution. Yet this young soldier's face burned with his blind faith in his leader, and that had to be good for China.

"Tiyo Willbee."

Reluctantly Theo turned his gaze to Feng. The big man was wearing his presidential ceremonial robes, embroidered blue satin over a quilted gold undertunic that made him look squarer and heavier than ever. A tall and elaborate black hat was perched incongruously on his bull-sized head and reminded Theo of the black cap of a hanging judge.

"Watch for the first man."

For a moment Theo did not grasp his meaning, but when a slow drumroll started up and from each corner a monk in saffron robes stepped forward and blew his long pipe in a loud wailing cry that alerted the restless crowd, he realized what Feng was saying. A string of eight prisoners was being led into the center of the square. Their hands were fastened behind their backs with leather thongs, their shirts stripped from their bodies so that they were naked from the waist up, despite the winter temperatures. Except for one. A woman. She was second in the string and Theo recognized her at once. The plain submissive face that had buried itself in the cat's mangy fur with such devotion. It was the woman on the boat, the one who had given him Yeewai. In front of her stood the master of the junk, the man who had made too free with his knife blade, and behind them stood six others, all from the same vessel.

"You see?" Feng demanded.

"I see."

Theo knew what was coming. He'd seen it before but it never grew easier to watch. The prisoners were made to kneel by the captain in the gray uniform and then kowtow to the president.

Feng sat stone-faced.

When a big man with a long curved sword stepped out into the middle of the square with slow dignity, the crowd roared its approval. He whirled the sword once around his head in a display of speed and skill and the action triggered two of the prisoners, no more than boys, to cry and plead for mercy. Theo wanted to shout to them that it was a waste of their last precious breaths. The sword rose and fell in turn on three necks. Gasps of awe flowed from the onlookers as the lifeblood spurted out. Suddenly a young woman rushed from the packed crowd of dark heads and hurled herself at Feng Tu Hong's slippered feet. She clutched them and kissed his ankles with a passion.

"Get rid of the bitch," Feng shouted, kicking out at her.

A soldier reached down and lifted her to her feet by her hair, so that they saw her face. It was beautiful but twisted with despair. She screamed, and the woman prisoner raised her forehead from the cobbles.

"Ying, my beloved daughter," she cried out and received a rifle butt in her throat.

"Please," the young woman sobbed, "great and honorable president, do not kill my parents, please, whatever you want of me, please, I am yours. I beg you, great one . . ."

The soldier started to drag her away.

"Wait." Feng lifted the staff of ancient ivory that lay on his lap. He pointed it at the Kuomintang captain.

The officer approached the platform in a stiff-legged march that did not attempt to disguise his hostility toward the president.

"Throw the old witch that is among the prisoners back in her cell for ten days, and then release her."

He flicked a hand in the direction of the young woman, and one of the attendants behind his chair led her away. She was mute now. Trembling. The captain bowed and snapped out an order. His face was stern with dislike. The female prisoner was escorted out of the square.

Theo leaned toward Feng Tu Hong. "If I offer good dollars for them all, would you do the same for the rest of the prisoners?"

Feng burst out laughing, showing his three gold teeth, and slapped his broad knee. "You can beg, Willbee. That would amuse me. I might even pretend to consider it. But the answer would be no. There is only one price that would buy their lives."

"What price?"

"My daughter."

"Go to hell."

"YOU ARE FANQUI. YOU SHAKE WITH THE DREAM SICKNESS. You caused the death of seven men today, so you will not sleep tonight, I think."

"No, Feng Tu Hong, you are mistaken. I will sleep like a babe in its mother's arms because around me will be the arms of Li Mei and the breast at my lips will be the sweet breast of your daughter."

"May the dragon bats devour your flesh this night, you foul-mouthed offspring of a demon's whore."

"Listen to me, Feng. The only reason I came to the square today was to make clear to you that nothing will make me give her up. Nothing, I tell you. Li Mei will never return to your house. She is mine to care for."

"She is your whore and she brings pissing shame on the name of her ancestors."

"She changed her name from Feng to her mother's name of Li because it is you with your evil trade who inflicts black shame on her. She asks how she can keep her feet on the Right Path when each day she must atone for the knowledge that her father is destroying men's lives with the dream smoke and his greedy violence."

"The opium is Foreign Mud. It was you and your kind who first brought it to our shores. You taught us how to do business. And now the shipments continue every night without the guidance of Mason's information about the movements of the patrol boats. They hunt down our night sails. So it is because of you that more men will be caught and more men will die. One by one in this Open Hand Square."

"No, Feng. Their blood is on your hands. Not mine."

"Wah, Tiyo Willbee, you can save them."

"How?"

"Go out with the night sails again."

"No."

"I swear their cries in the afterlife will haunt your dreams in the prison cell."

"Does that mean you have spoken with that bastard Mason?"

"Ah, indeed I have had that honor. It grieves me that because I will not deal with him alone, he intends to speak to your Sir Edward and deliver him your worthless neck. Tell me, Tiyo Willbee, who will care for your Chinese whore then?"

41

It was snowing. Large downy flakes that tumbled out of a hard white sky and made the pavement slippery. Lydia hurried. Not because of the snow, but because of Chang An Lo. She hated leaving him alone in the house.

"Can you fix it?" she asked in the dressmaker's salon.

Madame Camellia held up the green dress and eyed its sad and mangled state with the tenderness of a mother for her forlorn child. "I will do what I can, Miss Ivanova."

"Thank you."

The chemist in Glebe Street was next, with the row of tall blue and red and amber flagons in its window. More bandages, boric acid, and iodoform. By the time she came out of Mr. Hatton's shop the street was white and the cars crawled past gingerly with layers of snow on their roofs. Lydia was aware of the flakes soft on her cheek and blinked when they caught on her eyelashes as she hurried down Wellington Street to the little kiosk on the corner. Over the counter she bought a cardboard cupful of hot rice noodles and *bai cai* all wrapped up in a brown paper bag. Head down, she sped home.

"Lydia Ivanova."

She lifted her head warily. The corner of Ebury Avenue where she now lived came into view, and leaning against one of the big plane trees was the bulky figure of Liev Popkov.

"Liev," she shouted with delight and broke into a run toward him.

He stood there as solid as the trunk behind him, opened his arms, and folded her into a big hug. It was like being swallowed by a woolly mammoth.

"Thank you, Liev, *spasibo*, thank you," she whispered into his chest.

Her cheek was pressed hard against his overcoat, the same one that had sheltered Chang from the rain that day at the quayside, and it felt cold and wet and stiff, but she didn't care. She was so happy to see the big Russian again. Still clutching her bag of hot food, she wrapped her arms around him as far as they would go and squeezed tight. Suddenly from nowhere a great rush of emotion erupted inside her. Everything she'd been keeping a hold on broke loose and she was shivering uncontrollably. It turned her bones to water and her legs would have collapsed if Liev Popkov had not been pinning her to his chest.

He growled, soft and comforting, while the snow swirled silently around them.

As abruptly as it came, it was gone. Her bones came back. She hugged him tighter, then stepped away and offered him a shaky smile.

"*Luchshye?*" he asked. Better?

"*Gorazdo luchshye.* Much better."

"Good."

And that was all they said about it.

"Will you come in and meet Chang An Lo? He would like to . . . to thank you too." Her tongue struggled with the Russian words.

"Not dead yet then?"

"No. He's alive. *Poydiom.* Come."

She tugged at his arm, but he did not move.

"No, Lydia Ivanova. I care nothing for your Chinese."

"Then why did you help him?"

He shrugged his great shoulders. "For you." He lifted from his pocket a bundle of banknotes and thrust them into her coat pocket. She knew it would be the two hundred dollars.

"No, Liev. It's yours."

"I do not seek payment."

"But you helped me so much. I don't understand. Why risk your life searching the docks?"

His black beard twitched as he pushed out his chin. "Because you are the granddaughter of General Nicholai Sergeivich Ivanov." He raised his huge right paw to the brim of his fur cap and saluted.

"What?"

"It is my honor to serve you."

"Wait a minute. Are you saying you knew my grandfather?"

Before he could reply, the sound of an explosion ripped through the air, a loud whoosh of solid noise that made Lydia's ribs rattle. In the heart of the town a column of black smoke rose up over the snow-covered roofs and merged with the heavy clouds.

"Bomb," Liev Popkov said instantly. "*Bomba*. Go home. Quickly. *Bistro*."

"Wait."

But he was gone, his long lumbering stride carrying him away down the street. Lydia turned and ran to her house.

CHANG EXPECTED HER TO COME IN LOOKING FRIGHTENED, but she didn't.

"Your friend Alexei Serov spoke true," he said. "The bombs have started."

"You heard it?"

"The whole of Junchow heard it."

She had hurried into the room with an energy he envied, and instead of carrying fear in her face she brought with her a positive rush of *chi*. She glowed with it. Her cheeks were pink and her eyes sparkled. She was focused.

"Lydia," he said with a smile, "you make the room vibrate. More than the bomb."

She looked at him on the pillow, uncertain for a moment, and then laughed, tossing her flame hair at him. "For us it's good. As long as the Black Snakes are at war with each other, they'll leave us alone."

"A world lies outside this room, Lydia. You cannot ignore it."

"Today I can." She grinned at him. "Here, eat this."

HE DREAMED. AND ALWAYS THE DREAMS WERE OF FIRE. Sometimes the fire was in her hair, bright and flickering, but other times it was in his blood, burning him up. The fire of pain and the fire of hatred. Together they consumed him.

"Chang An Lo."

He opened his eyes. Instinctively he flinched. A hand was coming at his face. But it was only a damp cloth that touched his skin, cool and fragrant. Not a hissing red poker.

"It's all right." Her voice was low. "You were having another nightmare."

His heart was hammering. Sickness rose in his stomach but he fought it down. He knew he had already lost all face in front of this girl, he was so weak and helpless, his dignity gone, but he refused to vomit noodles over her bed and watch her clean them up.

"Here."

A cup brushed his lips. He sipped. Tasted the bitterness of Chinese herbs. They calmed him. The fires and sickness receded. He sipped again and knew the time had come.

"Lydia."

"Hush, don't talk. You need rest. I'll read aloud again if you like."

"The tales of Shere Khan are strong. But you must read of Mulan. She is famous in Chinese legend. You would like her, she's a lot like you."

"Poor and skinny, you mean." But she smiled.

"No. A risk taker. And brave."

She blushed and hid her pink cheeks behind a fall of hair. "You are mocking me, Chang An Lo. Be careful what you say or I might drop this cup of what smells like shark's gallbladder or something equally noisome all over you."

He gazed up at her, at the challenge in her eyes, at the exquisite roundness of them and their color of warm honey. How could she possibly think he was mocking her?

"Lydia, I must walk."

HE WALKED. THOUGH HE WOULD BARELY CALL IT WALKING. His weight was all borne by the fox girl, not by his own worthless legs, which crumbled the moment he asked them to do anything more than stand there. They felt as weak and unstable as the noodles in his belly. He was ashamed of them.

But she made it easy for him. First she brought in one of the long striped shirts that belonged to the new husband of her mother, and though it was too large for his fleshless body, it reached down over his thighs and gave him a sense of decency. It smelled of lavender, which surprised him, but she told him many people kept sachets of lavender in their wardrobe. Second she lit the second bar of the gas fire, so that the air grew warmer and his muscles less stiff. And lastly she slipped an arm around his waist as he pushed himself off the bed, and drew him to her, close against her own body, as naturally as if they were two halves of the same whole.

With his arm across her shoulders he dragged his feet into motion. Together they shuffled toward the door and back again, over to the window and back again, past the fire and back again. Walk. Foot. Move. Heel. Toe. Turn. Lift. Progress was unbearably slow. His head was spinning in a gray spiral and at times he lost his vision, seeing nothing but blackness in front of him, but he kept walking.

"Enough." Lydia spoke firmly. "Or you'll kill yourself."

"My muscles are weak, Lydia. I must give them strength." His voice was barely a whisper.

"What is the point of my healing your body, if you then make yourself ill again?"

"I cannot stop. Time is short."

"You must. Stop now, please. And we'll do some more after you've had an hour's rest."

"You'll wake me?"

"I promise."

He collapsed onto the bed and instantly slid down into a tunnel of fire.

"You have a visitor, Chang An Lo. A guest."

Before his eyes were even open, his hand slid to the long carving knife that lay beside him under the sheet. He had asked her to fetch one from the kitchen after that time her Russian visitor came, the one with the knowledge about the Kuomintang. If that man was back now, Chang would not die without a fight.

"Say hello."

Chang blinked in surprise, frowned, and started to smile. He never knew what this fox girl would do next. She was standing beside the bed holding a white rabbit. Its pink nose was twitching frantically at the scent of herbs in the room and its eyes were wide with excitement, but it sat happily in her arms and made no attempt to escape.

"Say hello to Sun Yat-sen."

"Sun Yat-sen? No. He is the father of revolutionary China. A great and noble man. You insult his memory by giving his name to a miserable animal."

"No, no, don't be silly. Anyway, how dare you say he is a miserable animal? He is a magnificent rabbit; just look at him. He is an honor to his namesake."

Chang looked. The creature was indeed a fine specimen. Its body looked strong and muscular, and its coat gleamed as white as snow in sunlight. Chang envied the animal its health. And its position in her arms.

"Very well. I greet you with respect, Sun Yat-sen." He bowed his head. "I am honored to see you here, but I hope one day to see you on a plate. With hoisin and ginger root."

"Chang!"

He laughed at her expression.

NIGHTTIME WAS THE HARDEST. SHE ALWAYS CHANGED THE bandages on his hands and the poultices on the burns on his chest before settling him down for the long dark hours. He did not let her know how much pain it caused or how long he lay awake afterward behind closed eyelids.

But pain was not all bad. It gave him something to think about when he was not thinking of Po Chu.

SHE SAT IN THE CHAIR AND LAY HER HEAD ON THE EIDER-down. He could feel the gentle weight of it on his hip, though he could scarcely see more than a faint outline in the darkness. Slowly he withdrew his right hand from under the sheet by the knife. He had made her remove the heavy bandages from that hand and instead bind it just in thin gauze that left the tips of his remaining three fingers and thumb free and mobile. Her chemist's sulfur had drawn out much of the poison and the maggots were long gone, so the hand was nearer its normal size and able to grip.

Like a thief stealing a chicken from its roost, he stole a lock of her hair. As the knife sliced off a curl at the back of her head, he almost expected her to cry out in pain but she didn't. Just murmured in her sleep. He wondered what dreams stalked her mind. He tucked the curl under the mattress for safekeeping and then stroked her head with a feather-light touch. She murmured again and shifted her body uncomfortably in the chair. His fingers crept forward to lie in front of her lips where they could feel the warmth of her breath. He closed his eyes. Then he tangled his fingers around a strand of her hair but it was not enough. The need for her was like a gaping cavern inside his chest. Ignoring the protests of pain that flared through his hands and up to his armpits, he lifted her head and the quilt and drew her whole body onto the bed, where he let the quilt settle over her. He held his breath but she didn't wake. She muttered, "I've spoilt the dress," which made him smile, but her breathing steadied into a slow easy rhythm.

She would not be angry, he told himself. There was a blanket and a sheet between his body and hers, and she was fully clothed, so it was not indecent. But he knew her mother would kill him if she found them like this, and that meant it *was* indecent. But the warmth of her body flowing into his flesh felt right. She spoke the truth when she said she would heal him. Not her potions or her herbs. Her. Just the musky smell of her was cleansing his blood, he could feel it.

In the dark he wrapped an arm around her and kissed her cheek.

42

SHE WAS AWARE OF BEING WARM. BUT WHEN SHE STRETched like a cat in the morning sunshine, she instantly realized where her limbs were lying. In his bed. Again. She opened her eyes and found his face only inches from her own, watching her. Again.

"Good morning," he said softly.

"Hello. How did I get here?"

"You needed sleep. Not in a chair. You feel better?"

"Much. And you? Did you sleep well?"

"Yes."

She knew he was lying, but it felt so odd to be having this conversation with him while she was flat on her back in bed with him that she didn't contradict him. He reached across and touched her ear for a brief second. She noticed that the swelling in his fingers was less and she wanted him to touch her ear again. Her ear, her face, anywhere he wanted. This close to him she could see a slight stubble on his jaw but it was only light, not like Alfred's. Chang's chest was hairless, and she decided she liked that. That smoothness.

They lapsed into silence, just staring at each other, but the silence was easy, not stiff or stilted. It felt as natural as the sunlight that spilled under the curtain, so that when she leaned toward him after a while and gently kissed his lips, there was no embarrassment, just a sense of wholeness. And a fierce sense of wanting more. The wanting was so strong it made her body ache. But just when she least expected it, he closed his eyes and shut her out. The disappointment made her swallow hard, but she reminded herself he was ill, seriously ill, and needed rest. When she slid out of the bed, he did not try to stop her. He lay there breathing hard, as if his chest hurt, his dark head immobile on the pillow that still bore the imprint of her own.

She gathered together some fresh clothes and went to the bathroom. *Gospodi!* She must stink. She ran a bath and emptied a stream of her mother's bright green bubble bath into it, plunged in, and scrubbed herself hard. To scrub the ache away. Afterward she wrapped her wet hair in a towel and put on her other dress and the new lambswool cardigan Valentina had bought her, all soft and primrose yellow.

She looked in the mirror above the washbasin, trying to see what Chang would see, but she couldn't. There was some flesh on her bones these days, which was an improvement. And it seemed that her mother was right because in the last few months the good eating, which was thanks to Alfred, had filled out not only her cheeks, but her breasts too. They weren't as good as Polly's but they were getting there.

She smiled. At the mirror. And was surprised by what she saw. It was a whole new smile.

WHEN THE DOORBELL RANG THIS TIME, LYDIA WAS HALF expecting it.

"It'll be Polly," she said and went down to open the front door.

"Hello, Lyd, I've come to see how you're getting on. Bit lonely?"

"Oh Polly, now is not a good time actually. I'm just . . ."

"Hello, Lydia, dear. My word, you are looking well. Positively blooming. And that color really suits you."

"Thank you, Mrs. Mason. No need to check up on me, honestly. I'm doing fine."

"I'm just making sure you are managing all right, as I promised Mr. Parker I would. We were worried the bomb might have frightened you yesterday, weren't we, Polly?"

"I wasn't. I thought it was exciting." Polly grinned. "I told Mummy you wouldn't be scared."

"Have you time for a few of your favorites?" Anthea Mason held up the cake tin in her hand and smiled enticingly. "Macaroons."

Lydia was not exactly in the mood for macaroons.

"Mummy made them specially," Polly said pointedly and beamed when Lydia stepped back into the hall, allowing them to enter.

She seated them in the drawing room.

"Isn't this a pretty room?" Anthea Mason said cheerily. "Adorable colors."

Lydia gave it a glance. "The colors are Mama's and the furniture is Mr. Parker's."

The cocktail cabinet and leather chesterfield were a bit dark and gloomy for Lydia's taste but her mother had already started to soften their impact with her own personal touches, warm textured cushions and curtains. But at the moment Lydia's mind was on other things. She remained standing, shifting from foot to foot, pushing a toe into the thick Chinese carpet.

"How's Sun Yat-sen?"

"Fine."

"And the cook? Is he looking after you?"

"Yes."

"So you're eating well?"

"Yes."

"But I'm sure you have room for one of these, don't you, dear?"

"Yes. Thank you."

"A cup of tea perhaps?"

"Oh. Right. I'll go and make one."

"Ask the cook to do it, dear. I know you've dispensed with your houseboy, though for the life of me I can't understand why."

"I won't be long."

She headed quickly for the kitchen, made a hurried pot of tea, carried it on a tray back into the drawing room, and froze.

"Where's Polly?"

"Oh, I think she popped upstairs to take a peek at your bedroom, dear. You don't mind, do you?"

Lydia dumped the tray and ran.

SHE WAS TOO LATE. POLLY WAS STANDING IN THE BED-room. Her cheeks were scorched red and she was absolutely rigid, staring at Chang An Lo. He lay in the bed and was clutching the carving knife in his hand.

"Oh, bloody hell, Polly, you should have waited." Lydia seized her friend's shoulder and swung her around to face her. "Listen to me.

You must say nothing. Do you hear? Nothing to anyone. Not even your mother."

Polly's eyes strayed back to Chang and regarded him in the same way she would a tiger in Lydia's bed. "Who is he?"

"A friend."

Polly's eyes widened. "Not the one from the alleyway? The Communist?"

"Yes."

"What's he doing here?"

"He's injured. Polly, if you tell anyone, it will be dangerous for him. You *must* keep quiet or he could be caught and killed."

Polly gasped and ran a nervous hand through her bangs, unintentionally flipping them up in a jerky gesture that revealed an ugly bruise on her forehead. The sight of it made Lydia angry.

"And don't ever tell your father about Chang An Lo either, will you? Promise me." Lydia put her arms around Polly. "It's all right, don't get in a flap about it. We've done nothing wrong."

Polly stared at her in disbelief. "Don't you think keeping a Chinese man in your bed while your mother is away is wrong?"

"No, I'm just nursing him, that's all. There's nothing wrong in it. Anyway, he'll be gone as soon as he's well enough, I swear." Lydia looked hard into Polly's eyes and saw something there that made her stomach drop.

"I still don't think it's right," Polly said quietly.

"Please, Polly."

"But if I told my mother . . ."

"No, don't tell anyone. You must remain silent about this." She held on to her friend's wrist and gave it a little squeeze. "For my sake." Suddenly she kissed Polly's cheek and murmured, "Please, Polly. Do it for me."

"I'VE BEEN THINKING," LYDIA SAID QUIETLY AS SHE LIMPED Chang An Lo up and down the room. "I've worked out what to do on Saturday."

Chang was sweating. The effort was killing him but he wouldn't stop.

"Saturday I leave."

Her throat tightened. It was the first time he'd said it. "No, that's my point. You can stay."

He turned his head and looked at her with a slow smile. "Ah yes, your mother and new father will be happy to welcome me as their guest."

"I want you to stay."

His arm around her shoulders pulled her closer but he didn't cease his shuffle.

"You see, I've worked out that you can stay in the shed, the one Sun Yat-sen is in. I've put a padlock on it, so no one will be able to open it except me. They'll never know you're in there. Alfred and my mother will be too busy with each other to notice and I've put all the gardener's things in the back of the garage, so . . ."

He chuckled. A rich mischievous sound that was so full of life it made her pulse thud with delight.

"I love you, Lydia Ivanova," he laughed. "Not even the gods can stop you."

H E HADN'T SAID NO. THAT WAS THE MAIN THING. HE DIDN'T say yes, but he didn't say no. She held on to that.

By the evening he was exhausted and seemed to fall into a deep troubled sleep. He moaned and muttered in his dreams, but it was in Mandarin. They had both been severely rattled by Polly's intrusion, but Lydia had assured Chang that her friend would say nothing. She was pleased her own voice sounded so confident and wished she could be certain of it herself. Polly had been shocked. No telling how she'd react when she'd had time to think about it.

"Polly," she murmured to herself, "don't let me down."

As the night rolled in, she gazed out the window before she closed the curtains and, considering the precarious position she was in, she felt extraordinarily safe. She knew it was absurd. So absurd it made her laugh out loud. A known Communist in her bed, her mother about to return and a prickly new stepfather coming to turn her world upside down, yet . . . still. She felt good.

She watched a bedraggled pheasant pick its way over the snow on the back lawn, scratching for grubs, and for the first time in her life it dawned on her what it was like to be on the inside. No longer a hungry creature out in the snow. She turned her head away from the cold wintry scene outside and studied her room. It was warm. It was softly lit by the green lamp. There was food on a tray and a white nightdress waiting on a chair. This is how people were supposed to live. But she knew it wasn't the nightdress or the tray that was making her feel so good.

It was having Chang An Lo in her bed.

HE WOKE HER IN THE NIGHT.

She was lying on the bed. Like the night before, under the eiderdown but on top of the blanket. She had cleaned her teeth, put on the pretty nightdress, and taken up her position beside him in the bed while he was asleep. The lamp was off and in the silent mix of shadows in the room her senses slowly grew more alert. She could hear his breathing and smell the male scent of his skin. She did not hurry to fall asleep.

"Lydia." His hand was on her arm, the grip strong.

Instantly she was awake. "What is it? Is the pain worse?"

He was shaking. She could hear his teeth. She sat up.

"No," he said. "Just the pain of the dreams."

She lay on her side and wrapped an arm over his chest, holding him tight to her. Even through the blanket she could feel the pounding of his heart. He rested his damp cheek against her forehead, drew a deep breath, and released it slowly. For a long time they lay like that.

"You never asked," he said at last into the darkness of the room.

"Asked what?"

"What happened?"

"I thought if you wanted me to know, you'd tell me."

He nodded.

"But maybe if you tell me now, it will be released and leave your dreams in peace."

He breathed deeply again and when he spoke his voice was flat and hard. "There is not much to tell. It was simple. They stripped me and put me in a metal crate. I survived. Three months, perhaps more. I'm no longer clear. A box with air holes. An arm's length square, the same high. They fed me when they felt like it, so most of the time they didn't. They only took me out of the box for amusement. Finger cutting. Chest branding. Other things. I don't want your ears to hear."

Lydia lifted a hand and stroked his cheek, his throat, long slow strokes. But she didn't speak.

"One day they grew careless. They left knives too close while they played their games with me. They believed I was a dead rag. No threat to them. But they were wrong. My hand still knew how to sink a blade into a well-fed stomach."

His words stopped. The shaking had passed. She could feel the anger in him, like a coat of steel under his skin.

"I escaped. But I could go to no one who was known to be my friend. It was too dangerous."

"So you went to Tan Wah."

"Yes. Nobody knew of him. The hovels are used by opium addicts. No one goes there. I thought he was safe." He let out a low-throated groan. "I was mistaken."

"No, Chang An Lo, no. You were right. He died only because of me. Because of my stupid coat and somebody else's greed. I'm sorry."

"We are both sorry, Tan Wah," he whispered.

The silence in the room was short-lived because Lydia's own anger was swirling up in her.

"Who did these things to you? Who are *they*? The Black Snakes? Or the Kuomintang? Tell me."

He moved his head on the pillow and looked at her. It was too dark to make out his expression but her fingers touched his face and she was amazed to feel a smile curving his lips.

"Why do you need to know, Lydia? Will you rush out and kill them for me?"

"It's what they deserve."

He gave a soft laugh and moved closer.

"Is it hard to kill someone?" she whispered.

"Lydia, you would kill a man if you had to."

Then he kissed her lips and it wasn't gentle this time. It was a fierce hungry kiss that made the ache flare throughout her body.

"Who was it?" she asked again when she drew breath.

"You never give up."

"Who?"

He sighed. "It was Feng Po Chu. His father, Feng Tu Hong, is the leader of the Black Snakes and the president of the council."

"Po Chu? The one who stole the explosives? Why did he do this to you?"

"Because I did something. It made him lose face."

"What kind of something?"

Chang was silent at first and she thought he was going to keep his secrets from her, but slowly he started to speak. "I walked him naked and bound to his father and made him beg. I thought I had the protection of Feng Tu Hong but . . ." He paused and traced a finger around the curve of her ear. "I was wrong."

Lydia abruptly recalled what Mr. Theo had told her about Chang making a deal with Feng, and she nodded. "Thank you. Now I know."

After a moment of thought she rolled away from him out of the bed, felt her way over to the small green lamp on the table, and switched it on. When she returned to the bedside, she stood quite still for a moment, gazing down at him intently. Slowly she slid the night-dress up over her head.

She saw his black eyes fill with desire.

SHE LIFTED THE SHEET AND LAY IN THE BED NEXT TO HIS naked body. He was warm. Like silk all down one side of her skin. She stroked a hand gently over his bandaged chest and down his thin ribs to his hips. She knew his body so well, each bone and muscle of it.

But suddenly, stupidly, she felt awkward. She didn't know what to do next. Her heartbeat was thudding in her ears and she was frightened he would hear it, but just when she was thinking she'd made a complete fool of herself by climbing into his bed like a common slut, he lifted himself up on one elbow and studied her face with a dark, serious gaze. So intense it stripped away her fears.

Slowly his lips found hers. Tentative at first. Small lingering kisses on her mouth, on the tip of her chin, the corners of her eyes and the sweep of her cheekbones. They made her whole body surge with something that felt almost like pain, it was so fierce, a burning heat. It swept from her lips to the tips of her breasts and rushed down between her legs. Her nipples ached. She heard herself moan in a soft mewing sound she had never heard before.

"Lydia," he murmured as his mouth claimed hers again. His hand caressed her naked breast and slid in slow teasing circles down the slope of her slender stomach.

It was as if her skin became something other than skin. It grew so alive it leaped out of her control, rubbed itself against his body, her hip pressing against his, her hands touching, searching, stroking, seeking out each bone of his back, his flat wide shoulder blades, the curve of his buttocks. Her lips opened to his and the unexpected sensation of their tongues entwining sent such a shiver of delicious shock through her body that it made him stop, lift his head, and gaze at her with concern.

But she laughed, almost a purr, and wrapped her arms around his neck, drawing him back to her once more. His lips explored her throat with open-mouthed kisses, as if he would eat her up, and his tongue started to lick her breasts, tasting her, discovering her, making the lines of her body melt until they molded perfectly to his. It amazed her that two bodies could do this. Become one.

As he bent his dark head over her breast she let her own tongue trail along the back of his neck, twirling the short hairs and nuzzling each bone of his spine. His skin. It smelled of herbs. But the salty taste of it set her loins throbbing. When he took her nipple into his mouth the heat inside her seemed to explode in her chest and the need for him became unbearable. Her hand reached down to where she could feel his penis thrust hard against her thigh but when her fingers curled around it, it startled her. This was not the penis she recognized, the one she had cradled in her hand before. This was different. Big. Too big. How could anything be so hard and yet so soft?

He moaned the moment her hand touched it. It twitched between her fingers as if electric shocks were sweeping through its blue veins and she felt a fierce choking desire to hold it, keep it, protect it, own it forever. It was as if it were a part of her. As he was a part of her.

Abruptly she could hold back no longer and she took his good hand, placed it between her legs. Instantly he lifted his head so that his mouth and his tongue could merge with her own, and his fingers started to caress the moist heart between her legs, gently at first, then firmer, harder. She moaned, and under it she heard a low breathless growl that was him. She lost track of time. A minute or an hour, she had no idea. She wrapped a leg up over his hip and felt his penis tight against her cleft, the pulse of it hot and needy.

And suddenly he was above her. His lips kissing her eyelids until she opened them and found his dark gaze looking down at her with an expression so tender and so full of longing that she knew she would carry it with her till her dying day. His mouth moved against her own.

"My sweet love," he breathed. "Tell me this is what you want."

For reply she bucked her hips so that the tip of him slid inside her and she heard his quick intake of breath. His teeth bit down on her lip. Slowly, gently, with infinite care he entered her. At one point a sharp pain made her cry out but he held her close, murmuring, whispering, eating her up.

She could barely breathe. All thought ceased. Her whole world became this one moment. A fierce pounding heat that crashed over her body, burning new pathways through her flesh. Through *his* flesh. Through *their* flesh. Molding it into one flesh. And when the final shuddering climax tore through them both, she thought she was dying. Literally dying. And that Chang An Lo's gods had carried her to a new afterlife.

No NIGHTMARES. NOT THAT NIGHT. SHE HAD BANISHED them.

Chang An Lo could not take his eyes off her, even in the dark. Her head lay curled on his shoulder as she slept and he brushed his cheek against her hair, just to feel it again, to touch its flames. His mind kept rushing ahead, twisting and turning around the hidden coil of the future, but he drew it back. Back to the present. To this moment. This now. This perfect point of time.

He struggled to center his mind. Focus his senses. But all he could feel was the joy of her, the physical wonder of her, the sweet smell of her. His fox girl. He relived each second in his head as he lay awake in the hours before dawn. Heard again the little yips of pleasure. Felt her teeth on his collarbone. The strong muscles inside her. That moment of certainty when . . .

No. He dragged his mind away and forced it to be in the now. Not in what had passed. Nor in what was to come. But now. To breathe each breath completely and not think about the next. The gods had granted him a treasure few ever come close to experiencing in this life. He would not waste it by fearing that some thief would come and steal it from him tomorrow or tomorrow's tomorrow. He touched her forehead with his lips and kept them there against her skin. It was warm and musky with sleep. His eyes held on to the shadowy tangle of her hair, and he listened to her breathing. He had to clear his brain. To think what was right for her.

"ARE YOU TIRED?" HER EYES WERE HUGE. GREAT AMBER pools of light.

"No." He smiled at her as she lay beside him on the pillow in the darkness. "I feel better. Much better. Strong inside again."

"Good."

He kissed her ear. "You have perfect ears. Priceless curls of porcelain."

She laughed and wrapped her leg lightly over his body. Instantly he was aroused. He touched her breast and felt the muscles spring to life under her skin. This time she made it easy for him. She sat astride him, rocking with an urgent rhythm while his hand caressed the soft swell of her breasts, firm and taut and infinitely inviting to his tongue. He watched her face. It was so mobile. It showed so much. He painted the picture of it into his head the way an artist paints a delicate portrait on a porcelain plate.

The freedom of her passion as she threw her hair forward and seized his lips with hers, arching over him with open longing, was something new to him, and it fired his need for her to even greater intensity. But it moved him too, deep down inside where no one else had ever touched before. And he wondered, as he danced his fingers down her sides and saw her tremble, whether he was the one who was the virgin.

43

LYDIA LAY VERY STILL. SHE DIDN'T WANT TO DISTURB THE darkness.

Everything had changed. Even her pillow smelled different. Her body felt as though she had swapped it for a new one overnight and she had to familiarize herself with it all over again because this body knew things and did things instinctively that her head could only observe with amazement. This body had no shame. In fact it reveled in these extraordinary acts of intimacy. And she was astonished that it knew no bashfulness in its nakedness, not even under the gaze of a man.

Not just a man. A Chinese man.

What would her mother say?

She smiled and a bubble of laughter escaped into the silent room. She pictured Valentina's face if she walked in now, her eyes and her mouth round with shock, then narrow with fury, but oddly none of it had the power to touch her. Not now, in this wonderful new body. This desirable body. This shameless body. She flexed its limbs, stretched its toes, clenched the newly awakened muscles between her legs and in the lowest part of her abdomen, felt a dull ache down there. Not a pain exactly, just a delicious ache that reminded her of what had happened to her. As if she could forget.

A virgin no more. The thought brought nothing but a shiver of pleasure even though she knew her mother would rant and rave and say that no man would want her now that she was spoiled goods.

That was such rubbish, she couldn't suppress a grin. She had been transformed from dreary back-of-the-shelf stock into shiny new goods. Glossy and glowing, inside and out. And who cared about what other men might say? She shivered with disgust at the very idea of another man's touch. It was Chang An Lo she wanted. No one else.

She put her ear close to his mouth to make sure he was still breathing. She didn't quite trust his gods. They might want him. But she wanted him more.

"TIME FOR BREAKFAST, MY LOVE. I KNOW IT'S NOT EVEN morning yet," she laughed and waved a hand at the black window, "but I'm starving."

He felt the warmth of her body disappear from his side.

"I want to eat only you." He smiled.

"No. Boiled egg and toast for you today. Got to keep your strength up. You never know when you might need it again."

She abandoned him with a mischievous chuckle, turned on the light, and trotted off to the bathroom. He was impressed by such luxuries in Western houses. He could hear her running a bath and singing to herself. He smiled, but knew he had to prepare her.

"TELL ME ABOUT YOUR CHILDHOOD."

She was perched cross-legged on the end of the bed eating yesterday's bowl of something she called trifle. Every now and again she leaned forward and slipped a spoonful of it into his mouth. Secretly he found it teeth-grating in its sweetness and was astonished she could relish it so, but he gave no sign of that.

"My childhood," he said. "It was very grand. Tutors, servants, and slaves. My father was a great mandarin. A peacock feather in the hat and gold-colored tiles on the roof as a mark of superiority. He was a trusted adviser to Empress Tzu Hsi, but after Sun Yat-sen . . ."

"My rabbit?" She grinned.

". . . after the true and noble Sun Yat-sen brought the end to the Ching dynasty in 1911, my family escaped death. Only because the new central government needed my father's financial skills. But," he felt his face grow stiff and expressionless, "the warlords slit each other's throats and came for him."

"And your family?"

"Dead. Each one of them. Beheaded in Peking. By order of General Yuan Shi-k'ai."

"I'm sorry. So very sorry, my love. To lose everyone . . ."

He shook his head, as if he could shake out the image from his mind. "I escaped. I had chosen to live with monks to learn a simpler way of life. In a temple up in the mountains north of Yenan."

"A temple?"

"Yes."

"But I thought Communists didn't believe in religion."

"You are correct. But it is not a simple task to root out superstition from the human mind." He reached over, drew her to him, and let his tongue lick a smear of custard from her lips. "Or love from the human heart."

"Is that what has happened to us?" Her eyes were solemn.

"Escape?"

"No. Love."

He stroked her chin and slid his unbandaged hand inside her blouse to where he could feel her heart beating strongly. "Can't you feel? Here."

"I feel a pain."

He laughed gently. "I love you, my beautiful fox."

Her eyes widened and focused on his, a small pulse vibrating at the base of her throat. "I love you, Chang An Lo. I won't let anybody part us."

A sharp pain erupted in his own chest. "Let us live now, my love. Nobody can ever part us from now."

"IT'S TIME TO MOVE."

"What?"

"To the shed."

"Why now?" she asked. "It's only Friday and not even morning yet." The first glint of dawn was fingering the curtain. "They're not due back until tomorrow, so we still have today and tonight to . . ."

"I'm sorry. I must move now. Today. Before it grows light."

"Why?"

"To be prepared. To be prepared is to stay alive. If they return early? They will summon police at once."

"Please. Don't."

"My precious love, you cannot keep me in a cage the way you keep your rabbit."

"But I want you safe, to give time for your body to heal and grow strong again. You are still feverish."

"I know I am weak."

"Not so weak last night."

"No. You see how you give me strength."

"Please, Chang An Lo. Wait till tomorrow."

SHE MOVED EVERYTHING IN THE LAST SHREDS OF DARKness. Sheets, blankets, medication, bandages, candles, food, and water. Together they made their way down the stairs and out to the shed, his arm across her shoulders, and he was shocked at just how weak he still was. He said nothing, but her face kept turning to him with concern as he dragged his feet over the icy lawn and his nods of reassurance were not as convincing as he meant them to be. The cook and his wife were lazy good-for-nothings while their master was away and were still in bed, so there was no danger of discovery, but his fear was that he wouldn't even make it as far as the shed.

What then? Could she drag him?

"You should have waited till tomorrow," she said crossly when he at last stumbled through the doorway and collapsed on the floor.

He crawled to the wall and propped himself up next to Sun Yat-sen while she made a rough bed for him on the wooden boards. His head was buzzing and his legs shaking. But he loved to watch her. The way she moved. Efficient and full of energy.

"Thank you," he said as she helped him into the pile of blankets and tucked a hot-water bottle under his feet. "Do not be angry."

"Hush, my love, I'm not angry. Just frightened you are leaving me."

"Look at me. Do I look strong enough to leap over your roof and fly away?"

She laughed, generous with her energy. "Go to sleep now."

"And you?"

"I'll go to the market as soon as it opens. To buy you some clothes."

He clung to her hand as her face slipped in and out of focus. "Peacock feathers and gold slippers would be nice."

She smiled. "I was thinking of a topper and tails."

He had no idea what she meant, but he raised her fingers to his lips.

She smiled at him. "And don't go holding any wild parties in here while I'm away."

SOMEONE WAS RATTLING THE PADLOCK. SILENTLY CHANG rolled out of the blankets. The long-bladed knife was already in his hand. He crouched to one side of the door.

"Missy Lydia? Missy, you here? Wai want you."

It was the cook, Wai. Chang breathed more easily. The man must be a piss-head if he couldn't see that of course she wasn't inside the shed if the padlock was fastened outside. The shed had no windows, just a small skylight in the roof, which meant no one was able to look in. He heard the cook move away, muttering about the cold wind, but Chang remained where he was. He forced the cobwebs from his mind. He needed to be alert. He listened for other footfalls but none came. Around him the air was dim and musty but he was aware of sunshine trickling into one corner, picking out the dust motes and sending a cockroach scuttling into the dark.

Gradually the light changed. Chang judged time passing by the speed with which the rectangle of light crept across the floor, brushing Sun Yat-sen's nose, then sliding over a huddle of wood lice and settling on his heap of blankets as though exhausted. Somewhere among the burlap sacks that leaned against one wall, a mouse pattered. With quiet concentration Chang observed a spider as it spun a web from one shelf of paint pots to another, and he would have given another finger to have the agility of its legs at this moment.

Because he sensed danger. How or when, he had no idea, but he could taste it. It was in the air.

When the sunlight finally sidled from inside the shed, he began to worry about Lydia. He pulled one of the blankets from the bed and wrapped it around himself and placed a handful of the medicines in the cloth case that was meant for the pillow, ready to move if he had to. With his right hand he carefully unbandaged his left. The time for cosseting was over. He studied both hands. The right was healing well now, but the left was still ugly and swollen, oozing pus from the hole where his smallest finger had once been. The sight of them offended him deeply. The balance was gone. They were lopsided. Even healed, they would possess no center point.

Rage reared up from where it lay curled deep in his stomach, but he controlled it, breathed slow, exhaled long. Steadily and unremittingly he began to exercise his fingers.

"I'M SORRY I WAS SO LONG. YOU MUSTN'T WORRY ABOUT me."

She had taken one glance at his face and seen beyond the welcoming smile he gave her. She bent and kissed his mouth. "What are you doing over here by the door? You should be in bed, resting."

"I have finished resting."

She gave him a look but made no comment. Instead she unwrapped her packages. Her wide grin filled the dingy shed with warmth and vitality, and he could feel it seeping into his own veins.

"They're not new, I'm afraid, but they're good."

She held them up. She was right, they were good. He was touched that she must have gone especially to the Chinese market in the old town because they were not Western clothes. A pair of loose peasant trousers, a quilted tunic, and a thick padded jacket, and in a separate parcel a pair of stout hide boots. A leather satchel, scratched and battered but still intact, pleased him most because it reminded him oddly of himself. Except he was no longer intact.

"Thank you. For these gifts."

"Your hand." She frowned. "What have you been doing? It's bleeding again. Let me bind it up."

"One twist of bandage. No more."

Again she gave him that look.

"In the English market where I found the satchel, I heard talk. About the bombs. Two more last night." She dug out the antiseptic boric acid and the pot of sulfur paste from the pillowcase. "Planning on going somewhere?" she asked lightly.

"No."

She nodded.

But it was an uneasy movement. "They say it's the Communists planting the bombs. Eight people were killed outside a nightclub and there's talk of scouring the district for union members. Everyone is angry."

"They're afraid," Chang murmured. He dismissed the pain as she dabbed at the wound on his left hand.

"Is it the Communists, do you think?"

"No. It is Po Chu. He is clever."

"But surely he gains nothing by—"

The door swung open and a brisk wind snatched at her hair. A strand of it swept across Chang's face, but he saw the tall figure standing in the doorway. Chang didn't move. Just his right hand. It picked up the knife.

Lydia leaped to her feet with an exclamation of surprise.

"Alexei Serov! What on earth are you doing here?"

She stepped right in front of the figure, blocking his view, but not before Chang had seen his sharp green eyes take in the rough bed, Chang's hands, and the dried bloodstain on the wooden floor.

"Come up to the house," Lydia said firmly and stalked out of the shed, forcing the Russian to retreat. She closed the door and clicked the padlock shut.

44

"Do you know what the penalty is for harboring a known fugitive?"

"Just one minute, what reason do you have for thinking he is a fugitive? He is a friend of mine who is wounded and needs help, that's all."

"In a shed?" Alexei Serov's tone was skeptical.

"I really don't see that this is any business of yours," she said crossly.

They were standing in the middle of the drawing room, but she didn't want to discuss things. She wanted him to leave. She had not invited him to sit, nor offered to take his immaculate gray overcoat and silk scarf.

"Anyway, what were you doing snooping around my shed?" Even as she said it, she had a feeling she could have put that better.

"Snooping? Miss Ivanova, I regard that as an insult." He drew his shoulders back stiffly. His short hair bristled. "I called at your front door and it was your servant who informed me that you were in the shed with your rabbit. He was the one who suggested I go down there."

Wai, the cook. Damn the lazy fool.

"Then I apologize. I meant no insult. I just feel that you . . ."

"Intruded?"

"Yes."

He looked at her with a cool questioning gaze and came a step closer, his hand tapping impatiently on the lapel of his coat. He spoke in a low voice. "I think you are taking a big risk. Yet again. These are violent times, Miss Ivanova, and you should take great care. The bombs that explode, the intrigues that cut the ground from under any agreements, the dangers to someone who doesn't know what they are involved in—these are things you know nothing about. People get killed every day for doing less than you are doing."

Some of her confidence evaporated, and it must have shown on her face because he said more pleasantly, "It's all right, I don't bite."

She smiled and made it look easy. "Thank you for your advice, but it is of no concern to me."

"What are you saying?"

He knew damn well what she was saying. "That it's all nothing to do with me. Of course I hear of what is going on here in Junchow, but . . ."

"But you're not involved?"

"No, I'm not."

"And that man in your shed is not a Communist?"

"No."

He laughed, tipped his head back, and made a soft mocking sound, blowing out air between his white teeth. "You are not a very good liar, Miss Ivanova."

She was stung. She'd always been a bloody good liar.

"What I'd like to know," she said curtly, "is what brought you over here in the first place. Why have you called on me?"

"Ah yes." He tilted his head in a polite bow, reached into his coat pocket, and brought out a card. He held it out to her. "From my own dear mama, Countess Serova."

Lydia accepted the card. It was ivory tinted, very thick, and embossed with a gold coat of arms at the top, an eagle with wings spread wide over a quartered shield. It wasn't hard to guess that it was the Serov family crest. On the card was an invitation to an evening of dance and entertainment at the Serov villa on Rue Lamarque on Monday at eight.

Monday? Monday was an age away. Much too far ahead to think about. First she had to get herself and Chang An Lo through this weekend.

"Just to make it official," he said amiably. But with that superior smile again.

"Thank you. I shall think about it, but I'm not sure of my plans for next week until my mother returns tomorrow."

A ripple of surprise crossed his face, as if he were not used to Serov invitations being refused, but he hid it smoothly. "Of course. I understand."

She walked him to the front door. When he strode out onto the drive the wind snatched at his scarf, but he ignored it and turned back to face her. His green eyes met hers, and for a long moment he considered her in silence. "Don't forget my advice, Miss Ivanova," was all he said at last.

But it was a step too far. "Alexei Serov, why don't you just look after your own life and leave me to take care of mine?"

She shut the door. All things considered, that hadn't gone very well.

"DARLING, SURPRISE!"

Lydia froze. She was in her bedroom. She had just hurried upstairs to fetch an extra sweater before going down to the shed to tell Chang An Lo how things had gone with Alexei Serov.

"Lydia, we're home."

"Mama." She ran down the stairs.

They were in the hallway, surrounded by luggage and packages. Shaking off their coats, laughing and stamping their cold feet, stirring up the air, and filling the house that had been so silent all week with noise and bustle. Bringing in the outside world.

"Darling." Her mother opened her arms wide and Lydia ran into them.

Something happened and Lydia was totally unprepared for it. Valentina wrapped her arms so tightly around Lydia it was as though she intended never to let go, and her elegant figure gave way to a deep tremor as she kissed her daughter's cheek. Suddenly Lydia's throat hurt, so much it felt like fishhooks caught there.

"Did you miss me, darling?"

"Oh really, have you been away? I didn't even notice."

"You wicked child." Valentina laughed and squeezed Lydia hard.

Alfred came over and patted Lydia awkwardly on the back. "Good to see you looking well, my dear. But where is Deng?"

"The houseboy?" Still she held her mother. Drew the scent of her perfume deep into her lungs. "I gave him the week off."

"Why on earth . . . ? Ah well, never mind. I'll take the cases up myself. Good exercise anyway."

She heard his footsteps tread heavily up the stairs, and she felt her mother's quick breath on her ear.

"Lydia," was all Valentina said. "Lydia."

"Mama."

They stood alone in the hall. Neither willing to release the other.

"YOU'D HAVE LOVED IT, LYDIA." ALFRED WAS BEAMING AT her and took a contented puff on his pipe, sending blue smoke coiling to the ceiling.

Lydia preferred the aromatic scent of the tobacco to the harsh smell of her mother's cigarettes. They were all seated in the drawing room after an excellent meal of fillet of pork followed by pineapple syllabub. Wai was showing off his wider menu now that his master had returned. Alfred had lit the fire in the drawing room, as there was no houseboy to do it for him, whistling the whole time, and Lydia noticed a marked change in him. No more nervous foot-shuffling silences. Lots of sounds coming from him. Humming or whistling or talking. As if the happiness inside kept flowing out of him in noise.

"One day, Lydia," Alfred said as he tossed a match into the glowing coals, "I will take you to the Yungang cave temples as well. You must see for yourself how astonishing they are and what wonderful building skills the Chinese possessed nearly two thousand years ago. Good Lord, in England we have nothing to compare with them. Quite remarkable."

"I'd like that."

"Oh *dochenka*, you really must see the seated Buddha. It's amazing. Sixty feet high and cut into a yellow cliff. I've never seen such a huge man." Valentina laughed and glanced teasingly at Alfred on the chesterfield beside her.

The radio was playing softly in the background, some new kind of syncopated jazz, and Alfred was humming again. Lydia was sipping a tumbler of lime juice with a handful of ice in it and trying hard to make conversation, but her mind was outside in the cold.

The hot-water bottle needed heating again. The poultices on the burns needed changing. The next dose of herb tea was overdue and . . .

"Darling, do listen. You look as if you're miles away. I was telling you about the system they have for their temples and tombs and things. It's called *feng shui*. They've used it for more than two thousand years. It's supposed to make sure the sites are . . . Oh, what was that word they used, my angel?"

"Propitious?" Alfred offered.

"That's it, propitiously sited."

Valentina was very animated. She seemed to have shed the cloak of cultivated indifference she used to carry around with her and taken on an enthusiasm for everything. Lydia found it quite odd. She couldn't decide whether it was something released from the inside or stuck on from the outside. But Alfred was clearly entranced.

"I know about *feng shui*, Mama. The trouble is that the Europeans haven't taken any notice of it at all. We drive railroads through their spiritual places, and missionaries build churches that throw shadows on ancient Chinese ancestral graveyards, disturbing their dead. Don't laugh, Mama. It really matters to them. And they believe our church spires pierce the skies with their sharp points and prevent the good spirits returning to earth. *Feng shui* means *wind and water*."

"Does it? How clever of you, darling. Don't I have a clever daughter, Alfred?"

"Yes, very clever." He beamed at Lydia again.

But she knew that if Valentina had asked him if her daughter was bright green with pink spots he'd have said yes just as willingly. Lydia chose her moment. She stretched casually and stood up.

"It's good to have you home again but I think I'll go to bed now, if you don't mind."

"So soon?"

"Mmm, I'm sleepy." She smiled at her stepfather. "It's the heat from this wonderful fire. I think I'll just pop out and check on Sun Yat-sen before I go up, though. He's still a bit nervous in his new home, so . . ."

"I don't think so, Lydia," Alfred said firmly. "I don't want you wandering around out there in the dark."

"But there's a moon. It's not too dark."

"No, you go to bed now, my dear. Leave the rabbit till tomorrow morning." He smiled at her but his eyes were serious, and suddenly she remembered the deal she'd made with him in exchange for the two hundred dollars.

Her heart sank. She looked to her mother for help, but Valentina was at the cocktail cabinet pouring a glass of vodka for herself and a snifter of brandy for her husband.

"Please, Alfred," Lydia said coaxingly.

"Not tonight, dear. You trot up to bed now and leave the bally rabbit till morning. There's a good girl. Sleep well."

Lydia nodded. "Good night, Mama," she said and gave her a light kiss. Then she did the same to Alfred, avoiding his spectacles.

Upstairs she drew a big letter A on a sheet of paper and stuck pins in it.

THEY LAY AMONG THE BLANKETS ON THE DUSTY FLOOR. Gently, soothingly, he stroked her nipple with his thumb. Together they watched the moon travel slowly across the skylight above them. Lydia yearned for it to be a full moon, a complete magical disk, so that they could wish on it but it was at least a week too early, its perfection marred by reality. Her head rested on his shoulder, their limbs so entwined she no longer knew where hers ended and his began. His skin a part of hers. Her breath a part of his.

"Lydia."

"Mmm?"

They had been silent a long time, wrapped comfortably around each other. The crisp rectangle of translucent light that the moon shed over them turned their naked skin silver and made shadows leap from one face to the other as their lips brushed. Earlier they had made love and it had been different. Fiercer. Hungrier. As if their bodies knew time was running out. Lydia had waited impatiently in her room until she was certain her mother and Alfred must be asleep, and then she'd crept downstairs and sped across the grass. Frost made it crunch underfoot. Trees lurched at her with spiky elongated shadows, and a bat flitted low over her head as she turned the key in the padlock.

"Are you all right?" he'd asked immediately. He was standing to one side of the doorway, a blanket over his shoulders.

"No. I'm not all right. Not remotely all right."

He kissed her mouth.

"My mother came home early, just as you said she might, and so I've been stuck up there in the house worried sick about you and what you must be thinking Alexei Serov will get up to. Damn the man. Why did he have to call? But honestly I don't think he'll betray us. He's helped me once before. I know he can be a real supercilious bastard at times, but he's not so bad underneath. The danger is that he might feel a strong duty to the Kuomintang and . . ."

"Hush, hush, my love."

His dark eyes searched hers and the expression in them made all the words tumble straight out of her head. He drew her into his arms, enveloped her in his blanket, and for the first time in hours she felt safe again. In the middle of a rickety old shed, freezing to death and with every possible thing going wrong. Yet she felt safe. And happy. She only had to look at him and she felt happy. And when she wasn't with him, she only had to think of him and her limbs turned liquid with desire.

"I must leave tomorrow," he said.

"No."

He kissed her hair and she could hear him breathing in deeply, preparing himself. She knew she should make it easy for him. Already she could feel that his body was starting to burn up again. The exertion of the day had been too much for his fragile state, but he hadn't allowed her to nurse him tonight, just drank the herb concoction for the fever. She mustn't make it harder. Mustn't.

"To leave you, Lydia, will tear my heart into a thousand pieces. But I can stay no longer. It is dangerous for you. I love you too much to risk that."

She held him close. Said nothing. She was frightened the wrong words would come out.

He caressed her ear with his fingertips. "I must leave Junchow . . ."

Everything inside her started to hurt.

". . . but it will be hard. Kuomintang troops check every road in or out. That means I must find somewhere else to hide . . ."

She breathed.

". . . until I'm strong enough to swim the river."

She closed her eyes.

"Kiss me," she whispered.

His lips came instantly to her mouth and his tongue found hers, soft and sensuous. His hand moved down between her legs, stroking the silky inner thigh. They didn't hurry, just took their time. In the moonlight.

THEY AGREED HE WOULD LEAVE BEFORE DAWN. SHE HAD brought what was left of the two hundred dollars and hidden part of it in his leather satchel, part bandaged to his thigh and part tucked inside his boot.

"No rickshaw," he warned.

"Why not?"

"The pullers have loose tongues. They are in the pay of the tongs. Black Snakes could track me. And you. I'll walk."

"I'll get Liev," she said quickly.

"No, my beloved. I want help from no one who leads to you. You see? I escaped from Po Chu. The loss of face will be worse than a blade in his belly and he will work to destroy anyone who . . ."

She put a finger to his lips and nestled close under the blankets. "Sleep," she murmured. "It's not dawn yet. Sleep. Grow strong." Their bodies clung together.

But when the first hint of gray tinged the skylight, Lydia knew Chang An Lo would be going nowhere today. The fever was back.

45

"THIS ROOM SMELLS ODD," VALENTINA REMARKED.

She was wandering around Lydia's bedroom, picking things up, putting them down, plucking copper-colored hairs from a hairbrush, straightening the curtain.

"It's herbs. I tried out some Chinese herbal teas while you were away."

"What on earth for?"

Lydia shrugged. "No reason."

She was sitting on the edge of the bed feeling tense. Her gaze repeatedly scoured the room for any telltale signs, but there was nothing that she could spot. She wondered what her mother wanted. After a rather stilted family breakfast all together, Lydia had bolted upstairs but soon afterward Valentina had drifted in. She was wearing a red wool dress that skimmed her slender figure and made her dark bob look more dramatic. On her wrist was a new bracelet of carved ivory. Lydia thought she looked tired. Finally her mother came to a stop by the window and perched on the sill, facing her daughter. Outside it was snowing again.

"So who is he?"

"What?"

"Who is the lucky young man?"

Lydia's pulse kicked erratically. "What on earth do you mean, Mama?"

"*Dochenka*, I am not blind."

"I have no idea what you're talking about."

Valentina reached into the pocket of her dress and for one awful moment Lydia thought she was going to bring out some piece of incriminating evidence, but it was only her cigarette case and lighter. She selected a cigarette, tapped its end on the tortoiseshell case before lighting it, and exhaled a plume of smoke in Lydia's direction.

"Sweetheart, have you looked in a mirror lately?"

Lydia glanced at the mirror in the front of her wardrobe, but all she saw reflected was her white nightdress on the chair. Suddenly she was nervous there might be blood on it.

"Mama, I want to go and feed Sun Yat-sen now. Is this important?"

"Ah, my wicked little liar. What were you up to last night? Don't look so shocked. I know you went to the shed."

Lydia felt her palms grow moist. She brushed them over the eiderdown. "How?"

Valentina laughed. "Because I couldn't sleep. I came in to see if you were lying awake, like in the old days in the attic, but you weren't here, naughty girl."

"Oh."

"Don't you *oh* me. You disobeyed Alfred. You went to feed your precious piece of vermin when you thought we were asleep, didn't you?"

"Yes." It came out as a whisper.

"*Dochenka*, a rabbit is not worth making trouble between you and your stepfather."

A heavy silence stilled the room.

"Is it, Lydia?"

"Of course not, Mama."

"Now," Valentina took a long drag on her cigarette and pointed its glowing tip straight at Lydia, "tell me who has got you looking like someone's lit a fire inside you. Come on, darling, tell your mama."

Lydia could feel her cheeks flush. "I don't know what you . . ."

"Don't be such a ninny, Lydia. You think I can't see? That I haven't got eyes? You and Alfred staring across the table over your tea and toast. You've both got it bad." She shook her head, setting her hair swinging in a girlish way. "The pair of you."

"Got what bad?"

"Love."

400 • KATE FURNIVALL

Lydia almost choked. "Mama, don't be absurd."

Her mother made a funny little grimace. "You think I don't remember what it feels like? Lydia, my sweet child, you have changed."

"How?"

"Your eyes shine and your skin glows and you give secret little smiles when you think no one is looking. Even your walk is different. So who is this fellow? Tell your mama. A boy from your class at school who has taken your fancy?"

"Of course not," Lydia said scornfully.

"Then who?"

"Oh, Mama, just someone I met."

Valentina came over and sat down on the apricot quilt beside her daughter. She took Lydia's face between her hands and looked into her eyes with a dark and solemn expression. "Whoever it is, you can keep it a secret if you must, but listen to me. No messing. You hear me? No messing with him. You have school to finish and university to go to, maybe even Oxford if we can get you to England in time. That's our plan, remember? So . . . ," she shook Lydia's head slowly from side to side, "you obey me this time, girl. No messing, absolutely none."

"Yes, Mama."

"Good. I'm glad we've got that straight."

Lydia tried out a small smile and Valentina laughed. "Don't fret, we'll leave it there for now. But you tell him from me that I'll dig his eyes out with a rusty spoon if he ever hurts my daughter's heart."

"Don't be silly, Mama." But she gave her mother a quick hug. "I missed you," she murmured.

"Oh yes? Like a cat misses a dog!"

Lydia held her mother's hand on her lap. It was the right hand, the one without the diamond ring, the one Lydia preferred.

"And you?" she asked. "Are you happy, Mama? With Alfred, I mean."

Valentina abruptly put on her enthusiastic face. "Oh yes, darling, he is an angel. The sweetest, dearest man who ever lived."

"And he adores you."

"That too."

"I want you to be happy."

"Sweetheart, I am. Really, look at me." She demonstrated with a big wide smile. She looked so lovely it was hard to believe it was anything but real. Only her dark eyes didn't sparkle.

"You'll have all sorts of nice things now. Just like you wanted."

"Just like I wanted," Valentina said. She stabbed out her stub in a glass dish on Lydia's bedside table and lit herself another. "But there's one thing dear Alfred wants me to have that I don't want."

"What's that?"

"A baby."

Lydia's mouth dropped open.

"You look like I feel about it, darling. Don't worry, it won't happen. Oh for heaven's sake, what's the matter? Why are you crying?"

"A baby," Lydia whispered as she wiped her face with the back of her hand. "I'd have a brother. Or a sister." It had never entered her head as a possibility before, but of course her mother was still young enough. "Mama, that would be wonderful. You'd love it." She tried to give her an excited kiss, but Valentina pushed her away.

"What? You're crazy, *dochenka*."

"No, I'm not. It would be perfect. And I'd help you."

"What do you know about babies?"

"Nothing, but I'd learn. Oh please, Mama, say yes. Tell Alfred. Yes. And he'd pay for an *amah* to do all the mucky work, so it wouldn't be too hard on you and I'd sing to him, or to her, the way you used to when . . ."

"Stop. Stop right now, little one." Valentina chafed Lydia's hand between her own and said with an odd little grimace, "I had no idea. That you would react like this. Are you so lonely?"

"No. But it would be . . . special. A brother or sister to love."

"As good as your filthy rabbit, you mean?"

Lydia grinned at her. "Not quite. But nearly."

"God preserve me."

They laughed together and for a moment Lydia thought seriously of telling her the truth about the shed. But with a sudden switch of mood her mother's eyes widened in horror. She jumped to her feet and faced Lydia with hands on hips.

"It's not that Serov boy, is it?"

"What?"

"Sweet Christ, I saw him drive away as we arrived home yesterday. Tell me he's not the one who has got you wagging your tail like a bitch in heat."

"Mama! Don't be . . ."

"Tell me." Valentina seized Lydia's wrist and yanked her to her feet. "Not him. You stay away from him."

"No, of course it's not him." She snatched back her wrist and rubbed it. "I can't stand Alexei Serov."

Valentina narrowed her eyes again and glared at Lydia. "Oh, *dochenka*. God strike your tongue black. How do I know when to believe you? You are such a good liar."

The doorbell rang.

TOO MANY VOICES. THAT'S WHAT ALARMED LYDIA. THIS couldn't be a visit by one of Alfred's friends because they would all expect him to be still on his honeymoon. No, this was something else. Something worse. Silently she moved out onto the landing and peered over the polished banister rail to stare down into the hall. That's when her lungs seemed to collapse inside her. This wasn't just worse. This was as bad as it could get. The narrow space was full of uniforms.

"I'm sorry, Mr. Parker," the English policeman with the pips on his shoulder was saying, "I do understand your objections but I'm afraid we have authority to search your premises." He held out a piece of paper to Alfred.

Alfred took the document but didn't even glance at it.

"This is a damned disgrace," he complained sternly.

Lydia slipped down the stairs. Panic made her fast but it was impossible to sneak past them. Valentina was standing just behind Alfred and grabbed at her daughter's arm.

"Oh, Lydochka, what excitement! A whole pack of them. Like wolves."

There were four English police officers filling up the hall, burly figures with polite manners but hard eyes, and snowflakes melting on their dark-blue shoulders. But it was what was outside that frightened Lydia. Five soldiers. Gray uniforms. The Kuomintang sun on their caps. Chinese troops. Waiting patiently out in the snow with cold, impassive faces.

Voices blurred. She had to get out. Now. Right now.

"Mama, what are they searching for?"

"A Communist, it would seem. A Chinese troublemaker. Some malicious creature has made up a story that's he's in hiding here. In our house, for God's sake. As if we wouldn't notice. Isn't that utterly absurd?" She started to laugh but as she looked at her daughter's expression, it died in her throat. She pulled Lydia to the back of the hall. "No," she breathed. "No."

"Mama," Lydia whispered with an urgent squeeze of her mother's hand, "you must make Alfred keep them here. Longer. I need time." She squeezed again, hard. "Do you understand?"

Valentina's face was as white as the snow on the doorstep, but she stepped closer to her husband again and slipped an arm around his waist. "Angel," she purred, "why don't you invite these smart officers to come into the . . . ," she glanced at the drawing-room door but to Lydia's relief seemed to recollect what the French windows looked out on, ". . . into the dining room for a drink and we can discuss this situation prop—"

"No, my dear." Alfred's mouth was drawn in a straight angry line. "Let them get this intrusion over and done with."

"Thank you, sir," the officer said formally. "We will disturb you as little as possible."

"No, Alfred, darling. I think this is . . . unacceptable."

Something in her voice made him look at her. Even through her panic Lydia was impressed. He saw what was in his wife's eyes, frowned, and touched his spectacles as if about to clean them, but didn't. Instead he cast a quick glance at Lydia, and then did no more than cover the moment with a cough and turn back to the dark uniforms.

"On second thought, I think my wife is right. How dare you come barging into my home for no reason? This needs more discussion."

"Sir, I have already given you the reason. We are cooperating with our Chinese colleagues, as it is out of their jurisdiction here in the International Settlement. There really is nothing further to discuss."

Alfred drew himself up, stiff as a board. "I must dispute that. And I will take it up in my next report for the *Daily Herald*." He waved a hand in Lydia's direction. "Leave us, Lydia." To the officer he said loftily, "I don't want my daughter involved in this . . . fiasco."

Mentally Lydia pulled out every single pin she'd stuck into the A on the sheet of paper last night. Without a word she left the hall.

"THE SOLDIERS. THEY'RE HERE. QUICK."

But he was already moving. He had risen instantly from the blankets but swayed on his feet, fighting for balance. His dark eyes blinked hard.

For one brief second she reached out and kissed him. "That's for strength." She smiled.

"You are my strength," he said, then seized his jacket. He was otherwise fully dressed, even wearing his boots. Prepared for this moment.

She scooped up the satchel that she had packed with his medicines last night and put an arm around his waist. "Let's go."

"No." The fever had dulled his eyes but not his brain. "Cover our tracks." He gestured at the blankets.

Quickly she grabbed them, stuffed them with the hot-water bottle into one of the dusty sacks against the wall, and then piled a heap of dirty straw from the rabbit hutch on top of it. To discourage probing fingers.

"Thank you, *xie xie*, Sun Yat-sen," Chang said solemnly.

Lydia would have laughed, but she'd forgotten how.

THE SNOW SAVED THEM. IT CAME SPINNING DOWN IN BIG floating flakes that blotted out the world. Pavements grew treacherous and sounds were muffled as cars and people faded out of focus into the swirling white world. Out through the garden door with the broken latch. On to the main road. They ran.

How Chang An Lo did it, she'd never know. The cold cut into her face. She was wearing no coat, just a thick wool sweater, but that was the least of her worries. The Kuomintang troops were at the house and once they found it empty, what then? They'd come looking. She kept glancing back over her shoulder but could make out no figures behind, and she held tight to the conviction that if she couldn't see them, they couldn't see her. Or could they? The snow turned the air into dense white sheets that blocked out any vision more than a few yards and it made everyone hurry, heads down, no interest in an odd pair rushing over icy pavement.

She had to think. Make her mind work for both of them.

Where to go?

Their feet pounded the pavement in fast rhythm together. Her heart kept pace. Her arm around his waist held him firmly against her side and she could feel him trying not to put weight on her, but once he stumbled. His damaged hand hit the ground hard but he said nothing, just hauled himself up and back to the running. The more they ran, locked in chaotic flight, the more she loved him. His will was so strong. And there was a calmness at the center of him that controlled the pain and exhaustion. Only the muscle that flickered in his jaw betrayed him.

Think. But it was hard when everything was slipping and sliding inside her.

She ducked down Laburnum Road to their left. Then right and immediately right again, zigzagging to confuse pursuit. Her breath came in quick, sharp gasps. As she drew Chang An Lo across the road, they were almost run down by a bicycle suddenly swooping out of the gloom, skidding in the snow, and it set her pulse pounding faster to realize how near the soldiers could be without her even knowing.

She could think of nowhere safe except the docks. Tan Wah's old hovel, if it was still there. Liev Popkov had destroyed its roof but it was better than nothing, anything was better than nothing. But it was a long way. Chang was weakening, his feet stuttering as if trying to give up on him.

"The quayside," she muttered, her breath flaring out in front of her in the icy air.

He nodded. Snowflakes were caught in his eyelashes.

"Can you make it?"

He nodded again. No waste of breath.

She slowed their pace to a hurried walk. She wasn't going to have him drop dead on her. Headed downhill. All they had to do now was cross the big junction of Prince Street and Fleet Road, then keep going straight down to the docks, but as they approached the crossroads she saw two policemen standing on the corner right in front of her. One was in British uniform; the other she recognized as French. They were huddled in their navy capes, heads close together.

Without breaking stride she steered herself and Chang through the crawling traffic across to the other side of the road, away from the uniforms, and thought she had got away with it. But the British one's head came up. He stared straight at her. At Chang. Said something to his colleague. Both immediately strode in her direction, carving a path through the sheet of white air. She couldn't run. Not with Chang An Lo. Instead she tried to come up with a good reason why a white girl would be stumbling along with a Chinese draped around her shoulders in a snowstorm.

She couldn't.

The police figures were closer, held up by a small burst of traffic, all shrouded in white. Death robes. A native man pushing a wheelbarrow with a child sitting in it swore at the car in front, which had slowed for the junction. It revved its engine ready to accelerate away, and the noise made Lydia glance across at the driver. She could barely see him through the sweep of snow-laden windshield wipers, but she saw enough. Instantly she stepped out onto the road, dragging Chang with her.

She tapped at the sedan's window. "Mr. Theo, it's me."

The window rolled down and Mr. Theo's gray eyes peered at her, narrowed against the cold wind. "Good God, what are you doing out in this?" His gaze shifted to Chang An Lo. "Bloody hell."

The policemen were almost at the car.

"I . . ." Her dry mouth tripped her up. She tried again. "I need a ride."

She saw his eyes notice the two uniformed figures now approaching the rear of the car. Beside her Chang An Lo's breathing came in convulsive gasps.

"Not on the run, are you?"

"No, Mr. Theo," she said quickly. "Of course not."

He knew she was lying. She could see it.

"Get in," he said.

46

Well, this was an interesting turnaround.

Theo was leaning against the doorframe of his guest bedroom and despite the sick headache that was a permanent fixture these days, he was smiling.

Po Chu was going to love him.

On the bed lay the young Chinese. Hell's fire. What a state the fellow was in. Looked terrible. *Don't die. Don't you dare die. I need you alive.*

The Russian girl was sitting beside the bed on a chair that was well over four hundred years old, not that she had eyes to appreciate its beauty right now. She was holding one of his mangled hands in hers and talking to him in a low urgent voice, the words too soft for Theo to hear. But that didn't matter.

Lydia Ivanova, you have brought me a prize indeed.

Theo drove her home. He'd almost had to cart her bodily out of the sickroom, she was so loath to leave, but Theo was having none of it. There was Alfred to face, so she had to go home and sort that out first. Anyway there was something so intense about the way she tended the Chinese young man that Theo was nervous that she was about to leap into bed with him, fever or no fever. What would Alfred say to that?

He left Li Mei bathing the patient's brow with herbs and potions from the hoard in the satchel and promised Lydia she could return when her mother and Alfred said she was allowed to. Not before.

She had almost spat at him with fury but fortunately had more sense and finally succumbed with ill grace. Her eyes watched Li Mei with naked suspicion, but in the end she had accepted that her Chang An Lo was in safe hands. No police.

"I give you my word on it," Theo said. "As an English gentleman. Li Mei will take good care of him while you're gone."

For a moment then, he thought she would bite.

To say Valentina Ivanova Parker was angry was an understatement. Theo was shocked. Never had he heard a woman use such language, and quite obviously neither had Alfred. She poured torrents of Russian and English abuse on her daughter's head. But the girl stood there and took it. She didn't cry and she didn't run. Her hands rubbed the sides of her damp skirt and sometimes her gaze lowered to her wet shoes but most of the time she looked her mother in the eye and said nothing.

By contrast Alfred's displeasure was muted. But he was British. Not like these crazy Russians. Theo attempted to leave but Alfred stopped him.

"Hang on a sec, old chap, if you don't mind. I want to hear the details of what happened, but first I must deal with Lydia."

So Theo waited and while he waited he went over to the cocktail cabinet and poured out three large whiskies. He sipped his own.

"Enough, Valentina. That's enough." Alfred spoke sharply and it got through to her.

She stopped shouting. Glared at both Alfred and Lydia, snapped something more in Russian, and then headed straight for the drink Theo was holding out for her. She knocked it back in one gulp and shuddered.

"I hate whisky," she said and filled the glass with vodka.

Alfred spoke quietly but sternly to his stepdaughter. "Lydia, you have only been a member of my family for a week but already you've brought disgrace on my name."

He paused, in case she had any comment to make, but the girl just scowled at the floor, the way Theo had seen her do a hundred times in class when reprimanded.

"Emotions are running high right now," Alfred continued with remarkable calm, "and we all risk saying things we may later regret, so I want you to go up to your room and stay there for twenty-four hours. To give you time to reflect on what you've done. Your meals will be brought to you. Now go."

"But I can't, I have to . . ."

"No *buts.*"

"Please, he's ill and . . ."

"Lydia, do not make this harder than it already is."

Theo saw the girl glance at her mother, but Valentina had turned her back on her daughter.

"Go," Alfred repeated.

She went. Theo was surprised. He had never found her so biddable himself at school. What special powers did old Alfred possess? Theo drank more of his whisky, though it wasn't yet noon. It was bloody indecent getting caught up in someone else's family palaver, even a good egg like Alfred. Damned bad business. He lit one of his Turkish cigarettes and felt the whisky start to dull the edge of the pains in his body. Christ, how long before they passed this time? Alfred was speaking, but Theo had trouble listening. He was thinking about Chang An Lo. And Po Chu.

"LEAVE IT, TIYO. LET A WORKMAN DO IT."

"No, it helps me."

Theo was sanding down the top of a desk. Two nights ago he had roamed the classrooms in an agony of pain and despair, his whole body shaking with need for the poppy's peace, unable to sleep, unable to think, unable to listen to Li Mei's words of comfort. The only thing that filled his mind was his loathing of Christopher Mason. It swelled in his brain until he thought his head would explode with the pressure of it, so he'd taken a sharp knife from the kitchen and carved on Polly Mason's desk the word *HATE* in letters six inches high.

In the morning he'd regretted it. The school Christmas break would end this weekend with the new term about to start, so he set himself this task of repairing the damage to the desk. The repetitive movement of the sandpaper, over and over along the grain of the wood, soothed him in some strange way. To erase hate. To create smoothness. It satisfied something inside him.

"Have you told Chang An Lo?" he asked Li Mei while his hands continued to move in rhythmic sweeps over the desktop.

"No."

"Will you?"

"No."

The rasping sound of the sandpaper was the only noise in the room. Li Mei perched on one of the other desks, tucked her feet under her, and watched him at work. She was wearing the lilac cheongsam he liked with an amethyst clasp in her black hair, and Theo knew she must be tired from nursing her Chinese patient all night, but still her oval face looked fresh and calm. Even the bruises were fading.

"If I tell him," she said at last, "that I am the sister of Po Chu, he will wish to leave."

"Yes, I can see why he would want to. Would that matter?"

"It would. My brother has wounded him and it is my duty to make amends. If I can."

Theo glanced up at her, his hands still at work. "You've been reading the *Analects* again?"

She smiled. "In the *Lun Yu* Confucius says much that is true."

"Po Chu will be angry if he finds out Chang is here."

"He won't find out." She paused. "Will he, Tiyo?"

Theo said nothing, concentrating on ridding himself and the desk of *HATE*.

"Will he?" Li Mei asked again.

Theo stopped, put down the sandpaper, and brushed the wood dust from his hands. "My love, after the brutal way Po Chu beat you, it pleases me to do anything that will hurt your brother. If Po Chu were to find out that Chang is here, he would come and have the satisfaction of killing him, but if he never learns what happened to the one who escaped from his clutches, it will always gall him. So no, he won't find out from me."

"Thank you, Tiyo."

He returned to the sanding once more.

"Tiyo?"

"Yes?"

"We both know you could use him to bargain. With my father. To make him stop Mason accusing you to Sir Edward."

"Yes. We both know that."

"Will you? Use him?"

"I've thought about it." For a moment he didn't know whether the rasping noise was inside or outside his head. "Which matters more to us, Li Mei? That I go to prison or that this young man dies? What does your Confucius say about that moral dilemma?"

Tears slid down Li Mei's pale cheeks.

HE PLACED A HAND ON CHANG'S FOREHEAD. IT WAS HOT. Instantly the black eyes opened and stared up at Theo with a wary expression.

"I am better," he mumbled thickly.

"I think not," Theo said.

"Lydia?"

"She's fine. But she can't come to see you. Her parents won't let her."

The young man's face tightened. He looked in pain. But Theo had a feeling it wasn't physical. He took pity on him. "Don't worry, she'll be here tomorrow because our school term starts. So I'll make sure you get to speak to her in her morning break."

The black eyes relaxed a little. "*Xie xie.* Thank you."

Theo nodded and started to move away.

"Why do you do this?" Chang asked.

"Do what?"

"Help me."

"Ah, why do you think?"

Chang's gaze was harsh. Theo felt it scour through him. "Because you need help. For yourself," the young man said in a low voice. "You help me and maybe someone will help you. It is about balance."

Theo found the comment unnervingly accurate. It was the same reason he'd taken Yeewai, the cat, from the woman on the junk. You reap what you sow. The gods of all religions seemed to agree on that.

He changed the subject. "Would you like something stronger for the pain?"

Chang shook his head on the pillow.

"Opium perhaps?" Theo offered.

"No."

"Good man."

47

Was he dead?

Or in a police cell?

Did he miss her?

Was he smiling at the lovely Li Mei the way he'd smiled at her?

No answers. Just questions.

If only she hadn't given her word to Alfred Parker in Tuson's Tearoom. She had promised to obey him in exchange for the money, but she'd lied to him before. Stolen from him. Thought nothing of deceiving him. So why did she feel so bound by this absurd promise? Why?

She was lying on her bed exactly where Chang An Lo had lain, her head where his had rested on the pillow, but she hadn't slept. As the night hours crawled by, she had time and again buried her face in the white Egyptian cotton of the sheets and pillowcase and tried to breathe in the essence of him. But it was too faint. Just the smell of herbs. She had risen from her bed as a dull dawn turned the sky from black to silvery gray, the clouds so heavy and low she could almost touch them. But it had stopped snowing. From her window just the sight of the shed sent a spasm of longing through her, and she stared for a long time at the flimsy wooden frame cocooned in white. The spindly claw prints of a bird trailed across the crisp crust of snow around it. Eventually she had retreated to her bed again and wrapped her arms around the pillow.

She could break her word. Creep out of the house before Alfred and Valentina woke. Though not that for one minute did she think her mother was asleep; no, she would be tossing and turning, listening and watching the light grow paler. Lydia was seriously worried about her mother. She'd never seen her so angry, so out of control. It made Lydia's chest hurt to think about it, so she concentrated on Alfred.

She could break her word to him.

She could.

She closed her eyes and tried to do deep breathing the way she'd seen Chang An Lo do when the pain was bad. In through the nose, out long and slow through the mouth. But her thoughts kept getting in the way.

She could break her word. She'd done so before.

No. No.

This was different. This was . . . she sought for the word . . . this was . . . fundamental.

In desperation she rolled onto her side and instead let her mind return like a homing pigeon to the feel of Chang An Lo's body next to hers, inside hers, on top of hers. The taste of his skin on her tongue. The look in his eyes when he said he loved her. He loved her.

But underneath it all she was aware of a deep swirling anger in her stomach. An acid. Burning her. Alexei Serov. He had betrayed her.

"Good morning, Lydia."

She didn't feel like speaking.

"I said good morning, Lydia."

She sighed. "Good morning, Alfred."

"That's better. Here, coffee."

"Thank you." She took the cup from him but placed it on her bedside table. Sitting cross-legged and fully clothed on the bed, she made no effort to stand up or be courteous.

"We need to talk," he said.

"Do we?"

"We all have to be very adult about this situation."

"Tell my mother that."

He looked at her sharply and removed his spectacles, polished them on his clean white handkerchief, and replaced them in a precise manner. He folded the handkerchief back into his pocket.

"Do you mind if I sit down?"

She was surprised he even asked. She nodded at the chair.

"Thank you." He sat down and folded his arms across his chest. Now they were on the same level.

She waited. He took his time.

"Lydia, what you did last week was very wrong and your mother and I are deeply upset about your behavior. You should be ashamed." His brown eyes studied her. "But I don't think you are. I have spoken to Wai and he tells me he hardly saw you all week and that you were always in the shed or in your room." He glanced around him as if he might yet find Chang behind the door. "Clearly you were with your Chinese friend. Is that correct?"

She nodded.

"And your friend is a fugitive Communist?"

She was more wary now.

"I do not intend to ask about the degree of . . . intimacy between you," a red flush of embarrassment made him pause, ". . . but I trust you sufficiently to know that you . . . well . . . that you would not do anything unwise. Immoral or unchristian," he added with sudden intensity.

"Alfred, he was ill. I nursed him. Is that unchristian?"

"Of course not, my dear. It is to be commended. The Good Samaritan, eh?"

"The Good Russian."

It made him smile. "Exactly."

He was showing signs of beginning to relax. Only a little, but it was something. She picked up the coffee.

"Mmm, it's good," she said. "Thank you."

He leaned back in the chair and unfolded his arms. "What we have to discuss is where we go from here. I don't want to cause any of us unnecessary grief."

She controlled her relief, keeping it from her eyes and her face. He was coming around.

"So I feel I must remind you of the promise you gave me in the teashop. Our bargain."

Her relief ebbed away. She brushed a hand across her face to hide her disappointment. "So what orders are you giving me?"

"Lydia, I don't like that tone of voice. I do not consider the word *orders* to be appropriate, but I am saying that you must not see this Chinese Communist again. It is too dangerous for you."

"No. Please."

"I insist."

Lydia could feel her face slowly fall apart. She hid it in her hands.

There was a long silence in the room. Then he was on the bed beside her. "There, there, my dear. It's for the best. Don't cry." He patted her shoulder.

She wasn't crying. Just dying.

"Alfred," she said through her fingers, "how would you feel if I said you must never see my mother again?"

"That's different."

"It's not."

"Oh Lydia, my dear girl. You are too young to be going through such despair."

"Please, Alfred. Let me see him."

He stroked her head, and she knew by the touch of his hand he was going to say no. She sat up and suddenly smiled at him.

"Mama told me you want a baby."

He blushed fiercely and looked away, at the snow on the sill outside where a sparrow was fluttering, its feathers ruffled against the cold.

"I think it's wonderful, Alfred."

"Really?"

"Yes, I do."

"Excellent."

He was delighted. She could see it in his eyes, and it touched her that he should care what she thought.

"So how about another bargain?"

"Pardon?"

"A bargain again. I'll do everything I can to persuade Mama to come around to the idea of having a baby, if you . . ."

"No."

"Let me say it. If you let me visit Chang An Lo while he's at Mr. Theo's house."

"Look, Lydia, I . . ."

"Mr. Theo can always be in the room. We'd never be alone, I promise. Please. I need to see that he's getting better and is still safe."

"I'm not happy about it." He frowned at her, but his eyes were softer.

"It matters to me so much," she said quietly.

He took a deep breath. Teetered on the edge.

"A baby would be lovely," she urged.

His mouth widened into a smile, despite himself. "You are a very persuasive young lady, you know."

"So I can see him?"

"Oh, very well, Lydia. You can see him. No, don't look so elated. I will permit you only one visit and not until tomorrow when you are at school. To say good-bye."

Lydia said nothing.

"I will speak to Willoughby and arrange it," Alfred continued. "Now, let that be an end to the matter."

Lydia reached out and gently touched his hand on the eiderdown. "Two visits, Alfred. Please let it be two visits?"

He surprised her by laughing. "You are a strong-minded miss, aren't you? Very well. Two visits. Under Willoughby's strict supervision."

"Thank you."

He kissed the side of her head, less awkward than before. "Right." He stood up.

"And you'll speak to Mama? Make her say yes to my visits?"

"Yes, of course."

"And I'll get her to agree to the baby. If you bought her a piano it would help."

For a moment their eyes met, and both knew a bond had been formed. Alfred nodded to her, not quite certain what to say.

"Alfred," Lydia said, "for someone who has never been a father, you are very good at it."

He blushed again and rubbed his chin self-consciously, but he was smiling as he left.

"MAMA."

No answer.

Valentina was holding a newspaper up in front of her face, but Lydia doubted that she was reading. It was her way of finding privacy. At intervals her foot in its velvet slipper would tap impatiently. Supper had been a stiff and stilted affair, but in the drawing room afterward Alfred had asked, "Lydia, do you play chess?"

"Yes."

"Would you like a game?"

"Yes."

"Good show."

He'd brought out a superb set of ancient ivory figures and proceeded to outmaneuver her with ease, but she learned from it. About the game. About him. And about herself. His patience was impressive but his mental discipline was too rigid, whereas she was impetuous. It was both her strength and her weakness. She needed to slow down.

"Thank you," she said when her king lay flat on the board.

"You've the making of a good player, my dear, if only you would . . ."

"Think more before I move. I know."

"Exactly." He smiled at her, his brown eyes warm behind his gold spectacles. "Exactly." He left the room to put away the box of chess pieces.

"Mama."

Slowly Valentina lowered the newspaper and looked coolly at her daughter.

"Did Liev Popkov know your family in Russia?"

Valentina's expression did not change, but Lydia could tell she was not pleased.

"He worked for my father. A long time ago," Valentina said shortly and raised the paper again. Subject closed.

48

CHANG AN LO OPENED HIS EYES AND SAW HER FACE. FOR A second he was sure it was another of the dreams of her that the gods granted him in his sleep, but he could feel her hand firm on his wrist and the tickle of her hair brushing the skin of his cheek as she bent over him.

"You are real," he whispered.

She smiled, that wide wonderful smile that stole his heart from his chest, and instantly he knew this was no dream. She bent closer and kissed his mouth, her lips soft and inviting.

"That's to prove I'm real," she murmured.

He held her close for a moment, felt her cool cheek against his hot face, breathed in the fresh outdoor smell of her hair and her skin, heard her blood pounding in his ears. So alive. So full of flames. To lose her would be like drowning in mud.

"How are you feeling?"

"Better."

"You look feverish."

"Inside I am better." He reached out and touched the fires in her hair. "The sight of you drives away the fever."

She laughed and laid her head lightly on his chest. She kept it there. His fingers stroked the silky, unruly hair that any Chinese girl would have oiled and fixed flat with clasps or bound into tight knots. He loved the freedom of her hair.

"Lydia," he said softly.

She lifted her head. "We don't have long," she murmured and glanced over her shoulder at the door.

It was open and the tall elegant figure of the schoolmaster in his black academic gown was leaning against it, but he was standing with his back to them, one of his foul-smelling cigarettes in his hand, a student's exercise book in the other. He made a point of reading it intently to indicate his ears were closed. Nonetheless they spoke in low voices.

"Your parents?"

"They have forbidden me to see you more than twice while you are here. But I didn't mention what might happen when you leave." Her amber eyes were full of light. "I have a suggestion." Suddenly she was shy. But excited.

A little of her bright light lifted the edge of the darkness inside him. He knew there could be no suggestions. He touched her eyebrow and her ear.

"What is it that puts a strong heartbeat into your words?"

She leaned closer, eyes fixed on his. "We could leave together."

"You are taunting me." But hope leaped unbidden into his throat and breathed life into his limbs.

"No, no, I mean it." She spoke in a whisper. "I've worked it all out. You said you must leave Junchow. I will leave with you. I have some money still and maybe I can get hold of more. It would be enough to hire a boat to row us across the river in the dark and then we could . . ."

"No."

"Yes, we'd be safe if we traveled by night and slept by day. It would take time, I know, but we could go far away from here to a remote village somewhere and I would wear a Chinese tunic and wide hat like at the funeral, so no one would notice and I'd learn Mandarin and . . ."

"No."

"Listen to me, my sweet love, it is our only answer. I've thought it through. You can't stay here, so there's no other way."

"Lydia. Don't, Lydia."

"I'm not foolish. It wouldn't be forever. I know that when you're better and strong again, you'll want to return to one of the Communist camps and continue to fight against Chiang Kai-shek. Of course I know that. But," he watched a soft pink flutter to her cheek like the shimmer of a flamingo's wing, "I will come too. I know women train and fight in Mao Tse-tung's army, so there's no reason why I can't become a Communist freedom fighter. Is there?"

AFTER SCHOOL THERE WAS A LOT TO DO. FIRST, THE DRESS. Lydia hurried right across town to Madame Camellia's salon.

"Thank you, Madame Camellia, it looks like new again."

The dressmaker bowed, a graceful dip of her groomed head. "You are welcome. Try not to let it get wet again."

"Please put the cost on my stepfather's account."

"Certainly, Miss Parker."

Miss Parker? *Miss Parker?* Lydia laughed and shook her head as she shot off toward the Masons' house on Walnut Road. Polly hadn't turned up for school today, so Lydia wanted to make sure her friend wasn't sick. The awkwardness between them last time over Chang An Lo still rankled and made it even more important to check that she wasn't just hiding at home because she couldn't bear to face Lydia. That would be awful. It was a long way to Walnut Road but at least it was a crisp bright afternoon. The sky was a rich clear blue that made the world feel bigger and though the wind was cold, the sun gave Junchow a glow that turned Lydia's usual disgust with the town to an amiable affection. Maybe it was the thought of leaving it.

As a Communist supporter. Lydia Ivanova, freedom fighter. She tried it on her tongue out loud and liked it. She even let her mind hold for just a brief second the sound of *Lydia Chang*, or *Chang Lydia,* as they would say in China. She let it reverberate around her thought waves, but that was a step too far into the unknown. She wasn't ready for that yet. Chang An Lo had said no. Of course he did. She knew he would. He was worried about her safety. But she'd seen the expression on his face. His mouth held tight in case it let out words that would betray him. The huge pupils dilated in astonishment. She saw something deep within him burst, and when she held his body tight in her arms she could feel the rapid beating of his heart.

He said no. But he meant yes.

★   ★   ★

SHE TOOK A SHORTCUT THROUGH ONE OF THE POORER DIS-
tricts of the International Settlement, down a snowy pathway behind St. Saviour's Church and across a small park. It was more a
patch of scrubland than a park, with a few creaky swings for children and too many overgrown bushes. It was as she was following
the footpath that she saw the car. Parked under a low bank of trees
that ran along the far side, away from the grimy terrace of nearby
houses. Lydia recognized it immediately. A big flashy Buick. It was
Polly's father's car. A cream and black sedan with wide running
boards, which in the late afternoon sun glinted above the dirty gray
snow in the gutters.

What it was doing here, she couldn't imagine, but if Mason was
going home he might as well give her a lift and at the same time he
could tell her what was up with Polly. She walked toward it. It was
parked facing away from her, so she was looking at the large spare
wheel on the back and the high rear window. The car looked empty.
But as she peered through the window she saw movement inside. She
edged around the side. To a clear view. A view she didn't want to see.
Christopher Mason in his shirtsleeves. He was stretched out on his
stomach on the front seat, the back of his slick brown head bobbing
and weaving, his hands moving over something under him.

It was Valentina.

Lydia turned and ran.

"HELLO, LYD." POLLY DID NOT LOOK ILL. NOR DID SHE LOOK
pleased to see Lydia on her doorstep.

"You weren't at school today."

"No. I was sick."

"Oh, I'm sorry."

"Something I ate."

"Right."

There was an uneasy pause. Lydia began to worry that Polly
wasn't going to invite her in.

"I've brought you the new term's timetable to copy out. And
some sketch maps we did today in geography." Lydia opened her
schoolbag and started to rummage in it.

"Oh . . . thanks." Polly stepped back, her wide eyes flicking away from Lydia. "Come on in. Do you want some hot chocolate? Mummy's out at her bridge club, but she's made a ginger cake if you'd like some."

"Yes, please."

Polly led the way into the kitchen. Most kitchens were dreary, meant only for servants, but because Anthea Mason so enjoyed whipping up soufflés or baking cakes and fresh rolls, the Masons' kitchen was modern and bright. Linoleum on the floor, tiles on the walls and a marbled enamel stove that was so much smarter than the usual black range. In the scullery behind it, Lydia could hear two servants working and talking in soft Chinese voices. Polly concentrated on heating the milk and scooping out cocoa into cups instead of talking.

Lydia filled up the silence with chatter about the first day back at school and how James Malkin had arrived with his leg in plaster after falling off his garage roof while retrieving a kite. Polly obliged with a smile. When they were both sipping their hot drinks Lydia felt the blood return to her chilled fingers, but her mind was still numb with shock.

Valentina. In the Buick.

Why?

But Polly was still avoiding her. Staring at the froth on her cocoa and blowing lightly to cool it.

"Polly, he's gone," Lydia said.

Her friend's worried gaze at last met hers. "Who?"

"You know who. Chang An Lo."

"Gone where?"

"I don't know."

"Did soldiers take him?"

"No. He escaped. So you don't have to worry anymore about . . . well, you know . . . what you saw."

Polly released a huge sigh of relief. "I'm glad."

"So am I."

They smiled quietly at each other, and then Lydia put down her cup on the table, went over and hugged Polly. All the stiffness immediately left Polly's slight frame and she squeezed Lydia tight. They laughed, the awkwardness sliding away, and took their hot drinks into the drawing room.

"Wait here, Lyd, while I just run up to my room with the maps and copy them out. I won't be long. Eat up the cake."

The moment she was gone Lydia abandoned the drawing room, tip-toed across the hall's parquet, and tried the door of Christopher Mason's study. It opened. In a weird sort of way, that disappointed her. If you leave doors unlocked, you can't have anything to hide, can you? She slipped in and shut the door behind her. The room was gloomy. The shutters were half closed and the tall bookcases along the wall looked . . . threatening. As if she were shut in. Trapped. A shudder rippled up her spine and she shook her head to clear it of foolish notions.

The desk. That's where she had to start. She nipped behind it and found Mason's leather-bound diary for 1929 placed neatly in the middle of the desk. She skimmed through the opening days of January and it was there, in bold black writing. Monday. Three-thirty. *VP.* Not *VI* anymore. *Valentina Parker.* Lydia wanted to hurl the wretched diary through the window.

Quickly she went through his desk drawers. Nothing of interest. Except a gun. In the top right-hand drawer under a fluffy butter-yellow dustcloth, it lay like a warning. Lydia picked it up. It was an army type, a revolver, heavier than she expected and smelling of oil. She squinted along the sights and aimed it at the door, switched the safety off and on again but didn't risk pulling the trigger, and then she replaced it. She rummaged some more. Just household accounts, stationery, two gold fountain pens that three months ago she might have taken, a few letters from England. Not helpful, just chat about someone called Jennifer and someone else called Gaylord. A jade paperweight. A box of cigars. Nail clippers. And in the bottom one, a photograph of his cat, Achilles. Disappointing.

A sudden noise. Lydia froze. Listened. A servant's footsteps crossing the hall. She breathed again, pushed the drawer shut, and looked elsewhere. An oak tallboy stood in one corner. Big brass handles. The first three drawers contained bottles of what smelled like chemicals of some sort, a sheaf of photographic paper, a cardboard box packed with reels and reels of negatives on top of which lay a silver hip flask. It dawned on her that Mason must be a keen photographer who developed his own work. It fitted with when she caught him in the library that time. He'd been looking at a book on photography then.

It was the bottom drawer that gave her a kick of hope. It was locked. Something to hide.

This was it. She took a moment to look coolly round the room. No keys in the desk. If she owned this room she would hide a key . . . where? The bookcase. Had to be. She listened intently for Polly's footsteps on the stairs. No sound. Quickly she ran her fingers over the books and the shelves. Any one of the volumes could be hollowed out to secrete a key. No hope of finding it if that's what he'd done. None. Instead she dragged over Mason's big leather desk chair, climbed on it and stretched up above her head to feel on the very top of the bookcase itself. Nothing. A smattering of dust. A dead spider. She shifted the chair further along, searched again. This time her fingers touched metal.

"Lydia?"

Polly's voice. Still upstairs. Lydia rocketed off the chair and opened the door a crack.

"Yes?" she called.

"Nearly finished."

"Don't rush."

"I won't be long."

Lydia shut the door again, leaped back onto the chair, and retrieved the piece of metal. A key. It lay on her palm. Her mouth was dry. She wasn't sure she wanted to know what was in that drawer. Already her head was filling up with suspicions. She took a long breath, as Chang An Lo had shown her, exhaled slowly, and then strode over to the tallboy and crouched in front of the bottom drawer. The key turned easily and the drawer slid open as if well used.

It was full of photographs. Tidy bundles of them in elastic bands. She rifled through them. Every one was of a naked woman. Lydia felt she should be embarrassed, but she didn't have time for that. She snatched up each pile in turn and inspected it quickly. The sight of a Negro girl mounted by a black greyhound made her shudder but she didn't stop, peering closely at the faces of the women. Most were hard and painted. Prostitutes, she assumed. She'd seen faces like that in the streets and hanging around the bars at the quayside. It was in the fifth bundle that she found it. A sultry picture of a slender white woman lying naked on a bearskin rug, one arm thrown in abandonment above her head, her hand twined in her thick long hair, showing off her breasts. The nipples were painted a dark color. Her legs were eased apart, one finger trailing in her dense pubic bush, a glimpse of something pale and glistening inside. The woman's full lips were smiling but the dark eyes looked dead.

Valentina.

A sob shook Lydia. A rush of anger that almost choked her and an avalanche of shame. Her teeth clenched together and she felt her cheeks on fire. She went through the rest. Four more of Valentina. Twenty of Anthea Mason. Two of Polly.

Lydia wanted to scream.

She pushed them into her schoolbag.

"Finished." Polly's voice. At the top of the stairs.

In a final rush Lydia scooped out the books from her schoolbag and dumped all the reels of negative film in their place. She threw the key into the bottom drawer, kicked it shut, and with her books under one arm and the bag under the other, she left the room.

"You don't mind, do you, darling?"

"No, of course not. I've got homework to do."

Lydia kept looking at her mother, her eyes following every flick of her finger—*that finger*—as she skimmed through the latest *Paris World* magazine and each toss of her hair as she lit another cigarette. Why? Over and over it squirmed in her head. Why did Valentina do it? Damn it, damn it, damn it. Why?

Her mother turned to Alfred. "We won't be back late, will we, angel?"

He exchanged a quick glance with Lydia. He had driven her to school that morning on his way to work, and she had mentioned that Valentina seemed a bit tense since the business with Chang An Lo and the soldiers. Maybe it would be a good idea to take her out this evening? A meal at the club? Dancing at the Flamingo? Alfred had jumped at it.

"Well, I'm not sure what time it'll be," he said with a look of open admiration at his wife. She looked stunning. An elegant new black and white evening gown that was cut low to reveal the full swell of her breasts. Lydia couldn't look at them. Not now. Not after what she'd seen.

Alfred handed his wife her mink muff and helped her on with her coat.

"Have a good time," Lydia said cheerfully.

The moment she heard the car swing out of the drive, she raced upstairs and pulled out the green dress.

"LITTLE SPARROW, *MOI VOROBUSHEK*, I THINK YOU'D FORget an old lady."

"No, *nyet*, I'm here. I even have an official invitation." Lydia waved the thick embossed card.

"So grand." Mrs. Zarya chuckled with delight, her broad bosom swaying dangerously close. She tucked her arm through Lydia's. "And quite lovely you look. So grown up now in your pretty green dress."

"Grown up enough to dance?"

Mrs. Zarya fluttered her own wide taffeta skirts in a strangely coquettish gesture. "Maybe, *vozmozhno*. You must wait to be asked."

THE SEROV VILLA AT THE FAR END OF RUE LAMARQUE IN THE French Quarter was even grander than Lydia had expected, with pillars and porticoes and a long sweeping driveway that was packed with cars and chauffeurs. The reception rooms were lit by ranks of crystal chandeliers and crowded with hundreds of guests in elegant evening dress. All around her swirled the lilting sound of Russian: *Dobriy vecher, Good evening. Kak vi pozhivayete, How are you? Kak torgovlia, How is business?*

She remembered to say *"Ochyen priatno," Pleased to meet you,* when introduced by Mrs. Zarya, but she did not listen to their names. She was here to seek out only one person. And he was not to be seen. Not yet. At first she stayed at Mrs. Zarya's side, reassured in this sparkling new world by the familiar smells of mothballs that wafted from her overheated figure. Old gentlemen with side whiskers and Tsar Nicholas's beard came to flirt with Mrs. Zarya and kiss Lydia's hand, while women in long white gloves toured the rooms, displaying their glittering jewelry and Russian temperaments. Lydia lost count of the number of diamond tiaras that glided past.

She wondered what Chang An Lo would make of all this. How many guns just one of those diamonds would buy. Or what number of empty bellies that fat woman's huge gold earrings would fill. Such

428 · KATE FURNIVALL

thoughts caught her by surprise. They were Chang An Lo's thoughts. Inside *her* head. That pleased her. That she could look around at all this wealth and see it not as desirable, but as a means of putting right an unbalanced society, was something totally new for her. Balance. That's what Chang said was needed. But she watched a man with the stomach of a well-fed pig and gold chunks on his pudgy fingers take a glass of champagne from a silver salver without even glancing at the Chinese servant holding it. The servant was gaunt-faced with submissive eyes. Where exactly was the balance in that?

A shiver of shock rippled through Lydia. It was not only new thoughts she possessed, but new eyes. It seemed she really was becoming a Communist.

"Lydia Ivanova, I'm delighted you could come." It was Countess Serova, regal as ever in her cream satin gown with high neck and full skirt, encrusted with pearls. "And tonight you are in a different frock, I see. I was beginning to think you only possessed one. How charming green looks on you."

Lydia found the mixture of insult and praise disconcerting. "Thank you for inviting me, Countess." This time she didn't bob a curtsy. Why should she? "Is your son here tonight?"

Countess Serova's cool blue eyes took the measure of Lydia, and without replying she turned her gaze on Mrs. Zarya. "Olga Petrovna Zarya, *kak molodo vi viglyaditye,* how young you look tonight."

Mrs. Zarya preened herself delightedly and dropped a curtsy, but Lydia did not hear her response because a young woman in black who was standing behind the countess, clearly an attendant of some kind, leaned close to Lydia and murmured in Russian, "He is in the ballroom."

Lydia excused herself and followed the sound of music.

THE WOMAN SHIMMERED. IN AN OFF-THE-SHOULDER SEQUINED gown she was seated at a grand piano at one end of the ballroom, her fingernails vivid red against the ivory keys. She was playing a modern piece Lydia recognized. Something by Shostakovich, something decadent. The pianist swung her silky blond waves in time to the rhythm. It annoyed Lydia instantly, that overdramatic way of performing. But why hadn't the countess invited Valentina to play? She turned away because whenever she thought of Valentina, the photographs in the drawer leaped into her head and made her feel sick. Instead she looked around her.

The room was beautiful. The high ceiling was painted with muscular heroes and nebulous goddesses who looked down on the pale polished-beech floor. Huge gilt-framed family portraits of people with long noses and arrogant eyes were designed to overpower guests of fragile nerve. Gleaming mirrors reflected thousands of pinpricks of light from chandeliers and threw them back into the room to highlight the dancers as they flowed with bright smiles from one end to the other. But Lydia's eyes were soon elsewhere, on a cluster of men in deep discussion in front of one of the long velvet drapes. One tall angular back in immaculately styled evening wear and with a head of cropped brown hair set Lydia's hackles rising.

She made directly for it.

"Alexei Serov," she said coldly. "I'd like a word." She touched the black ridge of his shoulder.

Instantly he turned, and the broad smile that greeted her only infuriated her further. She felt an urge to slap it off his face.

"Good evening, Miss Ivanova, how delightful that you are able to join us tonight." He snapped his fingers at a servant in maroon livery, standing to attention against the wall. "A drink for my guest."

"No drink, thank you. I won't be staying."

A frown crossed his long face at the coolness of her tone. His gaze studied her face, his eyes so intent on hers that she could see tiny golden flecks buried in the green irises.

"Is something wrong?" He ran a hand over the thick bristles of his hair and down the back of his head. It was the first time she had ever seen him betray the slightest sign of unease.

"I would like a word. In private, please."

His head drew back and he stared down his straight nose at her, half a smile curving his mouth. She did not care for the way he narrowed his eyes, his dark eyelashes used as a barrier between them. Another man with something to hide.

"Certainly, Miss Ivanova."

He placed a firm hand under her elbow and steered her effortlessly through the dancers to what looked like a mirror with carved gilded vine leaves around it but which turned out to be a door. More sleight of hand. They entered a small windowless room that contained nothing but a pale green chaise longue and a forest of stuffed animal heads on the walls. A wild boar with twelve-inch tusks glared at Lydia. She looked away and shook her elbow free of the grip on it.

"Alexei Serov, you are a lying bastard."

His composure was rattled, but he hid it well. His hand slowly stroked his jaw, revealing cuff links of gold scarab beetles. "You insult me, Miss Ivanova."

"No, it is you who insult me if you think I won't realize who it was who sent Kuomintang troops to my house."

"Troops?"

"Yes. And we both know why."

"I'm sorry, I don't understand what you . . ."

"Don't. Don't waste your breath denying it. Your poisonous lies crawl out of the gutter and only insult me further. Because of you I could be in prison now. Do you realize that? And my . . . my friend . . . could be dead. So I have come here tonight to tell you . . ." She could hear her voice sliding out of control, losing the iciness she'd planned. ". . . to tell you that your plot failed and that I think you are the lowest of the low. A filthy whore-boy to Chiang Kai-shek and his gray devils. Pretending to be a friend to me, yet . . ."

"Stop, Lydia."

"No, I will not stop, you bastard. You betrayed me."

He seized hold of her arms and shook her. "Stop this."

His face came close to hers. They glared at each other. She could hear the click of air at the back of his throat as he swallowed his anger.

"Release me," she snapped.

He removed his hands.

"Good-bye," she said, putting all the ice she could summon into the single word. She walked stiffly to the door.

"Lydia Ivanova, in heaven's name, what demon is inside you now? How dare you march in here with accusations and then refuse to hear my response? Who do you think you are?"

Lydia stopped, one hand on the heavy brass doorknob, but she didn't turn around. She couldn't bear even to look at the deceitful bastard. There was a moment's silence while the dead creatures in the room watched through glass eyes. She could hear her own heart thumping.

"Now listen to what I have to say." His voice was astonishingly calm. "I know nothing about troops at your house."

"To hell with your lies."

"I did *not* betray you. Or your wounded Chinese Communist. I told no one what I saw at your house, you have my word on that."

"The word of a liar is not worth spit."

His angry intake of breath satisfied her.

"I am speaking the truth," he said sharply, and she knew that if she'd been a man he'd have struck her.

"Why should I believe you?"

"Why shouldn't you?"

She swung around. "Because there was nobody but you to send the troops for Chang An Lo. You. Only you knew."

"That's plainly absurd. What about your cook?"

"Wai?"

"You think he didn't know? Miss Ivanova, you have a lot to learn about servants if you think they don't know everything that goes on in a house."

Lydia swallowed. "Wai?"

Alexei Serov was back in control. The stiffness seeped out of his body and his gesture was languorous as he waved a hand in the direction of wherever his own household servants camped. "They have eyes that see behind closed doors and ears that hear the thoughts in your head."

"But why would Wai . . . ?"

"For Chinese dollars, of course. He would be well paid for the information."

"Oh hell."

She felt her shoulders droop and her spine cave in. She sought refuge in staring at the feathery ears of a lynx's head. They were pricked, alert, ready to listen to her excuses.

"Bloody hell," she muttered.

"I swear I didn't betray him. Or you," Alexei Serov said quietly.

She made herself look him in the eye. This was hard. Angry came easy. Apologetic was much tougher.

"I'm sorry."

She wanted to get out the door. Out into the cold air before she melted into an ugly pool of shame on the smart marble flooring. Her tongue felt too big for her mouth. The words could barely squeeze past it.

"I apologize, Alexei Serov."

He didn't smile. Through his half-closed eyes she could not make out what he was thinking and anyway she wasn't sure she wanted to know.

"I accept your apology, Miss Ivanova." He gave a small formal bow. The little click of his heels scared her. It was the sort of noise you might expect from an executioner before he slices your head off. He held out an arm to her. "May I accompany you back to the party? This conversation is over."

She hesitated.

"And as a gesture of our renewed friendship, I hope you will do me the honor of the next dance." He smiled then, slow and teasing, as if he knew what it would cost her.

"Last time you said I was too young to dance with," she objected. There was only one person now in whose arms she wanted to float.

"That was six months ago. Then you were still a child. Now you look every inch a beautiful young woman." He raised one eyebrow. "Even if you don't exactly act like one."

She laughed, she couldn't help it.

"Oh God, Alexei, I'm sorry my mouth ran away with me. I can be quite respectable when I try, but somehow you always catch me at my worst."

" 'Filthy whore-boy to Chiang Kai-shek.' That was impressive."

She took his arm. "Let's dance." The quicker she got it over and done with, the better.

49

THEO SAT WITH THE CAT HEAVY ON HIS FEET. IT WAS COLD. Three o'clock in the morning. He could hear the wind shaking the windows and howling to come in, and it reminded him of the wind on the river at night and how it drove the scows as they nipped from junk to junk with their haul. He was reading in his study, trying to glean strength of purpose from the words of Buddha.

> *If you want to know your future,*
> *then look at yourself in the present,*
> *for that is the cause of the future.*

He absorbed that one.

His future would be decided on Wednesday.

Because on that day Christopher Mason had an appointment to tittle-tattle to Sir Edward with the story of Theo's involvement in opium trafficking. So he had twenty-four hours to decide.

> *Empty your boat, seeker,*
> *and you will travel more swiftly.*
> *Lighten the load of craving and opinions*
> *and you will reach nirvana sooner.*

Theo thought that was what he longed for, to travel light, but he was coming to the conclusion that he didn't know himself very well. The young Chinese man in the bed upstairs knew him. Knew his weakness. He could see it in his eyes. Chang An Lo was ready for what might come. Had already lightened his load. Prison was one path that might lie ahead for both of them, but could Theo really face the hell of a stinking cell, cooped up like a bird in a bamboo cage?

> *If you want to get rid of your enemy,*
> *the true way is to realize that your enemy is delusion.*

But neither Feng Tu Hong nor Christopher Mason felt much like delusion to Theo. The truth was that Feng could stop Mason. But Feng would want the young man in exchange, despite his disputes with Po Chu. Or maybe because of them.

And then? If Theo made the deal? What would Li Mei think of him?

What would he think of himself?

He leaned down and stroked the cat's head. It purred for a second before it remembered to sink its yellow teeth into him.

50

Lydia heard the click of her bedroom door. Quiet footsteps padded across the floor. She opened her eyes a slit but could see nothing in the darkness. She didn't need to see.

"What is it, Mama?"

"I can't sleep, darling."

"Go and disturb Alfred."

"He needs his sleep."

"So do I."

"Poof, you can sleep in class tomorrow."

"Mama!"

"Hush, I shall tell you about the Flamingo nightclub. One lucky woman was wearing a Fabergé brooch but her frock was quite frightful. Move over."

Lydia shifted position in the bed and Valentina lay down on it, under the eiderdown but on top of the blankets, just the way Lydia had done at first with Chang An Lo.

"Did you have a good time tonight?"

"It was bearable. That's about all."

"Did you dance?"

"Of course I did. It was the best part. When you're old enough I'll take you to a dance and you'll discover what fun it is. The band played the new jazz with . . ."

But Lydia didn't listen. She leaned her cheek against her mother's shoulder, let her musky perfume filter into her head. She wondered if Chang An Lo was awake. What was he thinking? She was frightened he'd leave. Just up and go. Without her. But they both knew that in the state he was in, he'd be caught. That he needed her. As she needed him. It was going to be hard. Of course it was. She wasn't blind to that fact or to the uncertainty of the future for them, but to be to-gether even for a few months while he healed would give them time. Breathing space. While they worked out the next step.

"So?"

Dimly Lydia became aware that Valentina had stopped speaking.

"So?"

"So what, Mama?"

"I said, so who is this Chinese Bolshevik of yours?"

"His name is Chang An Lo and he's a Communist. But," she added quickly, "he comes from a wealthy family under the last em-peror and is well educated. A bit like yourself in a way . . ."

"I am *not* a Communist and never will be." She spat out the words. "The Communists take a country that is great and noble and they smash it down with their hammers and sickles to the lowest level of a peasant. Look at my poor broken Russia, *Rus-matushka.*"

"Mama," Lydia spoke gently, "the Communists have only just started. Give them time. First they have to rid us of tyranny. Of the brutality that's existed for hundreds of years. That's what they're doing right now in Russia. And that's what China needs too. They are the only ones who will build a fair society where everyone has a voice. You wait, they will become the greatest countries in the world."

"Ah, you're crazy, darling. That Bolshevik boy has poisoned your mind and filled it with gutter slime, so that you don't see straight anymore."

"No, you're so wrong. I see clearer now."

"Poof! It is a two-minute infatuation."

"No, Mama, no. I love him."

Valentina drew in a quick breath. "Don't be absurd. You are too young to know what love is."

"You were only seventeen when you ran off and married Papa. You loved him, you know you did. So don't you dare tell me I don't love Chang An Lo."

There was a silence. The darkness grew heavy around them, press-ing down on Lydia's eyes, but she refused to let it into her head. She reached out to Chang An Lo with her mind and found him so easily, it was hard to believe he wasn't in the room with her. The connection was instant. And she was certain he was lying awake in Mr. Theo's house, seeking her out. She smiled and felt the inside of her head open up into a big bright airy room, full of sunlight, and the sound of Lizard Creek's water trickled through it. A place where she could breathe.

"Listen to me, Mama."

It was easy. At last to talk about him. She told her mother all about Chang An Lo. How he'd saved her in the alleyway and how she'd sewn up his foot at Lizard Creek. She told Valentina everything, the Chinese funeral and the search for him, even the quarrel in the burned-out house and the arguments over some of the savage methods the Communists used to achieve their aims. It all came spilling out. Everything. Well, almost everything. Two things she left out. The ruby necklace and the lovemaking. She managed to hang on to those. She wasn't *that* stupid.

When she'd finished, she felt as if she were floating.

"Oh my sweet daughter." Valentina turned and kissed Lydia's cheek. "You are such a fool."

"I love him, Mama. And he loves me."

"It's got to stop, *dochenka*."

"No."

"Yes."

"No."

Valentina's hand took hold of Lydia's under the eiderdown and held it as if in a vise. "I'm sorry, darling, your heart will break but there are worse things. You will survive it, believe me, you will. We have come this far, you and I. I am not letting you throw it all away just when I have set it up so that there is money for your education, for university. You could be a doctor or a lawyer or a professor, something great, something important. Something well paid. You'll be proud of yourself and hold your head high. Never will you have to be dependent on a man to put bread on your table or rings on your fingers. Don't ruin everything. Not now."

"Mama, did you listen when your parents told you the same?"

"No, but . . ."

"So neither will I."

"Lydia." Valentina sat up abruptly. "You will do as I say. And I say this business with the Chinese Bolshevik is over, even if I have to chain you to the bed and feed you bread and water for the rest of your life. You hear me?"

Lydia didn't mean to say what she said next. But she was angry and hurt. So she struck back.

"Maybe if I tell Alfred what I saw in the Buick today he would say the same to you."

She heard Valentina cough. The sound she'd heard a chicken make when its neck is rung. She wanted to cram the words back into her mouth. Valentina swung her legs to the floor but remained there, seated on the edge of the bed. Her back to Lydia. She said nothing.

"Why, Mama? Why? You have Alfred."

Her mother rustled in her dressing gown pocket and Lydia knew she was searching for a cigarette, but it was obviously empty because there was no snick of a lighter.

"It's none of your business," Valentina said at last in a tight voice.

Lydia rolled nearer and put out a hand. Her mother's stiff figure was blacker than the surrounding blackness. She touched her mother's shoulder and for a second had a flashback to reaching out and touching a male shoulder earlier this evening. Alexei Serov's. He had seen her home and she'd had to admit he'd been quite decent about her mistake. Sweet Christ, she'd made such a fool of herself. *Filthy whoreboy. Lying bastard.* He had every right to fling her out into the street. But he didn't. Just became even more arrogant with that conceited smile of his while she danced with him. Only one dance. She couldn't stand any more.

She could feel the warm silk of her mother's kimono under her fingers. "Why?" she asked again.

Valentina shrugged, as if it were nothing. "A fling."

"Mama, I've seen you with him. You hate him."

"Of course I hate that devil, God rot his stinking soul."

"Was it because of the photographs?"

Valentina stopped breathing.

"I've got them." Lydia stroked her mother's back. "And the negatives."

Valentina gave a brief sob. "How?"

"I stole them."

"It's what you are good at."

"Yes."

"Thank you." It was a whisper.

"So it is my business."

"Very well. You asked." Her mother took a deep breath. "There was no real scholarship to the Willoughby Academy. You'd spent four wasted years in the local charity school here and I knew you would just be smothered and die in that hellhole. So I sought out the best private school, the Willoughby Academy, and the chief officer for education in Junchow. Mr. Mason. And I made him an offer. Create a scholarship. Award it to you. In exchange for . . ."

". . . you?"

"Yes."

Lydia slid her arms around her mother and rocked her gently. "Oh, Mama."

"I couldn't get rid of him even after I married. Because of the photographs."

"I'll burn them."

"I'd burn him, if I could."

"Mama," Lydia moaned and tightened her embrace.

"So now you will do as I ask?" Valentina twisted around, her face close to her daughter's, two dark eyeless shadows. "You'll give up your Chinese Bolshevik?"

LYDIA PULLED HER COAT MORE FIRMLY AROUND HER AND stamped her cold feet on the rock-hard patch of lawn under the eucalyptus tree. She had been waiting an hour. The garage hid the house from her, just as it hid her from the house, and she'd had plenty of time to study the wall she was sheltering behind. It was made of red bricks and she'd counted how many lay in each row. Sixty-two. She had plucked three snails off the mortar and tossed them into the shrubbery, and watched a brown-legged spider cocoon a beetle that blundered into its web. There wasn't much else to watch.

A crow took off above her from the eucalyptus tree, making the silver leaves quiver, and with two slow beats of its heavy wings it drifted over the tiles of the garage roof and up high into the chilly air. She squinted up at it. The sky was a milky blue, full of soft swirls of white that reminded Lydia of a marble she'd once owned. She'd found it in a gutter, a bright patch of blue sky buried among the filth. She'd kept it safe in her pocket for four days, but in the end was tempted into a game of marbles by a gang of boys in the playground. She'd played and lost. When she saw her marble bundled with a handful of others into a grubby pocket, she felt she'd betrayed it.

A car door slammed. It was somewhere farther down Walnut Road and an engine growled into life. That was good. People were waking up, going off to work at last. It wouldn't be long now. It had been still dark when she'd put on her school uniform and slipped out of the house, a thin gleam of gold painted along the eastern horizon. She'd had the sense to leave a note. *Gone to library. To finish homework.* They wouldn't know it didn't open until eight-thirty, and actually it was a relief to skip breakfast with Alfred. He was awkward first thing in the morning and had a habit of looking up from his porridge with a frown, blinking hard behind his spectacles, as if wondering who on earth these two strangers were at his breakfast table.

Lydia thumped her gloved hands together and let out a long breath. Watched it curl away from her as solid as cigarette smoke. She drew in another deep breath, but it was an effort. Her lungs hurt. They just wouldn't work properly. It was her mother's words. They lay like a lead burden on her, crushing her chest.

It wasn't right.

"MR. MASON."

"Good God, girl, you startled me."

He looked so smart, so upright. A fedora and alpaca coat. A black lizard-skin briefcase snug under his arm, car keys in hand. The picture of respectability. Pillar of society. Lydia wanted to tear his eyes out and feed them to the crow.

"What are you doing loitering around my garage?"

"I'm not loitering. I'm waiting to speak to you."

"Oh, not now. I'm in a hurry to get to the office."

"Yes, now."

Something in her voice made him pause and look at her. His gray eyes grew wary. "Can't it wait?"

"No."

"Very well." He unlocked the garage and swung open the doors. The Buick's big chrome headlights stared out at her.

"I have the photographs."

His hand dropped the car keys. He bent, picked them up, tried to bluff it out. "What photographs?"

"Don't."

He pulled himself up tall, pushed out his chest, came and stood too close. "Look, young lady, I'm a busy man and I have no idea what you're talking . . ."

She slapped him. A long swing with her arm and then her palm full on his cheek. The crack of it sounded loud in the still air. She was shocked, but not as shocked as he was. His eyes glazed for a moment. The red imprint of her hand with fingers splayed was stamped on his cheek. His fists came up but she stepped back out of reach.

"That's what it feels like. To be knocked about, you wife-beating pervert. Taking nude pictures of your own daughter . . ."

He lunged for her. She dodged.

"What would Sir Edward Carlisle have to say about that?"

"Now you get this straight, girl, it's not . . ."

"Don't. I don't want to hear your lies, you piece of slime. Sir Edward will sack you on the spot."

His face grew ashen. He was having trouble swallowing, but his eyes remained shrewd. He held up one neatly manicured hand in a gesture of peace.

"All right, Lydia. Let's get down to business. You're no fool. I'll give you ten thousand dollars for the photographs and negatives."

Ten thousand dollars.

A fortune. Her head swayed.

"You can have it in cash. This afternoon." He was watching her closely and suddenly reached into his pocket and pulled out his wallet. He yanked out a thick wedge of notes and fanned them out like cards under her nose. "Here. Take this. As a starter."

Ten thousand dollars.

Ten thousand dollars would buy anything. Everything. Passports. Visas. Pianos. First-class boat tickets. She could take her mother to England and flee. Oxford University, just as her mother wanted. It was all there, in Mason's hand. All she had to do was say yes. And she could take Chang An Lo to safety with her.

But would he come? Leave China?

Mason's lips pulled into a thin line. It was meant as a smile. "Agreed?"

She opened her mouth to say yes.

"No."

"Don't be a bloody stupid fool. This is your chance."

"But you'd have the photographs."

"I'd destroy them, I promise."

"No."

"Why?"

She opened her hands to the sky, letting the money go. "Because you are scum. I don't trust you. As long as I hang on to those negatives, I can be certain you will never lay a finger on Polly again. Or your wife. Or my mother. Do you understand me?"

He scowled, turned away. She watched the money return to the wallet. Her throat hurt.

"Don't come near my mother anymore."

"Go to hell, bitch."

He walked to the car, his head sunk on his chest, and lashed out at one of the tires with a brutal kick.

"Mr. Mason."

He didn't look at her.

"Mr. Mason, leave Theo Willoughby alone too."

Mason made a harsh sound that sent a shiver down her spine. "Don't you worry about him," he retorted. "Feng and his son between them will look after Willoughby." His eyes crept back to hers, and the expression in them made her skin crawl. "Just like they'll look after you."

"What do you mean?"

"Now they know who took care of the Communist."

"What Communist?"

"Don't play innocent. The one they're after. The one you nursed."

Lydia felt ice spike her veins. "That's a lie."

"No. Polly told me."

"Polly?"

"Oh yes. Your loyal little friend. Still want to protect her, do you? Yes, she told me and I told them. Right now they're probably at your house." He laughed outright. "You didn't really think I'd give a bitch like you ten thousand dollars, did you? You and your whoring mother can . . ."

But Lydia was already running.

S HE BURST INTO HER HOUSE.

"Mama," she shouted. "Mama."

No reply.

The houseboy—what was his name? Deng?—she called out for him. He came running.

"Yes, Missy Leeja?"

"My mother, where is she?"

"I not know."

She pounced on him and shook his bony shoulders. "Is she here?"

"No, she out."

"So early?"

"She go with Master. In car."

"Just the two of them?"

His bright eyes were nervous of her as he held up two fingers. "Master and Missy."

She released him and he scuttled away, hunched like a beetle. Her tongue licked her dry lips. She'd panicked for nothing. But that didn't mean the danger wasn't there. It was. She walked into the drawing room and stared out the French windows. How the hell do you fight back when you can't see your enemy? She leaned her forehead against the icy pane of glass and thought about that. Something broke loose inside her. Everything felt too heavy. Too big.

Her gaze was drawn to the shed, and because it was the nearest she could get to Chang An Lo right now, she opened the glass door and walked down toward it. The air was cold and crisp in her lungs and her head began to clear. She became aware of a crunching noise. A rat was gnawing at one of the wooden planks at the bottom of the shed. Her pulse picked up. What was it after?

"Scoot," she shouted and the creature fled.

The padlock was still locked but the bolt attached to it hung uselessly on the door, the screws prized out. She gave a faint moan. Her hand reached out and touched the door. The wood was warm in the sun. Adrenaline hit her system. She pushed. The door swung open. She screamed.

Blood. So much of it. Red. Sticky. Everywhere. Walls. Ceiling. Floor. On the wire of the hutch and on the sacks. As if someone had painted with blood. The raw stench of it mixed with the stink of feces but Lydia didn't notice the smell.

"Sun Yat-sen," she screamed.

The rabbit was lying in the middle of a pool of blood on the floor, his white fur caked with bright crimson. Even his big yellow teeth were red. Lydia knelt beside him, careless of her school uniform, and tears poured down her cheeks.

"Sun Yat-sen," she whispered and lifted him into her arms.

He was still warm. Still alive. But barely. One leg twitched and a strange strangled screech whistled from his small pulsing body. His ears had been hacked off and rammed into his mouth, and his throat was cut. She pulled out the long, soft ears. Held him close. Rocked him and crooned to him. Until the final spasm stiffened his spine. His bloodshot eyes started to glaze.

Her head lowered over him, sobs raked her body. The blow, when it came, wiped out her misery. Darkness took over.

51

CHANG AN LO OPENED HIS EYES. SOMETHING WAS WRONG. He could feel it. Tight in his bowels like wire.

He lay very still, listening.

But the squawking children's voices as they played in the courtyard masked all other noises, and a soldier's boot on the stair would pass unnoticed. Silently he rolled out of bed. From under the pillow he took the curl of copper hair and from beneath the mattress he drew the knife.

He stood behind the door. The smell of blood in his nostrils.

LI MEI SHOWED NO SURPRISE. HER ALMOND-SHAPED EYES looked at the blade in his hand but her face remained calm.

"What is it?" she asked as she placed the tray she was carrying on a delicate chiffonier of honey-colored wood.

"A cold wind in my mind."

"All is safe. Tiyo Willbee is an honorable man. You can trust him."

Chang said nothing. He watched her pour hot water from a teapot with a bamboo handle into a bowl of dried herbs. He noticed she always did it in front of him, and he knew she was showing him that she added nothing extra. He need not fear poisons. He respected her for that. She cared for him well, coolly and calmly, with an observant eye, but he longed for the passion of Lydia's nursing, her determination to snatch him from the jaws of the gods and to breathe fire into his blood once more. He missed that.

"Any news?" he asked softly.

"The gray bellies are in the harbor, I'm told, hundreds of caps bearing the Kuomintang sun. They are searching ships."

"For Foreign Mud?"

"Who knows why?" She handed him the bowl and he bowed his thanks. Her hair was scented with cinnamon. "People say—but what do people know?—that Communists are being smuggled south by ship to Canton and to Mao Tse-tung's camps. The sound of guns is in the air today."

"Thank you, Li Mei."

She bowed. "I am honored, Chang An Lo." With a rustle of Shantung silk she left the room.

The smell of blood. It was strong in his nostrils.

"SHE HASN'T COME."

"No, Chang, I'm afraid she's not at school today."

"Is that not strange?"

"No, not really at this time of year. This is always the worst term for sickness and influenza at my school. Well, any school actually."

"Yesterday she was well."

"Don't fret, I'm sure she's fine. To be honest I suspect that blighter Alfred has shut her up at home to keep her away from you. You can't blame him really, old chap. She's still young."

"I don't blame him. He is her father now."

"Exactly."

"She needs guarding."

"Quite so."

"But not by him."

LYDIA'S LEG HURT. HER HEAD THROBBED.

But when she forced her eyelids up, the blackness beyond them was as dense as inside her mind. She tried them open and tried them shut. Nothing changed. She moved an arm and felt her elbow crunch against something hard. She touched her hip and thigh. She was naked. Shivering.

That's what decided it.

It was a nightmare. She was in one of those terrifying caught-in-a-trap nightmares. No clothes. Everyone staring. A splinter of hell. Stuck in her mind.

She closed her eyes and spiraled back down into nothingness, knowing she would soon wake in her own bed.

Strange about the blackness though.

52

"MY FATHER KILLED HIMSELF BECAUSE OF OPIUM."

Theo was shocked. To hear those words come out of his own mouth. It was not something he'd told anyone before, not even Li Mei. It was as though he'd vomited up a stone that had been stuck hard in his gullet for a long time.

The young Chinese was propped up in bed. He didn't look good. His gaunt face was gray, lifeless as ash, and bruised shadows circled his eye sockets. His limbs lay loose like a puppet's at his side, but his black irises were full of some dark emotion. Theo wasn't sure whether it was hatred or fear. He had a feeling it was hatred. But all Communists hated the foreigners in their land. Who could blame them? Yet it irritated Theo that they conveniently ignored the benefits Westerners brought with them. The industries. Electricity. Trains. Banking expertise. China needed the West more than the West needed China. But it came at a cost.

When the Chinese spoke, there was an edge to his voice. "I know this happens here in China. Death and opium, they share the same path. But I did not think it was so in England."

Theo shrugged. "People are the same wherever they live."

"Many *fanqui* think otherwise."

"Yes, that's so, and my father was one. He believed with all his soul in the supremacy of the British, and of his own family in particular."

"Grief hides in your words. An ancestral shrine for him in your house would honor his spirit."

"There's my elder brother too." The words kept flowing now that the stone was dislodged.

A shrine? Why not? Every Chinese home had one to keep the ancestral spirits well fed and happy. Why shouldn't he? Except of course he might not have a home much longer, and he had a nasty feeling prisons didn't go in for that kind of thing.

"He was handsome, my brother Ronald. Had everything. A Cambridge blue and the pride of my father's heart."

"Your father was fortunate."

"Not really. Papa gave over the family investment business to him, but it all went belly-up. My brother started on opium to help him sleep at night and . . . Well, it's the old story. He bankrupted the company and defrauded clients to cover it. So . . ."

Theo silenced his tongue. He could not understand why these memories had surfaced now. He thought they were dead and buried. Why now? Why to this Chinese Communist? Was it because, just like his father before him, both he and Chang An Lo faced the ruin of all their hopes and plans for the future?

"So?" Chang prompted quietly.

Theo reached for a cigarette but he didn't light it, just twisted it between his long fingers. "So . . . my father took his shotgun. Killed my brother. In his office, sitting at his desk. Then blew out his own brains. It was . . . frightful. Awful scandal, of course, and Mother took an overdose of something nasty. After the funerals, I came out here. That's it. Ten years and I'm still here."

"China is honored."

"That's a matter of opinion."

"I'm sure it is the opinion of the beautiful Li Mei."

Theo wanted to believe him.

"I would ask a question, please?" Chang said.

"Go ahead."

"Are problems of mixing a European and a Chinese very great? In your world, I mean."

"Ah!" Theo ran a hand over the minute hand-stitching on the Chinese gown he was wearing. He felt a sharp tug of sympathy for the young man. "To be brutally honest, yes. The problems are bloody huge."

Chang shut his eyes.

Theo patted his shoulder. "It's damned hard."

53

THIS TIME THE COLD WAS LIKE A SHELL AROUND HER. SHE pecked at it, picked at it, scraped her nail along it, but it wouldn't crack. Her mind couldn't understand why. It struggled. Grew weary. The organs of her body were shutting down, she could feel them inside her, one by one, going to sleep. Abandoning her. The cold. They hated it. It was only when she became aware of a sudden warmth between her legs that she woke up.

Her eyes opened. To total blackness. She tried to churn her thoughts into action, but all they wanted was sleep. Where had all this blackness come from?

Things came to her in bits and pieces. A pain in her leg. Her head sore and her cheek on something hard. Icy skin. Her knees up under her chin. Gradually it dawned on her that she was lying on her side curled up in a tight ball. Her hand risked stretching out into the darkness but it couldn't reach far because there were cold metal walls all around her. Her heart thundered in her ears.

Where was she?

She tried to sit up. It took three attempts. And when she'd done it, she felt worse. Not because of the pain in her leg that felt as if someone had kicked it. Nor because her head started to spin inside a crazy kaleidoscope, lights flashing behind her eyes, reds and blues and fierce brain-searing yellows. No, it was because she touched the ceiling one inch above her head and knew where she was. She was in a box. A metal box.

They put me in a metal crate.

Three months, perhaps more.

Chang An Lo's words.

Her stomach spasmed with fear and she vomited, sour acid in her throat. It sprayed over her knees, and the sticky warmth of it recalled to her sluggish mind the earlier warmth between her legs. Her fingers explored along the metal base under her. It was wet. She had peed.

Her mind went white. She started to scream.

SHE WAS FIGHTING HER WAY THROUGH COBWEBS. THEY stuck to her eyeballs, and a spider with a red speckled body and yellow pincers ran up inside her nostril.

She opened her eyes. And immediately wished herself back in the spider nightmare again. This was worse. This was real. Her body struggled into a crouching position and her hands inched along the four walls to discover the dimensions of her miniature cell. Long enough to sit up but not to straighten her legs, wide enough to touch both walls with her elbows at the same time. An inch of headroom when she was seated in a hunched sort of position. She then examined her own body. Her knees. They smelled. She remembered the vomit. The stink of stale urine scored the membranes of her nostrils, a lump on the back of her head, and high on her left thigh another one the size of a saucer. But no broken skin. No broken bones. No missing fingers.

It could be worse.

How? How in God's name could this devil's rat hole possibly be worse? How?

She could be dead. Think of that.

THE COLD DIDN'T INCREASE. IT DIDN'T IMPROVE BUT IT DIDN'T get worse. That was something. She worried about the constant shivering. It was using up so much energy, draining her reserves. She was exhausted already. Or was that the fear?

Her mind kept blanking out.

She'd be in the middle of trying to work out how long she might have been a captive in the dark, when her mind would suddenly slip away from her. Blank out totally. That terrified her almost as much as the box. Brain damage? From the blow to the head. *Please, no, not that.* Or was it sheer terror? Her mind escaping.

To find a tiny scrap of warmth she wrapped her arms around her knees and huddled tight, stroking her shins for comfort.

BREATHE. IN. HOLD FOR THE COUNT OF TEN. OUT. SLOW and smooth. In. Hold. Count. Out.

Control. Keep control. Concentrate.

Her thoughts felt like glass. The slightest touch and they shattered. Panic stalked her. Sprang out at her from the dark corners when she wasn't looking.

"Chang An Lo," she murmured, and was astonished at the reassurance the sound of her own voice gave her. "How did you keep yourself sane?"

She'd worked out three things. One was that she'd only been inside Box—she thought of it as a creature that had swallowed her whole—for less than a day. Otherwise she'd have peed more than once, though admittedly she'd not had anything to drink. *Don't think of that.* Her mouth was dust-dry and her throat parched. The screaming hadn't helped. Stupid that. Wasting strength. Anyway. Nor had she done . . . her brain shied away from the prospect . . . done more serious toilet matters. So. Less than twenty-four hours then.

The second thing she'd worked out was that she must be underground. In a cellar maybe. Or a secret dungeon. It was the temperature that made her decide that. It never varied. A constant cold, never warmer by day or icier at night. Not that she had any idea whether it was day or night inside Box. Just dark. And more dark. Cold. And more cold. No sounds either. If she'd been anywhere aboveground there would be sounds. Not this dead weight of silence.

Third thing. There must be air holes. Must be. Or she'd be dead by now. Her fingers started the search.

54

A STRANGE MAN.

Chang could not understand the schoolmaster. He had none of the wisdom that a learned scholar should possess. Sometimes he wore Western clothes, sometimes Chinese. Sometimes he spoke Mandarin, sometimes English. He ate Chinese food and bedded a Chinese woman, but Chang had seen him drinking in the Ulysses Club with his *fanqui* friend. He had books of Han-Shan's poetry on his shelves, yet he possessed an Englishman's foolishness over a foul-tempered cat. He swayed in any direction. Not even he knew which way he might go, hanging on the end of a thread.

That made him dangerous.

And the Foreign Mud. The opium. That too turned the schoolmaster into a spinning blade.

HIS DREAMS ABOUT HER GREW WILDER, STRONGER. HE WAS with her in a cave up in the mountains and wolves howled unceasingly. Blizzards ripped through the cave one after the other. Always noise and storm and roaring wind, but through it all they lay in each other's arms, the flame of her hair melting the snow and burning up the darkness. His hands were whole again when he drew her clothes from her body but there was a circular scar on her breast, the mark of a knife, and when he took her face between his hands to kiss her beloved lips, it turned into a white rabbit's with pink eyes. There was a wire tight round its neck.

"Chang An Lo."

It was Li Mei.

"Drink this."

He drank. "She hasn't come?"

"No." She laid a cool fragrant cloth on his forehead and bathed the sweat from his face and neck. "Patience. Tomorrow she will come. The fire-head loves you."

He closed his eyes and held on to the image of Lydia's laughing mouth and the excitement in her eyes when she described her plan to become a Communist freedom fighter. It threaded life into his chest, so that his heart drummed fit to wake the gods. He loved her. He wanted her at his side when he fought. She lay at the center of his being; she was in his breath and part of every thought. His skin was her skin. Love was too small a word. He reached for her with his mind but all he found was darkness. Coldness.

A thought whipped through him.

"Li Mei."

"Yes?"

"Ask the schoolmaster please to come here."

LYDIA FOUND THE HOLES. SIX OF THEM. IN ONE CORNER AT the top. Her little finger could just squeeze through. It came as a surprise to find something resting on top of the holes outside, something soft and thin. Some kind of fabric.

The awful kick of hope in her stomach made her feel sick again. She tried to squash it. Stamp on it. But it wouldn't go away. If she could remove the material, light might trickle into her black cell. Light. She craved it. Even more than she craved water. Without intending to, she found herself waving a hand in front of her face at intervals, but each time nothing had changed. She couldn't make out even the faintest shadow of movement.

Was she blind? Had the blow to her head destroyed her sight?

She choked on that thought and started to wriggle her little finger in one of the holes, digging up into the material and shifting it a fraction to one side. A fraction was all. A quarter of an inch if she was lucky, sometimes nothing. It was going to take a long time. She crouched there, finger aching, arm propped up by her knee, and tried not to hope.

★ ★ ★

WHY DID THEY WANT HER?

What was she here for?

Who?

Black Snakes? Po Chu? Kuomintang?

When would they come for her?

What did they plan to do to her?

Ask questions?

How?

With knives? With crowbars? Branding irons?

Or whips?

Rape?

Chang An Lo, my love, give me strength.

THE FABRIC WAS SLIDING. SUDDENLY THE WEIGHT OF IT took over and she could feel it slipping smoothly over the tip of her finger. And then it was gone. Nothing changed. No light. No grayness. No hint of a world out there. Disappointment crashed down on her and she burst into tears.

No. Not that. Not tears. No waste of precious fluid. No self-pity.

She made herself stop, but her shoulders kept heaving. It frightened her that a few miserable air holes mattered so much to her. They were trivial. What about the big things yet to come? The bad things. Really bad. To survive she had to get herself under control. She pushed her face into the corner with the air holes and breathed deeply. The air was fresher. Not much.

She licked the metal around the holes. It tasted foul but it was damp with condensation. Moisture. No more than a few smears of it, yet it set her brain functioning again. For the first time it occurred to her to think about rescue. What a fool. Of course she'd be missed when she didn't return home from school. Well, not immediately maybe, because they'd assume she'd gone over to Polly's house when she didn't show up, but eventually. By nightfall.

It might be the middle of the night already for all she knew. It certainly felt as though she'd been inside Box for a very long time because her body ached all over from the cramped positions her limbs were squashed into. So they could be searching. Right now. Out there with dogs and torches. For a moment she stopped shivering and lifted her head. Opened her eyes. No amount of listening or staring into blackness altered anything, but she felt she needed to be ready. For when they came.

Mama. Don't be casual about this. This is important. It's my life, Mama. Do something.

Do something.

VALENTINA'S HAND SLAMMED ONTO CHANG AN LO'S CHEEK. "You dirty yellow piece of pig shit. Where is she?"

Theo stepped forward to intervene, but she slapped the young face again and again. Punctuated by demands.

"What have you done with her?"

Slap.

"Where have your stinking friends taken her?"

Slap.

"Speak, you goddamned money-grubbing kidnapper. If she's hurt I swear I'll . . ."

She raised her hand to strike once more, but Theo seized her wrist and yanked her away from where Chang was standing in the middle of the room. "Enough, Mrs. Parker. This is not helping."

She swore ferociously in Russian and Theo expected a slap himself, but she shook herself free and glared at all three men in the room as if she would bite their balls off.

"Find her," she shouted. She dragged her hands through her disheveled hair in a gesture of despair, her face flushed with rage. "Communist, listen to me. You get out there and bring her back. Because if you don't, I will turn the police on you and you'll be hanged, so . . ."

"Let him speak," Theo said curtly. "Alfred, for Christ's sake, man, shut her up. The bloody woman is insane. Chang An Lo didn't kidnap her. He hasn't left this house and anyway, look at him." The Chinese was swaying on his feet. His face was gray except for the crimson imprint of Valentina's hand on his cheek. "He's about to drop."

"No," Chang insisted. "Mrs. Parker is correct."

"What?"

"I mean the search must start right now." His voice wasn't quite steady, and Theo wasn't sure if it was the fever and the shock of the attack by Valentina or because Lydia was missing. Either way, he looked bad.

"Call the police," Alfred said firmly. He'd been standing by the door, silent up to now. "They'll know how to handle it. They're used to kidnappings. They'll trace her and hunt down the culprits. If there are any, that is. Let's not panic yet, my dear. She may just have wandered off on some pet project of her own without telling you. You know what she's like."

"*Gospodi!* Don't talk like an imbecile." She swung back to Chang. "Tell me, Communist, what has happened?"

"I know nothing. But I suspect."

"Suspect what?"

"That the Black Snakes have her."

"What the hell are they?"

"It's a secret tong," Theo explained. "But why would they want Lydia, Chang?"

Chang did not waste effort on a reply. He was pulling on his boots. "You are right, Mrs. Parker. I will get out there."

"Steady, old fellow," Theo said quickly. "You're in no fit state to go roaming the streets."

Chang snatched his padded coat from the back of the door and spoke fiercely. "And what about the state Lydia is in?"

"The police . . . ," Alfred started.

"If you call in police," Chang said, looking only at Valentina, "they will be slow and heavy tongued. They might get her killed. You will have to tell them I was here and the schoolmaster will go to prison. It is against your law to help a fugitive."

Alfred stepped in. "Look, young man, that is not . . ."

Valentina sliced a dismissive hand through the air. "Mr. Willoughby can rot in jail for the whole of eternity for all I care, as long as I get my daughter back. Find her, Communist."

Theo did not take offense. Love was never rational. If it were, he wouldn't be with Li Mei. And out on the street, Chang's search methods would be more effective than those of the police, as long as he could stay on his feet.

"But first the police will want to question him," Alfred pointed out quietly, "to learn what . . ."

"You're wasting time, Alfred." Theo rested an arm on his friend's shoulder.

Chang opened the door.

"Godspeed," Alfred murmured.

But Theo put more faith in the knife up Chang's sleeve.

55

Lᴙᴅɪᴀ ᴡᴀɪᴛᴇᴅ. Iɴ ᴛʜᴇ ᴅᴀʀᴋ. Hᴜɴᴄʜᴇᴅ ɪɴsɪᴅᴇ ʜᴇʀ sᴇɴsᴇs. She knew they'd come for her eventually, when they were sure she was weak and helpless, and then they'd start their *amusement*—that's the word Chang An Lo had used for it. The thought turned her bones to water.

The only defense she had was inside her head, and she started working on it. Preparing. For questions. For pain. For how far she could go.

The nakedness. The cold. Even the absolute darkness inside Box. They had all seemed so important only hours ago, so crippling, but now she put them aside into a separate compartment in her head. She had gone beyond that.

It was a matter of focus.

Sʜᴇ ᴡᴇɴᴛ ᴏᴠᴇʀ sᴄᴇɴᴇs. Iɴᴄʜ ʙʏ ɪɴᴄʜ. Gᴏᴏᴅ sᴄᴇɴᴇs. Scenes with her mother when she was young. Bright shiny scenes of laughter. Of Russian tales at bedtime or of proudly playing the left hand of *Dance of the Cygnets* on the piano while her mother played the right. Swimming in the river on a hot summer's day and diving for fish skeletons to take home. Snowball fights in the schoolyard with Polly.

Why had Polly betrayed her? Lydia had begged her not to, had pleaded for her silence. And even if Polly believed she was helping Lydia by telling her father, what good was that to Lydia now? What use were good intentions inside a metal Box?

She forced Polly's name away. Good memories were what she

needed now. Lizard Creek. The touch of Chang An Lo's warm skin. The smell of his hair. His penis firm in her hand. Inside her. Good memories to build up good strength.

She could survive this.

She could.

She would.

THE NOISE CRACKED LIKE A GUNSHOT. HER EARS, SO USED to silence, misinterpreted the sound. It took an effort of mind to realize it was an iron bolt being drawn back. A door being unlocked. Shuffling footsteps on wood. Stairs? Someone descending toward her. She had prepared for this, run it already a thousand times in her head and taught herself to control the panic. Focus. Breathe.

But her heart rate exploded. Terror swamped her.

"Hello?" she called out.

A guttural stream of Chinese came in response and a thump on the side of Box, the sound of a palm hitting metal. She shut up. The best thing was the light. She focused on the tawny little trickles of twilight that filtered through the six holes and steadied herself by it. It was only faint. A candle? An oil lamp? But it was light. Life. She could make out her own knees, see a bruise on her leg, see her hand. Her eyes squinted after the utter darkness they had grown accustomed to but they wanted more. More light. More life.

A scraping sound, something dragging across the floor. She sat still, listening. The squeak of metal, then a *whoosh* and suddenly water was coming through the holes. The shock was total. Quickly she pushed her face under it and opened her mouth. The joy of feeling moisture in her mouth took over and she gulped it down, greedy and stupid. Then the taste of it kicked in. It was foul. Rank with dirt. Full of grit. She retched on the floor. Her mouth was full of grease and acid bile. She rubbed at her tongue with her wrist.

The water kept coming. She forgot about her mouth.

"Hey," she called out. "Stop it. Enough water."

A man's laugh and another bang on the side of Box.

"Please. No more water. *Qing*. Please."

The flow of water increased. It was inches deep already and her teeth were chattering so hard they hurt.

"Stop!" she shouted, but it came out as a wordless scream.

Focus.

Breathe.

Breathe deep. Fill your lungs.

The water rose. It crept up past her waist. She banged on the roof. "Please. *Qing.* Please."

But the laughter grew louder. Gloating. Gleeful.

She'd got it all wrong. They were going to drown her. The noise of her blood in her ears was deafening. Why drown her? Why? It didn't make sense.

As a lesson to Chang An Lo.

My love. My love.

The surface of the water rose to her chest, her neck, and she was ice cold. Her body felt paralyzed. She forced it to move, squatted on her haunches, pushing her face up against the metal and kept dragging air deeper and deeper into her lungs. Abruptly rage ripped right through all her focusing and her breathing, and she hammered uncontrollably on the metal roof.

"You let me out of here, you bloody murdering gutter scum, you filthy bastard son of the devil. I don't want to die, I don't, I . . ."

The water reached her mouth. She dragged in a last gulp of air. Held her breath. Closed her eyes. Water packed inside her nose, solid as snow. Spasms began in her calves and traveled up her body. In her mind she found Chang An Lo's smile waiting for her and she kissed his warm lips.

Box filled to the brim.

CHANG CROUCHED IN THE GARDEN. CLOSE TO THE SHED. Somehow it brought her nearer. Dawn was not yet anything more than a slight bleed in the sky behind him, but already a thrush was chattering its alarm call from high in a bare willow tree. A *fanqui* cat, a colorless shadow in the darkness, strolled round the edges of the frosted lawn staking out its territory, its thick fur ruffled by the wind from the northern hills.

The shed.

Chang had been inside, seen the blood, put a hand in the empty hutch. He promised Chu Jung, god of fire and vengeance, a lifetime of prayers and gifts in exchange for it being rabbit's blood. Not Lydia's.

Not Lydia's.

He had worked all night, seeking out those with eyes that see. Twice he'd used the knife because twice he'd been seized by hands that took Po Chu's silver. Fever had made his reactions slow but not that slow. The spiraling strike of his heel smashing a kidney, a tiger paw punch to the throat, a knife in the ribs to make sure. But before either of them went to join the spirits of their ancestors, Chang asked questions. Where was Po Chu now? His headquarters? His hideouts?

One gave answers and Chang followed the trail, but it led him into a black alley where only death lingered. Po Chu was being careful. It seemed he moved around, never long in one place, flitting at night, as alert as a bat to any threat. Chang couldn't get close.

"Po Chu, I swear by the gods that I will hound you down and make you eat your own blood-soaked entrails if you harm one hair of my fox girl."

He howled it. In the darkened streets of the old town where guarded eyes watched from hidden doorways but few dared show a face. There was the stench of blood on him and on his blade, and they could smell it.

Chang waited for dawn to arrive. His own blood felt like lead in his veins because he knew he had become a death bringer. It followed him, padded silently at his heels, its foul breath cold on his neck, first to Tan Wah and now to Lydia. He knew she was going to die. Even if Po Chu wanted to recapture him and was using her as bait, still that devil son of Feng Tu Hong would delight in killing her. He would slit her throat when he was finished, to punish Chang for the loss of face. If for one second he believed that Po Chu would release her in exchange for himself, he would be there on his knees, his knife tossed to the ground. But no. Po Chu would kill them both. After his amusements with them.

Chang seized a handful of brittle icy grass from the lawn and pulled it out, stuffed it into his mouth to still the scream of pain that gripped his chest. To love someone. It sliced open your heart. It made it soft and pulsating when the crows came to tear it apart with their savage beaks. He dropped his face into his hands. The bandages had been discarded. Love made you vulnerable as a kitten asleep on its back, its tender belly exposed to the world. That's how he felt. That weak. How could he fight when all he wanted to do was to protect her? Not China. Just her.

He bit on the raw place on his hand where his finger had once been and felt the pain of it dig into his mind, but still he couldn't shake free from the hook that held him. He reminded himself of Mao Tse-tung's doctrine that the needs of the Individual must be suppressed in support of the Whole. In his head he knew it to be the only way forward, but right now his head was as much use as a donkey in a gambling den.

His was a strong arm in the Communist fight and a strong mind. She was one girl. A *fanqui* girl.

But there was one last way he might find her. Save her. Though he would certainly die. Would that be too selfish? To give his life for the girl he loved, instead of the country he loved.

Lydia, tell them what they want to hear. Don't bare your teeth at them.

He spat out the grass. Rose to his feet and loped into the gray light of morning.

56

THEY DID THE WATER TRICK TWICE MORE. EACH TIME FOR longer. Her lungs burned. She retched up filth. Snatched at air. Vision blurred. She wanted to die, yet each time she fought for life like a wild animal.

The man with the gloating laugh enjoyed his work. He kept slapping Box's sides and chattering in high-pitched Chinese. Only when she knew that this time she would drown for certain, when stars flared in the black tunnel that filled her head and her lungs were seared by fire, did he dart around and slide a narrow slat from under her. The water gushed out and she curled very nearly dead on the floor of Box. Everything hurt.

When her bowels opened, she barely noticed.

SHE LOST TRACK OF TIME.

Sometimes she pinched her cheek to make sure she was still alive. Still Lydia Ivanova.

She was beginning to doubt it.

WHEN THE BOLT DREW BACK AGAIN, HER WHOLE BODY flinched. The footsteps on the stairs. She forced her lungs to drag in air, deep down, expanding even the tiny sacs at the end of each airway. She had to stockpile on air. Before the water came. Her skin felt numb with cold. With panic. She crouched. Ready.

But this time there was no sound of dragging hosepipe. This time it was the scrape of something wooden across the floor and the flickering light grew brighter.

What now?

Focus. Breathe. Don't cry.

Suddenly the world changed. The roof flew off. A hand reached in and grabbed her hair, wrenching it from its roots, hauling her to her feet. Her stiff body was sluggish and earned her a blow on the ear. She was staring into the face of an olive-skinned Chinese man with a pointed face and black eyes set close together. His teeth were red and for one crazy moment she thought it was blood, that he was eating some live creature, then she saw he was chewing on some dark red seeds that he held in his free hand.

"*Guo lai! Gi nu.*"

He yanked her out of Box and she looked around her, eyes screwed up against the dim light. She was right. It was a cellar. Two rats paused in a corner and inspected her, whiskers twitching. Box was a metal cube raised on a wooden plinth with a drain underneath and a small ladder propped against its side. She fell down the ladder, her feet too numb to guide her.

Don't cry. Don't beg.

Spit in his goddamn face.

SHE DIDN'T CRY. SHE DIDN'T BEG. SHE DIDN'T SPIT IN HIS face. She did as she was told. Her captor slipped wooden shackles on her wrists and a rope around her neck, then led her like a dog out of the cellar along a narrow dank corridor, slatted walls on both sides like some kind of passage between buildings. Up steps. Five of them. Should she try to break free? Here?

But it took everything inside her just to walk upright. When she stumbled or hesitated the rope was tugged tight with such force, she was under no illusion about the man's strength and knew her own body was a physical wreck. So. No. No escape yet. The narrow-faced man pushed open a door.

Warmth.

That was what hit her first. It flowed over her skin, silky golden waves of it, sucking out the cold from her bones. She wanted to weep with pleasure. She felt a sudden rush of gratitude toward her captors for giving her this warmth, but part of her mind insisted that was insane. She hated them. Hated.

Then came the noise. The room was so full of sound it made her head spin. Big voices. Boisterous laughter. It boomed inside her hollow brain and the bright lights cramped her eyeballs. She squinted, adjusting quickly, and tried to make out what kind of place she was in. A large high-ceilinged room, ornate carvings peering down at her from painted beams, red patterned tiles under her bare feet, small barred windows. The walls were covered in heavy embroidered drapes and lined with wooden settles. Full of Chinese faces. Jeering. Fingers pointing. Mouths spitting. Black figures everywhere. Too much black. Too much death.

The fact that she was wearing nothing except a primitive form of handcuffs and a rope around her neck did not distress her. She was beyond that. She cared no more about her nakedness than she would if she were standing in front of a pack of wild dogs.

A bunched fist swung lazily at her face. She ducked and it missed. The faces around the room split open into wide red caverns of laughter, but the man who had tried to strike her found no amusement in it. He was broad across the chest, solidly built, with a fleshy face and smooth oily skin. She was useless at guessing Chinese age, but he looked about thirty to her and carried himself with an air of authority. He had a high hairline and dark petulant lips. Oddly he wore a respectable black Western suit. It gave her hope. He stood in front of her and cursed in Chinese.

"You the filthy bitch whore of the shit-eater without the fingers." The English words startled her. "You lose fingers too. And eyes. And white putrid breasts. I feed to rats in cellar."

The threats came not from the smooth-skinned man but from a young boy, no more than fourteen or fifteen years old with long unruly hair and nervous eyes, as he mouthed the words with no emotion of any kind. He stood behind the shoulder of the big man who was cursing her, and it dawned on her sluggish mind that the boy was only the interpreter, echoing his master's words.

She switched her gaze back to the master and abruptly the cogs inside her brain turned faster. She recognized him. From the Chinese funeral Chang had taken her to. He was the one in white prostrating himself behind the coffin. Yuesheng's brother, Feng Tu Hong's son. It was Po Chu himself. She spat at him, the man who tortured Chang

An Lo. He hit her hard and growled something. *"Ni ei xi xue hui vhun."*

"You learn respect," the boy translated.

"Release me," she hissed, tasting blood inside her cheek.

"You answer questions."

"I am the daughter of an important British newspaper tycoon. Release me immediately or the British Army will come with their rifles to . . ."

"Bao chi!"

"Silence," the boy echoed.

The man's hand seized a hank of her hair and twisted her head back. He shouted in her face, his breath sour with alcohol, and his dark gaze roamed over her breasts and throat, down to her thighs and . . . She shut her eyes to block him out.

That was when he released her hair, reached down, and yanked out a piece of her pubic hair. The pain was sharp but brief and she didn't cry out. He held up the copper curl as a trophy for all to see, and the men around the walls cheered. Instead she thought of how Chang An Lo had twirled those same hairs around his good fingers and called them her fox flames. But what disturbed her more was the glimpse she got of her forearm when she struggled to free her hands. The skin was covered in bite marks. They were the marks of her own teeth where in the dark inside Box she'd been gnawing at a limb. Like a fox in a trap. That frightened her.

She made herself stand straight. "Sir Edward Carlisle will skin you all alive for this."

The boy translated. Po Chu laughed. *"Zai na?* Where Chang An Lo?"

"I don't know."

"Yes. You know. You say."

"No. I don't know. He ran away when the Kuomintang troops came."

"You lie."

"No. *Bu.*"

"Yes."

Each time the words came from Po Chu, with the boy echoing softly in English.

"Tell truth."

This time the question came with a slap.

"Tell truth." Another slap. "Tell truth." Slap. Slap. Slap. Again. Again. She lost count.

Her lip split. The space inside her head turned red. Her ears hummed.

Slap. Slap.

Harder. A knife point nicked the corner of her left eyelid and started to slide along the bottom of her eye as if to pop it out.

"He's dead." She screamed it.

The knife froze. The slaps ceased. She breathed. Small panicky gasps.

"When dead?" Po Chu demanded. In English. But she barely noticed. Her mind was struggling.

"How dead?" He ran the knife blade in a circle around one breast, and she felt the sting and the trickle of blood.

"From sickness."

"*Shen meshi hou?* When?"

"On Saturday. I took him to the docks. Nursed him . . . In an old shack . . . he died." Tears started to pour down her cheeks. It wasn't hard.

The boy translated, but it was the tears that seemed to convince Po Chu. He stepped back with a shrewd smile, flicked the knife spinning up into the air, and as it fell caught its ivory handle with an easy sweep of his fist. He stared at her.

"*Guo lai.*"

"Come," the boy said.

Po Chu seized the rope attached to her neck and dragged her across the room toward a screen that closed off one corner. Her eyes fixed on its panels inlaid with lapis and coral, ivory and mother-of-pearl, and she burned them into her memory. If this bastard was going to blind her, she had to make her last moment of sight go a long way.

"See, *gi nu.*" Po Chu thrust the screen aside.

She saw. And wished she'd drowned inside Box.

On a table, neatly laid out like precision instruments of surgery in an operating theater, were two rows of tools. Heavy tongs and blades, some serrated and some with needle-sharp points, and beside them lay small blunt hammers, chains and leather collars and cuffs. Her eye was drawn to a piece of iron with a long narrow shovel end and stout wooden handle. Not in her wildest dreams could she begin to guess its purpose.

Her inner organs turned to liquid. Nothing worked anymore. Her breathing stopped. She felt warm fluid dribble down the backs of her thighs and she knew her body was trying to flush out the fear. She felt no shame. She'd left that behind long ago.

"See, *gi nu*," Po Chu repeated. "Putrid whore. See."

Her ears still worked. They heard the anticipation in his voice.

"Tell truth."

She nodded.

"Where Chang An Lo?"

"Dead."

He picked up a pair of heavy iron-teethed tweezers, casually weighed them in his hand, lowered his thick black eyebrows in a frown of concentration, and clamped the metal teeth round her nipple. He squeezed.

She screamed.

Blood, bright red like paint. A burning pain in her breast. She screamed her anger and her hatred at him, bellowed it in his face, and would have hurled herself at him and bitten his eyes out if the rope around her neck had not been pulled tight from behind.

"Good." Po Chu smiled coldly, a spatter of her blood on his chin. "Now tell truth."

57

THEY HANDLED HIM ROUGHLY. GRAY UNIFORMS ALL OVER him like dung flies. A blow to the ribs, a boot in the groin, but Chang An Lo did not retaliate. Only when they thudded a rifle butt down on his damaged hand did he spit, but that was all. The headquarters was in a new concrete blockhouse on the edge of old Junchow, tucked into the shadow of the great stone walls, its entrance guarded by two fresh-faced young Chinese officers eager to impress their superiors. When Chang suddenly appeared before them out of the morning mist, their eyes widened in surprise. They stamped their boots and raised their rifles, expecting trouble, but when none came they led him quickly into their captain's office.

"You are the Communist dog we have been hunting," the Kuomintang officer said with relish. "I am Captain Wah."

He removed his cap, tossed it to one side, and rummaged through the chaotic piles of paper on his desk. After a moment's confusion, he pounced on a sheet that he held up at arm's length to inspect. It was an indistinct portrait of Chang's face, skillfully sketched, obviously sent out to all Chinese troop centers and police stations. Chang wondered bitterly which of his friends had obliged and for how much.

Captain Wah stared at Chang with cool, sad eyes and lit himself a thin cigar. "You will be interrogated first, gutter rat, and then a magistrate will order your execution. All you Communists are cowards who slither on your bellies, like worms under our feet. Your execution is certain, so do not add to the pain of China by worthless loyalty to a cause that is doomed. By great Buddha, we shall rid our country of you vermin."

Even with wrists handcuffed and the fever in his blood, Chang knew he could kick this man's teeth down his throat before the soldier at the door could draw his gun. It was tempting. But what good would he be to Lydia with a bullet in his brain?

"Honorable Captain," he said with a humble bow, "I have information to give, as you so wisely suspect, but I will give it only to one man."

Captain Wah's mouth narrowed with annoyance. "You would be wise to give it to me," he said in a sharp tone. He rose to his feet, tall and rangy in his dusty gray uniform, and leaned forward threateningly over his desk. "Do as I order, or you will die slowly."

"One man," Chang said quietly. "The Russian. The one whose words the Kuomintang listen to."

A change came over the officer. His cheeks sucked in, he rubbed a hand across his pockmarked chin, and his eyes grew more thoughtful. He bit the end off his cigar and spat it at the floor.

"I think," he said, "I will execute you right now."

"If you do, I promise you the Russian will have you whipped to the bone," Chang murmured with a bow.

58

THEO STEPPED INSIDE THE ROLLS-ROYCE AS IT PURRED TO A halt at the curb, and he inhaled the rich odor of leather and money.

"Good day to you, Feng Tu Hong."

"You asked for my time, Willbee. I am here. I am listening."

Theo slid onto the comfort of the maroon rear seat beside Feng and studied his enemy. Feng was wrapped in a long gray coat with a wide silver fur collar and pale gray kid gloves, but even in all his finery he still had the look of a buffalo ready to charge. Theo smiled.

"You are looking well, Feng."

"Well, but not well pleased."

"I appreciate your sparing a few moments from your busy day."

"Every day is busy for a man like myself who has so many matters to attend to and no son at his right hand."

Theo stared through the glass partition at the back of the chauffeur's head. Outside a few flakes of snow swirled in the wind. Feng had given him the opening but he had to tread with care.

"It grieves me to hear that Po Chu is no longer one of your household. A father's heart must hang heavy when his only son departs with harsh words."

"Daughter or son. A father's heart bleeds."

"It is about Po Chu I came to speak."

"He is a worthless beetle fit only for the sewers."

"I fear he will soon be in prison rather than in the sewers."

Feng sank his neck deeper into the fur collar and glared at Theo. "You lie."

"No, Feng Tu Hong, I speak the truth. Your son has kidnapped a *fanqui* girl. She is the daughter of a British journalist who will bring the might of the British Army down on Chinese heads in Junchow if the girl is not released immediately."

Feng's huge hand gripped the ivory cane he carried across his lap. Theo knew from Li Mei that it was a swordstick, though he had never seen the thin blade himself. Nor did he care to. Feng breathed heavily but said nothing.

"Such antipathy," Theo continued, "between our people would be bad for your . . . business."

Feng snorted. "What is it you want, Willbee?"

"I want to know where Po Chu is hiding her."

"Hah, you take my daughter and now you would take my son. Be careful, Englishman, that I do not take your head."

"No, Feng. It is the girl I want, not your son. If I can retrieve her quickly, Po Chu will not be harmed. I came to warn you of the danger he is in."

Feng turned his somber face away and stared unseeing out of the side window. On the pavement opposite, an acrobat was balancing on stilts while a stick-thin monkey in a scarlet jacket was holding out a cup for money. The chauffeur tossed in a coin.

"My son disobeyed me, Willbee. The way his brother, Yuesheng, did before him, and my daughter before that. He is banished from my house but . . . it grieves me, Willbee, because I can father no more sons however young and luscious the maidens I pleasure. My stalk is still willing but the seeds are shriveled and dry though I eat tiger meat. I grow old." He ran a hand over his sleek hair, touching the graying temples with distaste. "I need my son."

"The British courts will hang him."

Feng swung back to confront Theo and his eyes were dull with despair. "I want him alive, worthless as he is."

"There is a chance for him still if I can find her quickly before the authorities get involved."

Feng leaned close to Theo, and Theo had to work hard to keep his own anger off his face. He did not choose to forget that this was the man who had put Li Mei through so much pain and caused Theo's own problems with Mason.

"Very well, Willbee. I trust you because I have no other choice. Po

Chu is far too cautious to let any of my people come near, but you are different. Maybe you can speak with him because he will see you as no threat." He heaved a deep sigh that shuddered through the bunched muscles of his body. "My secret eyes tell me he and his followers are hiding in a farmhouse. Out near the Seven Woods to the east of town." His black gaze fixed on Theo. "Save him, teacher-man. For me. For his father."

Theo nodded. "When this is over, if Po Chu lives, I will name my price." He climbed out of the car.

"ALFRED."

"Thank the Lord you've come, Theo." Alfred's normally neat exterior was rumpled, his jacket creased and dark circles forming behind his spectacles. "Any luck?"

"I have news."

"You've found her?"

"Not yet." Theo shook his head and accepted the whisky Alfred held out to him. "How's her mother?"

"Beside herself with fury. Dear God, I can't bear to see her in such agony. The police are worse than useless, they're so slow."

"You shouldn't have involved them yet."

"Sorry, old man, but I had to. But look, I didn't mention that Lydia's Chinese friend was a Communist fugitive, so you should be safe from any charges. Quickly now, what's this news you have?"

"A farmhouse. That's where they're keeping her." Theo was uncertain quite how much to reveal to Alfred because he didn't want the police getting hold of the information yet, but he knew he was going to need someone to back him up. "I'm going out there in secret to try to bargain with Po Chu."

"Damn good."

"Come with me?"

"Of course."

"Bring a gun."

"ALFRED, LISTEN TO ME, TAKE LIEV POPKOV WITH YOU."

"Who?"

"Don't be so dense, you must remember him. The drunken Russian who stormed into our wedding reception. I know where he lives and can send someone to fetch him straightaway."

"Ah, yes. Right. Good idea. He's big."

"Take care, both of you. I don't want my husband dead, Mr. Willoughby."

"Don't worry, Valentina. I'll come back, God willing. With Lydia. She's my daughter too now."

"Oh, Alfred, if you do, I'll kiss the ground you walk on till the day I die . . . whether God's willing or not. Come here."

"Steady on, old girl. Theo's watching."

"Let him watch."

THE ROAD WAS ROUGH AND SO RUTTED IT NEARLY TOOK THE sump off Theo's Morris Cowley. It was little more than a dirt track that skirted fields that stretched bare and gray to the horizon. In the spring they would be a green swathe of young wheat shoots, but in winter they looked like a sea of ash. Depressing under an even grayer sky. Theo cursed and fought the steering wheel around to the left to avoid another pothole. Beside him Alfred was smoking his pipe in silence, and the calmness of each puff irritated Theo. His own heart was thudding like a steam hammer. Damn it, he wished he'd had a pipe of his own before he left, a dream pipe to quiet his nerves.

"Alfred, be a good chap, and put out the ruddy smoke signals, will you?"

Alfred glanced across, studied him for a moment before winding down the window and tossing his pipe out onto the stony track. "Better?"

Theo said nothing, just concentrated on the road. In the backseat the big Russian let out a loud guffaw and hunched forward with anticipation.

THE ROAD ENDED IN A GOAT TRAIL AND THEY LEFT THE CAR behind the few scraps of pine trees that Feng Tu Hong had called a wood. On foot they threaded their way to the far side of it and crouched down to observe the farmhouse that lay five hundred yards ahead. It was a cluster of single-story wooden buildings covering three sides of a square, with a courtyard at the center and the fourth side made up of a whitewashed stone wall with high arched gates of solid oak.

They waited thirty minutes by Theo's watch. A flock of ragged-winged crows dropped out of the gray clouds and settled on the flat lifeless soil in front of the house, where they strutted stiff-legged like old men and dredged for grubs. When one stretched out its neck and took to the air, cawing harshly and circling over the *fanqui* heads, Theo hoped it was not an omen.

"Nothing," he snapped when Alfred's timepiece pinged two o'clock. They were both staring at the gates, willing them to open. "We might as well get over there and take a look. Po Chu and I have old business to settle."

"You know this man?"

"Oh yes. He's Li Mei's brother."

"You should have said."

"I'm saying it now."

"So this is personal?"

"No, I'm here for Lydia."

"I see."

The one-eyed Russian abruptly shook himself and lumbered to his feet behind a huddle of trees. His black eye fixed on Alfred and then Theo. *"Zhditye zdyes,"* he said. "You here." He pointed at Theo's watch and indicated the movement of time. "One." He held up a thick scarred forefinger. "One. You here."

"One hour?"

"Da." Liev nodded.

"You want us to stay here an hour?"

"Da."

"And then?" Alfred asked.

"You . . . there." Liev Popkov pointed at the gate.

"And you? Where will you be?"

The Russian spread his lips, showing strong teeth inside his black beard, growled something in his own language, and slunk off back into the trees. In his matted fur hat and long gray coat, he merged into the landscape after only a few strides.

"Christ almighty," Theo muttered and settled down to wait.

Alfred removed his spectacles and polished them meticulously.

THEO BANGED ON THE OAK DOOR. ALFRED RANG A SMALL bronze bell that hung on a chain to one side and almost immediately a narrow slat slid open at face level. A pair of Chinese eyes stared out, but one was filmy and the other nervous.

"I have come to speak with Feng Po Chu." Theo spoke briskly in Mandarin. "Inform your master that the Honorable Tiyo Willbee is here. And be quick. The cold out here is the devil's breath."

The eyes grew wider and flicked uneasily from Theo to Alfred and back again. "Not here," he said and slammed the slat shut.

Alfred thudded his fist on the door, making it rattle in its lock. "Open up, damn you."

To their surprise his words were greeted with the sound of a key turning and a heavy bolt being drawn top and bottom, then the oak door swung open. In front of them an elderly Chinese man with a long old-fashioned braid lay unconscious on the cobbles, while beside the door stood a bearded man with a chunk of firewood gripped in his hand.

"Liev Popkov!" Alfred exclaimed. "How . . . ?"

"Never mind how he broke in," Theo urged. "Let's get searching."

He drew his gun. The Russian pulled a pair of well-used long-barreled pistols from his belt, and Alfred waved a small Smith & Wesson uneasily in the general direction of the buildings. Theo felt a kick of adrenaline in his guts. Almost as good as opium running on the Peiho on a stormy night. He raced toward the first doorway but found only empty rooms. They searched the place thoroughly, every building and every ramshackle outhouse. No Lydia. A farmer, his two burly sons, and a handful of women were the only occupants.

One of the young wives admitted readily, "Feng Po Chu has gone. Two days ago. Took his piss-making men with him."

The Russian let out a roar of frustration. They were too late.

59

LYDIA HELD ON TO THE PAIN IN HER BREAST. SHE SAT HUD-
dled over her knees, one hand pressed hard against the wound to stem
the bleeding. She never expected to be glad to be back inside Box,
but she was. She had cried with relief when they locked her up again
in the dark.

She'd stuck to her story. Chang An Lo was dead. If she could
make Po Chu believe it, maybe she would survive this. *No. Don't think
that. That's too far ahead. Think only as far as the next moment. Think of
now.*

He hit her a few more times, but that was all. It was as if the sight
and smell of her blood, the taste of it as he licked his chin, satisfied
some inner urge. For the moment. But like any addict, he would be
back for more. Her nipple throbbed, but somehow the pain had flicked
a switch in her head and woken her out of the torpor she had been
slowly sliding into, where Death stood waiting with a smile and open
arms. Life was more complicated. Harder to do. And pain meant life,
so she kept telling herself pain was good.

Chang An Lo.

Mama.

Sun Yat-sen.

Even Alfred.

Her slender army of faces to fend off fear.

And Polly's. Her friend's face came reluctantly, but it did come at
last.

I can do this. I can. Survival. That's what I'm good at.

★ ★ ★

THE SOUND OF THE BOLT AT THE TOP OF THE STAIRS.

She started to breathe deeply, ready for the water. But the footsteps were different, heavier, stumbling, and she felt her throat close with panic. The dim light grew brighter in the holes, the feet came closer. She stared upward. What this time? Water? Hot oil? Acid? Anything?

The roof flew off. She blinked. A hand grabbed her hair. Her knees felt like they were set in concrete but when the pull dragged at her scalp, she pushed against the walls with her hands and got herself to her feet. Instantly she was yanked over the edge and collapsed in a heap of flailing limbs on the cellar's dirt floor. A man laughed. She tried to stand, but fell. Another laugh. Loose and malicious. A booted kick on her bare buttocks urged her to her feet and this time she made it. She knew who her tormentor was even before she saw his face.

Po Chu. Back for more.

But this time was different. He was drunk. And he was alone.

She could smell the alcohol on him, *maotai* on his breath and in the sweat on his smooth skin, quivering in his muscles. He released his grip on her hair but seized her arm and thrust her back against the damp earth wall. She knew what was coming. His lips found her mouth, chewing on her flesh, and she let his big soft tongue enter her mouth and slide down inside her throat. She couldn't breathe. Choked.

He laughed, the high whinny of a horse. One strong hand gripped her wrist as his body crushed hers against the wall, grinding his hips into hers, his other hand forcing its way between her legs. Her flesh crawled at his touch. But she didn't resist. Instead she stroked his broad back with her free hand. He breathed hard as his mouth lowered to her breasts and he sucked on the wound, sending pain shooting up into her brain, but she kept stroking, mewing, arching against him, hands roving. Down to his hips. Into his trousers.

His groan of pleasure as her hand encircled his engorged penis disgusted her but at last he released her other wrist and wrapped his arm around her naked waist. Pulling her against him and dragging down his trousers, making it easy for her. She kept one hand busy on his penis to distract him while she slid the other up under his jacket to where she could feel the hard bulge of a gun holster under his left arm.

She opened her legs.

Instantly he thrust at her. In one quick movement she slid the gun out, pushed its muzzle against his ribs and pulled the trigger.

Nothing happened.

Po Chu screamed something at her, his spittle spraying into her face, and grabbed for the gun, but she snatched it away and slammed the heavy metal into the side of his head. He went down. Dropped to his knees. But his hands still clung to her and he started to rise, clawing his way up her, fingers digging into her hips.

Her breath had stopped. But her mind was clear. If she didn't end it now she was dead.

You would kill a man. If you had to. Chang's words in her ears.

She sought out the safety catch. Pointed the barrel right in his face. Fired.

The explosion set her head ringing and sent Po Chu hurtling back down to the floor. By the uncertain light of the oil lamp on the stairs she could see that his face had become an oozing black crater with shards of glistening white bone. She gaped at it. The gun was shaking in her hand. But in place of the horror she expected to feel, there was only a deep visceral satisfaction that came out of her mouth as a ringing war cry.

She started to run.

CORRIDORS CONFUSED HER. SHE TWISTED AND TURNED, seeking a door that would take her outside, but each time she threw one open it led only into yet another room. Voices behind her. She fired at their shadows. Again and again. A bullet grazed her shoulder. She hurled herself into a room where two frightened young Chinese children cowered under a tiger skin, picked up a stool, and slammed it into the window. Glass and shutters exploded. Cold air rushed in.

She leaped through the opening, dimly aware of pain in her feet, and found herself in a garden where winter vegetables were growing in neatly tended rows. It surprised her that it wasn't dark outside, the light a thin misty gray, but she had no idea whether it was dawn or dusk. Another bullet tore past her hair. She swung around, fired, aiming at nothing. Run. She ran. Over loose earth. Through a stableyard. Horses. Dogs barking. Run. Out. Into the open. Fields, a path, trees. More shots and men behind her, closer. Then suddenly in front of her a solid row of Chinese faces. A pair of hands seized her. No, not now. Not now that she was free.

"No," she screamed and raised her gun to the man's face.

"Lydia. It's me."

She stopped screaming. Lowered the gun. Squinted at the blur that was a face. Gray uniforms all around her.

"Here." A greatcoat was flung around her shivering naked body. "It's all right. You're safe now."

She blinked hard. The man's features settled into a familiar image. "Alexei Serov," she gasped and retched all down his chest.

60

"Mama."

"What is it, my darling?"

"You don't need to sit here all night."

"Shh, sleep now."

"I'm okay, you know."

"Of course you are. So shut your eyes and dream sweet dreams."

Valentina was seated on a low chair beside Lydia's bed, her elbows on the quilt and her chin propped on her hands, gaze fixed on her daughter's face. She looked tired, gray lines in a fine web around her eyes and mouth. For the first time Lydia could see what she'd look like when she was old and white-haired. She gave her mother a fleeting smile. They both knew the dreams were anything but sweet. In the hospital the doctors had kept her drugged with something that numbed the pain and the brain but let in the nightmares, so now that she was home she refused all tablets and instead remained awake.

Three nights her mother had stayed at her bedside, three nights of being there each time Lydia opened her eyes. When she heard Valentina softly humming the overture from *Romeo and Juliet* in the early hours of one morning, it made her cry.

"Where is he, Mama?"

"Who?"

Lydia put out a hand and cupped it around her mother's. "You know who."

The green lamp was on in the corner of the room, but Valentina had draped a ruby scarf over it, so that the light was muted to the colors of a winter's sunset. Enough to see her mother's eyes.

Valentina turned Lydia's hand over in her own and with one slender finger slowly traced the lifeline on her palm right down to her wrist. "He's a prisoner."

"Where?"

"How should I know, *dochenka*?"

"Who has him?"

"The Chinese, of course. You know what they're like, always at each other's throats."

"Do you mean the Kuomintang?"

"Yes, I suppose so, the ones in those dreadful peasant uniforms."

"Is he alive?"

Valentina sighed elaborately and her mouth softened. "Yes. Your wretched Communist is still alive."

"How do you know?"

"I made Alfred make inquiries. Don't look so happy, Lydia. He's not for you. You must forget him."

"I will forget him the day I forget to breathe."

"*Dochenka!* You've been through enough. Stop this madness."

"I love him, Mama."

"So you must unlove him."

"I can't. More than ever now."

Valentina sat up straight, placed Lydia's hand gently down on the quilt, pulled her kimono tightly around herself, and folded her arms.

"Very well, darling. So. Tell me. What is it that your stubborn little soul wants? What plans have you hatched in that convoluted head of yours?"

There was a long silence. Downstairs the grandfather clock chimed three. Lydia could hear her mother's breathing.

"Mama, I nearly died in that Box." She spoke softly.

"Don't, sweetheart. Don't."

"I'd always thought survival was enough. But it's not."

IT WAS SEVEN-THIRTY AND THE SKY WAS JUST GROWING light when Lydia went downstairs. Valentina was in the bathroom and likely to remain there for some time judging by the scent of bath oil wafting under the door, so Lydia knew Alfred would be alone and unprotected.

"Hello."

"Good heavens, Lydia, you startled me." He was sitting at the breakfast table engrossed in the newspaper, a bowl of steaming porridge oats in front of him. "Shouldn't you be in bed, my dear?"

She slipped into the chair opposite him. "I need your advice."

Alfred put down his paper and gave her his full attention. "Anything I can do to help, just say the word."

"Mama said you made inquiries about Chang An Lo."

"I did."

"I have to go to him. So . . ."

"No, Lydia."

"Alfred, if it hadn't been for him, I'd be dead."

"Well, really I think it's that young Russian gentleman who . . ."

"No. It was Chang An Lo. He was the one who got the Chinese troops searching for me. That's what Alexei Serov himself told me in the woods. So you see, I do need to speak with him."

Alfred looked uncomfortable. He picked up his spoon and stirred his porridge, added a sprinkling of sugar to it, then shook his head sadly. "I'm so sorry, Lydia, I can't help you. Chang An Lo is not allowed visitors."

"Where is he?"

"In Chou Dong Prison. It's down by the river. But listen to me." He pushed a rack of toast toward her and she took a piece because she knew he was trying to help. "This whole business of your kidnapping has caused a bit of a stink, what with the police looking into Feng Po Chu's death and everything."

Her head jerked up. "I thought they said I was in the clear. It was self-defense."

"That's true." He reached out and patted her hand, but she could tell his sense of order was dislocated. "You see, Sir Edward Carlisle feels that the sooner it all dies down the better because, to be honest, it has created a lot of tension between the Chinese and ourselves. If you go around complaining and making a fuss about this Communist down at the prison, well, it'll just stir things up even worse. So if you want my advice, I suggest you keep well clear. Get back to bed and stay there until this is all done with. I'm very sorry, Lydia, I know it's hard, but it's for the best, my dear."

Lydia spread butter on her toast. Drizzled honey on it. Snapped it in two.

"Best for who?" she asked.

"Best for you."

She looked at him. Behind his spectacles his eyes were full of concern.

"Will you drive me to the Serov villa on your way to the office today, please?"

"There's no need."

"What do you mean?"

"Alexei Serov calls here every morning. Nine-thirty sharp he's been arriving on our doorstep to ask after your health."

"*Chyort!* Why did no one tell me?"

"Come on, Lydia, you know what your mother thinks of him. She'll probably give me hell just for telling you."

Lydia allowed herself a little bright window of hope.

"ALEXEI, TELL ME WHAT HAPPENED. PLEASE. I NEED TO know."

The tall Russian looked relieved, and Lydia realized he'd been expecting a more difficult question. He was seated on the leather sofa, legs crossed, his gloves placed tidily beside him, his body as relaxed as ever in a dark well-cut suit, but his expression was tense.

"You're looking much better, Miss Ivanova," he'd said.

It was a lie but a nice one, so she let it pass. Their exchanges so far had been peppered with awkward silences. The usual words of polite conversation did not seem to be enough between them. Not anymore.

"Tell me," she repeated, "how you found me."

"It wasn't hard. But," he gave an easy laugh, "don't tell Sir Edward that. He thinks I'm a hero."

She smiled. "So do I."

"No. I just used my contacts. No heroics."

"But why did Chang come to you of all people?"

He leaned forward, green eyes suddenly very hard, and she could see the military man in him. "He learned of the split between Feng and Po Chu, heard a whisper that Po Chu was siding with the Kuomintang against his father. That meant their spies would know exactly where he was hiding out. So your Communist used his brains. Who was the one person who knew you but also had influence over the Chinese?" He shrugged and spread his hands. "Myself. And the only way he knew of finding me quickly was through the Kuomintang."

"But now Chang An Lo is in prison."

His long face studied hers intently. "Yes."

"Can't you do something? Please. To get him out."

"Lydia, don't be foolish, this isn't a game. Chiang Kai-shek and the Kuomintang army are at war with the Communists. They slaughter each other every day, sometimes hundreds at a time. Chang knew that when he walked into Captain Wah's arms. So no, I can't get him out."

"But Alexei, he stuck up a few posters, that's all. Surely not enough to . . ."

He barked out a scornful laugh. "Don't be absurd. He's a trained code breaker. One of their best. That's why the Kuomintang are interrogating him now before . . ." He stopped.

There was a silence in the room so crystal clear that Valentina's soft footsteps could be heard pacing up and down outside the door. It had taken a lot of "discussion" to convince Valentina that Lydia owed the Russian this courtesy.

"Alexei."

"Whatever it is you want, Miss Ivanova, the answer is no."

"You are in a powerful position, Alexei."

He stood up quickly and gathered his gloves to him. "Time for me to leave."

THE WALLS OF ALEXEI SEROV'S OFFICE WERE PAINTED bright yellow on the top half and a drab olive green on the bottom half. His desk was gunmetal gray and the floor just bare boards. Lydia regarded it with distaste as she sat silently on a bentwood chair in a corner and watched Alexei plow through a pile of paperwork. She noticed the way his brown hair, though still short, was starting to curl again behind his ear and the speed with which he scanned each document in front of him. But she was irritated by him. How could he sit there so calmly when elsewhere in the building Chang An Lo was . . . ? Was what?

In pain? On a rack? In chains?

Dead?

Twice she interrupted him. "Is he coming?"

Twice Alexei had sighed, lifted his head, and looked at her with disapproval.

"I've given the order for him to be brought to my office. That's overstepping my mark as it is. I can do no more. This is China. Be patient."

She sat there for two hours and forty minutes. Then the door opened.

LYDIA'S FACE MADE CHANG AN LO'S HEART BURST INTO life again inside his chest. Her smile filled the drab little room. Her hair. It set the air itself on fire. He ought to have known she'd come, that somehow she'd reach him. He should have believed.

She leaped to her feet, but the Russian at the desk gave her a warning look. So she stood quietly in the corner, her tawny eyes focused on Chang's face, her fingers tugging at her coat buttons as if she would tear off her clothes if she could. Behind him two Chinese soldiers stood at attention and he knew that if he gave the yellow-bellied worms the slightest excuse, they would delight in joining the imprints of their rifle butts to the marks already on his back. But he was certain their farm brains would know no English.

"Chang An Lo," the Russian said formally, "I have summoned you here to answer some questions."

Chang kept his gaze firmly on the Russian. In English he said, "The sight of you brings joy to my heart and makes my blood thunder in my veins."

The Russian blinked. A small sound escaped from Lydia but the guards behind him stood silent.

"I know not how long I will be allowed to stand here. So there are words I must say. That you are the moon and the stars to me, and the air I breathe. To love you is to live. So if I die . . . ," another raw sound from Lydia, ". . . I will still live in you."

The Russian could take no more. "For God's sake, that's enough," he snapped.

But Chang was barely aware of anyone other than Lydia in the room. He let his eyes move to the corner. Her gaze met his and he felt such a surge of desire for her that he knew he was not ready to die yet.

Abruptly the Russian was ordering the guards out of the room and following them through the door himself.

"You have two minutes, no more," he said briskly.

Chang An Lo moved toward Lydia. He opened his arms and she stepped into them.

61

THEO OPENED THE DRAWER AND REMOVED THE PIPE WITH care. He ran a hand over its long ivory stem and felt the ancient carvings on it talk to him through his fingertips. The need to keep it safe, to have it there at his bedside just in case, was so strong he knew he had to destroy it. Ever since that strange day at the farmhouse with Alfred and Liev Popkov he'd had an acute awareness that his life was too fragile to take risks with anymore.

Maybe it was all that crazy strutting about with a gun in his hand that did it. Or the violent death of Po Chu. Or the impending execution of the Communist.

Death was whispering in his ear.

Or was it the curt letter from Mason severing all future contact? That had mystified Theo. What in hell had changed that bastard's mind?

All he knew for certain now was that he wanted more from life. For himself. For his beloved school. And for Li Mei. He raised his gaze from the pipe in his hands and looked at her. She wore no jewelry, no face paint, and her hair was pulled back from her face in a severe knot, a white flower pinned to it, all signs of her mourning for her brother. She was sitting at the window, her hands folded over each other on her lap, her almond eyes watching him. Only the tick of a tiny muscle at the side of her mouth betrayed how much she wanted this.

Slowly he lifted the pipe up above his head, holding it with both hands like a sacred offering to the gods, and for a brief second his mind yearned again for the swirl of the sweet smoke. But Theo didn't

490 · KATE FURNIVALL

listen. The pipe came swinging down with force, right onto the brass rail at the foot of the bed. The ivory shattered. Pieces skittered across the room and one brushed against Li Mei's small foot. She kicked it away.

"Now will you say yes?" Theo demanded.

Her black eyes were bright with happiness. "Ask me again."

"Will you marry me, Li Mei?"

"Yes."

"Tiyo."

"What is it?"

"She's there again. At the gate."

"Who?"

"The Chinese woman."

"Ignore her."

"Perhaps she wants her cat back."

"You mean Yeewai?"

"Yes. The creature used to be hers. And now you say her husband has been executed and his boat taken, as well as her daughter, there's no reason why you couldn't give the animal back to . . ."

"If she wants the cat, let her ask."

"I don't like the woman, Tiyo. Or her cat. There are bad spirits around her head."

"Superstitious claptrap, my love. There's no harm in her. But if it'll please you, I'll give her a few dollars next time I go out."

"Yes, do that, Tiyo. It might help."

BUT WHEN THEO DROVE OUT, THERE WAS NO SIGN OF YEE-wai's previous owner and he gave her no thought. The traffic across town was slow, the streets full of Saturday shoppers, so it took him longer than he expected to reach Alfred's house and he was annoyed at being late. In the days that were to follow, he would go over these moments again and again in his mind, trying to get them straight and in the right order, to see if anything could have been done differently. But some were fuzzy and indistinct. His arrival was one of those. He remembered backing the Morris Cowley into the drive and leaving it near the open gates because Alfred's big Armstrong Siddeley was already taking up most of the space. But after that, nothing until Alfred was clapping him on the shoulder.

"Good to see you, old chap. I know Lydia is longing to thank you."

It didn't look like that to Theo. She was standing by the window in the drawing room, holding herself very stiffly. Either the girl was in pain or she was on guard. Could be both. Theo followed her line of sight to see what she was staring at outside. Nothing. Just an old garden shed. She didn't look well. Gaunt cheeked. Her skin transparent. Her mouth was pulled tight with strain and her amber eyes seemed to have turned several shades darker. Yet something in them gleamed, as if there were a bright light deep down there, a kind of fire he had not seen in them before. He remembered that, when he conjured up her image later. That fire.

"Lydia, come over and say hello to Mr. Willoughby."

It was Valentina who spoke. She was smiling enchantingly at Theo, and he got the feeling she was one or two ahead of him in the vodka chase. When he thought back later, it was her long cool throat he recalled, though he didn't know exactly why. She was wearing something bright, red maybe, that showed off her creamy white throat with its delicate pulse throbbing at the base. She kept touching it with her scarlet-tipped finger. Her mouth smiled a lot. And her eyes were genuinely happy, so that she looked younger than at the wedding only a few weeks earlier.

"We are so very lucky to have you home again, aren't we, darling? Safe and sound. Well," she laughed and the look she gave her daughter flickered with something more fragile, "nearly sound anyway."

"How are you, Lydia?" Theo asked.

"I'm well now."

"Good for you, young lady."

"Come on, darling, don't be so rude. Thank Mr. Willoughby."

"Thank you, Mr. Willoughby. For searching for me."

"Poof, what kind of words are those? He deserves better than that. He risked his life."

Lydia shivered. Then she smiled and something seemed to open up in her, letting out a young eagerness for a moment. She offered him her hand.

"I am grateful, Mr. Willoughby, really I am."

"It's your Russian bear you should be thanking. He was the one who did the dirty work."

"Liev," she said.

She raised the glass of lime juice in her hand and turned to where Liev Popkov was slumped in an armchair. He was peering with his one eye into the depths of a glass of vodka that was swallowed up in his great paw, but when he saw her look across he shook his black curls at her and showed his teeth. It made him look ready to take a bite out of someone. Valentina glared at him and muttered something under her breath in Russian.

"And Chang An Lo?" Theo asked.

"He's in prison."

"I'm so sorry, Lydia."

"So am I."

She went over and stood beside the big Russian, her knee only an inch from his elbow, and went back to staring out the window. They didn't speak, but Theo could sense the connection between those two. Odd that. He could sense Valentina's disapproval too. Obviously the invitation to Popkov had not been her idea. She moved off in the direction of the vodka bottle.

"Sounds like bad news for Chang," Theo said in an undertone to Alfred, who was looking particularly smart in a new charcoal suit. Valentina had worked wonders with the old chap.

"I'm afraid so."

"Execution?"

"Inevitable, it seems. Any day now."

"Poor Lydia."

Alfred took out a large white handkerchief and wiped his mouth as if to scoop up the words. "It might be for the best in the long run." He shook his head unhappily. "If only she would find herself a nice young English boy at that school of yours."

"Why so glum, my sweet angel?" Valentina said with a laugh.

She'd returned to slide an arm around her husband's waist. Theo was amused that his friend managed to look so pleased, yet at the same time so embarrassed by Valentina's open display of affection. But the way Alfred looked at her, so much love in one small smile, it haunted him afterward.

The next hour blurred in Theo's mind. But he knew the reason for that. It was shock. At what followed. It acted like a glass of water spilled over a page of writing, smearing all the words and making them run into each other like tears. So quite how he found himself walking into the driveway behind Valentina, he wasn't sure. Something to do with cigarettes. That was it.

"Oh damn," she'd exclaimed. "I'm out of smokes."

"Here, try one of mine," Theo offered.

"Good God, no. They smell lethal."

So he'd offered to drive her to the shop that sold her foul little Russian cigarettes and she'd been delighted. She'd gone over to her daughter, spoken softly in her ear, stroked her hair, obviously explaining why she was skipping off. Lydia nodded but made a face. Not happy. But in the drive he'd opened the passenger door for Valentina, that much he did remember. And the kiss. Her soft lips on his cheek and the smell of her scent, the light touch of her hand on his chest. She was so happy it was infectious, so brimful of life. It bubbled out of her. Her daughter was safe from both Po Chu and Chang An Lo, while Alfred lay curled in the palm of her hand. What more could she want?

As Theo climbed into the driving seat he saw two things that surprised him. One was Lydia standing in the doorway of the house. He couldn't imagine why she'd come to see them drive off. The other was the Chinese woman, the one who'd thrust the cat into his arms on the junk and who'd been hanging around his gates for the last two days. What the hell was she doing here? The foolish woman placed her stubby body directly in front of the car. He hooted the horn. Her broad face and narrow eyes twisted into an expression of hatred and she spat at the windshield.

"Aah, this crazy town is full of mad creatures," Valentina complained, but she wasn't alarmed. Nothing could dent her good humor today.

"I'll get rid of her." Theo jumped out, and that was when everything went wrong.

The woman swung back her arm and threw something under the car. He started to run at her, but she was already racing out of the drive at an astonishing pace. Theo put a spurt on and had made it as far as the gate when the world cracked right down the middle. He could think of no other explanation. The noise was like the roar of the devil. He was hurled across the road and felt his wrist snap as he landed. His ears seemed to implode. He couldn't hear.

He dragged himself off the tarmac and looked behind him. The Morris Cowley was gone. In its place was a crater and a few grotesque pieces of twisted metal. Behind it Alfred's Armstrong Siddeley was all hunched over as if it had been kicked in the teeth. Broken glass trickled down from the sky like razor-sharp rain. Ten yards away on the scorched lawn lay the tattered remains of Valentina's body. Her flesh turned to raw meat. Lydia was kneeling beside it, her mouth open wide in a scream that Theo couldn't hear, her hands cradling her mother's shattered face.

It was then that shock shuffled the images in his head and sent him spinning down into a cold black pit.

62

THE FUNERAL WAS A GHASTLY AFFAIR. THEO ALMOST DIDN'T go but knew he had to face it. He could have used his injuries as an excuse. Not deep injuries. But showy. Cuts and bruises on his face, a broken wrist in plaster. A strip of flesh missing from one ear. But he went. If it hadn't been for him, there would be no need of a funeral and he was going to have to learn to live with that fact. He honestly couldn't understand why Alfred and the Russian girl didn't whip him out of the church. But they didn't. Both wore severe black. And faces as gray as the earth that would soon swallow up Valentina. Theo took a place in the back pew, and beside him Li Mei sat with curious eyes and the white flower of mourning in her hair.

"Dear friends, let us give thanks for the life of Valentina Parker, who was a joy to us all." Standing in the pulpit with a wide smile was the old missionary, the one who was at the wedding, with hair as white as Abraham's. "She was one of our dear Lord's bright lights that sparkle in this world. And He gave her the gift of music to delight us."

Theo had no stomach to listen. He disliked churches. He didn't like the intimidation woven so skillfully into their magnificent architecture, all designed to make you feel a worthless sinner. But if Valentina was really one of this awesome God's bright lights, why extinguish her so brutally? Why make Alfred, who was one of God's most devoted servants, suffer this agony? It made nonsense of the concept of a loving God. No, the Chinese knew better. Bad things happen because the spirits are angry. It made sense. You have to appease them, which was why Theo had decided to follow Chang's advice and build a shrine in his house to the spirits of his father, his mother, and his brother. He would give them no excuse to harm his Li Mei the way they'd harmed Valentina. This was China. Different rules applied.

The Chinese boat woman with her grenade knew that. She had blamed him for the execution of her husband and for the suicide of her daughter in Feng Tu Hong's bed, and ended by blowing herself up with a second grenade. But that didn't mean she was no longer a threat. Theo had made Li Mei promise to speak kindly to the cat Yee-wai in future, just in case. Spirits were unpredictable.

When the congregation rose to sing "Onward Christian Soldiers," Theo remained seated and closed his eyes. His hand held Li Mei's tight.

THE FUNERAL RECEPTION WAS WORSE. BUT THEO WAS pleased to see Polly standing firmly beside Lydia the whole time, caring for her friend, warding off well-wishers. Alfred held himself together too well. It was heartbreaking to watch.

"If I can help out in any way, Alfred. . ."

"Thank you, Theo, but no."

"Dinner one evening?"

"That's kind. Not yet. Maybe later."

"Of course."

"Theo."

"Yes?"

"I'm thinking of applying for a transfer. Can't stay here. Not now."

"Understandable, my dear fellow. Where would you go?"

"Home."

"England?"

"That's right. I'm not cut out for these heathen places."

"I'll miss you. And our games of chess."

"You must come and visit."

"But what about the girl? What will you do with Lydia?"

"I'll take her with me. To England. Give her a good education. It's what Valentina wanted."

"That's quite a responsibility to shoulder. She knows nothing of England, don't forget. And you can't say she's . . . well . . . tame enough. To fit in, I mean."

Alfred removed his spectacles and polished them assiduously. "She's my daughter now."

Theo wondered whether the girl would see it like that.

"I'm sorry, Alfred," he said awkwardly. "I can't tell you how bad I feel that the hand grenade was meant for me. Not for Valentina."

Alfred's mouth went awry. "No, it's not your fault, Theo, don't blame yourself. It's this damn country."

BUT THEO DID BLAME HIMSELF. HE COULDN'T HELP IT. HE chose to walk home instead of hopping into one of the rickshaws that clattered through the streets, though it would certainly have eased the aches in his legs. But he needed to walk. Had to stride out. To drive the demon of guilt from his soul.

He was in no doubt that it would return time and again for years to come, and he would have to learn to find room for it in his heart. But in his clearer moments of mind he knew Alfred was right. It was this country. China had a history of thousands of years of violence, and even now its exquisite beauty was again being trampled underfoot in the stampede for power. They called it justice. A fight for equality and a basic wage. But really it was just another name for the same yoke around the necks of the people of China. They deserved better. It seemed to Theo that even the boat woman who threw the grenade deserved better. What kind of justice system served up freedom in exchange for your daughter's young body in bed? Or sold children into slavery?

"Willbee, you will put the other arm in plaster if you do not take more care."

Theo jerked back from the road where a flurry of wheels was speeding past, a noisy never-ending stream of motorcars and bicycles, rickshaws and wheelbarrows. Even a boy on a scooter hooted a Klaxon at him.

"Good day to you, Feng Tu Hong."

The black Rolls-Royce was murmuring at the curbside with the rear window down, but the man inside was not the one who had radiated so much strength and power only days before. One look at Feng Tu Hong's face and Theo saw the bewildered eyes of a father who has lost his son. He was wearing a white headband.

"I have been searching for you, Willbee. Please, honor me with a moment of your time. A brief ride in my worthless motorcar might ease the burden of the wounds you bear."

"Thank you, Feng. I accept."

They rode in silence at first, each man too full of his own thoughts to find the words to form a bridge. The streets were thronged with people going about their business in the bright winter sunshine, but the car attracted attention as it passed and several Chinese men lowered their foreheads to the pavement. Feng did not even notice.

"Feng, I offer you sympathy for your loss. I am sorry I was not able to help the situation, but the farmhouse was already empty when I arrived."

"So I learned."

"Your daughter also sends her father sympathy for his sorrow."

"A dutiful daughter would be at my side."

"A dutiful father would not threaten his daughter so savagely."

Feng refused to look at Theo but stared straight ahead in his own black world, his broad chest expanding as he took a deep breath to hold hard on his temper. It suddenly dawned on Theo that this man wanted something. It was not hard to guess what.

"Feng Tu Hong, you and I have a history of discord and it saddens me that we cannot put aside our differences for the sake of your daughter whom we both love. At a time like this when you are overflowing with grief for your last son . . . ," he lingered on those final two words, ". . . I invite you to my home."

He heard the big man's sharp intake of breath.

"Your daughter will be honored to serve you tea, though what we offer is meager compared to your own lavish table. But at this moment of sadness, Feng, there must be no raised voices."

Feng turned slowly. His bull neck hunched defensively. "I thank you, Willbee. It would please my heart to set eyes once more on my daughter. She is my only child now and I wish to cause her no distress."

"Then you are welcome."

Feng leaned forward, pushed the glass partition aside, and gave his driver new instructions. When he slid the glass back into place, he shifted uneasily on the leather seat and gave a deep cough in the back of his throat, preparing himself.

Theo waited. Wary.

"Tiyo Willbee, I have no son."

Theo nodded but remained silent.

"I need a grandson."

Theo smiled. So that was it. The old devil was begging. It changed everything. Li Mei now held the power.

"Come," Theo said courteously as the car pulled into the Willoughby Academy's courtyard. "Drink tea with us."

It was a start.

63

"Lydia!"

Lydia was in her bedroom. She had been staring out at blackness and rain. In a chasm of loneliness for so many hours, her mind had escaped the present. She was way back on a day when her mother had danced into the attic with a small square loaf of something she called malt bread in one hand and a whole block of bright yellow butter in the other. Lydia had been so excited by the strange new smell and squidgy texture of the loaf that didn't look a bit like bread, she had scrambled up on a chair to watch as Valentina spread great wedges of the butter on the bread. Then Valentina had fed the fruity slices piece by piece into Lydia's open mouth. Exactly as if she were a baby bird. They had laughed so hard they cried. And now it twisted something inside her as she recalled how her mother had eaten so little of their meal herself, but licked the last scraps of butter off the knife and rolled her eyes in delicious ecstasy.

"Lydia! Come quickly."

Lydia's instinct for danger was sharp. She snatched up a hairbrush as a weapon, raced onto the landing, and burst into Alfred's bedroom. She stopped. For one unbearable moment hope reared up inside her. The room was full of people and they were all her mother. Alfred was sitting bolt upright on the edge of the double bed clutching two envelopes in one hand, the other hand twisted up in a hank of sheets as if trying to hang on to reality.

"Lydia, look at these." His voice was breathless. "Letters."

But Lydia couldn't shift her gaze from the floor. Her mother's clothes were spread out all over it, neatly arranged in matching sets.

Navy dress above navy shoes. Cream silk suit with camel blouse and tan sandals. Stockings, hats, gloves, even jewelry, placed as if she were wearing them. Empty bodies. Her mother there. But not there. A scarf each time where her face should be.

It was too much. She choked.

"Lydia," Alfred said urgently, "Valentina has written to us." He wasn't wearing his spectacles, and his face looked naked and vulnerable. Though the bedside clock showed four-twenty in the morning, he was still in yesterday's rumpled suit, his jaw dark and in need of a shave.

"What do you mean?"

"I found them. Beneath her underwear in that drawer there. One for each of us." He abandoned the sheet and cupped the envelopes to his cheeks.

Lydia knelt down in front of him on the rug, placed her fingers lightly on his knees, and felt the shivers rippling through his body. She looked up into his face.

"Alfred, Alfred," she murmured softly. Tears were flowing down his cheeks, but he was unaware of them. "We can't bring her back."

"I know," he cried out. "But if God got His son back, why can't I have my wife?"

My Darling Dochenka,

If you are reading this I have done the worst possible thing a mother can ever do to her child. Gone. Left you. But then I've never been good at doing the mother act, have I, sweetheart? It's my wedding day today. I'm writing this because a horrible sense of foreboding has settled on me. Like a shroud. A coldness squeezes my heart. But I know that you'd laugh and toss your shining head at me and say it's the vodka talking. Maybe it is. Maybe it isn't.

So. I have some things to say. Important things. Chyort! You know me, darling. I don't tell. I keep secrets. I hoard them like jewels and hug them to me. So I'll say them quickly.

First, I love you, my golden daughter. More than my life. So if I'm already cold in the earth, don't grieve. I'll be happy. Because you are surviving and that's what counts. Anyway I was never much good at life. I expect to find that the Devil and I get along just fine. And for hell's sake, don't cry. It'll ruin your pretty eyes.

Now the hard part. I don't know where to start, so I'll just spit it out.

Your father, Jens Friis, is alive. There. It's said.

He's in one of Stalin's hateful forced labor prisons in some godforsaken hellhole in Russia. Ten years he's been there. Can you imagine it? How do I know? Liev Popkov. He came and told me the day you arrived home and found him with me in our miserable attic. That was also the day I'd said yes to Alfred's proposal of marriage. Ironic? Ha! I wanted to die, Lydia, just die of grief. But what good could your father be to you, stuck out somewhere on the frozen steppes of Siberia and probably going to die sometime soon? None of them live forever in those barbaric death camps.

So I got you a new father. Is that so bad? I got you one who would look out for you properly. And for me. Don't forget me. I was tired of being . . . empty. Thin and empty. I want so much more for you.

There. That's said. Don't be angry that I didn't tell you sooner.

Now. A secret I never planned to tell. The words stick in my throat. Even now I could take this one to my grave with me. Shall I?

All right, darling, all right. I can hear you shouting at me though the worms are in my ears. You want the truth. Very well. I give you the truth, my little alley cat, but it'll do you no good.

I've told you before that when I first saw your father, he was like a glorious Viking warrior, his heart beating so strong I could hear it across the room as I played the piano for Tsar Nicholas. Ten years older than I, but I swore to myself there and then that I would marry this Norse god. It took me three years, but I did it. However, nothing in life is simple, and when I was too young and silly for him to look twice at me, he had been busy at the tsar's court in the Alexander Palace at Tsarskoe Selo. Now this is the scorpion's tail. He was busy having an affair. Oh yes, my Viking god was human after all. The affair was with that Russian bitch, Countess Natalia Serova, and she carried Jens's child.

Yes. Alexei Serov is your half-brother.

Satisfied?

Even now it makes me weep, my tears blur his name. And the countess had the sense to get out of Russia before the Red storm broke over us, so she was able to take with her the child and her money and her jewels. And left her poor cuckolded husband Count Serov to die by the blade of a Bolshevik saber.

Now you know. That is why I would not have that green-eyed bastard in my house. His eyes are his father's eyes.

There, dochenka. I am confessed. Do what you will with my secrets. I beg you to forget them. Forget Russia and Russians. Become my dear Alfred's proper little English miss. It is the only way forward for you. So adieu, my precious daughter. Remember my wishes—an English education, a career of your own, never to be owned by any man.

Don't forget me.

Poof, to hell with this craziness. I refuse to die yet, so this letter will grow old and yellow wrapped up in my best pair of silk French underwear. You will never know.

I want to kiss you, darling.

*So much love,
from your Mama*

Mama, Mama, Mama.

A torrent of emotions hit her. She hid herself in her room and shook so hard the paper quivered in her hand, but she couldn't stop herself crowing with delight.

Papa alive! Papa. Alive. And a brother. Right here in Junchow. Alexei.

Oh Mama. You make me angry. Why didn't you tell me? Why couldn't we have shared it?

But she knew why. It was her mother's warped idea of protecting her daughter. It was the survival instinct.

Mama, I know you think I'm willful and headstrong, but I'd have listened to you. Really I would. You should have trusted me. Together we . . .

An image of her father leaped out of nowhere. It rose up and filled the inside of her skull. He was no longer tall, but hunched, gaunt, and white-haired. His feet in shackles and raw with festering sores. The Viking sheen she had always thought he carried so easily on his broad shoulders was gone. He was dirty all over. And cold. Shivering. She blinked, shocked. The image vanished. But in that moment before her eyelids closed, Jens Friis looked directly at her and smiled. It was the old smile, the one she remembered, the one part of him she still carried inside her.

"Papa," she cried out.

BY SEVEN O'CLOCK IN THE MORNING SHE'D BUILT A SHRINE. A big one. In the drawing room. Alfred sat and watched her in mute stillness as she swept everything off the long walnut sideboard and draped it with her mother's maroon and amber scarves. At each end she placed the tall candles from the dining room. In the center, taking pride of place, she stood a photograph of Valentina. Laughing, with her head tilted to one side and an oiled-paper parasol in her hand to keep off the sun. A happy honeymoon snapshot. She looked so beautiful, fit to enchant the gods.

Possessions next. Lydia worked out what Valentina would need and positioned the items around her. Hairbrush and mirror, lipstick, compact and nail polish, her snakeskin handbag stuffed with money from Alfred's wallet. Jewelry box, an absolute must. And right in front where Valentina could reach it easily, a crystal tumbler filled to the brim with Russian vodka.

More. She needed more.

On the right, a whole stack of sheet music and on the left, a book for her to read on Chopin's affair with George Sand, as well as a pack of cards in case she grew bored. A bowl of fruit. A plate of marzipan sweets.

What else?

She brought in a deep brass dish and placed it on the sideboard. Then she filled it with sketchy drawings on a sheet of paper of a house, a grand piano, a passport, a car, clothes, and flowers, lit a match, and dropped it in. A whoosh of flames carried them up to her mother, and she fed the flames with cigarettes, one by one. The smell was awful. When it was all over and the smoke had cleared, Lydia sprayed the whole shrine with her mother's perfume, squeezing the little rubber puffer over and over until the bottle was empty.

It was then that Alfred rose from the chair where he had been watching in silence and very gently, as though not wishing to disturb his wife, laid his wedding ring beside the picture of Valentina's laughing face.

★ ★ ★

"WELL, WELL, IF IT ISN'T LYDIA, THE LITTLE RUSSIAN *DYE-vochka* who doesn't know her own language."

"Countess Serova, *vashye visochyestvo, mozhno mnye pogovoryit Alex-eiyem?* I would like to speak to Alexei."

"Ah, so you are at last learning. Good. But no, you may not come in, as it is much too early for visitors."

"This is important."

"Come back later."

"I must see him now."

"Don't be impudent, girl. We haven't yet breakfasted."

"Listen to me. My father is alive."

"Go. *Yidi!* Go away immediately, child."

"*Nyet.*"

"NO. THE ANSWER IS STILL NO. HOW MANY TIMES MUST I say it?"

"Alexei, I'm asking you again. As your sister."

"That is unfair, Lydia."

"Since when has life been fair?"

They were striding through Victoria Park, heads lowered against the wind that had come howling down overnight from the wastes of Siberia and was tearing through the trees with a harsh whine. No snow yet, but Lydia could feel its teeth already. They had the place to themselves.

"This is too much."

"No, Alexei, it's not. It's a shock. But you should respect your mother the countess for admitting the truth, even though it pained her to do so."

"Pained?"

"All right, forget pained. It was like eating barbed wire for her. But she did it. She has courage."

"A Danish bastard is what I am. *Nyezakonniy sin.*" He lengthened his stride and veered off the path, ignoring the KEEP OFF THE GRASS signs and heading for the fountain.

Lydia gave him time. His pride was in shreds, and she'd learned from Chang the importance of a man's pride. She continued slowly along the gravel path, following its more serpentine route to the or-namental pond with the koi carp and the dragon fountain. Today the water lay still, ice already beginning to form with frayed fingers around the edges. Alexei was standing against the low railing, watching the silver and gold forms flitting like ghosts beneath the water. In his stillness and his long black coat he looked like a statue himself.

"The son of Jens Friis," she said quietly. "Not a Danish bastard."

"And who exactly was this father of ours?" Still he watched the fish.

"He was an engineer. A brilliant one. An inspired creator of new schemes. Tsar Nicholas and the tsarina adored him and used his plans for modernizing St. Petersburg's water system." She paused. "He played the violin too. But not well."

He turned and stared at her. "You remember him?"

"Only just. I remember the sound of his laugh when he threw me up into the air and the feel of his big hands when he caught me. Hands that I knew would never drop me." She closed her eyes to hug the memories closer. "And his smile. It was my world."

"I am sorry to hear about your mother."

It caught her off guard, and for a second she thought she was going to vomit down his front yet again. She flashed open her eyes and frowned at him. "Let's stick to our father."

He nodded, and there was something in those eyes of his that triggered a long-dormant memory of another pair of very serious green eyes looking into hers and a deep voice soft in her ear, telling her she must make no sound but hold on tight to his hand. She moved off around the railing, circling the whole pond, a hand trailing on the looped guardrail until she came again to where Alexei was standing, still rigid, hands in his pockets. She'd given him enough time. More than enough. The minutes were skidding by.

"Alexei."

He faced her. She looked into his steady eyes and tried to learn what kind of man he was, this arrogant brother of hers.

"Help me."

"Lydia, you don't know what you're asking."

"I do."

"If I help you, I will lose my job, do you realize that? And the Kuomintang do not take kindly to traitors."

"Why do you do it? Why work for them?"

"Because I hate the Communists and everything they stand for. They reduce everyone to the lowest level, they tear down all that is beautiful and creative in mankind and cripple the mind of the individual. Look at the devastation in Russia now. So, no, I have no wish to save the life of a Communist, even if he is a friend of yours. I do all in my power to help Chiang Kai-shek rid this breathtaking country of their curse and build a good strong government. And I shall continue to do so."

"You are so wrong, Alexei."

He shrugged. "I think we must agree to differ on that point."

His voice was once again crisp, no nonsense. He had good powers of recovery. She knew she had lost him. A cold numbness swirled inside her chest. Breathing grew hard. Her mind reached out to Chang An Lo, but all she could feel was a fragile heartbeat. The rest was as black as Liev Popkov's beard. With a sudden urgency she reached up and gripped Alexei's shoulder, swung him around to face her. Her hands seized his. Her fingers dug into his bones.

"Alexei Serov Friis," she said fiercely, "I am your sister, Lydia Ivanova Friis. You cannot deny me this."

64

ALL DAY LONG LYDIA WAITED IN THE SHED. SHE WRAPPED herself in her quilt. Alfred had gone off to his newspaper office and in her mind she admired the way he kept himself functioning as if life had not cracked open to a burning hell-pit under his feet. But at the same time a part of her heart wanted him to scream. To rage. To rant through the streets in sackcloth and ashes, to show the world that life without Valentina was unbearable. But no. He was English. Englishmen didn't believe in sackcloth and ashes. A dark suit. A black armband. That sufficed.

Lydia had chosen to wear one of her mother's white dresses. It was plain with a long row of jet buttons down the front and a large white lace collar. It looked all wrong on her, she knew, but she didn't care. It soothed a small part of the ache.

As she sat in the shed she made herself study the dried bloodstains on the wooden walls and floor, and thought about scrubbing them but decided against it. It would be like washing away Sun Yat-sen, and she wasn't willing to do that. But she did lay out the same blankets as before on the floor and sat down in the middle of them, gazing up at the skylight above her head. Though the hours crawled by and nothing happened, except the day grew darker, she kept calling his name softly.

"Chang An Lo, Chang An Lo, Chang An Lo."

If she stopped, something inside her knew he'd die. It was that simple.

THE HAIRS ON HER ARMS BEGAN TO PRICKLE AND SHE KNEW he was near. Above her the skylight was black as a grave while beside her a single candle burned with a flame that flickered and leaped, sending shadows careening around the walls.

She told herself it was the wind outside stealing through the shed's cracks and under the door. She wanted to believe it. But she could hear their breathing. The spirits.

Gathering.

HE WAS THERE. IN THE DOORWAY. HIS BLACK HAIR TOUSLED by the wind, an air of wildness about him, a grubby green blanket thrown over his shoulders in place of a coat. His eyes wanting her.

"Chang An Lo," she breathed and leaped into his arms.

He laughed, kicked the door shut, and carried her to the blankets. They didn't need words. No hows or whens or what ifs. They just needed each other. Their bodies so hungry they ached with the pain of it. Lips tasted each other again, sought out the hollows and sweet places that made moans of pleasure slip from their throats as their limbs entwined.

Her hands came alive as they explored Chang An Lo's lean frame once more, delighting in the long lines of his thighs and the broad planes of his chest. Her fingertips traced the familiar burn scars, as well as the vicious new bruises that sickened her stomach, so that she called down curses on Po Chu's name and that of the Kuomintang. So vehemently, he laughed. Until he saw her breast. Then the words that poured from him were unintelligible to her, in harsh Mandarin, and behind the fury in his black eyes was something hard and vengeful, something that had not been there before.

"I regret you shot Po Chu's face off, Lydia." He kept one hand cupped protectively over her damaged breast.

"But why? The bastard deserved it, Devil rot him."

"Because I longed to do it myself," he said angrily. "But only after I sliced off his seedless balls and stuffed them into his maggot mouth."

She kissed his chest and felt his heart beating strongly under her lips. Ran a hand over the sharp bones of his hips and down into the dense black bush of pubic hair. He bent his head and trailed his tongue over her pale stomach to the soft crease where it met the tender white skin of her thigh. Her body arched against his as he caressed and cradled, touched and teased, so that when he finally entered her the fire inside them forged them into one person. A perfect whole. Two halves molded into one. They lay locked together for a long time afterward, the warmth of their breath brushing their naked skin, their hearts finding a rhythm in time with each other.

"Lydia."

She smiled. Just to hear his voice say her name. But at the same time a sharp pain was starting in her chest. She curled herself up in the curve of his arm, her head resting on his collarbone, her leg entangled with his, breathing his breath, smelling his skin, and shut her eyes for a long minute. Imprinting the moment forever in her head.

She opened her eyes. "I know, my love. I know what you must say."

"I have to leave Junchow."

"Yes."

He held her tight to him, a shiver running through his veins. "I must leave you here, the light of my soul. Leave you safe."

"I know."

He kissed her forehead, his lips lingering on her skin. "I cannot take you with me, my love."

"I know." Her throat tightened and the pain in her chest was worse than a knife. "When I was captured by that snake Po Chu, I understood. The men there would be no different from a camp of Communist fighters. To them I would always be alien, a poisonous reminder of everything they were struggling to defeat. And as long as I was by your side, you would be in danger. I couldn't bear that. The enemy could use me to cripple you."

His hand touched her face, his fingers gently sealing her lips.

She forced the words out of her mouth. "I would be worse than shackles to you. So I know you must go alone."

"The only thing you shackle is my heart. And I swear I will return for it."

His eyes were brilliant in the candlelight. Free of fever. She saw in them the truth of the promise he'd just made but saw also the eagerness for what lay ahead of him, and the blade in her chest twisted a little.

"You'd better return," she laughed and tipped her head back, showing her teeth, "or I'll come charging up into the mountains to get you."

He kissed her throat. "The Communists and the Kuomintang

would both flee screaming in terror at the fury of such a fox spirit."

"I've made up a pack for you." She pointed to a bulging leather bag with a buckle and long shoulder strap propped against the heap of sacks by the wall. "Food and clothing. There's money in there too."

"A knife?"

"Of course. A good one."

He nodded his satisfaction. "I thank you, my love. Your father has grown more generous?"

"My father . . ." She heard the raw edge to her voice, swallowed, and started again. "My stepfather has other things on his mind." That was when she told him. About her mother. About the letter. And Alexei Serov. He held her close and she let hot tears flow for the first time since her mother's death. Something hard and knotted loosened inside her.

"Will they come after you again, the Kuomintang troops?" she asked at last.

"Like wolves scenting fresh blood."

"And Alexei?"

"When they find out he gave the order for my release, the Russian will have to answer to them."

She nodded.

For a moment his gaze fixed on her in silence, and then his eyes widened. He rolled up onto his elbow in one fluid movement and took her chin in his hand. He shook it in jerky little sweeps. She noticed that the wound where his finger had been was almost healed.

"You planned it well," he said. "And in a way that helps the Communist cause."

She nodded.

"The Kuomintang will lose their military adviser here in Junchow." His voice was calm but his face was very pale. "And you . . . No, Lydia. No. You will step into the dragon's jaws."

She smiled up into his intense black eyes and ran a finger along the sharp line of his cheekbone. "My love, it was from you I learned how to tweak the dragon's tail."

He stroked her hair urgently, as though he would stroke the thoughts from her mind. "You're returning to Russia."

"Yes."

"To seek out your father."

"Yes."

"It will be dangerous."

"I'll be well prepared, I promise."

"By the gods, yours will be a harder journey than mine. But I swear you'll travel with my soul in your pocket."

She felt a surge of exhilaration and kissed his eyelids. "Thank you, my love, for understanding. Just as you have to fight for what you believe in, so I have to do this."

"I hear your words, but fear chews at my bones."

"Don't. We'll get through this, you and I. I used to think survival was everything. All my life I've fought to eat and breathe in this stinking world, like the alley cat my mother always called me. But I've learned. From you. From dull old Alfred. Even from all that savagery in the Box. You have to survive for a reason."

Chang An Lo sat up and wrapped her in his arms, brushed his lips over the skin of her shoulder as if he would devour her. "Oh my Lydia, the wind of life blows strong inside you."

"Love," she said. "And loyalty. They're my reasons. Worth surviving for. He's my father, Chang An Lo. I want to know what reason has kept him alive for ten long years in a wretched Russian prison camp."

"The iron in a man's heart comes from his mind."

"In a woman's too."

Chang smiled, but not lightly. He reached to where his discarded clothes lay in a bundle on the floor. "I have something for you."

He pulled out a leather pouch and from it he drew a small pink pendant, which he placed in the palm of her hand.

"This is a powerful Chinese symbol. Of love."

She studied it carefully. "A dragon." It was exquisitely shaped, curled up like a kitten.

"Yes. Carved of rose quartz. Wear it always. It will protect you and ward off evil spirits until I return."

"It's beautiful, thank you."

She kissed him and they made love again, slow and lingering, savoring every touch and every taste, and then fierce in those final moments when they became a part of each other. It was at the point of her final shuddering release that something changed in him, she felt it, some instinct made him clamp a hand over her mouth and whisper close in her ear.

"Listen."

She listened. Heard nothing. Except the wind tearing at the trees. But her heart and stomach seemed to collide. "You'll need that knife."

THE DOOR WAS KICKED OPEN. IT SHRIEKED ON ITS HINGES and rebounded against the wall with a slam as a British army officer strode into the musty shed, his eyes quick and sharp. Behind him the gray uniforms of the Kuomintang hovered like leashed hounds on the trail.

Lydia leaped to her feet, wrapped in a blanket. "Get out! How dare you burst in here? This is private property."

"A warrant." The officer waved a piece of paper rudely in her face. "Don't play innocent, miss. Where is he?"

Already hands were rummaging through the blankets, among the boxes and cobwebs and old cans as if their prey might be hiding in one. It was when they yanked the sacks away from the back wall that the Chinese captain with the stone-hard face swore and yelled at his men to search outside. Where the sacks had stood was a gaping hole. The bottom of two planks had been carefully sawn through and re-moved. Lydia's afternoon of waiting had not been completely without purpose.

"Where is he, miss?" the English officer snapped.

"Gone," she said. And again softly to herself. "Gone."

65

THE TIME FOLLOWING THAT NIGHT WAS FRACTURED TIME for Lydia. The days passed but didn't exist. Images flashing by, blurred and meaningless. Only the meeting with Polly stood out and held her attention.

"Lydia, I'm sorry." Polly had turned up on the doorstep, bearing a gift of macaroons tied up in silk with a lavender ribbon. "Forgive me, Lyd. I only meant to do what seemed best for you."

It was hard. To let go of the anger. But Lydia told herself that if Polly's words had not drawn Po Chu's men to her in the shed that day, they'd only have found her some other day. Some other place. It would have turned out the same in the end. The Box. The water jammed in her throat. The iron-toothed tweezers on her breast. Nothing would have changed all that.

So she smiled into Polly's worried blue eyes and hugged her close. "It's okay, I understand. Really I do. You thought you were looking after me but it didn't go quite right."

"You see, my father . . ."

"Hush, Polly, hush. Forget it. It wasn't your fault. Your father does things sometimes that aren't always right."

But not anymore. Christopher Mason would not be doing things that weren't right with his daughter anymore. So Lydia kissed her friend's pale cheek and told her she would be leaving Junchow. Polly had cried, and they had clung to each other and promised to meet up again one day in London, in Trafalgar Square with the pigeons. Nothing else during those days was clear in Lydia's mind. Until the morning that she was standing on the railway platform with Alfred, clutching a net of oranges under her arm and a ticket to Vladivostok in her hand. Then everything came into focus. Pin-sharp. So bright it hurt her mind.

The oily belch of the steam engine excited her. All around them crowds jostled, travelers shouted to each other, carriage doors banged. A porter heaved bags. Vendors pushed trays of *baos* and hot roasted peanuts in her face, rang their bells, and yelled their wares. Interweaving through it all like a yellow river drifted five Buddhist monks in saffron robes, murmuring prayers and scattering incense. Lydia put a coin in their begging bowls. To please Chang An Lo's gods.

"I'll miss you," she said to Alfred.

"My dear girl, can I not persuade you? Even now?"

"No, Alfred. But I am grateful, really I am."

She meant it. He had been astonishing. When he realized he couldn't shift her from her decision, he pulled every string he could get his hands on and had turned Sir Edward Carlisle's neat bureaucracy inside out to acquire a visa and passport for her so fast. Both were in a name that still sat strangely on her tongue. *Lydia Parker.*

"A good British passport," Alfred had insisted. "That's what gets you places in this world. It will protect you. The might of the British Empire, you know, right there behind you."

He had a point. No doubting that. But she had more faith in herself than in his empire, so, unknown to her stepfather, another passport was hitched inside her waistband. A Russian one. Forged, of course. Name of *Lydia Ivanova.* Just in case. Part of the survival kit.

"I'll send you a wire, Alfred, I promise. As soon as I can."

"Do that, my girl. You know I'll worry."

She looked at his face and couldn't understand how it had grown so dear to her. He had lost a few pounds and his brown eyes seemed to have sunk deeper into his head than . . . before. How had she once thought them pompous? She leaned forward and hugged him.

"Sure you have enough money?" he asked.

"If I had any more golden guineas sewn into my clothes and glued inside the soles of my shoes, the train would need an extra engine to cart me over the mountains."

He laughed. "Well, you've got my solicitor's address in London, so you can always reach me and I can wire you money for a steamer ticket to England. I won't stay much longer. Not now. Not here in China."

She held on to his hand for a moment, trying to find the right words and failing. In the end she said with a smile, "Be happy in England. She'd want you to be."

"I know." His lips tightened. He nodded. Patted her arm. "Keep yourself safe, my dear girl. God be with you."

"I have my bear with me."

She glanced into the carriage. Liev Popkov was seated there. His great fist was stroking his beard and somehow managed to make even that simple gesture threatening rather than thoughtful. Her own small leather suitcase rested beside him on the bench seat, safe as the Bank of England. Probably safer. Even Alfred laughed when he saw two men back quickly out of the compartment when they encountered Liev's single black eye and outstretched legs, as if a buffalo had snorted in their faces.

The train guard started slamming doors. The smell of hot metal stung Lydia's nostrils as another belch of steam sent black smut swirling up the platform. The engine heaved itself into life. Whistles shrieked. This was it. Her heart was hammering in her chest, but at the same time something was tearing apart in there and she couldn't quite hold it together. She jumped up on the carriage step, and it was then that she saw the tall figure with the silk scarf, short brown hair, and lazy stride ambling along the platform, as if he had all the time in the world. He strolled up to her carriage and doffed his smart new fur cap to her.

"Alexei." She grinned at him. "I thought you weren't coming."

"Changed my mind. Not keen on this place anymore, a bit too chilly for me." He glanced over his shoulder toward the station entrance and though he kept it casual, she could spot the unease in his green eyes.

"Too hot, I think you mean. Come on, Papa will be glad to see you," she said and stepped to one side.

Alexei gave her a look that she couldn't read, but it didn't matter. Her brother was here. He shook hands with Alfred, who muttered, "Good man, look after her," and then Alexei leaped easily into the carriage beside her.

"We have company, I see," he drawled and stared suspiciously at the big greasy Russian.

Lydia laughed. This could get interesting. It was going to be a long journey.

The clouds overhead were moody and silver-edged as she took her seat. She leaned her head against the juddering window, drew in a deep breath, and released it slowly as Chang An Lo had taught her, watching the pane of glass mist up and obscure what was out there. What lay ahead terrified her. And thrilled her. She knew she could survive it. She'd said so many times. That was the one thing she was good at. Surviving. Hadn't she proved it? Well, now she was going to help her father survive.

She wiped a hand over the window. Cleared a swathe of glass.

Because now she knew that you didn't survive on your own. Everyone who touched your life sent a ripple effect through you, and all the ripples interconnected. She could sense them inside her, surging and flowing, doubling back and overlapping, all the way back to the beginning. And at the center of them all was Chang An Lo. She wrapped her hand tight around the quartz dragon pendant. He and she would survive this and would be together again when all the turmoil was over, of that she was sure. She stared intently up at the low ridge of hills ahead where rumor had it that the Communists camped out, as if she could keep him safe by sheer force of will alone. She sent out a ripple of her own.

The train growled to a start.